The Sol Empire
Volume 2 Fear

Vic Broquard

The Sol Empire Volume 2 Fear
First Edition
Copyrighted © 2018 by Vic Broquard
ISBN: 978-1-941415-83-2

This is a work of fiction. All characters, organizations, and events portrayed in this novel are products of the author's imagination and are used fictitiously.

What isn't fictional is the work that Humanity and Inclusion (formerly Handicapped International) is doing to help those who have suffered:
http://www.hi-us.org

Published by:
http://www.Broquard-ebooks.com
Broquard eBooks
103 Timberlane
East Peoria, IL 61611
author@Broquard-eBooks.com

For Morgan and L. Ron Hubbard

Table of Contents

Chapter 1 A New Client
Chapter 2 Unraveling
Chapter 3 Inhumanity
Chapter 4 A Deterrent
Chapter 5 The Meeting
Chapter 6 Strike Back
Chapter 7 Recoveries
Chapter 8 Key Decisions
Chapter 9 The Results of Fear
Chapter 10 Fear Fall Out
Chapter 11 Of Laws and Species
Chapter 12 Doomsday
Chapter 13 Armageddon Arrives
Chapter 14 The Federation
Chapter 15 Negotiations
Chapter 16 Brainwashed
Chapter 17 Texture Sensualism and the Offer
Chapter 18 Recovery and Actions
Chapter 19 Mom, What a Surprise We Have For You
Chapter 20 The Meeting
Chapter 21 Rulership Changes
Chapter 22 Boom, Wake Up
Chapter 23 Developments
Chapter 24 Perp Tracking
Chapter 25 The Drug Effect
Chapter 26 Change of Plans
Chapter 27 Secret Strike
Chapter 28 Recovery
Chapter 29 Decisions
Chapter 30 Solutions
Chapter 31 Recovery
Chapter 32 My Decisions
Chapter 33 Falling in Love Again

Chapter 1 A New Client

July 1, 2352, Chicago

"Molly Parkinson's Private Investigations and Security, Molly speaking. How may I help you?" I glanced at the clock: 9 a.m.

Déjà vu. Two years ago to the day—to the minute—I received the phone call that changed my life. Until that morning, I believed I was an orphan. That call led to the discovery I was one of fifteen female clones with a "lucky" gene in my DNA, but we think of ourselves as sisters.

I sat behind a refurbished desk in my office on the second floor of the Parker Skyscraper. The woman's voice sounded uncertain. No 3-d holographic video stream appeared on my phone. Conclusion: she wasn't wealthy.

"Are you still doing PI work?"

I sensed grief, worry, and fear in her tone. Because I've received much mental and spiritual therapy from my sister Celeste, I found it easy to sense the woman's emotions, even though I'd never met her and she'd only said a few words. My yellow touchpad vibrated from the distant roar of a ship lifting off from New O'Hare Spaceport.

"Yes. How can I help you?"

Although I felt a surge of adrenaline whenever taking on a new case, I kept my tone sympathetic, in between her grief and fear.

"Oh, thank heavens. You're my last hope."

It worked. I heard her exhale.

"It's my husband, Aaron Strawn. I'm Piper Strawn—a nurse at Central Chicago Medical Center. Aaron's a history professor at the University of Chicago. He's vanished, and no one can tell me what's happened to him. He led the downtown protest last week. It was on the news."

Within the past few weeks, protests had sprung up in various major cities and then last week here in Chicago. For two centuries, corporations forced people to retire at sixty, moving them into assisted living complexes. There, doctors gave them drugs that brought on severe dementia, thus killing them by age sixty-five. This corporate version of population control wasn't public knowledge until last month. Hence the demonstrations.

"You want me to find your husband?"

"Yes, oh yes, very much so," Mrs. Strawn said. Her words gushed out like a pyroclastic flow from a volcano.

"Okay, come by my office as soon as you can. Bring a 3-d holographic image of him."

"Thank you. I'll be there in thirty minutes." She paused for a moment and then said, "How much do you charge?"

Her voice changed from elation to hesitation. Because my sister's husband is a high school history teacher, I had a second clue the Strawn's weren't wealthy.

"How about a hundred up front? Twenty-five credits per day plus expenses. If I find him in less than four days, I'll give you a partial refund."

Again, I heard her long exhale and imagined her body relaxing. I'd pegged their financial situation. Damn, I'm getting good at this.

"Okay, see you in a half hour."

The call ended. I set to work verifying what she said. After the subterfuges and rampages of the Sixth Invaders over the last two decades and combined with Earth's inhumanity to man, I trusted no one—outside our extended family of clones, that is.

My PI license allowed me access to many corporation databases. I visited the Med Center's site and saw Mrs. Strawn was a blonde Galactic Doll.

The tall, gray, giant-breasted Sixth Invaders secretly ran the leading corporations for the last two decades. They used genetic mutation agents to turn most of Earth's women into the alien's idealized form of beauty, the Galactic Doll. Seeing Mrs. Strawn's image reminded me of my appearance.

That's what my body looks like. I have waist-length, wavy raven hair, blue eyes, a roundish face, bushy eyebrows, and full lips. Oh yes, a silly smile, too. Like all dolls, my breasts as large as my head. With a few exceptions, our mutated legs and feet force us to wear tall heels. Completing the image, we're supposed to keep our nails at least an inch long, painted to match our fancy gowns, and quite impractical.

Since last year's worldwide conversion of most women into Galactic Dolls, satin, form-fitting gowns have replaced all other types of women's apparel. Just two years ago, I wore slacks, shorts, flip-flops, blouses, tank tops, or skirts, for example. Besides having an image to uphold, women can't wear such apparel because the Sixth Invaders implanted us to only wear these fancy dresses.

Their implant technology compels behavior, and the person has no idea this pattern is imprinted in their mind or why they are behaving as they do. The implant uses an aesthetic wave in the kilo-yottahertz range that renders a person unconscious, at which time words are repeatedly spoken, recorded deep within their mind. Often, the Sixth Invaders combined this with drugs and pain, making this a lethal combination that cannot be disobeyed. When the massive conversion of women finished six months ago, we learned that even if a woman wanted to wear practical apparel, the Sixth Invaders' implant wouldn't let her.

My sisters and I exposed these Sixth Invaders' plots, but too late to stop the conversion. Three of my sisters developed a mental and spiritual therapy that erases physical and emotional trauma and these implants. I've had many therapy sessions that erased those implanted compulsions, but I still wear the doll gowns just to fit in.

Two minutes later, I had Professor Aaron Strawn's faculty 3-d holographic image displayed. His image didn't surprise me, though, for anyone living outside central Chicago, his appearance would be shocking. Why?

We learned that part of the Sixth Invader's plans included humiliating and discrediting the men who controlled the major corporations of the Sol Empire from here in Chicago. In the Invader's society, women ran everything, while their men handled domestic duties, and both sexes had enormous breasts.

The Sixth Invaders' Commander R'Ina had her Chief Science Officer develop a genetic mutation that changed men's bodies into perfect Galactic Dolls, though they still functioned as males. Their voices rose, a rib set dissolved, their pelvis expanded, their Adam's apple shrank, and their breasts rivaled those of any Galactic Doll woman. In fact, one couldn't tell the gender of a Galactic Doll without checking their genitals. The Sixth Invaders used this mutation agent on all males in central Chicago. While this wiped out Sol Empire male rulers—most of whom committed suicide—the Invaders hoped women would take over those vacated corporate positions.

Yet, the Sixth Invaders' plan for our men was worse than this, but because of my actions, they botched their original mutation formula. The genetic mutation should have also eliminated their arms, making our men handicapped Galactic Dolls. They planned to donate specialized robots to aid men's survival. My sister, General Beverly Blossom Blythe, confiscated that corrected biological mutation agent before someone could use it. Today, that agent is in the hands of Galactic Medicine for further study, against my vehement argument it should be destroyed.

Having seen that Mrs. Strawn's story seemed sincere, I logged into the Channel Nine News Archives. Now armed with Professor Strawn's image, I could track what happened to him. A dozen had shown up to protest, but that peaceful protest of corporations causing dementia and killing older people evolved into a demonstration, as more and more onlookers cheered them.

Seeing this reminded me that two years ago I lost my parents this way, and I wiped away a tear. Then, last year, I discovered all corporations did this and read the document that justified why they killed older people. Two hundred years ago, when people lived into their nineties or more, their medical and living costs bankrupted everyone involved, including corporations. By imposing this new age limit, they slashed health costs and ended the exponential population growth, though the Sol Empire colonization periods during the last two centuries cut Earth's population by over two-thirds. In Chicago today, people inhabit only one dwelling in three.

Many, including me, saw no reason to continue murdering everyone when they reach sixty. Professor Strawn's protest highlighted this inhumanity. I remembered seeing the rally on the news last week and telling Ted, my husband, that the protest wouldn't force the corporations to change their policy.

Just as I began viewing the 3-d holographic streaming images from the news archives, Mrs. Strawn entered my office. My latest client looked like her Med Center image. I relaxed; this time my client wasn't lying.

"Hi, Mrs. Strawn. I'm Molly. Please, have a seat."

She wore the usual cherry red, satin gown, but hers had a nurse's patch sewn onto her left shoulder. Piper's light blonde hair fell to her hips. With pink around her eyes, I wasn't wrong to conclude she vacillated between grief and fear. She twisted the leather strap of her purse while she talked.

"Just Piper, please. I'm so glad you'll help me find Aaron. I saw your news conferences—you know—when you were temporary head of Galactic Defense and uncovering the awful things they did to our people. Here's the hundred you asked for."

I watched her long talons as she slid the small bundle of credits across my desk before she resumed twisting the leather strap.

"Thanks. Can you tell me what happened? Why is Aaron still missing?"

"He—he never came home. I knew he planned to protest. How can they murder us when we reach sixty years old? It's criminal. Besides, we now know that older people's bodies rejuvenate when they're given the Galactic Doll genetic mutation agent."

She referred to the accidental discovery that happened two months ago. The Sixth Invaders spread their mutation nanoparticles across central Chicago and turned several million, men, women, and children into Galactic Dolls. The elderly in thirteen assisted living centers found their dementia cured and their physical bodies rejuvenated, though the men were now male Dolls.

I must have looked surprised because she continued. "Yes, it's just now becoming known. You see when women were mutated into Galactic Dolls—just after your own discovery that this mutation could regrow our soldiers' missing arms and legs—we noticed older women looked years younger. It's verified now. Galactic Medicine will soon announce that everyone's ID cards will contain both a biological age and a true age. Aaron's mother's ID card lists a true age of sixty-five, but a bio age of twenty-five. The mutation resets the body's clock to the mid-twenties—both men and women, though the men pay an awful price for regaining their youth."

After a momentary pause and a sigh, she continued. "Aaron has been having a difficult time adapting to looking like a Galactic Doll. But the hair and nail machines, along with the dressing robot, have helped him adjust."

I broke in with a broad smile. "But I bet your acceptance of his appearance and your encouragement helped him even more." My husband's a Doll, too, Ted Billings. Again, my hunch was dead on.

Piper grinned. "Well, that's true." Then, her face grimaced. "And if you and General Blythe hadn't stopped the Sixth Invaders from using their revised genetic nanoparticles, Aaron and all other men in Chicago would be armless. I don't think Aaron could have survived that. Anyway, I'm babbling."

"No, it's clear that you love him. I understand. Tell me what happened at the protest. How did he go missing?"

I saw tears welling up in her eyes, as she struggled to regain her composure. "From what I saw on the news, GD deployed members of our Local Defense Force. They fired stun guns at the protesters for no reason at all. Then several protesters fired their own stun guns back. Aaron and many others collapsed. Several EMACs arrived and carried the stunned away. I haven't seen Aaron since then."

She swallowed, retrieved a tissue from her purse, and wiped her eyes before continuing.

"I saw what had happened on the news at six that evening. When Aaron didn't return home, I called Galactic Defense in the morning. I've called every day since then, but I've gotten no response. All the spokeswoman would say is that GD has handled them." Her voice rose, "I don't know if he's alive, in prison somewhere, or dead. Molly, I've just got to know!"

"I understand, Piper. Let me see if I can find out what happened to him and get him back to you. I've connections with our new local Galactic Defense leaders here in Chicago. Give me your contact information and his 3-d holographic image."

She did so, transferring his and her images to my phone and touchpad. After thanking me, Piper left, presumably heading back to the Med Center.

These fifteen major corporations were vital to everyone's survival, for they sponsored all high school graduates. They paid for any occupational training or college degrees. Once trained, the corporation paid the person a monthly stipend for life, though it wasn't enough to get by on. One couldn't survive without a corporate sponsor. In return, the person had to follow any orders their sponsoring corporation might make of them at any future date. Failure to obey resulted in termination or loss of sponsorship, which meant no income or job, so it was better to be terminated.

For example, two years ago, my original sponsor, Galactic Defense, ordered me to kill General Fuller, the man behind the secret cloning project thirty years ago. I had to follow GD's orders, but the general helped me by snatching my gun and shooting himself.

I knew the new CEO of our local Galactic Defense corporation, Helen Hugo. But before paying her a visit, I needed to learn all I could about the protest and the aftermath.

Looking for clues, I reviewed the news footage of the protest and the conflict that followed. Because of the Galactic Doll mutations, everyone present looked like well-endowed women, though I knew most in the Local Defense Force (LDF) were male. In their tall stilettos and fancy gowns, their feeble attempts at fighting brought a smile to my face. When the LDF arrived, the onlookers fled.

The LDF fired their stun guns first. Protesters responded with shrill yelling before several pulled out their own stun guns and fired back. Those who collapsed should only be unconscious for a short time. No one used real guns like my Glock or the blasters our army soldiers carry.

I spotted EMACs arriving—the Electro-Magnetic Air

Cars, manufactured by my billionaire sister's company, Cartwright Enterprises. Deanna, an engineer and CEO, both made design changes to the EMACs and ran the corporation. These green vehicles are silent, need no fossil fuels, can carry dozens of people, and fly the skies. Most companies have EMAC parking lots on their skyscraper roofs.

The EMACs had the blue and gold logo of Galactic Defense on them. I watched the surviving LDF personnel and Galactic Defense security men carry the unconscious victims— both protesters and LDF men—into these GD transports. News coverage ended as the vehicles departed, leaving me with the key question: where did they take them?

Before calling Helen at Galactic Defense, I wanted to be as familiar as possible with these protests and riots. Once more, my acute sense of ignorance came to the fore. Unlike many of my sisters and husband, I was "uneducated." They had multiple doctorate degrees. Randi, Eve, and Celeste had three PhDs each. My Ted had two, a PhD in computer programming and one in robotics, and he worked for Galactic Robotics in their R&D department.

During the past two years, I've seen just how little I know. My naive high school wish to be a PI as a way to help people and prevent parents from abandoning their babies, as I once thought happened to me, has evaporated. No, people need more help and aid than a PI can offer, but I haven't figured out what I can do about it yet, so I compensate by doing in-depth research before acting, along with common sense.

Replaying the recording, I listened closely to what Aaron said.

"The corporations lie to us! They murder our parents! They kill everyone who retires! They move our older people out of their homes and into assisted living complexes. They give them drugs to bring on dementia so they can terminate them.

"Three months ago, my own parents stopped recognizing me. Guess what? After the Sixth Invaders spread their genetic mutation particles over central Chicago, my parents have recovered, just like everyone else. In fact, Mom looks like she did when she was twenty-five. Dad looks like a similar aged Galactic Doll. I call this a true miracle."

Pausing playback, I wiped my eyes. I missed my parents, victims of this older policy. But I couldn't help wonder how I would react if they had been rejuvenated as Aaron's parents had and were now my age. How weird. I continued the playback.

Professor Aaron continued yelling. "We must stop the corporations from poisoning our older people! It's criminal! Instead of making people retire when they reach sixty, let's make the corporations rejuvenate them. We know they make billions of credits in profits. Our salaries are low enough to prove that. They can afford to do this.

"Population explosion is ancient history. Earth has less than a third its historic high. Two in three homes in our city are vacant, as are three-quarters of small business buildings. More working people means more profits for everyone. So I say let's force these evil corporations to change their ways!"

The gathering crowd—now numbering at least fifty—chanted. "Change! Change! Change!"

That's when the Local Defense Force arrived, and the onlookers fled in all directions, leaving Professor Strawn's dozen protestors to face the LDF.

Instead of army divisions, every geographical area has its own Local Defense Force—more like a militia, ill-armed and poorly trained. Their main purpose is to help during natural disasters and the rare civil unrest, such as this protest.

Earth has only one ground army division, led by my sister, General Bev. Until the Sixth Invaders came, there had been no wars for centuries. Last year, Bev and our First Infantry Division defeated the robot soldier army of the Sixth Invaders. Then, a few months ago, they killed many of the alien Sixth Invaders here in Chicago.

Besides the army and the LDF, Galactic Defense has a large and powerful security force, considered the world's police, the most feared group on Earth. Also, other corporations have their own security forces. And most cities have local police—in our case, the Chicago Police Department—to handle routine crimes, though these days such are very rare. The usual robberies, rapes, and murders are infrequent because, when caught, Galactic Defense sentences them to either termination or a long prison term in the penal colony on Mercury.

Back on the video, Aaron's small group protested just outside the Chicago GD skyscraper. But when the LDF arrived, the nature of the chants and cries changed.

"You're the criminals!"

"What corporation lines your pocket?"

"Evil corporation puppets!"

"You should be ashamed of yourselves!"

"Wait 'til you turn sixty and get terminated!"

Until this point, the protest had been a peaceful one.

The leader of the LDF yelled. "Disperse or be arrested!" He waited for a second, if that, before he opened fire with his stun gun.

A stun gun only affects one person at a time, and it takes a minute to recharge. A brief firefight broke out, ending with the dozen protesters unconscious, along with six of the LDF personnel. I watched Aaron's body drop to the ground. They loaded the victims into two GD EMACs and departed.

Professor Aaron Strawn's protest rally was the first in Chicago, but Moscow hosted earlier protests, along with several other cities. Why Moscow?

At the bottom of the corporate hierarchy, local offices run the affairs of their geographical area, often that of a large city. Chicago's local offices are on the lower five floors of the hundred-story corporation skyscrapers. Earth has thousands of local offices, but Mars only has a dozen, and Ceres, only one.

Next up in the corporate hierarchy, the planet-wide corporation offices control and direct the many local branches. In Earth's case, the Moscow corporations supervise the thousands of local offices.

The highest corporation offices oversee the Sol Empire. Before the Sixth Invaders, those offices were in Chicago, and the Sol Empire Galactic Defense personnel, who issued orders to the many planets, moons, and space stations, such as Moscow or Mars or Pylon, occupied the upper ninety-five floors.

With the Sixth Invader's genetic mutations, the subsequent male suicides, and the discrediting of the men who ran the empire from Chicago, the Moscow corporations stepped in, temporarily handling the Sol Empire needs. A replacement strategy for this highest tier has yet to appear. That's why these initial protests began weeks ago in Moscow.

A call to our local CEO of Galactic Defense, Helen Hugo, led to an appointment. As I prepared to head over to the GD skyscraper, I wondered if this job was a harbinger of far worse things, just as that job had been two years ago.

Chapter 2 Unraveling

Once outside my office, I stepped onto the MTES—the Mass Transit Eco-moving Sidewalk system installed throughout the world in all but the smallest towns. Free and environmentally green, these horizontal moving sidewalks transported millions of people around the city each day and had replaced city streets and highways.

One could ride the MTES from Chicago to St. Louis, switching MTES systems at Peoria, and with no cost to the rider, though many brought along portable seats for the longer trips. The MTES system spanned out much like blood vessels and capillaries, often ending within a block or two of a residential street where one would walk to get to a home. Here and there, a wide street still had a single lane available for the tiny, obsolete electric cars or landing spots for maintenance EMACs. The MTES had a transparent roof that kept the weather off riders. It also had a fast lane for those in a hurry.

Overhead, puffy cotton balls dotted the morning azure sky. A fishy odor from the Lake assaulted my nose, as I joined a throng of people, many of whom recognized me—likely from my work exposing the alien Sixth Invaders plots—either nodding or smiling. Still pondering the déjà vu nature of this day, I couldn't help but notice the differences between two years ago and now. At first glance, I saw only shapely women wearing fancy gowns and tall heels. Many had their long hair up, but some wore theirs like mine, down and flowing in the gentle breeze.

Half were likely men, so different from Chicago's past or any other city on Earth. General Bev and I stopped the Sixth Invaders, though we didn't kill them all.

Towering concrete, steel, and glass-sided skyscrapers, each with flat roofs, dominated the horizon as I neared Lake Shore Drive. I spotted an occasional EMAC landing or taking off from one of these roofs. Unlike the distant roar of spaceships lifting off from New O'Hare Spaceport, these EMACs made no sound. As I approached the towering hundred-story Galactic Defense skyscraper with its identical Galactic Expansion building in the next block, the sky multiplied amid hundreds of reflecting glass windows.

I'd spent several months as the temporary CEO of Galactic Defense, brought in to sort out GD's corruption and illegal activities. While I did so, I also learned my involvement was part of the Sixth Invaders' plans to discredit the male leaders of the Sol Empire. They dismissed me when I got too close to their main plot.

As with most buildings, GD's doors opened as I approached them. I walked up to the receptionist who wore a bright blue gown. Two other women stood nearby wearing light blue gowns with gold trim, members of the GD security force. But were these men or women?

"Hello. Molly Parkinson to see CEO Helen Hugo."

"Yes, she's expecting you," the pleasant soprano-voiced receptionist said, handing me a visitor's badge. One can't tell gender from voices or body forms, making socially awkward situations around central Chicago. She glanced at my leather holster holding my trusty Glock and smiled.

I attached the badge to my dress and headed to the elevators, but one of the security guards accompanied me. Probably wanted to make sure I didn't get lost. I jest—really a matter of security.

"Helen, you're looking good." I entered her fifth-floor office. The vacant upper ninety-five floors used to house the Sol Empire-wide GD personnel.

As usual, she wore a red satin gown with matching heels and nails. She wore her
platinum blonde hair up. Her deep blue eyes captivated my attention as they always had. Helen wore three rings with large gems: one diamond, one emerald, and one ruby. Gold bracelets and necklaces adorned her arms and neck. Her husband, Casper, once was the Chief Finance Officer for GD.

"So good to see you again. Honestly, this job is taking up more time than I bargained for. Have a seat. How's everything? I heard you're expecting."

I don't know how she knew I was pregnant. "Well, yes. Next Valentine's Day—if I'm lucky. Say, is your art show still on for this fall?"

I discovered that, like many executive wives, her husband had suppressed her, forcing her into the corporate Galactic Doll role. Months ago, Casper shot my husband and abducted me, trying to turn me into his armless play toy. I foiled his attempts, and that's when Galactic Expansion's CEO appointed me to be the temporary CEO of GD, charged with rooting out corruption and getting justice. Helen and other GD wives requested their guilty husbands become armless Galactic Dolls. Within months, Helen and her friends soared back to life, throwing off the yoke of suppression from their husbands. I learned she had been an architecture photographer and had taken hundreds of photos around the city.

Helen's face radiated. "Absolutely. It's on for the first week of September. Here's six tickets for the opening night gala event. Been meaning to get them to you before now. I owe you so very much. In fact, all we wives do."

Weird. I suddenly saw Helen in the Art Gallery. She moved about the giant space hanging up mounted photographs while adjusting the floodlights to give just the right lighting for each image. As she passed a window, night had fallen, and yet the images I saw of Helen and the studio were vivid and colorful.

I must have been unresponsive for a minute because Helen kept touching the package of tickets to my right hand, nudging me into the present.

"Oh, pardon me." My face felt flushed and radiated heat. "You can count on me being there, Helen. Thank you."

What just happened? Those images of Helen were so real. Am I seeing things again? Pull it together, Molly. Focus. Focus. "I'm here today to ask about those protests we've been having."

"Yes, I've got questions, too," Helen said. Her forehead rose while she pressed her lips. "I don't know what's going on. Been dozens of similar protests in larger cities, such as New York, LA, St. Louis, and Moscow. The protests here began long after the others. From what I've been able to discover, the protest frequency and level of violence are increasing."

She raked a talon across her cheek and lips, before her eyes focused on mine. "Honestly, I support them. It's true, or rather verified, I should say. Those of us who had the Galactic Doll mutation have had our biological clocks reset. My body tests as being in its middle twenties, though I'm approaching forty."

I'm pregnant too.

That thought slammed into my mind. How? Who?

Helen hadn't noticed my reaction. "And I have good news too. I'm also pregnant, due next March."

That was her thought I heard. What's happening? I swallowed hard. "Congratulations, Helen. That's wonderful news. Yes, a nurse friend told me the older men and women in the assisted living homes are now in their mid-twenties. Even cured their dementia. Steep price for the men to pay."

We both chuckled. I waited to see Helen's response.

"We CEO's have been hustling to get those retired men and women back on working sponsorships. Some men have had to find different employment and sponsorship, since as Galactic Dolls, they can't handle heavy construction jobs. I side with the protesters. Rather than killing our older generation, we should rejuvenate them and make use of their knowledge and talents. Here in Chicago, people live in only a third of the existing houses. Besides, some of these men and women are highly educated and have made giant contributions to our world and empire."

"Wish my parents had had that choice, but it should have been their choice whether to have the mutations done. Still, isn't this going to throw a wrench into your sponsorship programs?"

"Petr Leonovich of Galactic Expansion has us working on the financial aspects. Here in Chicago, we could use many more normal men to help offset those who've become Dolls. Unfortunately, during these past couple months, I haven't been able to get many males to move here. That's about to change."

"Right, what normal man would want to risk coming here? We never eliminated all the Sixth Invaders. Sixteen escaped us, along with their spaceship."

Helen nodded, then smiled. "I've got good news for you. Petr decided he can't run the Sol Empire from Moscow. He needs the computer systems here and all the records and the databases. We're preparing the upper floors for their arrival. Tomorrow, these fifteen new Sol Empire leaders and their huge staffs are moving in. A week from now, this building will be the bustling hive of activity it's always been. I'm all for it. Personally, I couldn't see them trying to deal with empire issues over there in Moscow because everything they need is here in Chicago."

This was news. I knew how terrified men were of becoming genetically transgendered. Many adult men, especially corporation employees, chose suicide rather than adapt and live as male Dolls.

And having once been the temporary head of GD for a few months, I appreciated the massive computer systems and files stored here, along with the host of bureaucrats who assisted me in my search for information on criminal activities. I thought the Moscow corporations made a wise move.

I said, "Having normal men moving into Chicago will be good for everyone's morale."

Helen chuckled. "For us women, yes. For our men, I'm not so sure, though it's true our economy crashed since Petr moved the Sol Empire corporations' location to Moscow. Say, how's Leslie's male Doll apparel launch coming?"

When we first learned millions of men and boys of Chicago were going to be mutated into male Galactic Dolls, I had a vision of a line of clothing that helped men look more masculine. My sister Leslie, who owns CostumesRUs, and her husband, Felix, converted my ideas into reality.

"The launch date is this Wednesday. Already, they have thousands of pre-orders. The shirts have a western look and fasten with snaps. The pants come in denim and fancier suit fabrics—all with Velcro fasteners. Their tall heels have rounded toes and look as much like a man's shoe as possible."

"Casper has been hounding me to get him some. He hates dressing like a woman, but then most men do. Leslie will make a fortune."

16

For Helen's benefit, I said, "The dressing robot machine thing can handle these new garments. Leslie's made sure of that. Casper can use one to dress by himself."

She smiled and sighed. "Well, that'll be a big relief. It gets old dressing him all the time and caring for his needs. But I shouldn't complain. I have my life back, thanks to you."

I figured I'd done enough polite conversation; it was time to get down to business.

"I came by today to ask you about these protesters. What happened to them? I saw on the news that you sent in the LDF. They fired stun guns at the demonstrators first, but then protesters fired back. I watched the unconscious being taken away in GD EMACs. What happened to them after that?"

Helen frowned, took a deep breath, and exhaled before saying a word. "Well, to be honest, Molly, I've no idea. I have tried to find out, but Petr and Gregor are refusing to tell me. I can tell you this much. Bringing in the LDF wasn't my idea. I wanted to allow them to protest. But Gregor ordered me to send in my LDF and to order them to use their stun guns on the protesters if they didn't disband. I had no choice."

"That's what I guessed happened."

Helen flashed an appreciative-looking smile. "My orders were to take them to the Med Center and leave them there. I tried to find out what happened to them after that, but no one is talking—even made discreet inquiries with other local GD CEOs, but Moscow is keeping everyone ignorant. We took the victims to Med Centers; beyond that, I don't know what happened to them."

She said, "That's one thing I intend to find out from Gregor and Petr when they get here tomorrow." Helen promised to let me know.

After thanking her for the tickets, I headed back to my office. Besides knowing almost nothing more about the fate of the protesters, now I wondered what had happened to me— those images of Helen's were so vivid, so colorful, so real. Had I heard her thoughts? That occupied my mind until I got home.

I logged into Chicago's surveillance system, entering the

date and approximate time the EMACs would have arrived at the Med Center. Within five minutes, I watched a doctor checking on the unconscious victims in the EMAC. Then, he used a syringe to inject a victim, but that camera couldn't see the others.

So I found an alternative one that allowed me to see those inside the cargo hold of the vehicle. As I watched, the doctor continued to fill syringes from a bottle and inject the victims. After that, several orderlies carried the victims to another EMAC, this one with Galactic Medicine's logo on it.

I captured a good image of the doctor's face. I had a hunch where this new EMAC was heading. New O'Hare. Twenty minutes later, my guess proved correct. I watched other men loading the victims onto an Airliner. Zooming in, I spotted the tail number, which I typed into my yellow touchpad.

I paused the playback, fired up another task, entering the number and date. A PI license opened many doors for me. Soon I had the flight manifest displayed: mutation victims bound for Galactic Medicine, Moscow.

What did that mean? They took the unconscious protesters and the few LDF personnel to Moscow. Why? What did they mean by mutation victims? A strange turn of phrase. Most of us referred to them as Galactic Dolls or Dolls for short.

I made a cup of tea while I pondered this discovery. Would my PI license allow me to access surveillance in Moscow? If I was going to find out what happened to Professor Aaron Strawn, then I had to follow this Airliner no matter where it went.

It took hours, but I sat back, a pleased expression on my face. I'd done it—found a surveillance video of the Airliner landing in Moscow. There, men transferred the unconscious victims to another Med Center EMAC. But the EMAC didn't go to a Med Center, at least not right away. First, they stopped at a GD research facility. I couldn't read Russian, but the Internet translated for me.

What happened next was curious. Two men came out of the building with a Gurney. They picked up one unconscious victim, placed them on it, and transported them inside. The

EMAC driver sat on the ground, relaxing. After forty-five minutes, the two men brought that person back out, placing them on one side of the EMAC.

I watched them transport Aaron into the research facility. Like clockwork, they reappeared, bringing Aaron back out to the EMAC.

I counted eighteen victims, each handled the same way. Fifteen hours passed, and after four hours, another three men replaced the EMAC driver and the two workers. However, I didn't have to sit there that long; rather, I fast-forwarded.

Then, the EMAC driver took the unconscious people to a Med Center. I watched as personnel carried Aaron inside. I noted the date and time, comparing it to when I saw the doctor injecting the many victims. Since these Chicago people were already genetically modified Galactic Dolls, they shouldn't be in comas and certainly not this long. Had they been injected with a drug to keep them in a coma? Or was something else in play here? Why were they being taken to another Med Center? Why take them to Moscow in the first place? Why a research center? It claimed to be a behavioral science development center, whatever that translation meant.

I felt like a bulldog, jaws clenched on a pant leg. No way was I going to let go. Observation. That was my next action—that and patience. Aaron and the others were in a Med Center. A stun gun shot was harmless; they had already been in mutation comas because they were Dolls, either male or female.

I fast-forwarded through the surveillance video at the admitting entrance. I watched other EMACs arriving, depositing other patients. As the hours drifted by, I had an awful feeling about what might be happening. If so, it was the very thing I'd done everything to prevent from happening to us in Chicago—even to the point of glimpsing the future before it happened and using that vision to alter our future if that's the proper explanation of what happened.

My dogged patience paid off. I spotted a group of victims being ushered out of the Med Center and into a waiting EMAC. I gasped and cursed, before pausing the video and making a screen capture for myself, for Helen, and for my client. There was Aaron. He wore the same apparel as he had at the protest but his arms had vanished. So had the arms of the others, who wobbled like a line of penguins out to the waiting vehicle.

I zoomed in on Aaron as much as the grainy image would allow. Terror lined his face, but his lips continued to move. He was saying something, but not to anyone I could see. So were all the others. I made a video capture of this short sequence before noting the EMAC's identification number. When it departed, I guessed it was heading to Moscow's spaceport.

Within minutes, I found it landing there. The eighteen terrified victims waddled from the EMAC over to an Airliner. My heart went out to them, but I kept my focus and grabbed this vehicle's identification. When it lifted off, I didn't know its destination, but I reasoned it might head back to New O'Hare.

Their loss of arms made little sense. I felt sick at my stomach. While I had no concrete evidence, I suspected these men and women were subjected to the Sixth Invaders' corrected genetic mutation agent, the one designed to turn Earth's men into armless Galactic Dolls, just as the alien commander had announced in her pre-recorded video shown to everyone in Chicago. Thanks to my premonition or future-seeing, I had General Bev confiscate that repaired biological agent before it could be used on us in central Chicago.

Further, if my glimpse into the future had been correct, this repaired biological mutation was incredibly nasty—dominant over all other Galactic Doll agents known to date. These victims' missing limbs couldn't be regrown. This meant future children from such a parent wouldn't have arms—both boys and girls—quite unlike the other Doll mutation agents which also regrew missing limbs.

I remembered what Bev told me back while I was in the Med Center having my arms regrown. "I had to turn that nasty agent stuff over to folks from GMed. They said it would be passed out to other geneticists to study in hopes of finding more genetic cures."

Now, I doubted that had happened. I've learned not to trust our corporations or their leaders. But don't jump to conclusions. Get data. Get facts. Get a sample of Aaron's blood and ask Eve, one of my younger clone sisters, to analyze it. She could tell me if that terrible alien agent had altered his DNA. So I had an even more compelling reason to find out where they were taking Aaron and the others. I swallowed hard. Eighteen men and women just had their lives ruined. Someone would pay for this!

I'd had great success so far, but the supper hour approached. It could wait until tomorrow. We lived in one of the small apartments built behind Leslie's costume store. Leslie and Felix had moved back into her parents' home attached to the store. Our sisters, Eve, Randi, and Celeste lived in number one. Ted and I lived in number three. Felix and Ted were clone brothers. My sister Janine and Hank lived in number two, while our dear friends, Kyle and Holly Ann, stayed in number four. General Bev and her wife, Lieutenant Gail, resided in number five. Our other sister clone, Deanna, the billionaire, lived up north in a fancy estate.

Since neither Ted nor I could cook much, we often made use of the robot maid the aliens gave us. The Sixth Invaders provided a hair and nail machine, a dressing/undressing robot, and a maid robot for every occupied home in central Chicago. They had also sent a helper robot designed to assist the armless men. Via these machines, the aliens expected our armless men to survive. Since Bev and I stopped them from using that awful agent, people returned the helper robots to Galactic Robotics, where Ted now worked, but most kept the other three robot machines. The maid robot was also programmed to cook, and Ted and I used it that way.

However, Lieutenant Gail was a remarkable chef; often she and Bev had us over for dinner. Once we even dined on real food, not the usual synthetic goo with its many flavors and textures. While the machine set about preparing the synth chicken, potatoes, gravy, and peas, I waited for Ted to come home.

"Hi, dear. I'm back. Guess what?" Ted said as he walked into our apartment.

Ted is six feet tall without heels. He had been handsome, and even though he is now a male Doll, he's the love of my life. His brown hair reaches his hips, but he swears he'll cut it short as soon as Leslie's new male Doll apparel is available. And his face is square, highlighted with thick eyebrows. It's hard to tell Felix and Ted apart, and just as difficult to tell us sisters apart.

"Okay, what?"

"The Moscow corporations that took over as the Sol Empire leaders are moving to Chicago. Supposed to arrive tomorrow. Told you they wouldn't be able to run the empire from Moscow. Everything they need is right here. So how's your day been? Any new clients?"

"Yes. Do I ever have a story to tell you? Remember the protests?" I related what I'd uncovered, while the robot maid served up our supper.

"Well, dear, I can make sure Aaron and the seventeen others have one of those personal helper robots. They're programmed to feed them. Things like that. Not terribly useful, I suppose. Still, I'm sure this Aaron fellow will like that."

"Thanks. Tomorrow, I'll track down what happened to Aaron. He hasn't returned to his home yet, and he should've by now."

"So you think something else is going on with those victims?"

"Yeah. You know me." We chuckled.

After dinner, we headed over to Randi, Eve, and Celeste's apartment. Ted and these three younger sisters loved to spend evenings sharing what new things they'd learned each day. Yes, I always felt like the dunce, but Ted enjoyed these times. Tonight, I took Celeste aside.

"Celeste, something strange happened to me today." I described how real and colorful and vivid Helen's images had been and how I somehow read her thoughts.

She ran her hands over her face before replying. "Molly, we *are* getting somewhere. Telepathy. That's what's happening. You're developing the ability to read minds. Randi and Eve did it with me; that's how I would describe it. See, all these therapy sessions we've been running are working. You're becoming more and more able. I'll ask Randi and Eve if there are things we can practice to help you gain more control over it. This is exciting, Molly. No one has ever *made* a telepath. This is ground-breaking!"

Celeste's face glowed with excitement. I knew her life's goal was helping others via her therapy, derived in part from methods pioneered by Eve and Randi. While I always felt like a dummy around many of my sisters and Ted, they accepted me as I am. We all did. That's what made our extended family such a strong one, one that included Holly Ann and Kyle.

Chapter 3 Inhumanity

Some days, you just don't want to get up. Today was one of those. While Ted rose and dressed, I stayed in bed and grinned when he gave breakfast orders to our robot cook. Better him than me, since he's the robot man.

An awful gnawing feeling about the day ate at my stomach, because I suspected I'd find Aaron and the others. Then, I'd have to explain to Piper what had happened to him. Would she be able to handle the terrible mutilation of her husband? The agonizing suspicion that I would discover they'd used that revised alien mutation agent kept me in bed—the very one I'd foreseen as destroying our world via a vision in which Galactic Expansion (GPan) and GD poisoned everyone in central Chicago to terminate us mutated, handicapped people.

I joined Ted for bacon, eggs, muffins, and coffee, timing my arrival. The robot maid placed breakfast on the table as I sat down opposite Ted. I admit I found the robot useful since it also washed up the dishes when we finished. Perhaps, I could get used to these mechanical things; Ted has, but then his passion is designing robots.

Nine o'clock found me once more in my downtown office, watching surveillance videos. By ten, I'd proven they'd returned the eighteen victims to Chicago. In fact, I'd seen that terrified penguin march again—when they disembarked the Airliner and entered another EMAC. This one had no corporate logo markings, but it had a visible ID number registered to Phillip's Escort Services.

As I hunted for another surveillance system close to that company's location out near New O'Hare, my enthusiasm dwindled. They had arrived two days ago, so the people should have been returned to their homes and families by now. What did a prostitute ring want with these people? And how was I going to get Aaron away from them? I needed a plan.

After making myself a cup of tea, I pondered my next move. I could go to this place and "hire" Aaron, whisking him home to Piper. Or I could take Piper with me, but I rejected that idea as soon as I had it. Her reaction to Aaron's mutilation might make retrieving him more difficult. I sighed. Until I knew what the actual situation was, I couldn't devise a workable plan.

Worse, I'd never been to such a place. I needed advice and called my sister, General Beverly Blossom Blythe.

"Hey, Bev. Molly here. Got a wee problem."

"Hey, back at'cha. Wassup? Case?" Bev said.

"Yes, case, bad one."

I spent ten minutes outlining what I'd uncovered, along with my suspicions. Over a year ago, Bev had been one of the Sixth Invaders' female victims. While the captured men lost and arm and a leg, the women became Galactic Dolls, implanted to crave and demand sex. Only Randi and Eve's therapy could undo the implants, words repetitively spoken to them while they were unconscious and in great pain and which made the victims insane. That was the first time the Sixth Invaders unleashed their mental implanting technology on us—at least that I knew of.

"Don't do anything yet. Meet at my place at eleven," Bev said.

Her confident tone encouraged me. Of all my sisters, she and I are the most alike, in personality, that is. As clones, we all look identical, even more so after the Galactic Doll mutation.

"Trust me. I've got this," she said.

**

"Wow!" I said.

I walked up to the apartments behind the CostumesRUs store at eleven and saw two army EMACs with their 50-caliber blasters facing forward in their upper turrets. Sixteen men and four women stood at attention, armed for a battle. General Bev, Lieutenant Gail Jackson, Lieutenant Engineer Betsy, and the other women in the group wore their fancy blue satin gowns with gold trim.

"Okay, we've got mission orders. Let's go rescue these victims, but stay alert for Sixth Invaders in disguise," General Bev barked. "Mount up." She saluted them. They chuckled and dispersed into the EMACs.

"Molly, we're all set, ready for anything. You're with me. We've entered the coordinates into the guidance systems. Let's kick ass. ETA: five minutes."

I couldn't help grinning; neither could Gail. I followed them into the lead vehicle. After we buckled up, General Bev issued the takeoff order.

I liked flying in these ships. Not only were they silent, but also they were gentle. No jarring liftoffs or a vibrating sense of high speed.

We landed between the MTES and a row of low buildings a quarter mile from the edge of the sprawling New O'Hare Spaceport. The roar of ships landing and departing made talking challenging. We spoke in between ships. The MTES passed within fifty feet of Phillip's Escort Services and on a direct path from the spaceport.

As the troops disembarked, two spacers came out of the building, their faces flush and with smiles that faded the moment they spotted the soldiers. Without a word, they got on the MTES and into the fast lane, running back to the spaceport. General Bev and I took the lead and headed into the building.

Phillip's Escort Services occupied a two-story, concrete block building. A gaudy sign of a stripper flashed, beckoning everyone to enter. But there were no windows. Ugly brownish-red bricks covered what once had been windows, providing a sharp contrast to the gray walls. We entered through wide double doors.

A sharp perfume odor struck our noses as though someone had overused theirs. Or more likely, the owner wanted to cover up other, more objectionable odors. The entrance area held plush sofas and chairs while giant posters of exotic women and a few men lined the walls. A reddish carpet let to a round-topped door, now closed. To its right were a counter and a male Galactic Doll with a touchpad.

He wore one of Leslie's new male suits. I smiled. Today, her new product line went on sale. This man was first in line or had pre-ordered. As he looked up, his expectant smile vanished. Worry lines creased his forehead. He said,

"Welcome to Phillip's—"

I cut him off. "We're looking for the owner of this place."

He cleared his throat twice. "I'm—I'm Phillip. What do you want? I've done nothing wrong. There are no Sixth Invaders here, just beautiful escorts."

"You took in eighteen terrified armless men and women two days ago," I said. "We're here to take them back to their spouses and families."

My words registered. His face flushed before his whole body relaxed. I hadn't expected such a reaction, rather the opposite.

"Oh thank heavens! You can have them. Please, please, take them away. We can't manage them. They're insane, just like our female soldiers were—the ones we saw on the news from Brussels, Tau Ceti."

"Huh? What's going on? These are the protesters attacked by our Local Defense Force."

"Don't know about that, ma'am. Look, you're free to take them. I beg you; take them. We can't handle them."

My face must have appeared dubious to him. He said, "Look, I'll show you what GEnt gave me." He meant Galactic Entertainment, their new sponsors.

He rummaged in a drawer beneath the counter and retrieved a document. "Here, take it. It's what came with them. We're sure as hell not going to make any profit on these people."

He handed the paper to General Bev who handed it to me.

My turn to be flustered. GEnt was my sponsor. After GD tried to terminate my fellow clones and me, Deanna, our billionaire sister, worked a compromise. GD turned us into Galactic Dolls, and GEnt took over our sponsorship. Heck, GEnt led the way in exposing corporate wrongdoing and inhumanity. After we stopped the Sixth Invader threat, her husband, Russell Godwyn, now also a male Galactic Doll, took over as CEO of our local Galactic Entertainment corporation.

What had we stumbled into? I read the document as did Bev.

```
To:   Phillip's Escort Services
From: Galactic Entertainment

Re: 13903852
Disposition of Armless Sex Dolls

     Galactic Entertainment hereby gives you
these men and women who have been convicted of
unspecified crimes and have completed their
prescribed punishments. Their sponsorship has
been turned over to us. Thus, each will now
receive a monthly stipend from GEnt, as long
as they perform their assigned work for you as
armless sex Dolls. Based on their physical
condition, we conclude they cannot perform any
other line of work.
     Per GD Order 124383853, you may assign
them to various spaceships where they can ply
their trade on the long duration flights.
Additionally, this order allows you to sell
them to prospective buyers, reporting such
sales to GEnt so we can take them off our
sponsorship rolls.

     Vladimir Checko
     CEO Sol Empire GEnt
```

"Can I hang on to this?"

"Sure, if'em you take them all. I'll let GEnt know you've got them, so they'll send you their monthly stipends." He wiped his forehead. "I warn you. They're nuts."

I've never seen a person so eager to be done with something.

"Bring them out," General Bev said. She issued orders to the other soldiers. I had to smile. They looked so disappointed. No action. No battles.

A young woman opened the doors as the line of eighteen armless Galactic Dolls waddled out. I hadn't seen Bev when the Sixth Invaders returned her, but her face paled, while several of her soldiers cursed.

The Dolls' faces radiated terror or perhaps fright. I couldn't get the image of the wobbling penguin line out of my mind. Yet, all mumbled something about craving sex and were we here to do it with them.

General Bev swallowed hard. Her voice cracked twice while issuing her orders. "At least, they don't have arms to paw us. Get them into the EMACs now. Find out their names, too."

Gail's face blanched. Lieutenant Betsy, who also had been captured and implanted as a sex Doll, grimaced and held her hands over her mouth.

I guessed Phillip thought we might not take these victims off his hands because he handed me a paper listing their names. "In case they can't remember their names," he said.

Over a year ago, GD men kidnapped me. I woke up on the Padella doctors' South Pacific atoll only to find Dr. Janet Padella had amputated my arms trying to get my "lucky" gene to express itself. So I had a good sense of the shock, fear, and terror these men and women were experiencing while trying to walk in their tall heels with little ability to keep their balance.

General Bev and I brought up the rear. "What do we do with them?" she whispered.

"Is this—is this similar to the way you were? I mean when you got captured by the Sixth Invaders?"

"Mostly. Those fiends must be active again. I'm mobilizing the First Division, that's for damn sure!"

"Let me make a call."

I dialed Deanna. We couldn't take these victims to the Med Center, and we couldn't return them to their homes either.

"They gotta have Eve and Randi's therapy," Bev said.

"Hey, Deanna. I've got a real problem here."

I outlined what we'd done and the situation. She came through without my asking. That's the kind of sister and CEO she was.

"Bring them to the Cartwright Skyscraper. We'll house them on the living floor where you used to live. I'll call Ted and get robots assistants brought in today. Good lord, here we go again. I thought we'd seen the last of those Sixth Invaders," she said.

"Might not be Sixth Invaders, Deanna. I think it's our own people, our own corporations. I've got a signed order from GEnt. See if Russell can be there, too. I think he's got some explaining to do."

After calling her, I phoned Randi, Eve, and Celeste, telling them what we'd found. They promised to meet us at Deanna's skyscraper. I relaxed. If there was any hope for these people, it lay in their therapy. It had undone the Sixth Invaders' powerful mental implants. Bev and Lieutenant Betsy were proof of that.

Bev's EMACs landed on the roof of the Cartwright Skyscraper. As we unloaded the victims and led them to the elevators, two jumped off the roof. Five others tried to follow. Although taken by surprise, the soldiers reacted, preventing the other five from committing suicide. Amid sobbing, pleading to for us to kill them, and begging for sex, we ushered the remaining sixteen down to the forty-ninth floor and into the living quarters.

Deanna joined us, helping to get them settled.

That done, I asked her, "As bad as it was with Bev?"

"Similar, but not the same. Bev couldn't do anything but act out her implanted behavior, pawing every man in sight. These people are too frightened to carry out the implanted patterns. Lack of arms is limiting them. Are we facing those damned Sixth Invaders again? And what's GEnt got to do with it? Russell is on his way."

I showed her the incriminating document. Levelheaded Deanna cursed. She headed off to hire temporary personal assistants.

With a sigh, I called Piper Strawn. "There's no easy way to tell you this." I exhaled and outlined the condition of her husband, adding, "I'll see he gets the same special therapy General Bev and the other female soldiers received. There's a good chance that'll erase his insanity."

"Can I see him now?" Piper's voice sounded shaky, but since she was a nurse, I thought that a good idea. If nothing else, she could check on their state of health.

Next, Deanna and Russell arrived on the floor. I allowed them to inspect a few of the victims before joining them in the hallway. He'd been a victim of the central Chicago Sixth Invaders' attack. When I first met him before the genetic mutation, he was a big man, overweight, with a pudgy face and a countenance that demanded respect. Today, he was still a big man, but the mutation had cost him that extra weight. I smiled, for he too had just cut his hair short and wore one of these new "male" suits designed by Leslie and Felix. He must have pre-ordered along with thousands of other men. I couldn't blame him though his apparel couldn't hide his monster breasts, shapely body, and high-pitched voice.

I outlined my investigation and discoveries. Then, I showed him the official document from his corporation, rather the Sol Empire-wide GEnt. His corporation was our local one.

"This is the first I've seen of this. Looks like official document numbers. Let's go to Deanna's office so I can use her computer. We should be able to track this back to its origins," Russell said.

"I'll join you shortly. Piper's on her way. Besides, I want to see if Randi, Eve, and Celeste can work their magic on these victims."

Russell nodded, turned, and headed down the hallway. Deanna followed him while I waited for Piper.

She stepped off the elevator, her heels echoing just as Russell's had. Her pale face and forehead lines told me much. At least, her eyes weren't red. As a nurse, she'd probably seen it all.

As we walked down the hall to the room where I'd had Aaron Strawn placed, I outlined what I'd uncovered. "Brace yourself, Piper. It's grim. My sisters are on their way here; they cured Bev and many other female soldiers. There is hope."

We entered my old bedroom. Aaron was lying on the bed. When Piper entered, he tried to get up, but his arms didn't work, an action that brought a wall of tears to his eyes and another bout of terror to his face, all the while he kept reciting his implanted words. "Piper! Kill me, please. I can't live like this. I'm a sex Doll now. I crave sex. I need sex. Do it

31

with me now. I can't stand it any longer. I have to fulfill your sexual fantasy right now. Kill me. I can't take it. I'm helpless. Kill me, Piper. Oh no." He passed out.

Tears trickled down Piper's cheeks, as she reached for his hands to check his pulse. They weren't there. She touched his neck instead.

"Too much emotion. He's fainted. Just as good. I'll sit with him until he comes around. Should I take him home?"

"No. He stays here until we get him through his therapy and make other arrangements. GEnt is now sponsoring him. I'll see if Randi or Eve or Celeste can work on him soon."

I left her sitting beside his bed, rubbing her hands over his face and met the trio in the hallway. They'd arrived and had inspected a few patients. "Ah, thanks for coming. Verdict?"

Randi exhaled. "Goddamned implants! Yes, it's just like the Sixth Invaders implants. I think we can undo it, but it'll take time. Deanna said she's bringing in a cook and assistants. She's called Ted. He's sending over some of the Sixth Invader robot assistants that were to be given to the men and boys who lost their arms. Thanks to you and Bev that never happened."

"Okay. If one of you can do Piper's husband first— Aaron Strawn. Since there are so many of them and in such desperate need, I'll lend a hand, if you'll show me how to run the therapy on them."

My heart ached to aid these people. While I had helped them by discovering what had happened to them and arranging their rescue from the escort service, this seemed trivial compared to their physical situation.

Celeste chuckled. "About time, Molly. We'll hold you to that. Meanwhile, go sort out the causes. We'll see what we can do for them. Go. Go."

I thanked the trio and headed to the elevator. One floor up, I found Deanna and Russell at her computer installation.

"Ah, here you are, Molly. I've sent word of this to all Earth's GEnt local offices. No CEOs knew of this document, and several discovered they're now sponsoring many armless Galactic Dolls as escorts. A few CEOs reported that some victims are off their rolls, sold to off-world personnel.

Criminal, I'd say. I've backtracked these orders. Here, have a look." He handed me another document.

```
To:   Sol Empire Galactic Entertainment
From: Sol Empire Galactic Medicine

Re: 1499903852
Disposition of Armless Sex Dolls

     Galactic Medicine hereby gives you these
men   and   women   who've   been   convicted   of
unspecified  crimes  and  have  completed  their
prescribed   punishments,   per   GD   order
124383853.   We   have   verified   each   is   in
excellent  health.  As  armless  people,  their
employment  possibilities  are  limited.  Coupled
with  their  mental  state,  GMed's  opinion  is
they  can  best  serve  the  empire  as  sex  Dolls.
Thus,  we're  turning  their  sponsorship  over  to
you.  Dole  them  out  to  local  escort  services  as
you  see  fit.
     Per  GD  Order  124383853,  you  may  assign
them  to  various  spaceships  where  they  can  ply
their  trade  on  the  long  duration  flights.  This
order  allows  you  to  sell  them  to  prospective
buyers.

     Boris Yvette
     CEO Sol Empire Gmed
```

Russell continued. "I'm tracing it back further. Here's the order given to Sol Empire GMed. It comes from Sol Empire GD." He handed me the second document.

```
To:   Sol Empire Galactic Medicine
From: Sol Empire Galactic Defense

Re: 124383853
Disposition of Armless Sex Dolls
```

Galactic Defense hereby gives you these men and women who have been convicted of unspecified crimes and have completed their prescribed punishments, per GD order 124383852. Please verify their current state of health, both physical and mental. As armless people, their employment possibilities are limited. GD's opinion is they can best serve the empire as sex Dolls, but this evaluation is subject to GMed's review and findings. Thus, we're relaying their sponsorship to you. Dole them out to any local service as you determine they are qualified for and relay sponsorship to the proper corporation.

If you decide they may best serve the Sol Empire as sex Dolls, you may also assign them to various spaceships where they can ply their trade on the long duration flights. This order allows you to sell them to prospective buyers.

Gregor Mantovo
CEO Sol Empire GD

"Wow, this is wild," I said. "Can we find out anything more? Like who did what to whom?"

Russell chuckled. "On it. We've got the doc number. Bringing it up now. It's a good thing all CEOs have access to corporation official documents. We're not privy to private correspondence, mind you, only the official docs. I'll print you a copy too."

To: Sol Empire Galactic Defense, SolEmpire Galactic Medicine
From: Sol Empire Galactic Expansion

Re: 124383852.
Disposition of Protesters

Galactic Expansion has determined these protests in and around our offices are treasonous and disruptive. Hence, GD is authorized to order your local offices to use their LDF to capture these traitors. Stun them and take them to local Med Centers. While still unconscious, these traitors are to be injected with the Sixth Invaders genetic mutation nanoparticles that removes their arms. Once injected, GD is to transport them to Moscow and the GD research facility there, APEX.

APEX will implant sex Doll behavior patterns into their unconscious minds. We're working hard to be able to implant proper behavior patterns into our criminal elements. These will be an excellent test of our new behavior modification skills. Once implanted, take them to the Moscow Med Center, who'll monitor their mutations.

When they revive, GD will transport the rehabilitated personnel back to the cities of origin, transferring them to local GMed facilities. Give them this order: GD hereby gives you these men and women who have been convicted of unspecified crimes and have completed their prescribed punishments, per GD order 124383852. Please verify their current state of health, both physical and mental. As armless people, their employment possibilities are limited. GD's opinion is they can best serve the empire as sex Dolls, but this evaluation is subject to GMed's review and findings. Thus, we're relaying their sponsorship to you. Dole them out to any local service as you determine they are qualified for and relay sponsorship to the proper corporation.

If you decide they may best serve the Sol

Empire as sex Dolls, you may also assign them
to various spaceships where they can ply their
trade on the long duration flights. This order
allows you to sell them to prospective buyers.

Petr Leonovich
CEO Sol Empire Gpan

Stunned, Deanna couldn't curse. Russell's face flushed;
his fists tensed. He swore. I knew I had to do something and
fast.

"How soon can you arrange for me to meet Petr? Or are
you allowed to do so?"

Russell fumed. "They've gone too far, much too far. I
won't stand for this. Oh, CEO Helen Hugo of our local GD can
get you in to see him. She's handling receptionist duties while
these Russians move into the many skyscrapers. Good luck
seeing the beast. This has to stop now."

With that, he kissed Deanna, grabbed his copies, and
dashed out of the room. Figuratively, since in these heels, no
one dashes.

Deanna said, "We've seen man's inhumanity to man
these past two years, along with the Sixth Invaders'
barbarousness, but I never expected *this* from our own
leaders. Maybe Petr is now under the control of the aliens, just
as the others were. Do you suppose? How can we find out?"

"Could be. I'll see him and sort this out."

I stepped out into the hallway and called Helen, telling
her what I wanted: a brief meeting with Petr Leonovich, the
CEO of Earth Galactic Expansion or GPan, the corporation
that controlled the other fourteen major corporations.

"Yes, today," I said.

She agreed and promised to call me back. I paced up
and down the hallway outside Deanna's office, my heels
clicking on the tiled flooring. At her hyperspace relay comm
center room, I turned around and walked back. Five minutes
and a dozen loops passed before my phone rang.

"Hey, Molly. He'll see you in a half hour. They are
unpacking and getting organized, so he wants you to make it

quick," Helen said. "He wants to meet you—you being famous and all that. General Blythe, too."

I thanked Helen, glanced at the time displayed on my phone and picked up my copy of the documents. Fuming, I headed off to the Galactic Expansion skyscraper, one block over from GD.

Chapter 4 A Deterrent

I entered the GPan skyscraper, stopping at the main reception desk. "Molly Parkinson to see Petr Leonovich."

While she called up, I glanced at the lobby. One day, I must take their tour. The lobby contained models of various spaceships, the various moons and worlds of the Sol Empire, and even a history panel. Once more, I realized how little I knew.

The receptionist handed me a visitor's badge. "Take that elevator over there. Floor 100. He's expecting you, Miss Parkinson."

I thanked her, took a deep breath, and headed to the elevator, this time without a security guard escort. As it shot upwards, memories of my brief stint as temporary CEO of Galactic Defense returned, since I had to ride its elevator up the hundred floors to its top floor.

When the doors opened, I gasped. I saw dozens of men, some wearing GPan security uniforms, carrying boxes hither and thither. Real men. Until this moment, I hadn't seen a male that wasn't a male Doll—not for months.

A bass voice, familiar from our phone conversations, called out over the din. "Ms. Parkinson. This way. Excuse the mess."

Perhaps in his early forties, Petr Leonovich stood tall, though, in my heels, our eyes met, a fact neither of us missed. He had strong muscles visible through the open collar of his white silk shirt. His suit jacket and tie lay across the back of his tall desk chair. I guessed his suit cost more than my monthly GEnt stipend. His face was handsome. A black mustache lined his thick lips.

"My eldest son, Dimitri, is visiting his fiancé, Natalie, who is Gregor's daughter. This is my natural son, Ivan."

Ivan looked like a younger version of Petr, black hair and eyes, and a similar mustache. He had his dad's physique— a handsome man, likely my age.

A middle-aged woman walked into the office from the

attached living quarters. As expected, she was a Galactic Doll. As far as I knew, all women on Earth, except those in the assisted living homes and those still children, had been genetically modified, compliments of the Sixth Invaders and their schemes. A gorgeous woman, she was my height, with waist-length blonde hair and blue eyes. Rather her tiny waistline and lack of arms took me by surprise.

From Leslie and her fetish outfits, I recognized the cherry red outer corset but guessed she wore an inner wasp-waist corset. Her figure: striking, and she walked erect. Irina had a distinct accent.

"Are you going to introduce me, Petr?"

"Of course, my darling. Molly Parkinson, my charming wife, Irina, the perfect beauty queen."

I must have been gaping at her unique appearance, because he added, "She has the smallest waist of any Russian model. Irina was Miss Moscow when I snatched her up." A pleased look illuminated his face and eyes.

Irina interjected, "Only because I insisted Petr make me into a perfect female form." She batted her eyes and smiled.

I blinked and saw a much younger Irina. She wore a swimming suit with a banner that read Miss Moscow. A small diamond tiara rested on her head. I realized I'd just looked into Irina's mind, where she held onto an image of herself when she'd won the title.

"Ahem," Petr cleared his throat.

To these three, I must have looked spaced out or not-there. My face felt rather hot.

"Excuse me. Yes, I can see just how beautiful you are, Irina. You must have a personal assistant."

She smiled, "Ya, of course. But I expect you want to talk with Petr. Ivan, we should leave them be." To Ivan, she said, "Perhaps you should go next door and help your fiancé get settled in. Mary needs your encouragement. Bring her over for dinner tonight."

"Yes, mother. Just as soon as dad gives me his okay. There's so much unpacking to do."

She and Ivan moved out of the central lounge. Petr motioned me into his adjoining office, shooing several workers out. Boxes lay in various states of unpacking.

"What brings you to see me so soon? Once we get moved in, I planned to ask you to visit me. Please, just call me Petr."

Polite or argumentative? I had a choice on how to handle what I'd come for. I decided to be polite.

"Petr, I've come about this." I showed him the printed copies of the official orders.

"Yes, that *is* what I ordered. We can't have these hooligans protesting our treatment of our aged parents. If I took no action, soon we'd have riots in the streets—rapid criminality. No, I was being humane. I could have sent them to spend ten years at our penal colony on Mercury, but most would prefer death to that hell hole. I didn't think their criminal actions warranted a death sentence. I wanted them to become productive members of society again. Hence, those orders."

"But..." I protested.

He raised his hand, silencing me. "We have learned a good deal from these terrible Sixth Invaders. They've given us the best clues to human behavior modification. In Moscow, we've set up a research facility using these alien machines. Soon, I expect we'll be able to change the behavior of even the most hardened criminals on Mercury. In fact, I hope to close that expensive prison system in a decade at most. You must admit a simple behavior modification is far more humane than a lengthy prison sentence on Mercury."

I couldn't argue that point. "First, Petr, you're overreacting to the simple protests of the killing of our older people. Especially now we've discovered we can rejuvenate them. I assume you've seen the results on our central Chicago's older people's bodies—the ones exposed to the aliens' Galactic Doll genetic mutation agent—now they have bodies that are maybe twenty-five years old. In fact, Doctors Janet and Nelson Padella, our top geneticists, are now youthful and back researching more cures. We can make good use of our older people."

"Yes, yes, yes, but," Petr began. From his condescending tone, I knew he wasn't buying that argument.

"Earth doesn't need more garbage collectors and grounds tenders caring for the vast number of abandoned properties. I've ordered a study of those in Earth's assisted living homes. Those who have led valuable lives—our educated scientists and mathematicians—those we will make rejuvenation offers to— just not the bottom feeders."

Upon hearing that last phrase, my hackles rose. Was I a bottom feeder? Leslie? Janine? I changed the topic before I lost my temper.

"It looks like you've used that alien genetic mutation agent that General Blythe and I secured before the aliens could use it on central Chicago and the rest of Earth. You know—the one they planned to use to make men into armless Galactic Dolls."

"Ah, yes. We have you and General Blythe to thank for intervening before the aliens could rectify their mistake. Yes, that's the agent we've been using."

A rush of anger surged. "But that biological agent is horrible! It should have been destroyed, not used. My god, armless Galactic Dolls? What *are* you thinking?"

"They can be superb sex Dolls. My Irina's just wonderful, isn't she?"

I glared back. "We requested that biological agent be destroyed."

"No way! First, I sent samples to all local Galactic Medicine offices around the Earth. Then, I sent copies of it to all genetic research facilities and to most medical centers. The more people who are studying it, the more useful medical breakthroughs we'll have. Besides, no one in their right mind would use it as a weapon as the Sixth Invaders proposed. Only aliens might consider it a weapon."

I must have looked even angrier because he continued justifying his position. "Look, it's like the ancient atomic bomb. Back when there were countries on Earth, they stockpiled those bombs, using them as a deterrent. No one would be stupid enough to use them as a weapon. Oops. I guess the people in this geographic area, the USA I think it was called, used it on two Japanese cities. But after that, no one was stupid enough to use them as a weapon. They were a deterrent.

"So in like manner, this Sixth Invader biological agent that makes armless Galactic Dolls is being spread around Earth as a deterrent. No one will ever think of using it as a weapon, just as no one did with those nuclear bombs. We're perfectly safe. In fact, I hope that with the world's geneticists working with it, why, in a decade, we'll have many incredible genetic mutation agents available."

I fumed. Okay, I lost control. "Damn you! You're the stupidest man I've ever met. Don't you know this mutation is dominant? All children from any mating with one of these will result in the armless Galactic Doll physical form. You're dooming future generations. No one will use it as a weapon? Height of foolishness. That's why Bev and I wanted it destroyed, not propagated around the world. What are you going to do with a world of armless inhabitants?"

I ran down, but I picked up his thoughts, which again startled me. I sensed his concept of Irina as being the perfect wife and got the impression his son Ivan was marrying a version of Irina, but her image wasn't as clear as Irina's was.

His face reddened. "I think you're overreacting. You'll see. In a decade, why, we'll have many beneficial results from this mutation agent. Besides, we're civilized people, not the insane barbarians these vicious Sixth Invaders are. Our people would never use such a thing as a weapon. Now if you'll excuse me, I've much unpacking to do."

I knew I was dismissed and didn't protest further. He wouldn't listen. As I descended to the ground floor to turn in my visitor's pass, I felt pleased that I'd verified Petr was behind this latest inhumanity and learned two facts. One, he wasn't the brightest of leaders or ethical. Two, he wasn't an alien. Okay, three facts. A Sixth Invader wasn't occupying his body or that of Irina or Ivan.

If the Sixth Invaders were still around, they weren't merging with Petr's body as they had with Mr. Armstrong and Mr. Hardy of Galactic Expansion and Galactic Defense. Our new Sol Empire leaders were human men, not aliens in disguise. I felt relieved as I walked out of the skyscraper and breathed in the warm, fishy air from the lake. I headed back to

42

the Cartwright building to lend a hand with the sixteen victims. I promised myself to find out how many other similar victims there were. Could I do anything to help those victims?

When I joined everyone, my Doll husband, Ted, had arrived, bringing with him sixteen sets of personal assistant robots. These humanoid-looking machines performed two specific actions for these handicapped people. Foremost, their arm appendages handled feeding the victims, along with transporting food to the table. They also operated the person's phone for them, activating and placing the requested call in lieu of the person's thumb print.

Every household in central Chicago had a hair and nail machine, a dressing/undressing machine, and the maid robot that did cooking and cleaning. The original Sixth Invaders plan guaranteed the survival of the armless Dolls by providing them with these three machines along with the personal assistant robots.

"Hey, Molly. How'd it go? I brought the robots and got them programmed to respond to the victims—at least when they have recovered from their temporary insanity," Ted said. He gave me a welcome hug and kiss.

"Thanks. Not so good. Petr is behind it. He's a stupid ass, but he's not one of those Sixth Invaders as I thought he might be. I glimpsed his mind and his wife's too."

I told him what I'd discovered. "If you get the time, see if you can find out how many other victims there have been and if we can get them brought here to Chicago and if we can give them the machines and robots."

"And, therapy?" he said.

"Yes, if there aren't too many for us to do. I'll get Celeste to show me how to do it. Catch you at supper, dear. And thanks again. Darn fast response."

Ted laughed. "We have a million of those robot feeders sitting in storage, so it wasn't a problem. Catch ya."

He left, and I met with Celeste, who had made a list of the sixteen—their original occupations, personal contact information, and families. Leslie had already brought each of the men one of her new "male" outfits. So now it was time to help them over their traumas. If we didn't, they'd probably succumb. Worse, this mutation was dominant. Even though their future children would be similarly handicapped, I still thought life was precious and not to be wasted. Oops. In the vision I'd had, it was dominant, but here, no one yet knew that for certain.

"I want to help, Celeste. Show me how to do it."

Celeste grinned. "Okay. It's simple in theory. Note, we'll only try to erase the trauma they've recently suffered. We won't dive into their entire past as I did with you. We don't have hundreds of hours to devote to one person. Our goal is to erase the recent trauma. Get the terror and fear reduced, the command words desensitized so they aren't trying to have sex with everyone, and erase the pain and unconsciousness they endured during the attack and during the mutation process."

"Sounds like a tall order."

"Yes. The idea is to get them to return to the start of the incident where they were protesting. Then, have them re-experience what happened, telling you about it as they go through it. Remember, have them tell you what they are seeing, smelling, hearing, tasting, and so on. All the senses. Also, you know they are re-experiencing it when they are talking in the present tense. 'I see a nurse injecting me,' for example. If they use the past tense, 'A nurse injected me with,' they have bounced out of the trauma incident. So you nudge them back into it with questions like 'what are you seeing?'

"As nasty as this is—implant merged with stun guns and genetic mutation—expect the going to be very rough. It's likely to take many recountings to get it all erased. I'll keep an eye on you. Let's get started. Randi and Eve have already begun on Aaron and Sandy. We'll do Becky and Henry Dillard."

Becky was a third-grade schoolteacher, who had become a Galactic Doll like millions of other women late last year. Her parents were in an assisted living center north of the central Chicago area targeted by the Sixth Invaders a couple months ago. She'd protested, trying to save the lives of her parents. Becky taught at the same school complex that Kyle and Hank did, though the men taught at the high school.

Henry worked at A1 Food Distribution Center where he was a manager who oversaw the grocery delivery system. His parents were also in an assisted living center. Like Becky, he wanted to have GMed rejuvenate his parents, giving them more life. He and his wife had traveled down from northern Chicago to join Aaron's protest.

I pulled up a chair and sat close to Becky, who sat on the edge of the bed. Henry sat on the opposite side, across from Celeste. Working with these people turned out to be more challenging than I expected. Their implant forced them to act out the demanded behavior—that is, craving and demanding sex from anyone. Yet, their loss of arms and feelings of total helplessness caused them to oscillate between grief and terror. The duality made them almost unreachable with Celeste's therapy.

As I tried to get Becky to begin to re-experience her horror-filled days, I had another one of my futuristic flashes. It took me by surprise. I saw Becky and Henry returning to their home, but getting no therapy or training in how to use their feet as hands, though the helping robots went with them. Their terror vanished as I watched them trying to fulfill their implanted behavior patterns while almost helpless. Soon, they slipped from grief down to apathy, ending their feeble attempts to carry out their cravings. Days later, they sat on their bed doing nothing, not even eating. I watched them die.

I jerked my head, bringing myself back to the present, hoping that I'd not missed anything with Becky. Celeste cocked her head and raised an eyebrow. I sensed her slipping into my mind, and I showed her the futuristic images I'd just seen. She nodded. We both understood. Without successful therapy to erase their trauma, with no support group behind them, and with no training in using their feet as hands, they would succumb and die, unwilling and unable to overcome this huge barrier to life thrown so suddenly upon them.

Survive or succumb. When faced with terrible situations, each person has their own answer.

"Come on, Becky. I know you can do it. Let's go to the time when you went to Aaron's protest rally."

"I have to have sex now. I can't take it any longer. I can't live like this. Help me, please. I've got Henry convinced to come with me."

Above the implanted behavior and the terror of her helplessness, I noticed she'd obeyed my command.

"Good, Becky. Now move on through everything that happened to you. Tell me about it as you do that."

"I've got to have sex. I'm helpless. I'm holding a sign. Maybe this will work, I say to Henry."

I blinked but then realized she was doing it—re-experiencing what had happened to her. True, it was buried beneath the implant and other trauma, but if I listened, I could see she was moving through it.

Talk about slow going. By suppertime and with lots of encouragement and coaching, I'd gotten her through the entire several days once. True, she'd not gone near the underlying pain, unconsciousness, and huge loss, but she was calmer. Fear replaced her terror, and exhaustion forced us to end for the day. Henry, likewise. Hence, Celeste and I made sure they ate well and tucked them in for a good night's sleep.

Randi and Eve joined us for an evening tea and note comparing.

Eve said, "I got Aaron through the whole thing once. I can't believe I took eight hours to make that one pass. This'll take time to erase."

"It wasn't this bad with me, was it?" I asked, recalling my own reactions when I awoke and found myself mutated and armless, joining them and Ted on that South Pacific atoll of the Padella doctors.

Randi laughed. "Hardly. You weren't trying to carry out an implanted behavior pattern at the same time. We only had to deal with your panic and terror. No, they've done quite a job on these victims. My man was in the Local Defense Force, stunned by a protester. He's taking this hard. You know—feelings of betrayal by Galactic Defense on top of everything else. Quite nasty."

"If we don't succeed," I said, "many won't survive. I saw a flash of their future. They'll just give up and starve to death."

Randi validated me. "Yes, that would be my prediction. Give up. But some might try to commit suicide before dropping into abject apathy. And some would fight on and never give up. Life potentials differ from person to person."

What an insightful thought. I said, "What about the others who've had this done to them? I heard there have been lots of other protests in many other cities."

"If they are sold or working in escort services, we might not get to them," Celeste said.

That was sobering. I told them about my conversation with Petr. They reacted with curses.

So much for July 2, I thought, as I crawled into bed beside Ted, grateful to snuggle beside him.

I had to get up early the next morning because I wanted to get Becky's trauma erased. I felt compelled to do so, but any sentient human being should feel the same way if they had the technology to wipe out such awful trauma. But Ted rose sooner and had the news on.

"Dear, you've got to see what's on the news. I think Russell's making waves. Belay that. Russell's made a tidal wave," Ted called out.

I wandered out to the comm center and then smiled. Russell had made a worldwide broadcast, outlining what had happened to the protesters and why, relaying full details.

"Well, that's igniting a bonfire," I said.

Ted chuckled.

As we ate breakfast, I got a phone call from Helen Hugo, CEO of our local GD.

"Hey, Molly. Glad I caught you. You *must* meet a young Russian couple. One works for GPan, while the other works for GD. They're still unpacking, but trust me, Molly. You and Ted simply must meet them."

"Okay, Helen, but I'm tied up giving therapy to the victims. Can we get together later?"

"How wonderful. Any chance you can salvage their lives? I can't imagine living like that, though I've made my husband live that way as punishment for his crimes against you, me, and so many others."

"Lord, I hope so, Helen. So is Casper still an armless Doll? Is that working out as you wanted? He's not causing more problems is he?"

She chuckled. "He's calmed down a good deal, accepting the fact he's darn near helpless. He doesn't even try to find alternate ways to do things, not like you and Ted did. But that's fine with me. It's worked out for the best. He's no longer committing crimes against others or me, so it's better than terminating him or sending him to the penal colony. However, you've got to meet Dimitri and Natalie. I know. How about you and Ted joining us by the Lake for the annual Midsummer Fireworks on the fourteenth?"

"Yes, that's perfect. We'll meet you for supper and walk down to the Lake."

"Excellent. I'll make the arrangements," Helen said.

"What was that all about?" Ted said.

I explained Helen's call and our date to watch the fireworks. No one knew why there was a night of fireworks in July. Some suggested the tradition was an ancient one, going back many centuries to when there used to be countries on Earth, long before the corporations. Many thought Hank might know; he's our historian and Janine's husband.

I worked with Becky for another seven days before she erased the last part of her trauma and emotional loss. On day four, we uncovered the words spoken to her while she was unconscious and being bombarded with the aesthetic, white, very high-frequency energy. She heard a voice saying, "I am a sex Doll. I crave and need sex many times each day. My highest goal is to fulfill the sex fantasies of my clients. I must constantly remind myself of this."

That was all, just four lines. But those four lines along with everything else had altered her behavior. Had they only implanted her, I suspect she would have been content to be a sex Doll as the implant demanded. But combined with the shocking loss of her arms and feelings of utter helplessness and terror, she'd gone mad.

When we finished, she was sane and calm, though as soon as she had to do something, feelings of fear and fright returned, but those were natural. Ted provided each victim with a touchpad filled with all the how-to holographic videos that other armless men and women had made—the ones I'd watched while I was on the atoll and the ones the Sixth Invaders had planned to play over the comm centers for the millions of armless men and boys of Chicago. He and I figured with this video library to refer to they might have a good chance of independent lives. I encouraged her to go back to teaching grade school this fall, and I had Kyle and Hank work with her to do just that.

On July 11, I began therapy sessions on another victim, as did Eve, Randi, and Celeste. Four down and twelve to go. The other victims had had over a week to calm down, to get used to their new lives, and to watch the hours of how-to videos. Their therapy went faster. By suppertime of July 15, we had finished another four, sending them home, but we still had eight to go.

I was home when Ted got back from work. We changed clothes and headed for the elegant Loop restaurant where Helen arranged for us to meet these two Russians. After the meal, our extended family planned to meet up and join the throng by the Lake to listen to the music and watch the fireworks display, compliments of GEnt, who always sponsored this event.

Chapter 5 The Meeting

Ted and I entered Barnaby's, the most expensive restaurant in downtown Chicago. Their real food, superb, but far beyond our salaries. Thankfully, Helen picked up the tab. Upon entering, a waiter took us to Helen's table.

Helen rose as we walked up. She brought Casper along with her, the first time I'd seen him since he had Ted shot and had kidnapped me to make me into his armless toy Doll. That hadn't worked out the way he'd planned. After that, GPan installed me as temporary head of GD, and Helen had demanded his form of punishment. Today, Ted and I had our arms back; I suspected Casper would never have his back, not if Helen had her way.

As we walked up, his cheeks flushed. His eyes glared at me as though he could burn my soul with his vision.

I said, "Casper. Enjoying the night out, I see. We're doing fine, as you can see. Oh, my. Who are these two?"

Ted and I stared at the young couple who rose to meet us. I looked at myself while Ted looked at how he should have appeared or how Felix had looked before the alien mutation struck us all.

"I don't believe this," Natalie said. Her eyes opened wide while her hands rose to cover her mouth, revealing a lot of jewelry and five rings, each of which held large gemstones. She had my black hair, thick lips, and even the silly smile. She also wore a blue satin gown similar to mine. We shared matching tastes in colors.

Ted stared at Dimitri, who looked like a normal young man. I sensed Ted's reaction: jealousy or envy. Ted said, "Incredible."

Helen laughed. "For once, I've gotten you both good. Yes, this is Dimitri Leonovich, the adopted son of Petr and Irina. This is Natalie Mantovo, adopted daughter of Gregor and Dasha."

Natalie lowered her hands. "How can this be? You look exactly like me."

Ted laughed, "And Dimitri looks like I should be—before they genetically mutated me, though I shouldn't complain. The mutation regrew my arms. I'm Ted Billings. My wife, Molly."

Dimitri chuckled. "We'd heard about the alien mutations here in Chicago. Even saw the news images. Kind of wondered what I'd look like if it had been me. Glad it wasn't though. But how come you both look like us? Are we twins?"

"Yes, Dimitri," Natalie said. "That must be it. Twins. We thought we were orphans."

We sat. Helen had ordered for us, so we could chat. She had a very pleased expression on her face.

I said, "I guess I should explain. We're all clones. The Padella doctors cloned the men first and us girls two years later. All part of a Department of Defense secret cloning project to breed lucky soldiers. Since it failed, they moved on to the nano particle things, abandoning us until the DNA database project came along.

"So, Natalie, you have a lot of identical sisters. General Beverly Blossom Blythe, CEO Deanna Cartwright, me, Leslie, Janine, and our three younger sisters, Randi, Eve, and Celeste. Those three have a bunch of doctorates each while Deanna is a billionaire EMAC designer and engineer. I'm a private investigator.

"Dimitri, you've brothers, but mutations made them male Galactic Dolls. Ted and Felix. Ted has a couple doctorates, too. He's an R&D engineer at Galactic Robotics. For the last couple years, we've been searching for the rest of us. So tell us about yourselves."

"Incredible, Natalie. This is almost beyond belief," said Dimitri. His face, animated; his eyes, wide and bright. "So are we brothers and sisters then?"

Ted chuckled. "Long ago, we decided we're just normal people. Except for Leslie, who claims we're all very lucky. She might be right though. Casper here had his goons kidnap Molly and shoot me while we were sleeping. Fortunately, I fell asleep with my laptop on my chest, and the bullet shattered it and not me."

Natalie stared at Casper. "So why did you shoot Ted and

kidnap Molly? Don't you love Helen? From what I've seen, she's a wonderful woman."

His face turned crimson. Helen spoke for him. "He couldn't keep his thing in his pants. He wanted an armless play toy, someone he could dominate. So now he's paying the price for his crimes. Don't let money go to your heads. I'm doing a thousand times better now that Casper is under control. I have a photography art show coming up this September. Amazing what some of us gave up to become an executive's wife. Well, not anymore. Natalie, don't give up anything just to marry a future CEO."

Natalie laughed. "Hardly. I've been on Pylon, Epsilon Eridani for the last two years training to be a future leader in Galactic Defense. I'd love to talk with General Blythe sometime."

"Another soldier?" Ted teased.

"Not so much that as knowledgeable in ways and means of protecting our far-flung Sol Empire. Dimitri might not be a CEO though. His brother Ivan is in line for that position."

"Natalie's right. Ivan's on that path. Petr, Ivan, and I don't agree on many things. I'm quite the black sheep of the family," Dimitri said. He looked at Natalie before continuing. "I can't see having a trophy wife like mom. Mind you, she's nice enough, but Irina can't do much. It's true—she was Miss Moscow when dad met her and convinced her to marry him. Ivan's following his example, but I sure as heck won't. So you've got a doctorate?"

Ted smiled. "Two so far. One in computer programming and one in robotics. I'm in the research and development department, helping design robots that can help the handicapped. As you can see, we have an epidemic of armless people, but there are other handicapped people as well."

Natalie said, "You mean like the soldiers who lost and arm and leg fighting the robots of the Sixth Invaders?"

"Not necessarily. Our accidental discovery that the Galactic Doll mutation will regrow the missing limbs has pretty well restored those soldiers. Some people are blind; others, deaf, for example. I'm looking at ways a robot helper can aid anyone who has difficulties. I'm trying to show the world that a robot isn't a war machine like the Sixth Invaders used them."

Dimitri said, "Well, you must be good with computer systems. Helen said you and Molly rooted out GD corruption."

"Yeah, well, we botched it," Molly admitted. "We missed many other things."

"Don't blame yourself," Helen broke in. "The aliens mind-controlled people—that whole body swap thing. Does it work?"

"Yes, it works," I answered.

"How?" said Natalie. "We heard about it on the news."

I shrugged. "You should ask our dear friend Holly Ann. She's the one that figured it out."

Ted added, "It all has to do with that intensely white, pure aesthetic energy, in the kilo-yottahertz range. It's way beyond normal frequencies used in robotics."

I added, "The Body Swap machine and the implant machine both work on the same principles."

Dimitri said, "Yeah, that's what Petr said. With it, we can change human behavior. That's a step forward, isn't it? A good use of the alien tech."

"Hardly," I spat out. "You've no idea what damage it does to people. It's like adding a new compulsive behavior insanity or madness to a person. If you want to change behavior, this is the wrong way to go about it. Those poor victims Petr had mutated and implanted to be sex Dolls—my sisters and I spent eight days trying to undo their insanity so they can try to become normal people again. Now if they hadn't mutated them into armless Dolls, Petr might have gotten away with it for a while, before the implant wore down. But when it does, heaven help the perpetrators! There'll be hell to pay over this mess."

Casper spoke. "So when do I get my arms regrown? I'd like to be a human being again."

"When I'm convinced you've learned your lessons," Helen said. "If you had arms today, you'd probably shoot me." His face turned bright red.

"So what is this therapy thing of yours? It sounds powerful," Natalie said.

Helen looked at her watch. We'd finished our meal, though one of the robot assistants had fed Casper. "We'd better postpone that. There's always a huge crowd for the fireworks. Afterward, maybe you both can go back to Molly and Ted's place and meet the others."

"Can we? I've got so many questions," said Natalie. "Besides, I'd love to meet General Blythe."

I grinned. "Sure. Love to have you. You're one of our sisters now."

"And brothers, too," Ted added.

As we departed the restaurant, Casper whined. "Helen, keep your arm around me. I don't want to fall."

I smiled. Casper still had a lot to learn, but tonight, Helen had made my day. Heck, my week, my month. I couldn't get over the fact that two more of our clones had shown up—and in positions of future power too. Perhaps, things would get better. Yet I couldn't get a nagging thought out of my mind—that we'd only touched the surface of things. Maybe it was just the colorful explosions in the sky. I hoped so.

After the fireworks, Ted and I led Dimitri and Natalie to our apartments, surprising everyone. Even Deanna and Russell dropped by to meet our newest sister and brother. Natalie, Bev, and Gail had long talks. Near midnight, we had the two spend the night so we could chat more in the morning. Thank goodness we did that or as Leslie later said, "We're like lucky again."

Chapter 6 Strike Back

Mary Trout had just gotten her Ph. D. in genetics when the aliens began their program to convert women into Galactic Dolls several months ago. Hence, to be employable, she had it done, a small price to pay for her new job with Galactic Medicine. A gorgeous young woman with golden blonde hair and sky-blue eyes, she favored wearing light blue gowns that matched her eyes.

She began work at the Chicago Med Center where she learned this Galactic Doll genetic mutation was diabolical. Mary felt she had to tell someone about it. But who? Then, one day she ran into Ted and me. That was the day I finished my stint as temporary CEO of GD, rooting out corruption. Over cocoas at the coffee shop, she explained to us what she'd discovered.

"There's a big push on reworking the Padellas' nanoparticle genetic mutation sequences. However, there's something else that no one is talking about. The Galactic Doll is a genetic mutation. The Padella breakthrough causes a body to regenerate, like an injured fetus in the womb, but it's still a genetic mutation. So our children will inherit our Galactic Doll mutation. If you have a daughter, she'll be a Galactic Doll, too. But it's worse. If you have a boy, his body will also be a Galactic Doll. These genetic mutations are dominant.

"No one's talking about this side-effect—not until it manifests itself. Many of my peers don't think it will happen. In fact, they ordered me never to mention this. There's no proof, they say, but they're fooling themselves."

Mary sighed, took a sip of her cocoa, and continued. "Every girl sees becoming a Galactic Doll as being in her best interests. In fact, they've scheduled millions of graduating girls to have it done starting in mid-May. There's hardly an adult woman who hasn't done it or is waiting her turn. It's as though women have lost all common sense. Well, I shouldn't be so harsh. We're supposed to be beautiful Dolls. I've done it, but then we graduates had to set an example. Besides, I'm sure they wouldn't have hired me if I hadn't. And now, I'm sure women are supposed to be Galactic Dolls."

Mary felt rather confused when she said that last. Like most people, she didn't know the Sixth Invaders had used an overhead EMAC drone to implant every woman into desiring to be a Galactic Doll.

After a pause, she said, "Do you realize what this means twenty years from now? Everyone will be Dolls, even men. How will any heavy work get done? How can men perform as guards and soldiers? Gosh, the ramifications are enormous. It scares me, but what can we do about it? Who will listen? You didn't hear this from me. I'll get fired if they find out. Besides, women are supposed to be Galactic Dolls."

Again, Mary felt strange having made that last pronouncement. She left the coffee shop confident she'd done all she could to alert the only person she saw who might do something about the mess. She didn't know they had just dismissed me from GD. As she walked home on the MTES, a man came up behind her and injected her neck with something. Her body slumped, but the man caught her.

Mary woke up in the Chicago Med Center. Terror and panic flooded over her. She vomited and shrieked; doctors had amputated her arms. A nurse calmed her down a little. In the back of her mind, she presumed this was retaliation for revealing the secrets. Mary lived alone. Now she couldn't even dress herself. The only thing she could think of doing was to relay one more piece of information she'd just overheard. She had the nurse make the call.

Celeste and I checked Mary out of the Med Center and took her to my place. There, Mary told me she had learned the drugs they gave to people in the assisted living homes caused their dementia and thus deaths.

Mary said, "There, that's the last I've heard. I can't live like this. Please kill me because I can't do it. I'm ready to die."

She begged and pleaded with Celeste and me to end her misery. I tried to explain something about therapy, but that's when Mary's Uncle Fred phoned, saying he'd come pick her up. Mary had no choice but to go with him. I told her we'd stop by in a few days and give her the promised therapy. When we later called, we learned she'd vanished. With all that was going on, I admit I forgot about her.

***

Her uncle didn't take her home but to New O'Hare instead.

"Can you kill me here? I'm ready Uncle Fred."

"No, Mary. You're quite the beauty. They told you to keep quiet about something and you didn't. Anyway, a fellow in Russia wants to marry you, so I've sold you to him. It's a tidy sum that'll keep the misses and me on easy street."

A man walked up and handed him a small bag of credits. Fred peered inside and muttered.

Mary said, "Sir, will you please kill me? I can't live like this. I'm ready to die."

The man had a Russian accent and wore a purple uniform with gold trim. She recognized a GPan security guard. "Hardly. Come with me."

"I can't keep my balance. Please, this is frightening. Hold onto me," Mary begged. "Even better, kill me. Then you won't have to bother with me."

He only grunted and escorted her into an Airliner. Hours later, he whisked her off the ship and into the Moscow GPan skyscraper. When the elevator doors opened on the hundredth floor, Mary's eyes opened wide.

She entered a plush CEO's office and apartment. A woman who was also armless stood before her, a large smile on her face. Mary thought she must have been a model. She wore a red satin dress with a small diamond tiara on her head. Her long black hair draped down her sides, but Mary stared at the woman's waist. It was tiny, giving her incredible curves.

A pair of men stepped into the lobby. Both had a black mustache and wore hand-tailored, very expensive suits. The older man spoke.

"Ah, Mary Trout, here you are. I'm the CEO of Galactic Expansion for Earth, Mr. Petr Leonovich. This is Miss Moscow, my perfect wife, Irina. Our oldest son, Ivan, and your future husband. We've been looking for another perfect woman for Ivan, and now we've found her. Mary, you are nearly an ideal woman. We just need to reduce your waist before you marry Ivan. Welcome to our home."

57

"Dad, she's gorgeous. But I see what you mean. She needs to have her waist shrunk like mom's is. If she gets hers as small as yours, Mom, you'll have stiff competition."

Irina chuckled. "Mary, you're magnificent. Don't worry. We'll have your waist shrunk in no time. No pain, no gain. You'll have your own personal assistant to help you with everything."

"Can't you kill me now? I don't want to marry anyone. I'm not perfect. I'm helpless. I'm terrified and going to throw up again. Please just kill me. Put me out of my misery."

"Silly girl," Irina said.

"Son, why don't you escort her to her bedroom? Have Anna bathe her and get her properly dressed?"

"Hold me. I can't keep my balance." Mary begged him.

The thick carpet wasn't conducive to walking in tall heels. Reluctantly, Ivan did so, much to Mary's relief.

"This is your room and your assistant, Anna. Dad said to bathe her and get her ready."

Anna nodded but said nothing to Ivan. Soon, she had Mary undressed and into the giant bathtub complete with gold fixtures.

"Please, Anna. Kill me now. Drown me. I won't resist. I'm ready to die. I can't live like this. Please."

"Don't be silly. Anna wash you. Do hair now."

After drying her off and using the fancy hair and nail machine on Mary, she had her standing against another machine.

"Shrink waist. Machine tightens. You hold still."

Anna fastened the corset around Mary's waist, affixing the back laces onto hooks of the machine. As the machine whined, Mary felt the corset tightening around her.

"I can't breathe. Oh, you're killing me. Good. Hurry." Mary gasped.

Anna giggled. "No. Anna not strong enough to close it. Machine is. Miss Irina says it take months to get waist small to please Ivan so he marry you."

"I can't breathe. Please, just kill me."

"Irina breathes fine. Don't be silly girl."

Mary's emotional tone dropped downwards again.

Unable to change any detail of her now miserable life, the fear and grief gave way to a complete apathy. She no longer spoke or started any physical action of her own. For example, when joining the others for supper, her assistant had to make her body rise and then support it while walking, besides feeding her.

Frustrating the others, Mary no longer responded to questions put to her, let alone join any conversation. She even stopped begging to be terminated. Mary's life ended, but her body still lived, but only as long as her assistant kept putting fuel into it at meal times.

Petr took Irina to the Moscow Ballet and Theater every week. Ivan escorted Mary as well though Ivan saw a huge difference between his mother's vibrant behavior and that of the "dead" Mary. At the frequent balls that GPan held, this was even more evident. Irina played the hostess card with aplomb, dancing with everyone she could, constantly chatting, often about how perfect she was. Meanwhile, Mary's body moved to the dance steps as long as Ivan pushed and pulled her body with him. By early June, Ivan gave up on Mary as ever being the woman to marry.

Late June, Mary's assistant said, "Mary, we're moving to Chicago. Come and help me pack."

What the move might offer enthused her helper, but vegetable Mary sat in the last position in which Anna had put her. Yet one word registered in her closed-off mind: Chicago. There was something important about Chicago—if only she could make her mind work. Days and the long Airliner flight passed while Mary tried to work out the meaning of Chicago.

All around her, people unpacked boxes and arranged clothes, shoes, books, and toiletries, but Mary sat where her assistant placed her body. Then, from the nearby lounge, she caught a familiar name, Molly. Later, Molly's voice followed, impinging deep within her mind. Molly—she was important.

That was as far as her sub-apathy reasoning got before the Midsummer holiday arrived. Molly was important, very important. An original thought flashed in her mind. *I need to see Molly.* Unfortunately, her assistant chose that moment to move her body out to the dining room for supper, ending her cognitive processes.

Her assistant touched a bite of food to her lips. Mary's mouth opened, her teeth chewed, her throat swallowed, a marvel of automatic responses. Then, everything changed.

Mary noticed her assistant had slumped onto the table, her head lying on her own plate of food. Mary's eyes moved around the table in a slow-motion sweep. Everyone's head rested on the table. *How strange.* Then, her eyes landed on Irina, whose head was also lying down. Several minutes passed before Mary realized Irina wasn't chatting away as she always did at mealtimes.

Mary duplicated the "no action—no movement" of her environment. *Am I finally dead? They are, but I'm not. Just my luck. Everyone else is dead, and here I sit alive. There's no justice in this world.* At first, Mary didn't realize she was thinking again.

Her curiosity rose. For a minute, she stared at the blood vessels in her assistant's neck, checking for a pulse the only way she could.

"Darn, not dead. Rats," she said, the first words uttered in weeks.

To her left, her voice roused Irina. "Oh, I must have fallen asleep." Irina's eyes shot around the table before she shrieked, causing Mary to jerk.

"What's happened to everyone?" Irina said. "Is everyone dead? Oh, Mary, you're awake."

"They're breathing," Mary said. Her voice sounded stretched or thin.

"Help! Somebody, help!" Irina yelled.

No one came, even though Irina kept shouting for a minute. Molly's emotional tone rose higher. That Irina was disturbed by everyone being asleep registered.

As Mary became more alert and awake, her training as a geneticist awoke. She studied those around her. Then she took the first voluntary action she'd taken in months. She got up, moved close to each person, and examined them.

"Whatever are you doing, Mary? We need help here. Perhaps we should try the elevator. There are hundreds of others in this building."

"Comas." Mary uttered the word that culminated her observations of the small group.

"Huh? What are you saying, Mary? You aren't making any sense."

"I think they're all in comas. Maybe they were injected with the genetic mutation agent."

"Oh, don't be silly, girl. No one's been in here with syringes. No one's been injected with anything. But I wish this awful smell would go away. Petr never said we'd have to endure such an awful Chicago city stench. Don't they have proper sewers? I'll ask Petr to check on that. Honestly."

"We should get help. Molly. Yes, she's the only one. I've got to get to Molly."

"What? What are you saying? You mean that Miss Parkinson—that private investigator? What's she going to do? Mary, we need real help here. Where are you going?" Irina watched Mary wandering out of the room. She added, "Wrong way. The elevators are that way."

She couldn't point. But Mary stopped and turned around. Irina nodded, attempting to show the right direction. Mary headed off the other way.

"But we can't work the elevators. We need our assistants for that. Mary? Mary?"

Mary didn't answer but kept on walking. She spotted the elevators. Wham. Recognition of her helplessness slammed into her mind again, thrusting up from where her sub-apathy had buried it for so long.

"This is important. I must tell Molly before I die. Perhaps, she can terminate me."

She bent her knees so her nose reached the buttons since her double corsets didn't let her bend. When the doors opened, she stepped inside. As she turned around to face the doors and the array of floor buttons, she saw Irina walking toward her.

"Oh. When you find someone, send them up here. Tell whoever you find we need help fast. Thank you, Mary."

Mary started downward. She pressed the 1 Button, hoping that meant the ground floor. While the meaning of Irina was clear, Mary didn't intend to go floor by floor looking for someone. No, her full attention focused on what she had to tell Molly and then be terminated.

When she reached the first floor, she saw four security guards slumped over their desks. She checked on them. "Comas." She headed for the main doors, wondering if she could open them or if she'd be trapped inside.

The moment she reached the doors, they slid open. A faint smile flashed across Mary's face, the first since she'd been attacked months ago. She stepped out into the dark Chicago night though the many city lights from the vast MTES system made it seem well lighted. The fishy odor from Lake Michigan registered, bringing back more memories.

For a minute, she paused outside the doors getting her bearings. So many tall skyscrapers. Then she spotted Galactic Medicine's ninety-story building, where she'd spent long days in study. Oriented at last, she tried to recall where Molly lived. She'd first talked to them at StarLight's Coffee Shop. When she had awakened in the hospital, Molly and one of her sisters had taken her somewhere, but where?

A memory surfaced. The Cartwright skyscraper. A trace of a smile appeared. Mary headed off to find Molly, her steel-tipped stilettos echoing on the concrete outside the skyscrapers. Almost no one was around, but she occasionally heard spaceships landing or departing from New O'Hare. She stepped onto the MTES, thankful she didn't have to walk the whole distance.

She shuffled to the main doors of the Cartwright building. The doors opened. She stepped inside, and a security guard looked up. "How can I help you, miss?" he said. "Out rather late, aren't you?" He wore Leslie's new line of male Doll apparel.

"Molly. I must see Molly Parkinson."

He smiled. "Sorry. She's not here. She has her own apartment now." The guard noticed Mary's crestfallen expression and added, "I can phone her for you if it's important. Otherwise, try her tomorrow."

"Oh please, call her. Tell her Mary Trout is desperate to see her right now. Please, it's very important."

"Sure thing, miss." A minute later, he said, "Hey, Molly,

this is Sam over at Cartwright's. An armless woman named Mary Trout just walked in here. She is desperate to see you yet tonight. Okay. I'll tell her."

He slipped his phone back into his pocket. "Molly said she'll be right over. I'm to make you comfortable until she gets here."

***

"Who was that? It's midnight," Ted grumbled.

"It's Mary, Mary Trout. You remember—that poor geneticist who warned us about the long-term effects of these genetic mutations, the woman who was attacked and lost her arms."

"Oh yeah, the one who begged you to kill her. I remember. Didn't her uncle take her?"

"Yes, she's back and is desperate to see me. She's at Cartwright's."

"Want me to come with you?"

"No, you go back to sleep. I'll try not to wake our guests. Back soon, dear." I leaned over and gave Ted a kiss before slipping out of the house.

Minutes later, I entered Deanna's building and saw Mary. She still wore sky blue gowns. Her golden hair was just as glowing as I remembered. In spite of her mutilation, she was one gorgeous young woman.

"Mary, so good to see you again. I tried to call you but your Uncle Fred said you had moved out and gotten married."

I hugged her and slipped a steadying arm around her thin waist, noticing the restrictive corset. Questions popped into my mind but she spoke first.

"Molly, something awful has happened over at the Galactic Expansion building. Everyone's in a coma. It happened while we were eating supper. I came to later—hours later since this nice man told me it's midnight. Irina's still conscious and needs help, too. Everyone else is unconscious, including the night guard on the front door. Now I've told you this bad news, can you please terminate me? I can't keep on living like this, a helpless vegetable. Please."

"Comas? Everyone? Shit. Guard, see if you can rouse someone over at GD. If not, call GMed and tell them they might have a widespread biological attack at GPan."

He snapped into action, whipping out his cell. "GD isn't answering. Trying GMed now. Are we in danger here too—like the last time the Sixth Invaders struck?"

His face twisted. While he was now a male Doll, I suspected he didn't want to suffer what the Sixth Invaders had promised the men of Chicago. He glanced at Mary and cringed.

"No way of knowing. Tell GMed to check GD, too. I'll call GD's CEO Helen Hugo."

I grabbed my phone from my waist belt, which also held my 9mm Glock.

"Helen, sorry to wake you. Are you inside the GD skyscraper? No? Good. I think there may have been a biological genetic agent attack on those inside GD. We're sending GMed over there now. For heaven's sake, don't go inside GD until you get GMed's okay."

Just then, a loud Whoop! Whoop! Whoop! echoed through the building.

"What the hell is that?" I said.

"Crap! Oh, that's the new warning system our electronics genius installed. Holly Ann said it's an early warning device. She must have detected those Sixth Invaders again. There, it's off."

A dozen other guards rushed down to the front desk, alerted by the warning. "We're supposed to evacuate the building," one said, ushering us outside.

I started to dial Holly Ann when she called me.

"Molly! My alarm just went off. The Sixth Invaders are back."

"I know. I'm at the Cartwright building. You've roused all the guards. We're outside like you asked. What's going on? Are we being attacked?"

"I'm on my way there now. Let no one back inside until I get there. It worked. Yahoo, I'm a genius. Cya soon." She hung up.

One of the nearby guards chuckled. "That's just like her. Don't worry. I'm not about to go back inside. I think we should scan the skies for the Invaders."

While heads looked up, I called Deanna, letting her know what was going on. Then, I, too, gazed at the sky.

"Hey, look. Isn't that one of the drone surveillance EMACs?" a guard said.

"It's smoking. I hope it doesn't crash into a building," another commented.

As we watched its wobbling orbit, one thing was clear. Something catastrophic had happened to it. The vehicle descended into the Lake. We got a break there.

While we watched it between two buildings as it splashed, a horde of other people rushed to us. Leslie, Felix, Hank, Janine, Celeste, Randi, Eve, Bev, Gail, Ted, Kyle, Dimitri, and Natalie arrived, led by an exuberant Holly Ann.

"There it goes! Yahoo. It worked. I've detected and neutralized one of the Sixth Invaders. Plus one for Holly Ann!"

"You did that?" I said.

Holly Ann straightened. "Yes, it's my latest invention. We know we didn't terminate all the Invaders. I didn't want any more of those nasty nighttime attacks in which they mutated us. So I worked out a signal jammer or a signal short-circuit mechanism. That ship must have had one of their implant machines on it because that's what the jammer goes after. I designed a positive feedback loop in the kilo-yottahertz range."

Celeste interrupted. "You used Chaos Theory?"

"Exactly. Positive feedback. It overloaded their circuits. Looks like it disabled the EMAC, too. I take it my warning system here worked," she said to the security men.

One laughed. "No kidding. I almost fainted when it sounded. Good going, but does it need to be so loud?"

Holly Ann smiled. "Have to make sure you get woken up."

Dimitri interrupted, "Mary Trout? What's Mary doing here? She's Ivan's fiancé."

"Comas. They're all in comas. I came to warn Molly. Now, I'm ready to be terminated. Molly, please use your gun. I'm ready."

Molly filled in the few details Mary had told her. She finished when Deanna arrived, landing her two-man shuttle on the sidewalk just outside her building, and then joining them. After she verified her building was safe, she suggested we head toward GPan to see if we could see anything. Okay, we are a curious bunch. Besides, I knew Dimitri and Natalie wanted to go. Their parents were in there.

We stopped a block away. Flashing lights from several CPD EMACs and a dozen emergency responder vehicles illuminated the areas around both GPan and GD buildings. As we watched, two people wearing yellow biological containment suits moved toward the doors of the buildings, one entering each building. Before one reached the GPan entrance, the doors opened revealing Irina.

"Mom!" cried Dimitri. "That's my mother."

A police officer heard him and motioned him forward. "Son, if that's your mother, best have her walk over here. If this is one of those biological mutation attacks, you don't want to get too close."

"Mom. Mom. Irina, over here." Dimitri waved his hands, getting her attention.

She made her way to her adopted son. "Help. We need help, Dimitri. Everyone's unconscious. Maybe comas. Oh, Mary. Here you are. You brought help."

"Yes, and now they will terminate me."

"Mom, are you all right? Come here." He slipped a steadying arm around her waist. "You look different."

Irina puffed up. "You noticed! Good boy. Yes, I look twenty years younger—just as I looked when I was Miss Moscow and met your father. Isn't this amazing? I feel younger too. Your father will be most pleased when he wakes up. I'm even more perfect now."

She wasn't lying. Even in the MTES lights, she looked much younger, early twenties, I'd guess. That recognition produced a sickening feeling in my stomach.

Helen Hugo arrived, spotted our group, and joined us. "Why, Irina, you look—younger. Dimitri, Natalie. They said an EMAC crashed into the Lake."

After we told her what we knew, the person in the bio-containment suit reappeared at the entrance to GPan, walking toward the emergency vehicles. Several more EMACs hovered overhead and one landed; Galactic Entertainment arrived, filming for the morning news.

We were close enough to overhear the emergency person reporting. "Yes, it's a biological genetic agent attack. I've samples for the geneticists to analyze. It's a gas this time, spread through the air circulation system. Hundreds are in comas throughout the building. Best cordon off several blocks and evacuate anyone in the nearby buildings. I've no idea how this will spread. Best be safe."

A minute later, we listened to a similar report from the GD skyscraper.

I said, "Gang, let's head over to the Cartwright building. We should be all right there. I need a coffee. We have to get on top of this. Are we under another citywide attack? Helen, good to see you're here, too. Bev, we should get the First Division mobilized. We don't want to have the whole city mutated again, let alone the rest of Earth. Does anyone know how to contact our space fleet?"

At that moment, we heard a loud popping sound. I felt a sharp pain in my head, followed by a flood of intense pain. Everything went black before I found myself outside my body's head, looking down on it. Blood rushed out of its head. Realization struck. I'd been shot!

Emergency personnel swarmed, racing my body to the Med Center. That's what saved the body's life. Me, I was stunned. My baby. My life. I had to face the fact it was over. I had no idea who had done this or why—no way to find out.

Chapter 7 Recoveries

Captain L'Grina led the surviving sixteen members of the Sixth Invaders Recon Force 125. She was intimately familiar with Earth's defenses, having spent decades in the body of GD's CEO Hardy. After Molly and General Bev killed her commander and were interrogating their Chief Science Officer, she had him murdered to keep him quiet.

The aliens were tall and thin, with gray skin tones and coal-black eyes and hair. However, both their males and females had enormous breasts. In their society, males handled domestic duties, including nursing their young, while women ran all else, though a few science officers were males but had no authority.

For the past decades, these Sixth Invaders had followed their commander's grand plan, which was to have the recon force conquer the Sol Empire long before the real invasion force got around to doing it. If so, they would become famous. They almost succeeded and would have, except for the constant interference of Molly Parkinson and General Beverly Blossom Blythe.

The thwarting of the commander's plan to make the men of central Chicago into armless Galactic Dolls was pivotal. Molly's interference had rushed their Chief Science Officer, who, as a consequence, made mistakes in his mutation formula. By the time he corrected his error, General Blythe had struck, murdering their commander.

Almost thirty years ago, the Sixth Invaders had arrived in a cloaked light cruiser, which they parked in woods many miles from Chicago. After General Blythe's actions, Captain L'Grina took her remaining forces and fled to their ship. For a time, they hovered undiscovered in a low orbit, eavesdropping on Earth's communications.

Thus, Captain L'Grina learned the Moscow corporations took over control of the Sol Empire-wide corporations. The Invaders still had many of their implant machines and their body transference machines. They could begin anew with these men in Moscow, but Captain L'Grina didn't want to start over. Besides in six months, their long tour of duty ended, and they'd go home. Another recon force or the main invasion fleet would replace them. If anything could be salvaged, she knew it must be done within this short time span.

Worse, the supply of the corrected genetic mutation agent had fallen into the Earthling's hands. She reasoned if she could get that agent spread over the Sol Empire's ruling city, Chicago, making men and women almost helpless, the fear of that would make the rest of Earth capitulate and surrender to her. She was confident of that outcome if only they hadn't lost the mutation agent and their Chief Science Officer, the only one who could make more of it.

Compounding matters, while it would be a simple matter to steal a sample of the mutation agent, they no longer had access to Earth facilities where they could mass-produce it. Captain L'Grina faced serious difficulties, but she hadn't risen to captain by being a dummy. Within days of learning the Moscow corporations were taking over for those who died in Chicago, she formulated a new plan.

She explained to her small group, "Essence of simplicity." Which it was, considering they had personal invisibility shields, disguise devices that made them look like the average of the surrounding humans, and other such contraptions. Their implant machines could install suggestions or orders into human minds.

Days later, Captain L'Grina roared. "These stupid humans. Their new leader—this Petr fellow—he's doing what we need by getting our mutation agent duplicated and spread over this planet. One less thing for us to do. Now to get it mass produced. We'll need quantities of the stuff readily available. Let's implant a few ideas with those who have access to G'Karn's mutation agent."

Her crew spent a few weeks traveling to several major facilities where they pretended to be humans. They used their implant machines at low power to "suggest" the researchers make large quantities of the serum. That went without a hitch since many independent labs and researchers wanted samples to study. A little encouragement produced results.

Next, Captain L'Grina focused her efforts on spreading word of what the corporations had been doing to older people. Disguised as humans, her crew visited bars and other hangouts in major cities. They told everyone they could about how the corporations were drugging those in the assisted living homes so they'd develop dementia and be terminated by age sixty-five. They also related the remarkable rejuvenation of older people in the assisted living complexes of Chicago—dementia cured, while bodies were twenty-five-years-old once again. Also that the Chicago GMed facilities now issued dual ID cards—one with real age and one with apparent age.

Captain L'Grina stoked the fires of rebellion. Later, as men and women voiced such opinions, she ordered their implant machines to "push" them into protesting against the major corporations. It took little nudging because most people recognized the inhumanity and unethicalness of these corporate policies.

How the corporations should handle these open protests arose. Disguised as a human, Captain L'Grina observed the first one which took place in LA. The local CEOs ignored the whole thing because these local men couldn't do anything about such policies. Either the Earth-wide corporations or the Sol Empire-wide corporations could establish them. Frustrated, the Captain returned to her cloaked ship to make further plans.

Captain L'Grina and her crew had no familiarity with Moscow or its corporation personnel. She saw this geographical shift as a disaster to their plans.

By early June, her crew installed an implant machine in CEO Petr Leonovich's GPan office. With the device set to low power so as not to attract undue attention, she installed two key ideas into his mind. First, the protesters were traitors, so arrest them, inject them with the armless Galactic Doll agent, and implant them as sex Dolls. Make them useful members of society again. Second, they should move their offices into the abandoned Chicago offices, since all the Sol Empire-wide data and connections were there. After three attempts, the light implant took hold.

From Captain L'Grina's point of view, things then progressed rapidly. Protests broke out in many major cities, handled as she desired. These actions fueled further protests because she knew someone would discover what was happening to the protesters, making that known. On his own initiative, CEO Russell Godwyn of GEnt did that for her.

Although Petr announced their move to Chicago, he still hadn't worked out a replacement for his original group, the Earth-wide corporations, an action that suited the Captain. She brought her small group back to Chicago and began preparations for their final action: the conquering of Earth.

On 2 July, Captain L'Grina screamed. "Not her again!" A soldier informed her that Molly Parkinson discovered what was happening with the abducted protesters. "That woman just keeps meddling in our affairs. She's got to go. We don't have time for her interference; we only have a couple months before we're off this miserable world."

"Your orders, sir?" one of her soldiers said.

She calmed down, though continuing to pace the control room of her light cruiser.

"Okay, we've got to push the plan along. We don't have time to find a new angry protester and implant him with the revenge idea, so this first time, we'll do it ourselves. Give these stupid Earthmen the right idea. Round up the required volume of the bio agent."

"How much?" she said.

"Um, we'll do the GPan and GD skyscrapers. That should be enough to plant this idea into many other minds in other Earth cities. If not, we'll repeat it. Have one of our remaining scientists work out the volume needed. Those two skyscrapers are twins; each is one hundred stories tall."

"Should we steal the agent from facilities here in Chicago?"

Captain L'Grina thought for a moment. "No, get it elsewhere. We want to make sure others in this city can steal it and follow our lead. Make it happen."

"Aye, sir."

It took longer than expected to prepare the attacks because the science officers didn't know the amount of bio

71

agent needed. That depended on the method of delivery. It was one thing to inject the agent into a body and quite another to release it in the air system of a giant building. As they narrowed these factors down, Captain L'Grina learned Molly and her group had undone the recent sex Doll implants made at the Moscow research facility.

"That woman has interfered for the last time! Terminate her! Someone, tail her."

Delays slowed down the Captain's plans. When all was ready, she chose the night of the Midsummer fireworks; the inherent noise would cover the activities in the two skyscrapers.

Captain L'Grina issued her parting orders. "Make sure you document how you inserted the bio agent. We must pass that info along to other Earthling protesters so they can do our work for us."

Wearing their invisibility shields, six of her soldiers landed on the roofs, three on each. Giant circulation fans pumped in volumes of air, so it was a simple matter to attach the cylinders to each unit. While cutting the holes in the metal made noise, the festival down by the Lake obscured it. When each group finished attaching the cylinders, they took a photograph of the hookup. This way, they'd have an easy way to show other protesters how to do it. The genetic mutation agent attached to nanoparticles far smaller than the air filters could trap drifted down into both skyscrapers. The gas affected those on the upper floors first.

That done, the two teams gathered on the streets opposite the two buildings. From here, they could see anyone fleeing the buildings. Still invisible, they waited. Everything depended on infecting everyone inside the two skyscrapers. If half the people escaped, the dosage would have been too low and must be corrected in future attacks.

Just as they were about to call it a total victory, they spotted someone walking out of the GPan building. The time: midnight. Two moved closer to identify the person but discovered she was one of the two armless women the GPan executives kept. This, they reported to the Captain who ordered them to continue observations.

"As soon as our drone completes its implant run over the two buildings, you can return to the ship," she commanded.

"Oh no! Molly Parkinson is interfering again," one soldier reported. "She's brought her entire group here. All the emergency vehicles are here. What's that? Something's happening to our implant drone. It's smoking. Looks like it'll crash land."

Captain L'Grina said, "We're on it here. The controls are fried. We must recover it from the Lake and examine it. Oh hell. Forget it. We'll just make a new one. Science Officer, make a new implant drone at once."

"Sergeant, if you can see Molly Parkinson, put a bullet in her head! Don't use our weapons. We want it to look as though an Earthling shot her."

"Aye, sir. Moving into position now." A minute later, she said, "It's done. Got her in her head. She's down. Molly won't be interfering in your plans any longer. From their emergency responders, we know the dosage was correct. They're reporting that everyone inside both buildings is in a mutation coma."

"Excellent. From what we can tell, the drone made a couple passes over the buildings, so maybe the implant will hold. We'll see in about a week. Good hunting. Return to base," Captain L'Grina ordered.

***

I became aware again. My body lay in the Med Center on a bed. A white bandage encircled my head. Spooky. I rested on the ceiling looking down at my body and the others gathered in the room. Celeste, Eve, and Randi were off to one side, conferring. Ted stood beside the bed, eyes bloodshot. Also, Mary Trout sat in one corner, complaining it should have been her since she wanted to die. Holly Ann arrived and walked over to my three sisters.

Silly me. I should have been using my telepathy. I sent, 'Eve, what's happened to me? I'm on the ceiling.'

The others saw her looking up at me. She said, "Hey guys, Molly's aware again. She's up on the ceiling. Using telepathy. Great going, Molly. Are you able to hear us?"

'Yeah, I hear you. Tell Ted, I'm all right.'

"Ted, she said to tell you she's all right."

He responded. "She's not all right! Look, the doctors got the slug out of her head, but her brain is so damaged she'll never wake up again, but our baby is still fine."

'Eve, what's the doctor say about my recovery? Is he right?'

"She's asking for more data, Ted. Yes, the bullet damaged your brain. They don't think your body will ever recover, but for the sake of your baby, they want to keep your body on life support until the baby comes and then terminate the body. Is that okay with you?"

'Shit. My baby. Is it going to be okay?'

"Yes, the doctors said the baby is doing fine."

Holly Ann looked up at the ceiling, shook her head, and interrupted. "Hey, Molly. There's another choice. Mary desperately wants to die and not spend her life handicapped as she is. What about a body swap with her? Eve can help her find a new baby body. We're in the Med Center after all."

Mary said, "Please say yes. No one will help me get terminated. That's all I've ever wanted since I woke up in this Med Center. I'm begging you, terminate me."

I focused on Ted. 'Dear, is that okay with you? If I take Mary's body?'

"Wow, way cool. She's talking inside my head, too. Sure, I want you back and our baby, too. I'm greedy."

'Eve, let's do it. Tell Holly Ann and Mary. Do it as fast as possible. The Sixth Invaders are back, and I want to help defeat them before it's too late.'

Eve said, "She agrees. Holly Ann, get your Body Swap machine. Let's get Mary's chair moved closer to Molly's bed. Mary, we'll help you, so don't worry."

"What do you mean helping me get a new baby body? I want to die."

"You can't die. You're immortal—a spiritual being, a ghost, a personality. We're a composite. Being plus physical body plus mind. Don't worry. It'll become clear once we do this."

"Okay," she said. "As long as I don't have this

handicapped body."

I relaxed. Soon, I'd have her body, and though it was armless, I'd still be able to work, to act, to help others fight these vicious Sixth Invaders. That's what mattered. I wasn't about to be out of the game while a new baby body grew up for twenty years. I doped off for a time.

An hour later according to the wall clock, Holly Ann returned, pushing a cart with her Body Swap machine on it. I watched as she hooked one head harness onto my bandaged head. Then, she attached the other one to Mary's head. I thought these looked more like metal hats.

The pure white, incredibly aesthetic energy swept over me, the being, not the body. I felt incredible. Such beauty. Such purity. And then the light faded. Oh, how I didn't want it to diminish. Can't it go on forever?

"That's so beautiful," I said. I gasped, for I was talking from Mary's body. Everything felt so different. Breathing was difficult, too. I blinked and tried to rub my eyes, but that failed. No arms. "It worked. How's Mary doing?"

Celeste said, "Welcome back, Molly. We'll run lots more therapy sessions on you."

I grinned.

Ted said, "Molly, is that really you?" He stared at Mary's body—me now.

"Yeah, it's me."

Randi said, "Eve is handling Mary. She's decided she wants to be a girl again. They're in the maternity ward choosing one. I think this surprised Mary but she got her wish. Also, Deanna is calling for a meeting of everyone tomorrow at ten at her Cartwright building. She'll be pleased you're back, Molly. Now, it's darn late. We best get home. We'll travel as a group, Deanna's orders."

As we rose to leave, Ted whispered in my ear, "What's your motto now? Do you remember?"

"Of course, silly. Stop and think how. But I'm wobbly. Keep an arm around me. Besides, I can't breathe right."

Once home, Ted got me undressed and out of the corset. That's when I appraised my situation. When GD security men kidnapped me and took me to the South Pacific atoll of the Padella doctors, Janet amputated my arms, thinking that might help make my lucky gene express itself. Thus, I had no choice but to learn to adapt, which I did. However, this new body was stiff, inflexible, and lacked the coordination and balance I'd developed before.

"Honey," I said, "it'll be a challenge to get this body able to do what I could do when we were on the atoll."

"Kind'a figured that. Don't fret. I'll be here just like I was last time. I'm so thankful I haven't lost you. Besides, this body is even prettier than your other one. Let's get you bathed and in bed. It's late."

The next morning was awkward. While I tried to use my feet and toes to do everything I used to do with them, this body refused to cooperate—more or less. Ted chuckled.

"Dear, we have to get you limbered up. Slow and easy does it. The Sol Empire wasn't built in a day. Let me help you."

I sighed. "I know. It's frustrating. I used to be able to do these things, brush my hair, feed myself, but now..."

"Remember back on the atoll? We worked together. Heck, we practiced all day for six months. Patience. We'll get you back to speed. Come. Everyone's getting ready to head over to Deanna's skyscraper. We've never had a big meeting before. I've been wondering what she's got in mind."

"We've lost our ruling CEOs again. I'm worried the Sixth Invaders might win this time. Okay, keep a steadying arm around me. I didn't know getting used to a new body was this challenging. It feels so different. Its senses are just enough off to confuse me. Okay, patience, practice, and time. God, I hope we have enough time, dear."

Chapter 8 Key Decisions

Deanna chaired the largest meeting we'd had. I didn't grasp how critical our decisions would become. I realized Earth was in big trouble. No top leaders.

Bev and Gail, wearing their First Division uniforms, joined us. Besides our extended group, also present were Dimitri Leonovich, his mother, Irina, and Natalie Mantovo. Two local corporation CEOs joined us, Helen Hugo of GD and Deanna's husband, Russell Godwyn of GEnt.

Russell began the meeting. "I've sent out newscasts explaining this new Sixth Invader attack on our Sol Empire corporations. By the end of today, word will have spread around the world. I'll continue to keep the world informed. Deanna, this is your meeting."

He gestured toward his wife. I knew he hated being seen in public and talking. When we first met him, he'd been a very public figure. After being genetically mutated, he preferred to stay in the background, even though he was now a local CEO. I sensed his embarrassment over being transgendered, though he never talked about it.

"Right." Deanna took charge. "We're facing very serious problems. We must act. Earth must act. If we don't, the Sixth Invaders could end up controlling our world."

"Huh?" Ted muttered.

"I'll explain what I mean. Russell and I were up most of the night discussing these issues. Let's start with the attempted assassination of Molly."

"Yes, why go after her? She's done nothing," Ted said.

He was angry, and I couldn't blame him. Besides, I had the same question. Why kill me now? Revenge?

As if reading my mind, Deanna said, "Revenge? Could be, but it's more likely they see Molly as a formidable enemy, though General Bev might be right up there with her. Those two foiled the aliens' original plans. Since these Sixth Invaders are back, Russell and I are of the opinion they wanted to take Molly out of play, fearing she could mess up their current plans. As a result, General Bev has done two things."

She nodded to Bev, who smiled and spoke up.

"Righto. As of now, I'm invisible. No one will know where I'm located. I've already canceled the division's furlough—summoned back all soldiers. Probably some won't show up, but Gail and I figure we'll have at least half the division available. I'm keeping our location a secret. The second we discover the aliens' location, the First Division will swoop down on them. We'll blast them into oblivion."

She sat down, basking in the cheers and applause we gave her. Okay, I could only voice my approval. Frustrating.

Deanna continued her meeting. "Next, we have about seven days to work out what to do with the many victims in the two buildings. Incredible luck is on our side."

Helen said, "You're right. If we Chicagoans hadn't been out celebrating with the fireworks, all your local GPan and GD personnel would be in comas, too. So your local corporations are still in operation. Well, not exactly. We can't get into the buildings and to our computers yet. But we're using phones to stay in touch with other local corporations."

Deanna continued. "In seven days, we must handle one thousand two hundred six victims. Since the buildings are contaminated, the victims are being left in the two skyscrapers. Those in the bio-containment suits counted them, removed their clothing, and made the victims as comfortable as possible. We've far too many to transport—not until the buildings are free of the bio agent. No predict when that will be."

She said, "As far as the victims go, the counts are:
406 men
400 women less Mary and Irina
400 teens, children, and babies
Rescue personnel brought out three newborn babies that are now in the Med Center but they aren't expected to survive."

Everyone sighed. I glanced at Helen, and she, me, both of us thinking of our own unborn.

Deanna said, "Galactic Robotics has already said they'll give each survivor their own personal helper robot and the usual three household ones. And Leslie has offered to clothe

the men with her new line of male Doll clothing. But that's not the problem. Molly, would you tell everyone about your vision of the future back when we first faced this alien mutation agent?"

I cleared my throat. Gosh, my voice sounded so different. "Well, I was in the Med Center. Their Chief Science Officer—that G'Karn fellow—he injected Ted and me with the bio agent to regrow our arms, forcing us to stay in the Med Center for a month while they finished conquering Earth. That's when I had a view of future Chicago after they unleashed their armless Galactic Doll mutation on central Chicago. It was ghastly. We all died, but I'm getting ahead of my vision. This mutation ended up being dominant over all other genes. Future children from any of these mutated parents ended up being armless Dolls. So in ten years, there were millions upon millions of armless people, threatening Earth's survival. They predicted within a few generations, there wouldn't be an armed person on our world. Thus, GPan had no choice but to terminate all armless mutations. They used cyanide on us while we slept. That's what I saw. With Bev's help, we stopped them from using that awful agent on us."

Eve defended me. "While we've yet to analyze this new agent, I can say initial tests suggest this form of mutation will be dominant over all others. She's right. Future children will carry that body form forward. Grim."

Deanna said, "So not counting the protest victims around the world, we've another twelve hundred to handle. Based upon what happened here the first time when men mutated into male Dolls, my guess is this time it will be far worse."

"What do you mean?" said Dimitri. He and Natalie sat beside his mother, Irina, listening to our every word.

"Most of those who worked for the fifteen major corporations committed suicide. Only two dozen of the executives survived, and only a few returned to their former positions. Russell is an exception. So what I'm saying, Dimitri, is when these men wake up, they won't want to live, let alone run their corporations."

"What? But I'm the perfect Doll," said Irina, interrupting Deanna. Her face displayed the perfect protest. I wondered if she had practiced it in front of a mirror. Or perhaps she had been an actress. "Petr will waken and be as perfect as I am. Don't be silly. He won't want to die."

Deanna ignored her. "A few months ago, these Sixth Invaders mutated central Chicago, affecting over a million men. You've seen the final report. Adult men had the highest suicide rate, while younger boys seemed better able to accept what's happened. We'll know more in two months when they return to school for the first time. Hank and Kyle are high school teachers; they'll keep us apprised of that aspect. Leslie's new line of male apparel will help.

"What I'm saying is that this time, expect much higher death wishes. Molly and Holly Ann did live independently without their arms, but Molly had the benefit of all those holographic how-to videos and six months of intensive practicing. So how to care for this many victims is our initial problem. Galactic Robotics will donate the necessary robots, and we must find personal assistants for each one until they can learn to care for themselves. So expect death wishes among the eight hundred adults.

"This brings me to the point Mary Trout kept bringing up. After her attack and mutilation, she wanted to die and begged everyone she saw to help her do it. So I ask you, does a person have the right to die when they wish? If so, who will do it and how? Couple that with the dire prospects of having mutated children, then perhaps the more who die the better."

"Morbid, just morbid," Hank said. Janine nodded, agreeing with her husband.

"Doesn't a person have exclusive rights to his or her own body?" said Celeste. "If I remember my history, women's battles for those rights and equal pay took centuries to win. Isn't this just an extension of that? It's our own body, not the corporation's or anyone else's. We ought to be able to do with it as we wish as long as what we do isn't criminal or unethical."

I spoke up. "I agree with Celeste. It's their choice—to live or die. It isn't fun trying to survive this way, even with the robot assists, but with diligence, how-to video guidance, and months of practice, we can become productive members of society. The crux of the problem is that most people believe they are only bodies. They've forgotten they're immortal spiritual beings and thus can't die. Celeste and I wanted to give Mary therapy sessions so she could discover that for herself because then she could make an educated, non-reactive decision about her life. But there isn't any way to give that many victims such therapy. So far, we've only handled about half of the recent Chicago protest victims."

Randi said, "Suppose we could get each victim to see they were immortal beings. I predict they would then be even more eager to let this mutilated body die, knowing they could get a new baby body. Only those people with a powerful drive to get things done, to see something completed, will carry on, like Molly here or Holly Ann. For that, we thank you both."

Dimitri stirred. He said, "Don't we have to consider the corporations? They sponsor us. I mean no disrespect, but I suspect there are very few jobs mom or Molly could do. I can see why dad shunted the protesters into the sex escort trade. But we don't need more people in that arena or do we, Russell?"

"Hardly," he said.

"Some could teach," I said. "But I see Dimitri's point. Earth and GEnt don't need another two thousand prostitutes, even for the space ports."

Deanna summarized, "So our rulers must reach a decision on whether to do as these victims ask. Terminate them. And this brings up the next vital point."

Natalie broke in. "Wait. Who will run the Sol Empire and Earth-wide corporations? Dad and Petr kept putting off any decision about replacing their positions. This is a double whammy. No one's leading Earth or the Sol Empire. All that's left are the thousands of local level outlets. We're leaderless. Not a good thing with the Sixth Invaders attacking us."

Hank, a high school teacher working on his doctorate in history, agreed with her. "Natalie has identified the critical aspect of this whole mess. Local corporation offices handle the day-to-day needs of their geographical areas, but they aren't prepared to deal with Earth defenses let alone Sol Empire needs. What does Helen know of the defense needs of Pylon, Epsilon Eridani?

"From what we learned from G'Karn before they terminated him, these Sixth Invaders are trying to set up Earth to be conquered either by themselves or by their space fleet. We need effective rulers today before it's too late."

Hank had an attentive audience. I nodded, as did many others. He continued.

"But things are far worse. During the centuries of corporation rule, there have been no checks on their actions and decisions. Today, people are discovering the terrible things corporation rulers have done. We don't know all the unethical or criminal actions they've committed. Perhaps we never will. Maybe that's a good thing." He sighed.

"While the Sixth Invaders carried out this attack, soon other protesters around the world will follow their example. I predict copycat attacks on local corporations focused on GPan and GD. This nasty biological agent is available worldwide, albeit for genetic studies."

Deanna interrupted him. "Hank, are you saying our own people will steal it and use it to attack other local offices?"

I shuttered, recalling how I pleaded with Petr, telling him this bio mutation agent wasn't a deterrent, but an ultimate weapon. He insisted no one would consider using it that way. Ha. The aliens had. And if Hank was right, Earth's own people would use it against our corporation leaders. Still, hearing these ideas vocalized by others caused me to gasp.

Hank said, "If I had to estimate the chances, Deanna, I'd give it a ninety percent likelihood of happening."

Russell wiped his forehead. "I shouldn't have had GEnt broadcast the details of this latest mutation attack. I've given protesters new ideas."

Hank said, "Relax. If you didn't tell the world about it, I'm sure the Sixth Invaders would have let people know. As Natalie says, our real problem is that we're leaderless in a time of covert war. Does anyone know if there's any procedure for installing new ruling corporation personnel?"

Dimitri, Natalie, Russell, and Helen swept their heads

Helen said, "No one ever expected the total loss of an entire corporation's bureaucrats and leaders. Promotions often come up the ranks. When GD went down a few months back, Gregor allowed me to take over our local GD office because my husband used to be the Sol Empire-wide Chief Finance Officer. I suspect Gregor thought I knew more about GD than I did. Besides, with the deaths of so many men here in Chicago, women had to step up."

Hank's face tightened. "Conclusion: there is no protocol for getting us new world corporation leaders and necessary bureaucrats in short order. Correct?"

They nodded. "So," he continued, "we're at a crossroads. If we do nothing or let the other local offices tinker around working out who will take over these key corporations, then Earth is ripe for conquering by these Sixth Invaders."

I spoke up. "I hope you've got an alternative, Hank."

He smiled. "In history, great battles are won by great leaders, like Alexander, the Great, Napoleon, Attila, the Hun, and even the dictator Hitler had he stopped with France. Nowhere in recorded history has a corporation ever won a battle. Even on Brussels, Tau Ceti, General Bev planned and executed the decisive attack on the Sixth Invaders' robot army. It's always a single leader that wins battles, not a group, though that leader would be wise to accept input and advice from others."

Hank saw he had an attentive audience. With a smile, he said, "What can we do? Install single leaders who have power over the corporations."

Russell laughed. "So now we put all power into one man's hands instead of the long arms of the corporations."

I frowned. That was our current corporation situation: concentrated power with no means of justice or adjudication or even protest.

"We need," Hank said, "a form of rule in which there are checks and balances on those in power. We need a system that values and protects human rights, not just on Earth, but all other worlds and moons we contact."

Randi said, "Now that I can agree with. That mining ship committed genocide on Bahira, Ross 248 about twenty years ago. They wiped out a primitive people just so they could mine rare earths."

"Precisely. We need a new form of government with single leaders who are held responsible," Hank said.

Ted piped up. "Hey, we're missing another key point. Don't forget these Sixth Invaders body swapped into the CEOs of GPan and GD for the last twenty-some years. They know every secret, every policy, we've got."

What a sobering thought—I'd forgotten about that aspect. Our enemy knew everything about our civilization.

General Bev said, "Not everything, boys. They don't know what I've done with the First Division. But yes, they know how we're armed. Rats."

I spaced out—another one of my unpredictable premonitions. I saw a newscast in which six local corporate groups battled over who would become the next Earth-wide and Sol Empire-wide corporations. While they argued, positioned, and bargained, the Sixth Invaders took control of Earth. No, not by a massive space battle nor even by a conquering ground assault. No, their weapon was fear—fear of also becoming armless Galactic Dolls. I saw newscasts of the

84

greater LA area being infected with the airborne agent and later watched as millions died, for there were no able-bodied persons left to help the victims recover. Captain L'Grina had won. Resisting their rule meant becoming a helpless Doll. Fear was a powerful weapon in the hands of these Sixth Invaders.

I jerked and came out of my spooky trance, wondering how long I'd been out of it and if anyone had noticed. They all had. Silence greeted me. And everyone stared at me. My face flushed.

"Okay," I said. "I had a flash of a future."

"Tell us about it," Deanna insisted.

Heads nodded. I did, ending with, "So if we do nothing and let the other corporations work it out, fear of future mutation attacks will subdue the entire world. My god, millions of men, women, and children will die in LA alone. That huge city will be devoid of people. After that, everyone'll do what the Sixth Invaders tell them to do out of fear of that happening to them. We must do something."

"But what?" said Deanna. "Did you see an alternative future like last time?"

Her face, like many others, looked so hopeful. I hated to dampen that. I replied, "Not this time. It's obvious we have to do something drastic and different. It can't be business as usual. I wish I had paid more attention to history in high school."

Hank said, "History shows us we need a single leader, but also that we need checks and balances on his or her powers. And for good or ill, we need to do this in a manner that the local corporations will accept. We can worry about the rest of the Sol Empire later."

Whoop! Whoop! Whoop! Holly Ann's warning system activated again, startling everyone.

"To the roof," yelled Holly Ann, who dashed off. We followed, but Irina and I brought up the rear.

As we walked, Irina said, "I miss my personal assistant. We must have one, Mary, er, I mean Molly. I'll have Dimitri find us one yet today. We can't live without one, can we?"

"Yes, we can, Irina. I want my independence. I wonder what the Invaders are doing now."

When she and I reached the roof's EMAC parking deck, the visual sight was over.

Holly Ann said, "My jamming device just shorted out another one of their implant drones. Guess they weren't through trying to change our behavior."

"Well done, Holly Ann. Keep on inventing ways to stop these beasts," I said.

"Dimitri, Dimitri," Irina barked, "I want you to find me a new personal assistant right now. I simply must have someone to assist me."

"I'll see what I can do, mother, but we've more important things to handle first."

Once we reassembled, I took control of Deanna's meeting. The situation reminded me of our high school senior dance. I was on a committee with ten other girls. Our task: plan the dance. That's when I learned a group rarely decides on any path, at least not swiftly.

"Look," I said, "we must do something now—today. If we don't, then either the Sixth Invaders will take advantage of us or other CEOs will make a mess of things. Since Hank says we need a single leader, I hereby appoint Dimitri Leonovich as the Sol Empire Emperor of Expansion and Natalie Mantovo as the Sol Empire Empress of Defense. You two are the sole surviving operational personnel of the empire-wide GPan and GD corporations. That should help sell the other corporations on your new positions. Hank says we need checks and balances so we'll set up a Sol Empire Inspection and Justice Czar. I'll volunteer for that post."

Ted said, "Hold on, Molly. If you use your name, then the Sixth Invaders will know you've body swapped. They're sure to shoot you again. Why don't I take that post and be the front person? You'll still run everything, but quietly for a time."

"Okay. You have a point, dear. So, Dimitri, Natalie—are you willing to take on this much responsibility?"

He sighed and rubbed his hands across his face. "Well, I hoped to one day make a difference, but this is one tall order. Natalie, I'll try, if you will."

"I'm game," Natalie answered. "I just returned from

advanced training on Pylon. Defense must be our current focus. General Blythe, we should work together. Dimitri, our first task will be to put together a working staff. It's possible we'll be able to get a handful of our parents' staff to help us after they recover from their comas."

Dimitri snorted. "I'll wager we won't get one, but we'll see. They'll be helpless."

I interrupted him. "Dimitri, we aren't helpless. We have different ways of doing things, and we need help with different things than you do. I did fine as a PI before G'Karn regrew my arms. Yet, I see your point. Many may not have the will to live independently. People react in different ways to handicaps."

His face flushed. "I'll contact my friends in Moscow and see if they're interested. We can use the funds set aside for the Sol Empire-wide GPan and GD corporations as our initial operational capital."

Natalie said, "Excellent. I concur. But what about punishments for those who fight back, the criminal elements? Current studies show most prefer death to being sent to the penal colony on Mercury. Worse, maintaining that prison costs close to five hundred thousand credits per inmate per year."

"Good lord!" I said. "That's my monthly stipend for the next several decades. I didn't know it was that expensive."

Natalie smiled. "Few do. Worse, the recidivism rate is close to ninety percent. The few who don't resume their life of crime are too old to do so. Perhaps, we should adopt termination as the only penalty."

That sounded way too harsh. I said, "Look, local crime rates are low, except those committed by corporation members. We've already seen most of those convicted men choose termination. Yet, has that stopped corporate crime?"

Dimitri chuckled. "Hardly." He snickered. "Dad skimmed one percent off the top of GPan's budget for himself. Ted, once you dig into the goings on of the major corporations, you'll uncover many unethical and criminal activities."

I laughed. "The goal of police, security guards, justice, and law is to find something the criminal fears enough to make them cease committing crimes. Obviously, we've not done that. Wait, what about threatening to turn any convicted criminal into an armless Doll? Use the same argument the Sixth Invaders are using with us."

"Isn't that inhumane, too?" said Deanna.

"Termination isn't the answer," Celeste said. "What you fail to realize is that we're spiritual beings. So when you terminate a guilty person, they're free to grab the next baby body and begin again. True, they're sidetracked twenty years while the new body grows up, but soon they're back again. They've not changed their ways. Termination isn't the answer. Locking them up on the most inhospitable planet in our solar system isn't working either. While Molly's proposal isn't all that humane, it gives us something important. Breathing room. Turning them into armless Dolls will keep them alive and from committing more crimes for perhaps forty or fifty years. Maybe by then, we'll have developed a better way of handling them."

Dimitri said, "I like that idea. But Celeste, we already have a better way. Our research facility outside Moscow is experimenting with the alien implant technology. I've seen how it can alter the behavior of people. I propose we also experiment more with that approach, too."

Celeste frowned. Many of my group did too. I knew from personal experience that mental implants were detrimental to the overall well-being of a person. Still, Dimitri and Natalie believed implants worked and wanted to try further experiments.

With that, the meeting broke up. Celeste, Randi, Eve, and I headed back to deliver more therapy sessions to four more of the protest victims. Ted, Dimitri, Natalie, Deanna, and Russell continued to discuss how they could find the staff they needed and how they would break the news to the other corporations of Earth. For now, they didn't worry about the other worlds in the empire.

Why did I push Dimitri and Natalie into these critical positions? I'd only just met them. They hadn't seemed very surprised to discover they were clones. Did they already know that detail? If so, why hadn't they contacted us before now?

Neither had protested their new appointments. I didn't

have to persuade them to take the positions. I guess their fathers heavily influenced them. Was I picking the best people to be emperor and empress? I doubted it.

Yet, we had to have leaders today, ones who had a chance of correcting the unethical and inhumane decisions of their predecessors, and ones who could act swiftly. By putting Ted and me in charge of investigations and justice, I hoped we could keep Dimitri and Natalie on right paths. A failure to act now would allow the Sixth Invaders to conquer Earth. And that I wasn't about to let happen.

Chapter 9 The Results of Fear

The days passed swiftly for me and followed a certain routine. After eating breakfast, I ran therapy sessions on the next protest victim. After lunch, I let that person relax while I worked on a second patient. Then, after supper, I went back to the first, continuing their therapy.

Even though Dimitri, Irina, and Natalie stayed with everyone in the Cartwright Skyscraper, I saw little of them. I heard a few newscasts, thanks to Ted who recorded them for me to watch while we got ready for bed each evening.

Just as suspected, copycat attacks sprang up around the world, affecting other local GPan and GD corporations. By the time Petr and the others came out of their mutation comas, LA, New York, Peking, Singapore, and Caracas had been attacked by presumed protesters who had stolen quantities of the bio agent and who had inserted it into the buildings' air circulation systems. Several of the perpetrators made mistakes, becoming victims of their own attacks, so we knew the Sixth Invaders weren't involved in these crimes.

As Chicago's men, women, and children woke to their nightmare without end, thousands of others were in similar comas. By this time, we finished the therapy of another eight Chicago protest victims, leaving the last four waiting for their turn; they had seen the therapy benefits in their fellow victims.

Natalie and Dimitri convinced fifty men and women from Moscow to come to Chicago to help them with the situation. Together, they were ready to handle the thousands when they came out of their comas.

Irina insisted on being with Petr and Ivan when they awoke. Since Dimitri needed to direct the rescue operations at GPan, Ted and I volunteered to stay with Irina after Dimitri took us to his father and brother. Celeste accompanied Natalie when she went to check on her parents in the GD building.

The scene was the opposite of being beside Hank when he awoke to find himself a male Doll. The mutation process had regrown his missing arm and leg. Elation swept over

Hank. In contrast, months ago, we had seen the reactions when millions of central Chicago men and boys awoke from their mutation comas, discovering their bodies were now male Dolls. Many committed suicide. I suspected this time would be worse, but its magnitude shocked me.

As we rode the elevator upwards, Dimitri covered his ears with his hands, as did Ted. Irina and I couldn't. By the time we reached the top floor of the GPan skyscraper, we'd lost track of the number of terrified screams.

"Why are they screaming? They're perfect Dolls, just as I am and you are," Irina yelled above the noise, as the elevator passed between floors and the volume subsided slightly before increasing as we passed another floor.

I decided not to answer her. I doubted I could yell over the din. By the time the doors opened on the one-hundredth floor, Dimitri's face appeared bleached. The rosy color had faded from Ted's cheeks, too. As the doors opened, soprano screams greeted us. A new experience slammed into us; I'll try to describe it as best I can.

Every person experiences their own emotions. For example, we feel grief when someone we love is terminated. But have you ever sensed the emotions coming off or radiating from another person? By the time we stepped out of the elevator on the top floor, my stomach was in a knot. The overwhelming emotions of fear and stark terror coming from so many people echoed or resonated within us, the rescuers. For a moment, I wanted to scream and run—run as fast and as far from here as I could.

"I don't think I can do this," Dimitri said, his voice shaking. His whole body twitched.

Ted's hands shook, though he kept them around Irina's waist, supporting her. Irina's face turned a ghastly white.

"What's the matter with my legs?" Irina said, her voice trembling. "Why are they screaming? They're perfect Dolls now. Well, maybe not perfect, but tight-laced corset training would accentuate their magnificent curves."

No one answered her. Each experienced the pure terror emanating from over five hundred people. Worse, it didn't let up, not for some time. When Natalie, Celeste, and her workers entered the GD skyscraper, they experienced that, too.

"Oh, there you are, Petr," Irina said.

She moved over to her husband who was lying naked on the floor. His original clothes lay in a pile nearby, right where the rescue person in the bio-containment suit had left them. In time, I planned to gather up the apparel, donating it to goodwill charities in other cities, since these people could no longer wear such clothing.

Petr looked up at her and continued his shrill shrieking. His now armless male Doll body shook violently on the carpet.

"Oh, do hush, Petr. And get up. You're just perfect, too. After all, you've always told me I'm the perfect Doll, and now you are, too. Please, stop screaming so. I can't take it any longer. You are perfect. Please stop yelling. I can't cover my ears."

"I'm not perfect! I'm helpless. I can't live like this. Dimitri, Dimitri, kill me, please, I beg you," Petr cried out.

At least, he ceased screaming. He couldn't do both at the same time.

"Dad, let me help you up," Dimitri said.

"Oh god, I can't stand up! My feet," he said, before vomiting on the carpet. His feet were like all Doll's, unable to lie flat on the ground. He needed to wear the usual tall heels that we wore. I think he realized this, along with how helpless he felt as his son helped him up, and that caused his stomach to lurch so violently.

"Petr, stop being such a baby. You have a perfect body now, but I suppose we can start you on waist training so you can get your body even more shapely and perfect, like mine is," Irina said.

I watched her closely since Ted headed off to help Ivan who was lying in another room. Irina's body still trembled. Her lips quivered, but her eyes took in every detail of Petr's body from his giant breasts to his widened hips to his distorted feet, finally resting on his waist-length black hair.

"Dimitri, kill me. Take pity on me. I can't live like this. Please, son, I'm begging you."

"It's okay, Dad. I understand. It'll be done soon. I promise," Dimitri whispered, holding back watering eyes.

I watched Irina, expecting a wild reaction. Her face tightened for a moment before she slumped into a nearby chair. Uncharacteristically, Irina didn't say another word, not to Petr, not to Ivan, not to Dimitri, and not even to me. She sat in the chair, her eyes oblivious to everything around her.

Dimitri said, "Dad, I've got to go check on Ivan. Back soon."

As he left, Petr sobbed. His terror had yielded to fear, and now he slumped down into grief. When Ted and Dimitri returned, Ted shook his head. I assumed Ivan didn't want to live either.

"How's Ivan taking it?" I said for Irina's benefit, but she didn't seem to notice anything around her.

"He's begging to be terminated, too," Dimitri said.

Upon hearing that, Petr's sobbing ceased. I looked over. He'd slipped down into apathy. He sat there, his back against a table leg. No motion, no talking, nothing at all. I'd seen such reactions before and knew he had slipped into the sub-apathy emotions, waiting for death to take his body.

Dimitri tried to discuss the GPan situation with Petr, but his father appeared not to hear him.

"What's the matter with him?" he whispered.

I told him the truth, even though it hit him hard. "He's gone now, Dimitri. He's waiting for death to take him. I've seen that look before, right after the Sixth Invaders' attack on central Chicago."

"Can't—can't anything be done for him?"

I shrugged. "He's made his decision, Dimitri. I always hoped we would have a right to the disposition of our own bodies. If he doesn't want to continue living with his body, then it should be his right to have it die. He's doing his best to kill it by becoming oblivious to everything."

Dimitri sighed. "Well, I issued that order. Anyone wishing to be terminated shall be, but I had hoped no one would want that. I'm gonna throw up, too. I can't take much more of this."

"Look around you, Dimitri. It's other people's terror and fear you're feeling. I've never seen such strong emotions flooding a place as here. Look at the ceiling. Okay. Now, look at that table." I had him noticing things around the room for several minutes.

"Thanks. I feel better. I best lead the rescue operation. Can you and Ted lead mom home? Can you give her your therapy? I don't want to lose her, too."

"We'll get her home, Dimitri. I'll see if she'll accept therapy. Take heart. Unless I'm wrong, you'll find the younger children much more accepting of their fate. We observed that happening before."

"I swear I'll listen to your advice more often, Molly."

With that, he left the suite. Ted helped Irina rise, though Ted carried her. She'd had a shock, but I didn't realize how much this had affected her. As we descended, the noise level was only a little less. My stomach felt as though tied in a tight knot, but I realized I sensed what these unseen men and women were experiencing. As we left the building and breathed in the fishy lake odor, I wondered if the walls of the building would retain any trace of that violent emotion. Was that even possible?

Once back at the Cartwright Skyscraper, Ted suggested, "Dear, perhaps you should work on Irina today."

He moved her body over to a sofa. She stood there until he used his arms to force her to sit. In doing so, her body fell into it. Irina had dropped to the sub-apathy emotional levels, waiting for death. She'd given up on life. I didn't know if I could reach her, but I had to try to help Dimitri's mother.

"Irina, close your eyes. Okay."

Great. Now, what do I ask for? Her current loss?

"I want you to return to the moment when Petr awoke from his coma."

The trigger of her emotional trauma must have been his reactions upon waking up. Anyway, that was my rationale. I soon discovered that time runs excruciatingly slowly for those who are in the sub-apathy emotions. After hours and only two passes through it, I asked for an earlier trauma.

"Irina, is there a similar trauma that happened earlier?"

Suddenly, she shot up to fear. "Yes, that accident I had. My Miss Moscow reign is ending. Petr is taking me on dates and to the ballet. I wake up in the Medical Center. My shoulders throb. I've lost my arms, but Petr is there beside me. I'm now a perfect woman. He's telling me he has a personal assistant to help me. Petr jokes about asking for my hand in marriage, but I didn't have any."

I had her go back over it several more times, wondering if the details of her accident would appear since such an event must contain pain and unconsciousness. Irina yawned and yawned.

Suddenly, she sat up. Her eyes opened wide. "Damn that bastard! I didn't have an accident! He drugged me and took me to the Med Center. He ordered them to cut off my arms. He kept whispering in my ear. You are a perfect woman. Over and over. My god. He brainwashed me. Oh no. I'm anything *but* a perfect woman! I can't do much except talk. Wow. That bastard! Well, you should make him live and not allow him to be terminated."

Irina laughed. She looked straight at my face. "Molly, can you please have someone terminate me? If what you say is true and that I'll come back in a new baby body, then that's what I want to do. No way am I going to live a second lifetime handicapped like this."

I ended our session. "Let's tell Dimitri what you discovered and what you want to do. If he agrees, then okay. I get your point."

"Well, let's do it soon."

As we walked out of the bedroom, Ted had a pair of robot assistants prepared and waiting for us.

"Thought you two were never coming out. Irina looks bright and cheerful," he said. "I've got these helper robots ready to go. Supper's already been delivered. Dimitri and Natalie said to eat without them. They'll be here later on. Guess they have a real mess on their hands."

"A good day for the morticians," Irina jested.

Since I'd met her, that was the first joke she'd made, so I hoped she might change her mind about desiring death.

Around eight, the exhausted pair arrived, collapsing on the couch. Irina, Ted, and I joined them.

Irina said, "Dimitri, I want you to terminate me as soon as possible. I don't wish to live another helpless lifetime. I've just discovered what your father did to me. He's a sadist. When my Miss Moscow reign ended, he drugged me, took me to the Med Center, and had my arms amputated. Worse, while I was unconscious, he kept whispering in my ear telling me I was now a perfect woman and that I'd always have a personal assistant. Ha. I've lived his lie for one lifetime. I'm not about to live it another. So, Dimitri, I want you to terminate me. I've been exposed to this new bio agent, so they can't regrown my arms. But it would be nice if you forced Petr to stay alive for the rest of this lifetime so he can appreciate what he did to me all these years."

"You're kidding, mom. Right?" Dimitri ran his hands over his face and then his head, before pulling his chin down. "He said nothing about this."

"He never told me what he'd done. You wouldn't expect him to tell you or me. It's not something that brings respect. The bastard." She spat.

"Well, I watched them both die. It's been a hideous day, and I'm numb. So is Natalie. Mom, I hear what you're saying. You aren't alone. Between GPan and GD, only three families wanted to continue living. The eight hundred adults that came with us from Moscow—all are now dead except six."

His voice cracked. Natalie's head slumped as though it weighed more than her neck could support. After a pause, he continued.

"Three hundred three teens and children want to live. We only lost ninety-four of them. I can't believe how brave and how well they're taking this. Now, we've got to find homes for three hundred youngsters."

"Good god," I said. "Where are they now? Ted, have you been able to get them personal assistant robots? And all the other machines we need?"

"We're housing them on GD's living floors, at least for tonight," Dimitri said. "I have a dozen nurses and helpers staying with them, but I promised them better accommodations by tomorrow."

"My idea," Natalie said. She sighed, her body slumping further into the couch. "I think we need to find families who want to adopt these children. They need mothers and fathers.

Dimitri and I are planning to get married soon and adopt needy children. Tomorrow, I'm going on a GEnt newscast to encourage others to step up and adopt a child. I know they're handicapped or physically challenged, but they are still people. We have to help them; I feel so badly for them."

"We don't need pity or sympathy, Natalie," I said. Perhaps, I was too harsh with her. "Yes, we have different ways to do normal things, and we need help with things that armed people don't. We need to be treated like a person and given the same opportunities."

Ted said, "And remember the motto: stop and think how."

I smiled. "Will the families receive financial support, a stipend to help raise the children? Will there be safeguards in place so the foster parents don't take the money and do nothing for the children? You know, I'd also like to run a day camp for the survivors, showing them the many holographic videos the Sixth Invaders intended to play for us. I want to have a hands-on day camp where we all practice together."

Natalie's ashen face broke into a wide grin; pinkish color returned to her cheeks though the gray-black around her eyes remained. "Oh Molly, that would be most welcome. I didn't know if I had the right to ask you to do something like that or not. We can use the giant conference room on Floor 50 of GD. It can hold five hundred at one time."

Dimitri flashed a brief smile but still looked downcast. "Things aren't getting better around the world. There have been more mutation attacks by protesters. This time in Paris. Worse, many corporations are refusing to accept our new positions as emperor and empress over the Sol Empire. I've gotten suggestions that Brussels or Pylon should now rule the empire. Even the smaller moon colonies are protesting the changes."

"I figured they would," I said. I wished I had words of wisdom to share, but I couldn't think of anything. From all I'd seen, most corporation men were corrupt and self-centered, though after what I'd learned about Irina, perhaps more than I'd ever imagined.

He continued. "I've been trying to arrange an Earth-wide conference of top local CEOs, but they're terrified of coming to Chicago—becoming the next victims. These Sixth Invaders have created an aura of fear. Tomorrow, I'll see about making it a teleconference meeting. If they go for that, Ted, I could use your help to set it up."

"I'll get on it in the morning. I think Holly Ann will volunteer to help."

Help. That reminded me of a key point. "Say, Ted, when we were on the atoll, having five of us together allowed us to do what one of us alone couldn't easily do. We should keep that in mind as we find homes for the kids."

Natalie asked what I meant, and I spent several minutes explaining our time on the atoll.

She said, "I'll see what we can do about that. I also had several calls from GD CEOs in LA, New York, Peking, Singapore, Paris, and Caracas. They want to send all their surviving victims here to Chicago. Make Chicago the sole location where these handicapped victims live, along with the many male Dolls. Keep everyone in one location. Plus, they're frightened of having to deal with the aftermath—so many victims and their enormous needs."

"It has merit," Dimitri said. "But I'm worried someone could kill us all, just like that vision you once had, Molly. Scary."

I cautioned. "Let's not get ahead of ourselves. If we adopt these children, we'll need larger homes. We've much to do tomorrow."

***

"Quite a crowd," I said to Ted. Over thirty gathered in the auditorium of the Cartwright Skyscraper for the GEnt broadcast news conference. I didn't recognize many of the men, though I found it strange to observe un-mutated males here in Chicago. Ted and I sat before the cameras, along with Emperor Dimitri and Empress Natalie. Dozens of large monitors stretched around the room. Each displayed other Sol Empire corporation leaders.

Dimitri explained, "We have CEOs from Brussels, Tau Ceti, and from Pylon, Epsilon Eridani. The time delay between us and them is five minutes or more. We'll discuss issues for

98

ten minutes and then wait five for them to hear us and another five for their replies. When you hear them talking, please cease speaking. Allow our counterparts on these distant worlds of our empire to air their grievances, too.

"First, I wish to repeat my earlier declarations. No one is to be forced into retirement when they reach sixty years old. No one in the assisted living homes is to be given the drug that brings on dementia. Those who have assisted in these criminal acts have immunity, but only if they cease such actions now. Beginning next Monday, anyone discovered administering those terrible drugs will be prosecuted.

"Second, would be protesters, please cease your genetic mutation attacks on your corporations. As of today, anyone committing such hideous crimes will be prosecuted. There is no need. We have heard your complaints and protests, and we have acted to end these atrocities.

"Third, as of today, I've issued orders to all assisted living centers and Med Centers to offer anyone who has reached sixty years of age a free Galactic Doll mutation. Those who have it done may expect their bodies to rejuvenate to about twenty-five years old."

He sighed and said, "I've listened to the requests of other CEOs around Earth. Their suggestion is to send their recent armless genetic mutation victims here to Chicago, where we can deal with their needs, removing such a burden from many other cities. Further, normal male Dolls can also be relocated to Chicago. Doing this is cost effective, too.

"Finally, I want to close our penal colony on Mercury. To do that and to reduce the high levels of recidivism, I'm instigating a new policy. Those convicted of serious crimes will be given the Sixth Invaders' genetic mutation that turns them into armless Dolls. That way, they cannot commit further crimes. Termination is too easy on them."

"Now, I want to introduce Ted and Molly Parkinson-Billings, our new Investigations and Justice leaders. Molly helped to thwart the recent Sixth Invaders' attacks on Earth. She uncovered massive crimes committed by members of the Chicago Galactic Defense corporation. Molly is well suited for this challenging job. Yes, she may look different to you. The

Sixth Invaders attempted to murder her, but she swapped bodies with another victim who wished to be terminated. Molly wants to say a few words about how we're handling this latest Sixth Invaders mutation attack."

The camera panned to me. Since the allotted time was just about up, I decided to let those on the other worlds respond before I spoke. A man in the middle of the room stood. Dozens of chairs surrounded him. Some of my extended family smiled and waved at me.

But I sensed hate radiating from the unknown man. While I mused on that, the illusion created by the device around his waist ended. There stood one of the Sixth Invader female soldiers. She held a disintegrator rifle in her hands. I saw a blinding blaze of yellowish energy flying from its barrel heading toward me. Then, intense pain flooded over my body. I think every muscle in my body tensed or contracted as hard as it could to try to stop the tidal wave of pain from wracking my body. I was thrown out of my head, landing on the ceiling where I blacked out.

I must have been knocked out only a moment because I watched the reactions that followed. A dozen of the strange men stood up and fired their own hand disintegrator pistols at the Sixth Invader soldier. She had a protection field around her, a force field generator Holly Ann later explained. Bluish energy illuminated a zone or shell around her body about three feet away from her. As the other disintegrator beams hit, the protective shell shrank. Then, her shield dropped, and giant holes appeared in her head and chest areas. Her rifle gun dropped to the floor, and her body followed.

A soldier said, "Compliments of your First Infantry Division. Only fifteen more Sixth Invaders to go. Bring them on, you cowards."

Whether he would have said more wasn't known. At that instant, the Sixth Invaders took over one of the comm channels. The image of Captain L'Grina appeared on a monitor. Via the teleconference, every comm center on Earth received it, not just those in the conference links. Her well-muscled body and gray-skin contrasted with her short jet black hair that matched the color of her eyes. Her bosom was gigantic, each breast the size and shape of a soccer ball. Each hand had six fingers, long and dexterous. She wore a space fleet uniform, comprising a black shirt, pants, and knee-high boots. A four-star patch on her collar showed her rank in the service.

"That takes care of Meddling Molly. Now then, I'm giving you Earthlings until August 1st to unconditionally surrender to me. If you do not yield, then beginning August 2nd, you may expect every day thereafter we will expose one major city to our genetic mutation agent that leaves everyone as armless Dolls until you do surrender. We will monitor your comm channels, awaiting your surrender."

The connection ended. Pandemonium broke out, but Natalie brought order. I had a good overhead viewpoint and watched her.

"Okay, soldiers, carry Molly's body out. Ted, you go with her; check with Irina. Security guards, fan out around this facility. Stay alert for more of these foul creatures from Hell. If you see any of these Sixth Invaders, shoot to terminate."

White. Ted's face echoed his shock. Twice he'd seen my body shot. He rose and followed four soldiers out, two carrying my deceased body. I followed Ted, unwilling to risk getting lost or separated.

Five minutes later, Holly Ann had my dead Mary Trout body hooked up to her Body Swap machine. Celeste led Irina into the room.

She said, "Okay, last chance. Are you sure you want to be terminated and get a new baby body?"

"Absolutely. Besides, I can help Molly. And there's no way I want to live an entire second handicapped lifetime. So let's do it. Will it hurt? How will I find a new body?"

Celeste smiled. "It's painless. Randi will help you get the perfect new baby body for you."

Ah, that incredible, pure, white energy. So aesthetic, so wonderful. It made me feel like a god or something. Only I awoke to find myself in Irina's body.

"Oh god, I can't breathe! Ted, get me out of this corset mess. Holly Ann, thank you, thank you."

Ted chuckled. "Not quite what I expected you'd say. But

you gotta promise me to stop getting shot. I don't think I can take it again. Come. I'll get you out of it. Randi is helping Irina find a new body back in St. Petersburg. Then, let's get you a full medical checkup."

"Oh here you are, Ted," General Bev said. She marched into Holly Ann's lab, where we'd gone to do the body swap. "I'm glad I had a squad of my soldiers in your audience. We got another Sixth Invader. Too bad about Molly."

"Thanks, Bev. I'm here. Irina's given me her body, only it can't breathe."

"Oh, great. Now you have a very hot body!" She teased, and Ted's face reddened.

"Glad to continue to be in the game," I said. "There is too much to do to start over as a baby."

"Righto. Well, I've got to find better ways to keep you safe, Molly. By the way, count Gail and me in on adopting some of the children. Gotta run. Duty calls. Check with you later."

***

An hour later, the Med Center doctor placed two large x-ray images side by side on his monitor. "This one was taken when Irina arrived in Chicago, a few days ago. The one on the left is today's. See this? It's the missing rib. Irina's medical records showed she'd had her lower set of ribs removed so she could have a tinier waistline. She was exposed to the new mutation agent, which is regrowing that missing set. That's why all the pain. As long as you can avoid wearing such a tight corset, you should be fine. Next month, we'll take another x-ray to make sure all is well."

I thanked him. Ted and I left the Med Center, relieved to know the source of my discomfort.

"I've no intention of trying to have a tiny waist, Ted, so don't go getting any weird ideas."

"Hardly. Now I'm married to Miss Moscow. Woo hoo. Hot body."

"Consider yourself slapped." We chuckled and headed home.

Breathing in the Chicago air, I felt alive. I'd cheated death twice. Was it because of my lucky gene?

"Ted," I said, "we need to help these many new victims. Bringing them all here to Chicago from all over the world gives us a chance to help them learn alternative ways—like I did while on that atoll. But then what? Even Holly Ann returned to her home city, Chicago."

"Out of sight, out of mind," Ted said.

"Huh?"

"That's the feeling I got from hearing Dimitri relay the wishes of those in charge of the other cities. Move all the victims from their city to Chicago—out of sight. Then, they can forget about them."

"You're as cynical as I am." I teased, and Ted laughed. "But your point's made. They won't have to see armless Dolls and transgendered men in their cities. Out of mind. But sending them to Chicago isn't good for us, not in the long term. Plus, with us in one location, they could use cyanide, eliminating the problem."

"You haven't seen that in our future, have you?" Ted turned to stare into my eyes.

"No, dear. I'm being paranoid." I returned his gaze and added, "From the survivors' point of view, trying to adapt to a new city on top of everything else isn't optimum."

"But the kids—they must be placed in foster homes or adopted," Ted said. "I don't see how we can find that many foster parents. Let alone ones who can understand and help these kids. I think we need to take it one step at a time. First thing has to be to get them a touchpad with all those how-to videos on them."

"And work with them practicing the actions," I said.

"Precisely. Drill into their noggins: 'Stop and think how'—just as we did with you on the atoll. We need to get them ready to go back to school this fall. Education will be their salvation."

I often felt embarrassed because I didn't have any degrees. He was right. We rode in silence.

Two weeks. We had two weeks before these Sixth Invaders promised to wipe out an entire city. I didn't see how we could stop them, let alone help all the current victims. It seemed hopeless, but perhaps those feelings came from this new body, for that must have been how Irina felt.

The next morning, Ted headed off to work, promising to send over video-loaded touchpads for each victim. He made sure I could handle my grooming before he left. After that frustrating struggle, I headed off to meet with the three families and the three hundred teens and children housed in the GD skyscraper.

I found them assembled in the giant auditorium. Three dozen women, along with the new personal assistant robots, handled their breakfasts. As I looked them over, already changes had happened. Someone had cut the men and boy's hair. Leslie's promised male apparel had arrived, and I noticed how much this heartened the males in the group. Then, I gave my speech.

"Hello, everyone. I'm so pleased to see so many survivors. Look around at your neighbors. Realize you're looking at the best of the best. Those whose will to live and thrive cannot be destroyed by these vicious Sixth Invaders. We are survivors. We don't want other people's sympathy or pity. Rather, we want to figure out how to carry on, live independent lives, and do well. I'm here today to help each of you succeed.

"Contrary to popular opinions, we aren't helpless people. Yes, we face challenges that normal people do not, but that doesn't make us helpless. Each will receive a touchpad loaded with hours of holographic videos made by others like us, showing how they do nearly everything. We have to learn to use our feet and toes as hands and feet. Yes, that will take time, practice, and patience.

"While it may take us longer to carry out a task, we can do it. Each of you has to memorize our motto. Stop and think how. Rather than curse when a challenge comes our way, we have to stop and think how we can do it. Some will say we're physically challenged. Okay, so we are. That only means we need to use our brains more than the next person does. We have to think how we can do something. It's not easy. It can be frustrating. I won't deny that. Patience and practice become the answers."

Men arrived with hundreds of touchpads. I paused

while each person received theirs. They even gave me one. Next, I had everyone examine the main menu of videos. I began by having everyone, myself included, working with our toes and the silverware. Later after someone brought in paper and pens, we worked on writing our names.

Mid-afternoon, Deanna dropped by, her face pale. "Molly. There's been another attack. At Galactic Robotics. That Terri Torelli woman—the one who went insane when the robot aliens butchered her husband—the woman you and Bev prevented from unleashing this bio agent on Chicago."

"Is Ted all right?"

"She unleashed a container of the mutation agent in the labs. Fifty-nine are in mutation comas. Ted's among them. He'll be all right. Terri is also in a coma, so her revenge will cost her. Natalie issued orders she is not to be terminated, but forced to live out her life."

"Oh hell. Where's Ted now?"

"They sucked out the air in the labs and have transported them to the Med Center. I'm told since Ted's already a modified Doll, his coma should be a short one. When you're done, I'll take you to him."

"God, when is this ever going to end?"

"Not until we put an end to these Invaders."

"Okay. I might as well finish up here first since he'll be in a coma."

"I'm so sorry, Molly. That's true. I'll drop by around six after these people have their dinner."

I smiled. "Thanks. I want to help them learn to feed themselves without having that silly robot do it."

"I don't know how you can do these things. You and Holly Ann. Remarkable women. Inspirational, too."

"Thanks, Deanna."

Natalie rushed in. "Oh, Deanna. Have you told her..."

Deanna nodded.

"I'm so sorry, Molly. I checked with Helen Hugo. Maybe you're right about our behavioral modification implant. Torelli was given one at the Moscow Center, following the practice ordered by Petr. Something must have gone wrong."

"Revenge can be a powerful driving force," I said.

"Look, she saw her husband being butchered by the supposed Sixth Invaders only to find out those were robots built with Galactic Robotics corporation parts and controlled by Galactic Defense personnel. Her life was destroyed. Then, Bev and I thwarted her plan to get revenge on the corporations. No amount of implanting will erase that drive in her psyche. At least, she's no longer going to be a threat."

"Will you be okay with Ted being..." Natalie said.

"Sure. We got by fine before. It's a pain but we can do it again. Glad you're here, Natalie. We need to talk. Long term. These kids deserve better than to be dumped here in Chicago, far from Moscow and their uncles and aunts and grandparents."

"You think so?" Her eyebrows rose. Her eyes drilled into mine.

"Yes, definitely. But not until they're proficient dealing with life on their own. Once able to effectively use their feet and toes, they stand a good chance of making it in Moscow. Besides, as Ted pointed out last night, how can we expect to find hundreds of foster parents here in Chicago who know how to handle us? We don't want sympathy or pity, but that's what everyone gives us."

A blush flashed across her cheeks. "Good point. I'll talk with Dimitri about this."

"Ted said these other corporation executives are doing an out of sight and out of mind thing with all the mutation victims. That's not good for anyone. Except it might be wise to bring them here so I can help train and educate them on ways to live independently."

"Okay. I'll relay that. We'll have another teleconference tomorrow. You must come. This time, its location will stay a secret until the last minute. Plus, Bev will provide heavy security."

"All right. Count me in. We have to get the other corporations to accept you and Dimitri. We've also got to come up with a plan to stop these fiends before August. Have you got any ideas how?" I said.

She shook her head and left.

After supper, Deanna returned to take me to visit Ted.

She, too, was impressed at how quickly so many children were picking up the techniques for feeding themselves.

As we walked to the Med Center, she said, "I'll come by tomorrow around nine and pick you up. We'll take my two-person shuttle craft."

"Wow. I've always wanted to see what one looked like. Bet they cost a fortune."

She laughed. "True, but they are convenient."

When we walked into the giant Med Center, the receptionist said, "Two doctors want to see you."

Down the long hallways, our heels clicked in unison. First stop, visit Ted, except they moved him into the same room where they had my brain-dead body on life support. By the time we entered, his doctor joined us. Also a male Doll, he wore Leslie's new line of apparel; that brought a smile to my face in spite of the grim situation.

His eyes stared at my unusual form. I suppressed an urge to say "So what?"

"He's doing fine. We've verified the alien mutation agent used in this attack. It's the same as the one used earlier at GPan and GD. In about a week, his body will finish absorbing his arms."

"He's all right otherwise? No gunshots?"

"No, no. The official report is that a crazy woman unleashed the attack, but Ted and several others tackled her, preventing a much wider spread of the agent. They saved hundreds of other Galactic Robotics personnel from being infected."

Deanna said, "Is the official count still fifty-nine?"

"Yes. About equally divided between men and women, all younger workers, all highly educated. That includes the perpetrator. Already, we've received orders to keep her alive no matter what her wishes may be when she awakens."

He looked at me. "We'll call you when he'll be coming out of his coma."

I thanked him, and he departed. We turned to leave when Dr. Janet Padella entered. The Galactic Doll mutation had done much for this woman. Before, she was anything but attractive. Homely fit her and her husband. Now, she looked not a day over twenty-five, and her face wasn't unattractive any longer.

"Ah, Molly Parkinson, I presume," she said, looking at me, though she saw Irina.

"Yes, Body Swap."

"I see. Interesting, but then you'll find this even more interesting. Molly, I've taken the liberty to conduct an experiment on your deceased body there. I heard what had happened and that they were keeping it alive so your baby could survive. Admirable. Amazing what modern medicine can do."

"Dr. Padella, what did you do to my body?" That sounded strange, but my body lay there, a multitude of tubes connected to its many orifices. "Who gave you permission?"

She smiled. "No one ever gives doctors permission for experiments. I felt I owed you something for what you've done for Nelson and me. We have our lives back and our youth—a second lifetime. Anyway, Nelson and I determined this new alien bio agent is much stronger than any version we've created. Hence, I've injected it into your body. If you look, you'll see it's in a coma, just as Ted's body is."

I gasped and looked. She continued. "I believe the fetal regeneration process of the mutation agent will repair all the damage the bullet did to your brain. When the mutation is finished and the body comes out of its coma, I predict your body will be perfectly fit and not dead. What you do with it then is your own business. Consider our debt to you paid in full."

My mouth waggled, but I couldn't think of anything to say. She pivoted and left the room. I called out a parting, "Thank you."

"What the heck just happened? Am I going to have two bodies in a few days?"

Deanna said, "I'm calling Celeste and Eve right now."

Chapter 10 Fear Fall Out

Neither Eve nor Celeste had any idea about how one being or person could operate two bodies at the same time. Nothing like this had ever happened before, and we took a wait and see approach, though Celeste promised to give me some sessions to erase the two shooting traumas. But considering the needs of so many other victims, I declined for the time being. I focused my free time helping the hundreds of victims practicing using their feet. Besides, I needed the practice, too.

In the morning, Deanna landed her two-person shuttle outside the apartments. I stepped out to meet her, awed.

"Wow. This is incredible. So tiny and so cool."

Deanna smiled, "Agreed. These are convenient for getting about swiftly, though EMACs are far more practical. Come. The meeting awaits. I have a hunch this will be a pivotal one."

She helped me into the small ship, strapping my safety belt. I stared at the panel of controls.

"So how do you drive it?" It looked vastly different from my ancient electric tiny car. I only saw dials and gauges. No steering wheel.

"It's voice or touch operated. You say Main Menu or touch here." She pressed the big M button. A series of choices appeared. "I've entered all the usual destinations I visit. This morning, I had to add this new one. Bev called with the new location. Touch it. Everything is automated. We're taking off now. Computers control all aspects of the flight. Nothing can go wrong. But it's darn expensive. Molly, it's so easy to use that you could fly it."

"This is incredible. I can see so much of the city. Oh, there's the Lake. Wow. Okay, so where's the meeting?" I said. "I could ride around up here for days."

Deanna laughed. "I did that when Peter bought this one for me a couple years ago. Tell you what. We'll do that later today if there's time. We're meeting in an abandoned warehouse on the south side. They've got a hundred giant monitors set up, so all corporations across the Sol Empire can get in on this meeting. Ah, we're landing now."

I looked down and saw hundreds of well-armed soldiers surrounding the warehouse that once shipped mattresses if the faded and pealing sign was right. An invisible Sixth Invader would bump into a pair of soldiers if they tried to get in around them. I smiled, figuring Bev had thought of this detail. She was thorough when it came to security. Deanna and I entered, after two soldiers encircled us, ensuring that no invisible Invader was trying to sneak in behind us or with us.

Inside the huge space, chairs filled the central area, while giant monitors hung from the walls. Many video cameras and lights focused on the chairs, broadcasting to those not in attendance. Teleconferencing gone mad, I thought.

Dimitri and Natalie arrived and had me join them at the front of the wall of chairs. "After all," she said, "you represent the Inspection and Justice Division, Czar Molly." She grinned, and we chatted about how Ted was doing.

One by one, live images of various CEOs of many corporations from around the world appeared on the monitors. Top men from every other planet, moon, and space station in the Sol Empire joined them. Then, the central monitor came alive with the image of the Communications and Control Center of the Battleship Atlantis and Admiral Aldo Rossi himself, the man who controlled the entire Sol Empire battle fleet.

I whispered to Natalie. "Now we're getting somewhere."

Dimitri rose. "Welcome, everyone. I'm the Emperor of Galactic Expansion, Dimitri Leonovich. With me are Natalie Mantovo, the Empress of Galactic Defense, and Molly Parkinson, Czar of Inspections and Justice. Joining us are Admiral Aldo Rossi and General Beverly Blythe. Natalie has tight security around us today. She instituted new security protocols since all existing ones have been compromised by the Sixth Invaders. They body swapped into our top CEOs for several decades."

After each of us nodded a welcome to the cameras, he continued.

"Today, Earth and our young Sol Empire are facing its worst challenge since overpopulation and global warming nearly destroyed our world. The Sixth Invaders threaten our existence. We cannot and will not let these evil aliens destroy our world. They must be stopped. If Earth doesn't, then the rest of our empire will be next.

"We can't let fear control our decisions. You heard yesterday there was another biological agent attack on Galactic Robotics here in Chicago. The perpetrator was the wife of a soldier who had been hacked to death by the Sixth Invaders' robot soldiers on Brussels, Tau Ceti. She wanted revenge. Several brave men stopped her before she could cause widespread mutations. Fifty-nine are now in a coma, including Molly's husband.

"This has to stop. I'm requesting every facility that has any of this mutation agent, the one that makes armless Dolls, either destroy the samples or secure them. If the Sixth Invaders cannot steal the mutation agent, then they can't infect any city, nullifying their threat to do that. So lock up this terrible agent. Use your tightest security. I'll pause for ten minutes to give our other worlds an opportunity to reply."

Chaos broke out. No one waited for the more distant worlds to respond. "Surrender to these Invaders now. My god, man, you're dooming millions of us to horrible mutations," yelled one CEO.

So many talked or screamed at once that I couldn't tell their cities.

"Who gave you the authority to take over the Sol Empire?"

"You've got to surrender before their deadline!"

"We're holding you responsible for the Invader genocide of our city!"

On it went. I've never seen so many hostile men. But I couldn't blame them. Not really. This mutation was insidious and affected our future generations. They had a right to be terrified. The consequences were terrible to contemplate. But they shouldn't have duplicated this bio agent and made it so widely available. Only a fool would have believed Petr when he said it would never be used as a weapon or fall into the wrong

111

hands.

On the positive side, there were only about fourteen of these alien invaders left. I hoped so few could be stopped.

Admiral Aldo Rossi listened to the yelling chaos for a minute before he acted. When I was in high school, I'd seen pictures of him. He looked older now, probably in his early fifties. Square-faced, his bushy, black eyebrows, and piercing brown eyes gave him a commanding appearance, befitting our top space fleet admiral. Just looking at his face, one got the notion here was a no-nonsense man, one who couldn't be bought. At least, I hoped so.

A loud "wheeoop" sounded, drowning out everyone. The Admiral laid his bullhorn down, a smirk on his face.

"Listen up, you fools," Admiral Rossi barked. "We're at war. Wars demand leaders. Not groups of CEOs who can never agree on anything. Except spending money. I and our entire Sol Empire fleet are backing the Empress of Galactic Defense, Natalie Mantovo. She has finished her advanced training on Pylon and is qualified to defend not only Earth but our Sol Empire. Empress Mantovo and I have worked out new defense protocols, ones the enemy doesn't know about. We need leaders, not corporations or committees.

"I support Emperor Dimitri Leonovich and Czar Molly Parkinson, too. It's obvious that Earth needs a Czar of Inspections and Justice. In fact, Mrs. Parkinson's objectives are vital and centuries overdue. Hence, I'm sending her some assistants to help her flush out the corporate system that is little more than a den of corruption. Major Airla Baker will join her later today."

He cleared his throat, rubbed his face, and continued. "Now then. About our defense and finding this lone alien ship. I've put my best, brightest minds on the problem. How to detect a cloaked or invisible spaceship. They've re-purposed the M.A.D. system."

"What's that?" I said. I had no idea, but I listened intently. Until this instant, I'd never thought much about our space fleet and their personnel, let alone how they were trained or even who might be members. I felt like the dummy I knew I was until I saw many other heads nodding.

"Mass-Anomaly-Device. It's a satellite device that's used to search the surface of Earth for possible archaeological sites long lost to jungles and such. It measures spots where there is a local mass anomaly, such as a stone temple. Spaceships weight a lot. So even if it's parked invisibly on the Earth's surface, the M.A.D should detect it, showing an outline of its shape on the screen. We're surveying the entire Earth's surface. They can hide their ship, but not for long."

Loud applause and yells forced him to stop, a smug look on his face. "We've installed a new early warning system. The second the main Sixth Invader fleet appears in Sol Empire space, we'll know about it and destroy them."

He smashed a fist into his hand. The loud smack sound emphasized his point. I flinched, but so did many others.

"Now you local Earth corporations—you figure out who will be the new Earth-wide corporations. GPan in particular. I want a much larger space fleet. Two more battleships, three heavy cruisers, and ten light cruisers. You figure out how to make that happen. That is all."

I had no idea how expensive a battleship was, but the amount must be gigantic. Which made me wonder if the size of our current armada was up to defending us against the Sixth Invader fleet. Were we about to defeat this recon invasion force only to be defeated in the skies and space around us? Again, I felt ignorant.

Pylon and Brussels leaders, along with other off-world men, asked Admiral Rossi about this very point. In a condescending tone, he responded.

"Yes. Yes. No need to worry about that. We'll attack them the moment one of the Sixth Invader ships is spotted in your area. But we're not prepared for a lengthy war. So build me those new ships."

After his speech, the CEOs discussed his request, pointing out its expense and asking who would pay for the ships. That got nowhere as I suspected. After that, all but the Earth-based leaders signed off. For a time, they remained and discussed how to replace the lost corporation staff and how to decide who would replace the Moscow corporations and lead Earth.

Deanna and I left them. As we departed the old warehouse, she said, "Molly, you'd best get a building to house your Inspections and Justice Department."

"Duh. You think? How am I supposed to buy such a thing? I know how badly it's needed because GD once ordered me to murder General Fuller. I bet there's a zillion crimes to be uncovered. But how am I supposed to start?"

"By using your head. We need a building first. Then, we need office equipment for workstations. Once we've zeroed in on that, you can begin hiring. Organization. That's my thing."

"Makes sense, Deanna. I guess I'll just charge everything to GD for the time being."

We both laughed. She stopped and looked at me. "Say, the Westcott Building is vacant. It's near the Loop and New O'Hare. Needs remodeling."

"I've seen the building. It's two blocks from my office. Got time to check it out?"

"Sure. Let's walk. I need air. I've been meaning to ask you. How's Irina's body working out for you? That sounds so weird. I mean what's it like suddenly having another body?"

A sheepish grin swept over Deanna's face. I sensed what she wanted to know.

"It's damned weird. This body is stiff and not so flexible. It feels funny, strange-like. Sometimes I feel like it's not me. Mary Trout's body was only a little better. I shouldn't complain. God, I can't believe I've been killed twice now. Er, rather my body was killed twice. That sounds so freaky."

Deanna laughed. "I can't even imagine what you're going through. Russell and I talked about this whole body swapping thing. Neither of us can fathom what it must be like. But I have to admit I've no idea how you and Holly Ann could get by with no arms, let alone how you and all the others can adapt to it. It's—well, I can't imagine how I could cope—not at all. I know how you hate others feeling sympathy or pity for you, but I can't help it. I do. You're my sister. If I had a way to undo this vicious mutation, I spend my fortune to do it."

"I know you would. I have sympathy for the victims too, but I keep it to myself. Focus on getting them to see that they can live independently again, that their lives still matter, and that they aren't helpless. Sympathy and pity have no role in that. Still, when I see these young children barely school-aged—my heart goes out to them."

Deanna said, "I keep thinking, there but for the Grace of God goes my daughter. They could just as easily have attacked my company."

We arrived outside the Westcott Building, which stood five stories tall and occupied the block. On the boarded-up windows, a relator had nailed a For Sale sign. Deanna dialed their number, so I didn't have to. Again, I sensed sympathy coming from her.

Within twenty minutes, an EMAC sat down on the sidewalk. If we bought this building, we'd only have to walk a block to the MTES. I liked that aspect. The young woman gave us a tour. While it was in rough shape, last occupied twenty years ago, maybe more, it had potential. Deanna made the arrangements to buy it and hired a remodeling firm, the one she often used for her renovations at the Cartwright Skyscraper.

***

While we waited for the renovation contractor to come by the building, Major Airla Baker found us.

"Ah, here you are. I've been all over looking for you, Mrs. Parkinson. I'm Major Airla Baker, now retired from the space service. Admiral Rossi sent me."

"Hey there. Yes, he told me you were coming to help me. Pleased to meet you," I said.

I didn't know why the Admiral wanted to install one of his personnel in my new department, so I was reserved. She hadn't had the Galactic Doll genetic mutation and wore flats. Her curly brunette hair just touched her shoulders. Deep blue eyes looked up and into my own eyes. Her confront was excellent—that much I could tell already. Yet, I couldn't sense her mind and mental attitude toward me. Strange.

"You look so different from your images taken a couple months ago. And Mrs. Cartwright—good to see you, too."

"Body swap. The Sixth Invaders killed my last two bodies. Crazy thing is that Dr. Janet Padella is trying to restore my original clone body. We'll see if that happens in a few more days. We've just bought this building and are arranging the renovations."

"Excellent. Personnel. Have you given any thought about hiring personnel? What their requirements should be?" she said.

"Not yet. They need to be honest and dedicated."

"I've been giving this a lot of thought since getting this assignment. Honest, dedicated. Excellent attributes. Might I make a suggestion?"

"Airla, you don't need to ask; you're a part of the team."

"What about hiring some of these men and women who have been victimized by the Sixth Invaders' nasty genetic mutation? They're proven survivors. I don't think you can find more dedicated and honest employees. Besides, they need jobs they can do and do well. We'll be using advanced computers. Those are even more automated than your laptop or touchpad."

My face broke into a huge grin. I couldn't help it. I've never had an assistant, except for Ted and Bev, but those two depended on me giving them specific orders to follow.

"Brilliant! Incredible. Yes, that's a fabulous solution. Besides, the last I heard, the other cities are sending their victims to Chicago. This will give them real hope for the future and a rewarding job, too."

Airla smiled. "Good. We see eye to eye. Now then, I've been checking on how many victims will be sent here and where they'll live. What do you think about buying an assisted living complex? All in one place, more or less. I've heard it's possible each can help the other with things. Not too sure about that. You're the expert on such issues."

"Yes, four or more adults living more or less together works well. But our problem is most will be teens, grade school children, and preschoolers."

"Yes, I saw your proposal to have many Chicagoans adopt these handicapped children. Admirable. But will it work?"

"Love works," I retorted. I didn't like her hinting that adopting such a child made the person a hero.

"What I mean is will they give the kids the support and

love they need?"

I shrugged. "Ted and I will. I can only hope others do. Otherwise, I don't know what we'll do with so many children without parents. You'd think their other relatives would want to take them into their homes."

Airla shook her head. "Not that I've been able to tell. I think they don't want the challenge of raising such handicapped children. Besides, what future will these kids have? I've been wondering that ever since I saw the first protest victim's situation."

"A bright future. Our minds aren't crippled. We have different ways to do things," I said, growling.

"What about schools for the children," Airla changed the topic.

I sighed before responding. "I had hoped local families would adopt them and send them to local schools. But if other cities send us their victims, then that won't work."

Airla said, "I expected this. The abandoned Oakbrook Academy is available as is the nearby Ace Leisure Acres apartments, which used to be a home for retirees, so everything is on the first floor and automated for senior living. I know it hasn't been used for forty years, but with a little refurbishing, it could handle many thousands of residents. I took the liberty of commandeering both for our use. If they don't meet with your approval, I'll cancel the contracts. GPan is paying for both buildings."

I laughed. "You are the epitome of efficiency. Let's check them out, and then I best head back. I'm supposed to be helping the victims learn new ways to do things and giving therapy sessions."

An hour later, I was back doing both. The academy would make an excellent school for the children—both grade and high school. The living center was a large array of identical buildings, each housing ten separate families, but with an adjoining central community room.

Airla took charge of getting them cleaned and upgraded.

Chapter 11 Of Laws and Species

"This is too confusing. I can't handle it. How can anyone run two bodies at the same time?"

Ted and I awoke from our comas within hours of each other, surrounded by our extended families. All eyes focused on my two bodies. How would it work out with having two bodies? Many thought I'd not even be aware of my original body; Holly Ann and Kyle held that opinion. But I was aware of both.

Imagine looking out of four eyes, speaking with two voices, hearing from four ears. Freaky and unnerving. Okay, I couldn't handle it. The doctor injected a sedative into the Irina body. Once she was asleep, I felt much better.

"Thanks. I feel like my old self again."

The doctor said, "Yes, Dr. Padella was correct. This new alien genetic mutation agent is powerful enough to regenerate severely damaged brain tissues. I want to run a full set of tests before I release you."

While the doctor began the tests, I said, "Well, Ted, thanks for stopping Terri Torelli. If you hadn't, she would have harmed more than just fifty-nine lives."

"I know, dear. That's why I tackled her and held on until we both passed out. I guess it's back to stop and think how for the both of us. What's been going on while I've been unconscious?"

Deanna filled him in while the doctor poked and prodded me, testing my reflexes.

He finished up and joked. "Mrs. Parkinson, I guess whenever you and your clan are involved with the Med Center, we should come to expect new breakthrough medical procedures. First, it was limb regrowth and now brain regeneration. We'll keep Irina in a stasis unit for a month, just to make sure there are no side effects."

I smiled. "Just keeping you folks sharp. Can we go home now?"

Deanna signed the release papers for both of us.

Accompanied by my clan, Ted and I left the Med Center for our apartment. After they settled us in and departed, except for Eve who wanted to chat, Airla dropped by with facts and figures. And I knew we had decisions to make.

"We have one hundred-seven adults," Airla said, "coming in from LA, New York, Paris, Singapore, Peking, and Caracas. That includes those here in Chicago, except they don't count the latest fifty-nine who worked for the R&D Department of Galactic Robotics. Ted thinks they'll resume their work, once they have enough recovery time."

She continued, "Of these, some are qualified to be teachers, which we'll need. I'd like to hire the others to work for the Investigation and Justice Department."

"What about the children?" I said.

She sighed. "Grim. High school: eight hundred nine. Grade school: six hundred eighteen. Preschool: four hundred twenty-five. There are another fifty-eight living with their parents who are here, too. They, like the fifty-nine, aren't in the totals."

I said, "That's a lot. Okay, we should have all the adults move into the new Ace Leisure Acres apartments and have the children go to this new Oakbrook Academy school. We'll need teachers and books and supplies..."

"Already on it," Airla broke in. "I've brought in a workforce from St. Louis to expedite the renovations. We'll have everyone moving in by Monday. Two weeks from now, six teachers from South Chicago will help groove in the new high school and grade school teachers."

"Thanks, Airla. You are the essence of efficiency."

She smiled. "Time isn't on our side. I hope there aren't more victims. That this reign of terror is over." She paused and bit her lip. "You victims—do you realize you're a new subspecies? Everyone else is homo sapiens sapiens."

"Huh?"

Eve spoke up. "She's right. I've analyzed Ted's DNA and yours, sis. Also, three dozen other victims. Your DNA is sufficiently different to classify the armless Doll victims as being in a new subspecies. Technically, you aren't homo sapiens sapiens any longer. I've checked with several anthropologists. All agree. The question is what to do about it?"

Airla said, "She's right. You survivors have different DNA from the rest of us."

"But I don't feel any different. I'm the same person I was before I got shot and mutated. I've lost my arms and have to do most things differently than before, but that's all. Holly Ann was born with a birth defect. Does that make her a new subspecies?"

Eve laughed. "No, it's just a birth defect. All evidence suggests any baby born from one of you armless Dolls will inherit your form. That's what one would expect from a new species—breeding true."

"Crap. Our baby will be like us." I grew annoyed with this mutation business. There were becoming too many of us. Unlike before, I hadn't yet had any premonition that someone would murder us in our sleep to remove the mutation problem.

"That's correct," Eve said. "So sorry, Molly, Ted."

"I hope they don't use cyanide on us," I said.

"That would now be genocide," Eve stated.

"She's got a good point. It would be genocide," Airla said. "And that brings up the next major point, Molly. Laws. What are the laws people have to follow?"

I laughed. "Duh. Good one, Airla. Well, let's see. Murder is against the law."

"Is it really?" said Eve. "Didn't GD order you to murder General Fuller? Galactic Mining ordered the mining ship to exterminate the primitives on Bahira."

"Crap. Point taken. Gosh, the only laws are those the corporations make—no, what they order you to do is what's legal," I said. I rather wished I still had hands. I would have slapped them on the table to emphasize my point.

"That's the precise detail we have to handle," Airla said. "One has to do whatever the corporations order you to do. Beyond those orders, most people assume they shouldn't murder other people, beat them, rob them, or rape them. But there isn't a set of legal laws anymore. Over two centuries ago when there were such things as countries on Earth, each one had their own volumes of laws. Most laws weren't comprehensible to the ordinary person. And they filled many books. It took a lawyer to know what was or was not against the law."

I chuckled. "That's what Ted and I faced when they hired me to bring order into GD after the robot plot was uncovered. Whatever a corporation leader says is acceptable becomes okay to do. I decided on my own that if an action harmed another, then it was illegal and punished the perpetrator. Most people have enough common sense to understand that."

"Precisely, Molly. But if we're to handle Investigations and Justice, everyone must know what is proper conduct and what is illegal," Airla said.

"How do we figure that out?" I said.

"In ancient times, they had elected officials who made the laws. We have nothing like that, so I suppose we must do it," Airla said.

Eve said, "If you're going that route, then do it on the basis of does an action harm more than it helps. An action could harm one's own survival or it could harm or hinder one's marriage and children. Or it could harm the group that one is a part of or even a whole species, like genocide. Or it could harm or hinder the survival of plants and animals, especially those we use for food. Or it could damage physical things, such as shooting down an EMAC. Or it could even be detrimental to spiritual beings. I put those mental implants in this category since without our therapy the implanted behavior follows you into your next lifetime."

I laughed. "Wow, Eve. That's a lot of them. Seven?"

"Yes. So if an action that one does or that they fail to do harms more of these than it helps, it's a harmful act and shouldn't be done. I think that's a good meter stick for you to follow."

"I agree," said Airla. "I'm not sure what these spiritual beings things are, but the other six make sense. Genocide should be illegal. So, since you and the other victims are technically another species, you should be protected. That's why I brought it up. We need to get the victims classified as a new subspecies. Perhaps, that will guarantee others won't try to exterminate you."

"What a strange juxtaposition, but I agree with her," said Eve.

"That sounds weird, but it makes sense. Go ahead with it. I'll be pissed off if someone tries to add to our misery."

***

July 25 became mass moving day. Ted and I moved into No 1A of Ace Leisure Acres. We had three bedrooms, two baths, a kitchen, dining room, and a small living room-comm center. The living room opened onto the giant commons. Ours was one of the ten suites, all sharing this same commons, filled with tables, chairs, couches, and the giant screen comm center. Becky and Henry Dillard moved into No 1B, our closest adult neighbors. Sasha and Yuri Petrova moved into No 1J. Another hundred-five adults, some married, moved into other buildings of this large collection of condominiums. However, eighteen hundred teens and children also moved into these suites, supervised by the adults.

Ted and I adopted thirteen-year-old twins from Caracas, Isabella and Bernardo Torres. Both had raven hair. Hers was curly, trimmed at her waist, while Bernardo had a crew cut. They had thick, bushy eyebrows, and angelic faces. I found their eyes enchanting, but full of fear. They wanted to be in Eighth Grade this fall.

Likewise, Becky and Henry adopted Sandy and Buck, while Sasha and Yuri adopted Nessa and Adrik, but she was also pregnant with their first child. We six adults were also responsible for the other thirty teens and preteens who lived in the other seven adjoining suites, just as the other adults were in the nearby and identical buildings.

Centrally located among all these single-story buildings was the giant auditorium or meeting hall. Couches and chairs replaced the pool tables, video games, and other entertainment facilities. Here we could all meet as one giant group if one didn't mind the crowding.

The morning hours were chaotic, with movers bringing in apparel, computers, various robots, bedding, cooking supplies, and of course synth food. They also dropped off many bags with shoulder straps, the only way we could carry most things. Each of us received four bags, compliments of Leslie, who embroidered "Lucky" on our bags.

In the afternoon, everyone met in the auditorium, but twenty grade and high school teachers also came, along with Randi, Eve, and Celeste. I started the meeting.

"Hey there, everyone. I'm Molly Parkinson-Billings, a Private Investigator by training and the new Czar of Inspections and Justice. First, I want everyone to look around at your neighbors. Really look at each person. Yes, each of us is a real person. We aren't freaks. More importantly, each of us is a survivor, and that alone makes us very, very special people. Many lost parents. We didn't give up, did we?"

Several yelled out "No," while others hollered.

"We're all in the same boat. Together, we must help each other and become independent, productive people. I'll let you in on a secret." I lowered my voice and watched the many eyes and heads leaning forward in anticipation of hearing something special.

"We've a motto, one that no one else has. It's: stop and think how. We will run into many frustrating things that are hard for us to do, things we used to do, sometimes without even thinking about them."

A myriad of yeah's echoed and interrupted me.

"Don't curse or get flustered or angry. Stop and think how can I do this? We use our minds, our brains. Doing that will make us much better people in the long run because we must be smarter than everyone else. Stop and think how. Let's all say that out loud."

I coached them into repeating it until I had them shouting it back at me. Yes, I had a rush when I sensed their enthusiasm over this simple saying.

"School will start in about another month. Between now and then, we must practice so we'll be ready to go to the new Oakbrook Academy school. Every day, your new parents and adult supervisors will work with you. If you get stuck, ask one of us or your companions. We're in this together.

"Many of us adults have volunteered to become your teachers. Just try to hire a hundred new teachers on a few weeks' notice."

Several adults laughed. I continued.

"So those who want to be trained to be teachers are to join the teachers who've come to help set up the classrooms."

After many adults departed, I talked to eighteen hundred children.

"Kids, these are my three younger sisters, Eve, Randi, and Celeste. They are plenty smart. They each have three doctorate degrees. If they can do it, so can you. But they're here today to show you how to run their special therapy, which will help erase the trauma and horrible losses you've endured."

I chatted about it before turning the meeting over to Randi. She was amazing. Most of the children accepted her as a substitute mother. I've no idea how she did that. Impressive. She taught them how to perform her therapy, kept her language simple, and explanations, direct.

I was flabbergasted. Fifteen minutes later, everyone paired up with the person sitting next to him or her and to run out the terrorist attacks—the mutation trauma, the severe loss of their parents, and waking to find themselves almost helpless, not to mention being shipped off to a strange city. We four walked around the giant room, helping here and there, offering words of encouragement.

Buckets of tears flowed. Cries and shrieks reflected the pains they'd uncovered and endured while in their comas. Yet, the children responded to the therapy far more rapidly than the adults had. Becky had taken a week to erase her trauma and losses, and I thought we'd never make it. By suppertime, most of the kids had finished up.

Randi left them some parting words. "Kids, remember, anytime you fall down and get hurt, feel angry, frustrated, sad, or anything else, have someone near you use this therapy on you and erase it. If you run into trouble with it, let Molly know, and she'll get one of us to help. Never stop until the person is cheerful and happy. That's the answer, along with your motto: stop and think how."

***

I allowed the maid robot to fix our supper and carry the dishes to the table, but I insisted Isabella, Bernardo, Ted, and I carry our own plates, cups, silverware, and napkins to the table. I explained why.

"At school, it's okay to let the robot helpers feed you and such. Here at home, each of us must learn to be independent. It takes lots of practice and many flubs."

Isabella said, "But you and Ted—someone said you didn't have arms before."

"That's right. The Sixth Invaders and mad doctors got to us. So yes, we lived independently for quite some time before our arms got regrown."

"But I want my arms regrown," Bernardo said. His lips puckered.

"Who doesn't? This Sixth Invaders' mutation is dominant, which means all previous cures won't work on us. But many people are working on cures. I expect in time they'll find a way to regrow our arms. Until that happens, we must take care of ourselves. That's what's important. Look, kids, Ted and I conducted the Galactic Defense investigations when we didn't have arms, rooting out the criminals. We can do most anything if we put our minds to it."

Ted said, "The most important thing is for us to stick together and help each other. Don't always take the easy way out and use the robots. We're a family now. Come next Valentine's Day, Molly will have a baby, too. Then, we'll all be extra busy."

Bernardo said, "Are you being honest with us? Are we really going to be normal people? With real jobs, a sponsor, and all that?"

"Absolutely, son. But only if you practice using your feet and toes as others use their hands and fingers. Heck, Celeste, Randi, Eve, and I didn't have hands for years, and yet each of us got two or three college doctorate degrees. I still work in the Research and Development Department of Galactic Robotics, but I get time off to get used to being armless again before I go back to work."

"Yeah, but I wanted to be a chef—a famous chef and own my own restaurant," Bernardo countered.

"Yahoo," I said. "Go for it. I've never been able to cook much at all. Ted's so bad at it that he uses the maid robot. Oh,

I see what you mean. I'm sure you can do it, only you'll need patience and do a lot of thinking how. Hey, as soon as you want, you can cook for us."

He smiled before frowning. "That's not gonna happen anytime soon. I can barely feed myself."

"It takes time, patience, and practice," Ted said.

Isabella, who had been silent, said, "But I want to work on hyperspace engines."

"Why not?" Ted said. "That would be a great job, but you'll need lots of math. Just don't ask Molly about such things."

I laughed. "He's right. Aunt Randi is the person to ask. She's got doctorates in math, astrophysics, and hyperspace theory and applications."

"Really?" Isabella's eyes opened wide.

"Yeah. Women are just as bright as men, maybe brighter," I teased.

After supper, we worked together to do the dishes. Then, we sat and talked, allowing Isabella and Bernardo to tell us about their lives and deceased parents.

***

Two days later, the new teachers and those who were training them met with the school kids in the auditorium. They wanted to give each student an IQ test and a Standard Achievement test. Armed with these results, they could better place them in the correct grade and courses.

Their first attempts proved futile. Timed tests failed because the children weren't skilled enough to mark the answer sheets fast enough. We knew we were in trouble when the highest IQ wasn't even up to the moron range.

"Why don't we bring in some with arms and let them mark the answers for the kids?" I suggested. "Either that or get rid of the time limitation."

After a discussion, those with hands marked the answers for the children. It took several days to handle everyone. The results: shocking and inexplicable. The lowest IQ was 130, a borderline genius, while the highest was almost off the charts. Thus, several teachers believed something was wrong with the test or with our administration of it.

However, Eve had an idea. We looked up my test results. When I was in high school, I'd taken the same test. My IQ was 120, nothing spectacular. Ted's was 140, but I always felt he was a genius.

"I want to do a little experiment. Molly, take the test again. Celeste, you and Randi also take it. I'll mark the answers for Molly. James can mark them for Ted. Let's compare the results."

An hour later, Eve sat back looking at the results. "This is unbelievable. Molly, your IQ today is 150. Ted, yours is 160. Celeste and Randi's results agree with their scores from the tests they took back in high school. Something has radically improved Molly and Ted's IQ scores."

"The mutation..." Ted and I said in unison.

Everyone laughed. Eve said, "It's possible the mutation triggered a sharp increase in IQ level. It's also possible so much therapy caused the sharp rise in IQ. I've asked a friend to compare the before and after mutation scores of a few of these children. We should be able to compare maybe eight hundred results. Schools test IQ in seventh grade. Trouble is that it won't distinguish the cause since all the kids have had the therapy."

An hour later, Eve received an email with a spreadsheet showing the results. They omitted student names, providing only the before and after mutation IQ scores in two columns with the statistical averages across the bottom. The average IQ increase was twenty-five points.

"That's incredible," I said. "I didn't think IQ scores changed much."

"They don't."

"So those of us who've had this mutation have had our IQ raised. How interesting. I wonder if their Chief Science Officer intended this effect."

Eve said, "Possibly he did. You must be smarter and brighter to think how." I chuckled. "But it could result from the therapy sessions."

At the next assemblage of the kids, I explained the startling results. "See, now you have proof you're smarter and more intelligent." That brought a smile to many faces.

Counseling came next. I discovered they scheduled Isabella to take Calculus this fall. Her Eighth Grade schedule looked nothing like mine had. I never took Astronomy or Physics when I was in high school. I was impressed.

Bernardo had Algebra, Menu Design, and Food Properties, among the usual courses Eight Graders received. The academy tailored courses to meet the needs of the students. I suspected this curriculum change would help the kids since they'd need more time to learn how to accomplish the tasks in their fields. Still, I felt proud of the twins.

When we sat down for supper, Isabella said, "Mom, I keep hearing Bernardo's thoughts in my head."

"Hey, don't blame me," Bernardo said. "I keep hearing yours."

"Huh?" I said, looking at Ted, who also had a funny look on his face.

Chapter 12 Doomsday

August 1ˢᵗ, LA GPan CEO Don Hamid, along with five other corporation CEOs took to the universal airwaves.

"Sixth Invaders. This is Don Hamid, LA GPan CEO. With me are five other CEOs. We surrender to you. I repeat. We surrender. Don't attack our city. It's yours. Please respond." He repeated his message for five minutes.

When he finished, London CEOs gave their surrender pleas, followed by Paris, Caracas, Peking, Singapore, Indianapolis, Boston, and a dozen more cities around the world.

"Are you seeing the comm displays?" I said. After seeing the first one, I called up Natalie, but her staff had already notified her.

"Cowards. The lot of them," she spat. "Don't worry. We're not surrendering. General Blythe is on it as is Admiral Rossi. Gotta go." She hung up.

"What's she say?" Ted said. He and Bernardo were practicing their writing skills while Isabella was doing math exercises.

"She knows about it. Bev and Admiral Rossi will do something, but she didn't say what."

"Well, those creeps are paranoid the aliens are gonna mutate them. That's what I think," he said.

"It won't do them any good," Isabella said. She looked up from her papers on the floor.

"Why not?" said Bernardo.

"Cause who's gonna care if they bomb Colorado Springs? No one. If they take out LA, London, Paris—those will make big news. Scare the crap out of millions," Isabella said.

I said, "Those men—they're afraid. That's why they're doing what they think might save them from the Sixth Invaders and their mutation threat."

"It won't work," Isabella said, before resuming her calculations.

"Hello, everyone. I'm Dimitri Leonovich, Emperor of Galactic Expansion. Contrary to the cowardly men you've been hearing on the comm sets, Earth isn't surrendering to these Sixth Invaders. Not today. Not tomorrow. Not ever. You're seeing the fear and panic these aliens have instilled in cowards. We're prepared and ready to fight them to the bitter end. Earth never gives up. That is all."

"You tell them, Dimitri," Bernardo said to the monitor.

I smiled. Our kids were brave teens. But I wondered if we could defend ourselves.

***

In Earth orbit, Admiral Rossi watched the action in his Communications and Control Center on the Battleship Atlantis. For days, his crew manned the M.A.D. device, looking for large mass anomalies, sweeping methodically over the spinning globe below them. After this main pass, light cruisers then monitored the searched areas on the chance the Sixth Invader ship tried to land.

"Chicago is clear, Admiral. Searching Wisconsin now," a junior officer reported.

He nodded and glanced at his watch. Noon, local time.

"Sir, we have something," the officer said.

Admiral Rossi rushed to the display unit to see for himself—not that he could recognize an anomaly when he saw one. Protocol required that he verify the search results.

"Where?"

She pointed out the triangular shape. "Estimated size: five hundred meters from point to base and two hundred meters across at its base. Sir, that has to be the Sixth Invaders."

"Excellent work." He picked up his handheld comm device and barked. "Now hear this. Alien ship sighted. Battle stations. Inform the Battleships Kiev, Lexington, and Shanghai. Send them the coordinates. Inform me when you have a firing solution."

Warning sirens sounded throughout the ship. Men and women dashed to their posts, but those on the main armaments were already there and had been all during the search. They'd manned them in eight-hour shifts.

"Blasters armed and locked on."

"Laser cannons locked on."

"Disruptors armed and locked on."

One by one, the main gunnery batteries acknowledged target acquisition.

When the other battleships reported they'd received the coordinates, Admiral Rossi said, "All batteries: continuous fire on that ship."

Booms and rumbles echoed around the giant ship, accompanied by slight hull vibrations as the three dozen batteries fired on the cloaked enemy ship. It had landed on a grassy meadow within a forest preserve just outside the greater Madison area. With so many weapons firing, the optical images being relayed to the Admiral's monitor soon showed nothing but an enormous gray cloud.

After five minutes of continuous bombardment, a giant ball of light flashed. When the dust settled, Admiral Rossi announced, "Cease firing. We've destroyed their ship. Major Chan, take a search party down there, but stay alert for survivors."

To his phone, he said, "Conference call Natalie, Dimitri, and Molly."

Molly answered her phone, surprised to see the holographic image of Admiral Rossi emanating from her phone. He had one of the expensive phones.

"Good news. We've just located the Sixth Invaders' ship and have destroyed it. Massive explosion. I'm sending a video stream to GEnt for widespread broadcasting. No idea how many aliens are dead. A search party is heading down now. Battleship Lexington reported seeing several tiny radar anomalies just before the ship blew up. Possibly some aliens fled. More later. That is all." He hung up.

"Kids, did you hear?" I said.

Ted, Isabella, and Bernardo cheered.

***

Captain L'Grina cursed and cracked a wooden table in half. She'd just watched her light cruiser being destroyed. Her four crew sent her streaming video of the attack—three were men and domestics of little importance. The four evacuated in four

131

Vic Broquard

escape shuttle pods just as the defense shield gave out. The Captain wasn't worried about being stranded on Earth; she expected their main fleet would arrive soon, perhaps within a few weeks.

This setback angered her because she was so close to achieving total victory. Already ten large cities had broadcast their surrender. Others would follow—except those infernal Chicago leaders who had brought the Sol Empire space fleet into the action.

Captain L'Grina had thirteen fighters with her, along with five domestics and two science men, whom she kept busy making the mutation bombs as she called them. They'd taken up residence in an abandoned warehouse in South Chicago not too far from the obsolete Argonne Laboratory and Fermilab near Joliet.

A recon force always carried all the latest electronics and technology. Each soldier wore a ULTU, a Universal Language Translator Unit, and a Morph Unit, which would alter their appearance to the average of the local humanoids around them. They also had personal invisibility devices, but only four personal defense shields remained.

"Captain, there isn't enough of the mutation agent available to wipe out an entire city," the lead science man protested. "If we had a year and access to this world's production capabilities, we could prepare enough to wipe out several cities."

"Of course there isn't, you fool. We need to focus on Chicago. The only resistance is here," she barked.

"Aye sir, but we haven't been able to crack their new security protocols," her second in command said. "We've no clue where those three self-appointed leaders are located. They aren't in the two skyscrapers. Our scout patrols have verified that. Any ideas where we can search for these holdouts?"

"None. But I promised we'd wipe out a city, and by Fringle's Ass, we're gonna do that," Captain L'Grina said. Her face, taught. Her cheeks dimpled inward. "Okay, here's where we'll strike. North Chicago. That's where all the wealthy have their mansions. Mutate them and they'll force these pesky upstart leaders to surrender. Have we located the water supply insertion point?" She directed the question to the cowering male lead science officer.

"Well, yes. They have good filtration and purification protocols in place, but—"

"But what," she interrupted, glaring at him.

"Well, we've found an insertion point after the water has been treated. If we inject there, it should work."

"Okay. Take three soldiers with you. Make it happen. Wipe out all North Chicago," Captain L'Grina ordered.

Her facial muscles relaxed. After the four left the warehouse, the four escape craft landed. She ordered them brought inside while she debriefed her soldier. "So by Fringle's Ass, how did they find the cruiser?"

The shrugging replies didn't satisfy her. Not remotely. Whether she would have chastised her soldier isn't known, because at that moment, one of her guards sounded the alarm.

"Enemy ships are closing in on us!"

"Fringle's Ass! How? Did you lead them here? Okay, pack up. Take all shuttles. Leave the remaining mutation agent. We'll release it into the atmosphere. That'll make a mess of this area. Meet up at the secondary site."

She raced to her ship and departed. Once the craft was hovering, she headed out the main warehouse doors. Overhead, she saw dozens of Earth ships swooping down in attack formation. The cloaking device worked, and she slipped her small ship between the attacking vessels. Behind her, she heard a massive series of detonations. Pivoting, she saw a huge ball of flames where once the warehouse stood.

"Crap. There goes any chance the mutation agent will get airborne. So how did they find us? Can they track our cloaked ships?"

She arrived across town at LeRoy Oakes Forest Preserve, just outside the burb of St. Charles. There, she parked her shuttle. After making sure it was cloaked, she loaded up her backpack with all her gear and headed off to the cabin retreats, where she had stockpiled food and supplies. She'd also had her crew install a comm video system patched into the greater Chicago and Earth system. True, the Earthlings had changed protocols on her, locking her out for a time, but her science men had burrowed into the system. From here, she had a direct patch into the system. She sat and prepared her next video cast speech, to be delivered after Earth's leaders discovered the widespread mutation comas of the wealthy.

Boom. Boom. Explosions echoed dangerously close to the cabins. The dense trees obscured any chance of seeing the cause. Three soldiers dashed through the trees to the cabins.

One cried out, "They've followed the escape craft here. What do we do now?"

"We hold out here. Set up the perimeter blasters. How are they able to follow us? I double-checked. My craft is and was cloaked."

"Dunno. Must have some new tech, but we're all that's left, except the four heading for the water plant."

Captain L'Grina cursed. "Prepare to hoof it to our last backup location. Maybe they won't get wise to these cabins. They're damned remote."

***

Casper Hugo, Jr. sat before the giant monitor in his luxurious living room of the Hugo mansion in North Chicago. Hours ago, Helen left, helping coordinate the defense of Chicago and Earth. Still mostly helpless, he watched the news. As he saw the video of the attack on the cloaked Sixth Invaders ship, he realized how badly he'd erred when he'd been GD's CFO.

"I've been the biggest fool ever! CEO Hardy was a Sixth Invader, and he allowed me to get away with everything. Boy, have I ever screwed up! It's a wonder Molly didn't terminate me. I can't imagine what Helen still sees in me. I'm a total loser."

"What's that? Water? Tea?" called out the maid, Lucy, who came by twice a week to clean the spacious mansion.

She brought in two glasses of water, brimming with ice cubes. One had a straw in it which she placed within easy reach of Casper. She sat down next to him.

"Taking a break. Anything on the news?" she said, taking a long drink.

"Thanks," he said.

Lucy looked up. Until now, Casper had never thanked

her for anything. Her eyebrows rose.

"I think our space fleet is destroying the Sixth Invaders. They've been showing footage of a strike on their cruiser. I think it's blown to smithereens. Now, they're going after smaller escape pods or something. Maybe..."

Casper dozed off, his head drooping over. He awoke, groggy, as though he'd had an ill night's sleep, wishing he could rub his face. He turned and wiggled his right shoulders against his eyes and forehead. That's when he noticed Lucy sitting unconscious beside him. He bumped into her, trying to wake her up. The news channel was on, and he glanced at the time. He'd lost an hour.

"Lucy. Lucy, wake up." No response. "Something's wrong." He saw his phone lying beside the comm center's main box. He took a deep breath and rose to his feet, being careful not to lose his balance. Casper walked over to his phone that Lucy always operated for him. Now, he'd have to do it himself, if only he could figure out how. He struggled to speed dial Helen by using his nose.

"Helen, something's wrong here. Lucy is unconscious on the couch. We were drinking ice water when we both passed out. I woke up an hour later. She's still unconscious. Helen, we need help. Oh, and I'm very, very sorry for all the crap I've put you and Molly through these many years. I've been the biggest fool ever."

"Unconscious? Okay. I'll send a medical crew right away," Helen said.

"Can you patch me through to Molly? Please, Helen. I have to apologize to her, too. And to Ted. I've been the Earth's biggest fool for years. Please, Helen."

"All right, Casper. But if she complains about this, I'll cook your goose."

Moments later, Casper said, "Hello, Molly? Good. This is Casper Hugo. I wanted to apologize to you for all the foolish, wicked, and dumb things I've done, not only to you and to Ted but to so many others. I've let everyone and the entire Sol Empire down. For that, I'm sorry. I'd like to help defend Earth and our empire. I heard Admiral Rossi wants us to build him more ships. As you know, I was the CFO. So I know how to make that happen—finance-wise, I mean. That's what I was good at—finding the ways and means to finance major expenses. I'd like to help, but I don't know if I can physically do it, but I'll try my best. If only you and the others will give me a chance. I have to make up all the damage I've done over the last quarter of a century. Please, Mrs. Parkinson-Billings, please."

"Okay, Casper. I'll relay your request to Natalie and Dimitri. Apology accepted. Why this sudden change of heart?"

"I have been following all the action on the news channel—the blowing up of the Sixth Invader ship. I realized how foolish I've been. It's like I woke up from a decadent fog. We're under attack, and we could even lose this war. I want to help. I'm the go-to money-man or used to be. I can make financial things happen. That's what I've done all my life. I need a chance to make things better. Also, something weird is happening here at the mansion. Lucy, our maid, and I—we were having a glass of ice water when we both fell unconscious. I was out for an hour, according to the comm channel. Helen's sending an emergency crew to check on Lucy. Oh, they're here. Gotta go. Thank you. Bye."

"Coming. It's open. I can't move fast. Come on in," Casper yelled. "She's here on the couch in the living room."

Two medical technicians walked in, both wearing Leslie's new male Doll fashions. By the time Casper joined them, having walked the few feet from the comm center and his phone, they'd found her and reached their conclusion.

"She's in a coma. You were drinking water you said?" one said.

"Yes, hers fell on the floor. Mine's still on the end table."

The other man spoke into his phone. "Mutation coma suspected. No odor in the air. I'm bringing in a water sample. Can the stuff be in the water? Over."

"Okay. Bring her to the Med Center along with the water. We're sending out police officers to check on nearby residents."

"I'll get the Gurney." He left, while the other fetched her purse and ID card.

After they left, Casper sat down to watch more of the

news. "Yes!" he exclaimed, watching the video of the smaller cruisers blasting a warehouse and aliens to rubble. "Go get them all!"

"We interrupt this newscast to report another alien genetic mutation attack. If you live in the North Chicago area, do not drink the tap water. The alien armless Doll mutation agent is in the water supply. Already, hundreds of men, women, and children have been transported to various Med Centers around Chicago. Security forces are inspecting the water distribution system to determine how the aliens infected the water. This warning is only for North Chicago at this time. Prudence dictates no one in the entire Chicago area drink any water that doesn't come from sealed containers purchased from your grocery stores. I repeat..."

The message repeated along with a scrolling banner across the bottom of the monitor warning everyone to avoid drinking tap water. Casper realized what had happened.

"Oh God! I've been mutated, too! That's why I was only unconscious for an hour. I'm already an armless Doll, so there wasn't much in my DNA to change. Thank heavens Helen wasn't here. Our baby is safe. I've just got to help defeat these beasts." He would have pounded his fists on the couch had he had them.

**

"Empress Natalie Mantovo, Admiral Rossi here. Your strategy is working. We're able to track the ion trails of their smaller ships. They regrouped in a warehouse outside Joliet. I've sent word to General Blythe to secure the area and ascertain casualties. By god, we'll get them all."

"Don't get too hasty. If they abandon their ships and travel on foot, we've no way to track them. Still, getting a body count is imperative. Molly's count was sixteen soldiers remaining after they killed that alien science officer. I won't rest until the body count is sixteen female Sixth Invaders," Natalie said. "I've received word the aliens have launched another mutation attack. This time, they put their agent in the North Chicago water supply. Hundreds are in comas. Helen's husband, Casper, reported it."

"How come he wasn't affected? He didn't drink the

water?"

She heard him issuing orders to monitor the Med Centers around Chicago.

"He's already an armless Doll."

The admiral smirked and signed off, leaving Natalie to pace around her secret office in an abandoned office building south of the Loop and guarded by an entire battalion of soldiers. On the whiteboard, she had drawn sixteen stick female figures. Several already had an X through them. She called General Blythe.

"Natalie here. Updated body count, please."

"Working on it, Empress. Call ya back when tallies are in. We're on our way to another site. Admiral Rossi has blown up more fiends. Okay, being relayed now. Four confirmed dead along with what was their main spaceship. Female and three males. We're heading out by Argonne Labs now. What's that, Gail?"

Natalie suspected the general was handling several calls at the same time. A bit confusing, but critical.

"All right. Got it. Oh, Empress, we're weeding them down. Some kind of small one or two person shuttles this time. Blown to bits. Got a platoon poking around the remains now. Let's compare counts, shall we? Otherwise, how are we going to know if we got the last of the beasts?"

An hour later, Natalie thrust a hand into the air. "All right! Gang, listen up." She pointed to her whiteboard and 'X'ed out stick figures. "The Sixth Invaders are down to their last three soldiers and one male. Today, we almost got all of them. Well done, but stay vigilant. Those last three could still cause significant damage."

Over a hundred soldiers cheered the news.

"What's the report from the Med Center on this latest mutation attack?" she asked one of her new aides.

"Empress, only sixty-three victims this time. Forty-one women, two men, and twenty children. We got lucky this time."

"Yes, we did, thanks to Helen's husband—that Casper Doll. His timely warning and GEnt's quick newscast prevented thousands from being infected. How are they coming on flushing those water lines?"

"Going to take a couple days to make sure it's out of the lines. They're recommending every home and business run all taps for an hour. A boil order is in effect until further notice. A platoon of the Local Defense Force is going door to door handing out bottled water. CEO Helen's coordinating it."

"Excellent. I heard that Casper fellow wants a word with me. Have Helen bring him to Location C, say around seven tonight. I'll have Molly and Dimitri join us. It's almost champagne time and would be except for those three remaining Sixth Invaders," Natalie said.

She ran her hands over her forehead, before pulling on her lower jaw, easing the tension from her face. If only she could ease the stress from of the rest of her body. Today had been trying, but in this male-dominated world, she'd proven she was up to the task of world security, if not that of the empire.

***

"Hi, Gail. So you're my escort to Bev, eh?" I said. I received Natalie's phone call and agreed to meet with everyone after supper.

"Hey, Molly. Yes, fabulous day. We've terminated most of these wicked Sixth Invaders. Bev and Natalie think there's only three female soldiers left and none of their tiny shuttles."

Lieutenant Gail looked stunning in her blue uniform with gold trim—very businesslike. I felt envious of the 9mm gun she had in her waist holster. Ah well.

"So they're on foot? Like the rest of us?"

We chatted as she led the way out of our new complex to the waiting EMAC, parked on the sidewalk just before the MTES.

"That's our current theory. Thanks to the Admiral's ion detection system, they have a way to track the cloaked tiny ships. Not sure how it works. Only that it does. They tracked a bunch of them to just outside Argonne Labs and blew them up. Bev sent in several patrols to search for survivors and counted the dead aliens. Now, she's got her recovery platoons there, trying to confiscate anything left of their fancy devices. I'd like Bev to have one of their personal defense shields."

I chuckled. "Hey, I'd like one too. I'm tired of being shot and killed."

"They can't get you. You're lucky. Leslie keeps telling us that. She might be right."

We both laughed as the vehicle lifted off. Minutes later, it landed on the roof of an abandoned factory. A squad of soldiers surrounded us as we stepped out of the EMAC. We went down an elevator, but to my surprise, we slipped out the back of this rusting hulk of a factory and into the warehouse next door.

"Like our preventative measures?" Gail teased me.

I couldn't help but sense her surface thoughts. 'Got to keep Bev and our baby safe.' I smiled. My telepathic abilities continued to grow. I was picking up other's thoughts easily. No straining. Still, I did my best to keep from prying into people's private thoughts. What bothered me was that Ted, Isabella, and Bernardo were also showing signs of having telepathic abilities. Well, they were twins, and I'd read that twins sometimes knew what the other was thinking. Still...

Gail escorted me into a back room. We passed by another platoon of soldiers, who made sure no invisible aliens were trying to sneak in behind or beside us. General Blythe was already there. I caught a thread of unspoken communications between the two, which brought a smile to my face.

Bev looked dominating in her fancy uniform. Her demeanor demanded respect from her soldiers, aided by her lengthy list of accomplishments against these invaders. Natalie wore a sky blue gown, but her hair needed a brushing. I sensed she'd been preoccupied all day. Well, I would be too if I were in her position.

Dimitri entered, also escorted by a squad of Bev's soldiers. I didn't need telepathy to sense what they exchanged via their eyes. Rather, I wondered how soon they'd get married. They hugged but avoided a public display. Major Airla Baker's arrival surprised me. She kept a steadying arm around Sasha and Yuri Petrova. I knew she was planning to hire armless Doll victims for our Inspection and Justice Department, but seeing my condo neighbors surprised me.

"Molly, meet our two newest employees," Airla said.

I picked up Sasha's surface thoughts. 'Don't know if we can do anything, but we gotta try, if only for the kids.'

"Welcome aboard, Sasha, Yuri. I'm sure you'll work out fine. Just remember. Stop and think how," I said. "It's anything but easy."

I picked up Yuri's response. 'It's goddam hard, but I've got to. If only for the kids and Sasha.'

Strange. I picked up no thoughts from Airla, who greeted Natalie, Bev, and Dimitri. Helen and Casper Hugo entered, her arm around his waist. I put my attention on Casper and picked up his thoughts.

'I'm scared. But I have ta do this. Hope they don't laugh at me. Oh, there are two more like me. Maybe there's hope.'

"Hey, everyone. Great job today. I hear you nearly got all of them," said Helen. "Oh, this is my husband, Casper, who used to be the Chief Finance Officer for GD Sol Empire. He claims he's paid for his crimes, has come to his senses, and wants to help. I admit I was shocked when he called Molly and Ted to apologize. Anyway, Casper, this is Empress Natalie Mantovo of Galactic Defense, Emperor Dimitri Leonovich of Galactic Expansion, General Beverly Blythe, First Infantry Division, and Molly Parkinson of Investigations and Justice Department. Molly, who are these other three?"

Natalie, Dimitri, and Bev nodded to Casper.

"My second in command, Major Airla Baker, and two of our investigators, Sasha and Yuri Petrova."

Sasha said, "Is that the fellow who shot Ted and kidnapped you from your bed?"

"Yes, Casper Hugo, Jr. He called me earlier today and apologized. To Ted, too. We accepted it."

Natalie said, "Please, have a seat. Casper, we're meeting with you only because you've apologized to Ted and Molly. That act of contrition has gained you this audience. But I should caution you not to expect to have your arms regrown. As of today that's not possible. You've been exposed to the new armless mutation agent. You're now like the other recent victims. Thank you for calling in the alarm so rapidly. Thanks to you, only sixty-three people were affected. It could have been thousands this time. Many people owe you their lives. So thank you."

Casper's face clenched before he sighed and relaxed. "I've accepted the fact this is the way my body is. I know I've committed many crimes, but that was in the past, and I'm not going to claim those aliens took over my body like they did with Hardy. No, I did the crimes of my own volition.

"But today—I don't know how to explain what happened to me. As I watched the events unfolding, I woke up. Came to my senses. Something like that. I feel awful about what I've done to Ted and Molly. Worse, there's nothing I can do to make amends for what I put them through.

"Anyway, I want to help. After hearing what Admiral Rossi wants—all those new spaceships—I realized I know how to make that happen. It's all in the financing methods. That was my specialty. Financing. Arranging things. I'd like to have the chance to help get him his new ships if you'll have me.

"I'm rather helpless, but I can do the financial work on the holographic computers which I can manipulate with voice commands. Please, I want to help."

Okay. I admit I used my budding telepathic skills on Casper the entire time he spoke. Why? I was looking for insincerity, lying, deceit—anything that might suggest he had other motives or purposes. Until this moment, I didn't trust Casper. Yet, I sensed he was honest with us. I picked up his thought. 'God, I hope they let me help.'

Natalie glanced at me. I sensed she wanted my acceptance or okay before she gave hers.

"Casper may have learned his lesson. Natalie's right. From what we've seen, Casper, there's no way to regrow the arms of recent victims, so you'll have to adjust as we all do. Meantime, we must build the new spaceships Admiral Rossi needs. From what little I know of these Sixth Invaders and what their Chief Science Officer G'Karn told me, I'm certain their main invasion force will arrive soon. If Casper thinks he can work out the financing, I'm all for it. Only someone should watch him. No embezzling funds."

His face flushed. I picked up his thought. 'I've no need to steal credits.'

Natalie cleared her throat. "Well then, I'll agree to let Casper join my GD empire-wide staff. Admiral Rossi wants two battleships, three heavy cruisers, and ten light cruisers. We want them built and operational as soon as possible. We must man them, too."

Casper exhaled, very relieved. He said, "Finding more personnel for the space fleet is part of the overall financial operation. It's pointless to build a ship and not have a trained crew to man it."

Dimitri chuckled. "He's got a point there. Whenever we build a new exploration ship, we also acquire and train its future crew at the same time. Welcome aboard, Casper. Mind you, don't screw this up. If Molly says their main invasion fleet will soon be here, we should believe her."

"Okay then. Tomorrow, have Helen bring you to GD when she comes," Natalie said. "Molly, perhaps you could drop by and show Casper how he can run his computer."

"All right. I'll be by, say at nine."

"Thank you. I won't let you down," Casper said.

For the first time, his complexion looked normal. Worry lines that had defined his face vanished. He seemed relaxed. All this left me wondering. Could a criminal, a pervert, a sadist change their behavior?

As I watched Helen lead Casper out of the room, I couldn't detect the kinds of feelings from him that I'd had when he kidnapped me. Still the same man, the same mind, but Casper wasn't acting out the urges that had gotten him into so much trouble. I made a mental note to check with Helen. She'd be the best judge of any real changes in him and if he was playing games with us. I also decided to chat with Celeste about this whole situation.

Chapter 13 Armageddon Arrives

"Use your toes and nose, Casper. Like this," I said.

As agreed, I joined him. We sat before his computer system in his former office on the ninety-fifth floor of the GD building. His system handled virtual holographic projections both faster and easier than my cheap laptop. Okay, I envied his fancy computer.

Casper first tried to run it via verbal commands. While those would work, such was cumbersome. "Like this." I maneuvered the images around, opening tasks, expanding sections, and so on by using my feet and toes.

"It's so hard."

Water swelled up in his eyes. His whole face grimaced, and I picked up his thoughts. 'I can't do this. But I have to do this. Oh god.'

"Yes, it's hard, but with practice, you can do it. We all can. Practice. Practice. Practice. It would help if you studied the how-to videos we've accumulated. Helen says they're on your laptop. Getting frustrated is part of the game. Like I keep telling others, remember our motto. Stop and think how. No one cares if you take an hour to do what once may have taken a couple minutes. The vital point is you got it done."

"Easy for—" he started to say but stopped himself. "I'm a stupid fool. I should have been watching them and practicing these past many months. Instead, I sat on my ass feeling sorry for myself. But I feel bad for my assistant Lucy, who's in a coma. Life will be awful for her when she wakes up, won't it?"

"Just as it has been for thousands."

"I know why so many chose suicide. That's what I wanted to do for weeks after I woke from my coma."

"And now?" I said.

I found Casper's total change in personality striking. Was he for real or did he have another plan in mind? Well, thanks to the Sixth Invaders, he had no way to get his arms regrown. Was that stark realization behind his behavior change? I couldn't discount it. It was one thing to know that at any time someone could inject him with the curative version of the Galactic Doll mutation agent to regrow his arms and quite another to be facing a potential lifetime as an armless Doll just as we were, thanks to the vicious Sixth Invaders.

"I'm alive and want to stay that way. I've got to help, somehow, someway, and I can't sit around and be useless to everyone, especially Helen. I've seen how happy she's been these past months. Both our bodies are rejuvenated, but she's the same vibrant, alive woman I met and fell in love with so many years ago."

"What happened to her back then?" I probed.

"I screwed it up. That's what happened. I can't believe I forced her to give up her photography and everything else. Yeah, I happened to her. This time—this time, I've got to become independent enough so I'm not the albatross around her neck."

"Well then, Casper, practice, practice, practice. Treat her with admiration and respect, just like my Ted does me. Back to this computer. Let me see you use those feet and toes."

Once more, I couldn't sense any disingenuous thoughts or lies. When I first met him last year, I described him as creepy, covertly hostile, and stuck up with his own self-importance. From all the therapy sessions Celeste had given me, I knew back then he had been acting out a persona contained within a traumatic event of his past.

For example, when I was a youngster, I got food poisoning and was deadly sick at my stomach. My dad and mom discussed whether to take me to the Med Center. He kept saying, 'I've got to help others today. You know that, so you'll have to take her.' Hence, in grade and high school, I just knew I had to help others, which is partly why I became a PI. It was either help others or feel sick at my stomach.

I wondered what kinds of trauma Casper had endured and what had shunted them aside—at least for now. Would he revert to his old ways? Probably not, since I doubted Helen or Natalie would ever give him the power he once had as GD's CFO.

"This is so frustrating," Casper said. His wrinkled forehead and tense jaw line told me how angry he felt.

"Yes, that's one of the more common reactions we have, Casper. Frustration. Persist. Get it done. Remember, accomplishing something matters, not how long you take or your difficulty in doing it."

"I suppose you have a point," he said. I watched him relax. The red faded from his face. "Get it done. I'll remember that."

That reminded me of my own frustrations when I awoke on that South Pacific Atoll and found they'd amputated my arms. Celeste, Eve, Randi, and Ted meant well, but I was so frustrated back then. Only Celeste's therapy sessions and Ted's constant support, suggestions, and help got me over it. I realized Casper had no one to support him, not like the rest of us who had moved into the new Ace Leisure Acres where we could back up each other with support and help.

"Casper, how would you like to attend my how-to sessions?" I explained what they were. When a recent victim woke up and was ready, I held group sessions, instructing and showing them how to do the basics of life, modeled on the holographic videos stored on the laptops and touchpads Galactic Robotics, via Ted, gave to each victim.

"Could I? Yes, yes, a thousand yeses. But will I ever be able to be independent again? To do all the normal things of life?"

"It isn't easy, Casper, but with lots of practice, yes, you can become independent."

In a lowered voice, he changed the topic. "Say, this is gonna sound—well, strange. But when I took the elevator up here, I sensed something, kinda like terror or fear—like I shouldn't do this. At first, I thought it was my own nerves, but the more that I'm here, the more it seems to come from the building. I even wandered around a couple floors looking for someone who needed help. Found no one, except possessions that haven't been picked up yet. Do you sense anything strange?"

"Yes, you're picking up the terror residue from the five hundred recent victims who woke from their mutation comas. When we came inside to rescue them, their screams were deafening. I can sense it, too, Casper. Now, back to practicing.

We need those new warships."

I worked with Casper and many others. During the next two weeks, the recent victims awoke to their terrifying futures, but these people wanted to survive. I added the forty-one women, two men, and twenty children to our daily practice sessions. Major Airla Baker convinced the men and ten women to join our growing Investigations and Justice Department. I allowed Airla to handle the daily duties. For me, helping these recent victims get a handle on how to live took priority. The crimes would still be there next week, next month.

August 20. Armageddon Day dawned, a typical dog day of late summer. After practicing with and instructing several groups, I headed over to GD to spend time with Casper. My task: make sure he wasn't doing anything illegal. Already he had contracts let for the construction of one battleship and one heavy cruiser. Natalie and Dimitri asked me to make sure everything was acceptable. Both faced extreme backlash against their assumption of power over the corporations.

Looking over Casper's shoulder, I watched him finagle several corporations on Pylon to finance the construction of a light cruiser. Just as he completed the financial specifications, Helen rushed into the office room.

"Quick, you two. Into the living room and the comm center. It's on the news. GEnt is on top of the action."

"What's happening?" I said.

"The Sixth Invaders are coming—a whole damned fleet of them!"

Casper and I rose and followed her into what had once been their living room when they'd lived in this suite. I flinched as I walked past the bedroom in which I awoke when Casper had kidnapped me. Then versus now, I told myself.

"... at the very edge of Brussels, Tau Ceti space. Initial counts from our spy drones put the number of Sixth Invader ships at nearly one hundred. Empress Natalie Mantovo has ordered our entire fleet into action. We should soon see our forces appearing around Brussels, defending that world from these monsters.

"Repeating our top story of the day, Admiral Rossi's secret advanced warning system has worked. An estimated hundred Sixth Invader ships dropped out of hyperspace some ten light years from Brussels, Tau Ceti, the most distant world of our Sol Empire. Tau Ceti is about a dozen light years from Earth, so these beasts are twenty-two light years from Earth. They are at the edge of Brussels, Tau Ceti space."

Helen lowered the volume. "They are the same cigar-shaped ships that have attacked our merchant ships," she said.

"Yeah, they are, honey. Damn. I hoped we were done with these fiends," Casper said.

"Those ships sure look funny," I said.

Casper chuckled. "They're different from our spaceship designs. Ours are shaped more like flying delta wings. Flying triangles, I used to tease the fellows at work. Not so funny now. We don't have a hundred fighting ships in our fleet. This is bad, really bad."

Once more, I felt my ignorance, my acute lack of knowledge embarrassing me. I had no idea of our ship design or that of the aliens ships either, only what few glimpses were shown on newscasts.

"So it's likely to go south? I mean when they attack. They outnumber us," I said.

Casper sighed. "Likely. As far as I know, we were more or less holding our own when only one or two of their ships attacked ours. But this. It's a whole new ball game. I wish Admiral Rossi had asked for the additional ships years ago."

Helen said, "He wouldn't have gotten them. Don't forget. The aliens were inside Hardy's body. That's still creepy. Don't you think?"

"Scary, honey, damn scary," he replied. "I wonder how we're able to see such good images. Does he have a ship out there monitoring space?"

"Dunno," Helen said. "I'm sure Natalie knows, but she's not likely to share that with me. I'm only the local GD CEO."

We three stared at the monitor for some time. Then, to our surprise, the screen split. On the new half, one by one, our own ships appeared, dropping out of hyperspace. The announcer hinted they were within Tau Ceti space, standing by to repel the invasion force.

I counted thirty of our ships. Only now did I grasp what

Casper had already realized. They had a hundred to our thirty. Bad, bad odds. Still, I thought our ships looked prettier. I found their delta wing shape aesthetically appealing. But that was the least important aspect of our ships.

"Why aren't they attacking?" Casper said. His voice wavered, and I didn't need telepathy to sense his fear.

"Dunno. It's hard for us to fight back, Casper, but we can kick."

I watched his shoulders sag under the biggest sigh I'd seen. I'd nailed what he was thinking because I was thinking much the same thing. He and I wanted to fight the aliens, should they land here, but we felt an acute sense of helplessness. We couldn't hold or fire a gun, let alone engage in a fistfight.

"This is the end, isn't it?" Helen whispered.

She ran her hands over her face, stretching her skin as she did so. The GD CEO added, "I should have learned how to shoot a gun."

"We're outnumbered," Casper said. "Three to one, maybe more. Doesn't look good. Damn it! If only I'd spent my time building up our space fleet all these years instead of goofing off and being a dick head."

"You couldn't have gotten that past your leaders," I said. "Both top men were under the total control of the Sixth Invaders. Body swaps. Remember? They would have vetoed any such plans, Casper. Once they land, we have our ground division to protect us. Not so good for the moon bases and the other planets if they land there."

"You don't understand," Casper whined. "They don't need to land. Not at first anyway. No, they'll dump their terrible mutation agent on us all. After we're all helpless Dolls, then they'll land."

I bit my lip. "Why would they do that? Makes little sense. If they want to conquer our worlds, don't they want to make us their slave laborers? You and I can't do much physical laboring."

Helen cracked a slight smile. It faded, and she pointed to the screen, gasping. Another spaceship appeared, and the screen split three ways. This new one lay halfway between the giant Sixth Invader fleet and our own fleet. Again, I marveled at the technology Admiral Rossi had set up for advanced warning.

This ship was unlike any Sol Empire delta wing or the cigar-shaped Sixth Invader ship. Its cross-section was hexagonal. Its main body consisted of dozens of these long hexagonal cylinders, joined like jigsaw puzzle pieces. What looked like giant gun turrets bristled along its surface, so many I couldn't count them. Compared to this ship, our battleship was a mere cruiser, as were the many Sixth Invaders ships.

We watched the Sixth Invader fleet retreat about a light year before again remaining stationary. Whose giant ship was this? Helen used the zoom feature to expand the ship's image, focusing on what might be an identifying marker. We saw a rising blue sun on a yellow background.

Helen said, "Sixth Invaders markings are a black, clenched, raised, six-fingered fist on a gray background. Our empire's logo is a yellow sun on a green background."

Again, I felt ignorant for I knew no such things.

"I bet Admiral Rossi and Natalie know," I said, covering for my lack of knowledge.

"Nobody's attacking," Casper said, his voice shaking.

Helen, who had been twisting her hands together, stopped. "You're right, dear. That has to be a good sign, right? I better head back down to my office. I bet the switchboard is being flooded with calls though I surely don't know how to answer them. You better come with me, dear; Molly, you too."

"Okay. I'm glad I'm not a GEnt reporter," I joked. "How do they know what to say? How do they know this is Armageddon Day?"

Helen shook her head and turned the comm center off. Together, we headed down to the fifth floor. We walked into a rain of confusion. No one had any answers, but they sure had questions.

I headed on home. As I rode the MTES and gazed at the azure sky and puffy clouds, I wondered if all this would soon change. Would they drop bombs on us? The crew of one small scout ship had almost conquered the world. What would those hundred ships do? It seemed hopeless. For the first time in my life, I felt doomed, depressed, and helpless.

Chapter 14 The Federation

"Ah, here you are. I've been looking for you," Major Airla Baker said.

I was just walking up to the main doors of our condo when she came out. She was five inches shorter than me, but in my heels, the difference was almost a foot. Airla wore flats and a professional woman's outfit: a white blouse and black skirt.

In a rush of words, she said, "Have you seen the news? The appearance of the strange spaceship?"

"Yes, I was helping Casper. We saw it. Any ideas whose it is?"

"No, but Admiral Rossi has summoned us. Come. I'll let him know we're on our way."

"Where? What's up?"

"Don't know. It's big, though. Natalie and Dimitri will join us. General Bev too."

"Okay, but where're we going?"

"New O'Hare Spaceport. General Blythe's soldiers are escorting us."

A dozen heavily armed soldiers appeared behind her. They surrounded me. After making sure an invisible Sixth Invader wasn't trying to slip in behind us, they ushered us to a waiting EMAC parked beside the MTES outside my new home.

Three minutes tops. We landed at New O'Hare Spaceport. Funny thing is I've heard ships landing and departing all these years, but I've never been to the spaceport. I had no idea it was this large. As we walked from the EMAC to the waiting spaceship, I saw how vast this complex was.

Automation was the key to its efficient operation. Conveyors carried cargo crates hither and thither, scanning their bar codes as they routed packages to their destinations. I spotted machines handling the loading and unloading but saw very few people. As we walked, the roar of a departing cargo ship was deafening. I promised myself one day I'd return and have a tour of this facility. Again, it reminded me of just how uneducated I was. Sobering.

We entered a commercial transport, a three hundred foot long liner—a cylinder attached to a large delta wing. She told me it could carry a hundred passengers divided into two seats on either side of the main aisle. A cargo hold followed, but most of the ship consisted of engines and fuel tanks. Impressive, especially since I'd never seen one, let alone rode in one. A giant screen and a help yourself bar were up front.

Major Baker explained, "All our cruisers are out on the defensive line, so we've confiscated a commercial liner. Probably more comfortable."

She led the way as though she'd done this many times. Since Airla had been in the space fleet, I presumed she had. After we walked up the entrance ramp, our soldier escort departed. Natalie and Dimitri were already on board, as was General Blythe, who stood beside the bar.

Bev said, "Molly, isn't this something else? Never been on one of these—just the military transports. We didn't have leather seats or this well-stocked booze lounge."

Airla fastened my seatbelt while I responded to my sister. "Hey, Bev. Don't get drunk. I think this will be really important. Did you see that weird spaceship that just appeared?"

"Yeah, I know. Still, I can have just one drink. Maybe two. Settle my nerves before they jump into hyperspace. Always hate that. Weird sensation. Did ya know you're nowhere when in hyperspace."

I laughed. "I've no idea, Bev. Been in Chicago my whole life, and I've never visited this spaceport. How silly is that? I can't get over how big it is."

Major Baker said, "One hundred acres. All fully automated. Cargo ships can land here from Brussels and be unloaded, the goods shipped around the world—almost with no human intervention. Galactic Robotics set up these space ports."

She talked on while Bev poured herself a drink. I felt a lurching sensation, as though my stomach was going one way and my head, another.

Bev belched. "We're in hyperspace. That was the jump.

See what I mean?"

I laughed. "No need to get drunk, sis, but it's a strange sensation."

"Travel around a lot and you'll get used to it," Natalie said.

"Well, I feel positively ill," Dimitri declared, holding his stomach.

His complexion paled. Bev handed him a bottle; he took it and gulped the whiskey.

Natalie said, "Now that we're in hyperspace, I can tell you what's going on without fear of alerting the few remaining Sixth Invaders. That new ship was from another alien civilization calling itself the Federation. We're joining Admiral Rossi to meet with their ambassadors. From the initial exchange with him, if the Sol Empire joins the Federation, they'll protect us from the Sixth Invaders. We'll see about that."

Bev belched. "Little green men?"

"I think they're yellow and brown," Natalie said. "At least, that's what the Admiral said."

"Where are we going?" I said.

"We're joining Admiral Rossi. Together, we'll take this transport on over to that Federation spaceship," Natalie said, pouring herself a vodka over ice. "I know that's risky—all our top personnel visiting these unknown people. But I okayed it. What choice do we have? If the Sixth Invaders attack our fleet, they have better than three to one odds. We'll be wiped out. Both the Admiral and I noted the Sixth Invader fleet backed up at least a light year when this Federation ship appeared as though the Sixth Invaders fear these people. Of course, it could be a ruse, and we're going to our deaths, but Admiral Rossi and I decided we didn't have a choice. We have to take this gamble."

I sensed Dimitri felt left out of the decision-making process. I picked up his thoughts. 'You should have asked me, Natalie, not ordered me. This could be a trap. Nothing like taking down the key leaders in one shot. How can we even trust these aliens? We've never heard of this Federation.' His stern face reflected his thoughts.

Curious, I checked on Bev's thoughts. Reading surface thoughts had become easier for me to do. 'Blaster? Check. Glock? Check. Laser knife? Check. Knife? Double check. If this goes south, I gotta protect Molly and Natalie. God, I need another drink.'

I turned to check on Major Airla Baker. How strange. Again, I picked up nothing. No thoughts at all.

Then, my stomach lurched in the opposite direction of my head.

"Dropping out of hyperspace," Bev said.

Our ship docked in the huge bay of the giant battleship Atlantis. Fascinated, I watched as our pilot maneuvered us into the portage. The ship's delta wing design was like the other warships in our fleet, at least the ones I'd seen, except the scale was all wrong. Major Baker once told me its crew numbered one thousand. I believed her, but I had no real way of estimating the dimensions of Atlantis.

We didn't get out. Rather Admiral Rossi boarded us. As soon as he entered the passenger area, our pilot departed. Once more, I barely sensed the motion. The introductions to Admiral Rossi distracted us during the brief jump into and out of hyperspace. A few minutes after he boarded, we began our approach to the alien ship.

Admiral Rossi said, "I received an official call from Admiral Baba Skaggs of the Flagship Kanika. He claims to be the leader of the Federation Space Fleet, and he said if we join the Federation, they'll protect us from the Sixth Invaders. He claims he's had previous run-ins with them. On board are several ambassadors who want to discuss the situation with us. We shouldn't be hasty. As General Blythe has cautioned, it could be a trap; this whole Sixth Invaders thing could be a scheme to force us into this Federation, whatever it is. Oh, crap!"

He gazed out the window and saw our approach to the Kanika. We gasped. The sheer size of this spaceship was staggering. I guessed you could put the entire GD skyscraper into the ship. It dwarfed the Atlantis. Constructed of joined hexagonal tubes, here was a town in space.

"Prepare for culture shock," Admiral Rossi said, as he

handed out waistbands containing Universal Language Translator devices. "My shipboard anthropology and xenology person warned me and suggested we wear these. They translate between our language and several others, but she said the Federation people would have their own such devices. So these might prove useless. Still, be as prepared as possible."

He continued, "I'll handle space battle discussions. General Blythe, you handle any ground-based battle commentary. Czar Parkinson, as our Inspections and Justice Czar, I want you to stay alert for lies and deceptions. You're our private investigator."

"But what about our Emperor and Empress?" I said. "Shouldn't they handle something as important as this?"

"They'll handle the negotiations, but you observe. Point out troubles just as you did when you were the temporary CEO of GD, only this time as they come up in the talks. We don't have the luxury of time. Ah, we've docked. Good luck. All of us."

A giant of a man in a green uniform stood outside our transport's door. He spoke but his voice came out of a box around his waist. That's not correct. The sounds from his voice were undecipherable but the translator box spoke English. This was my first exposure to language translation devices though I had read they were common among anthropologists and our exploration ship personnel.

We walked down a long metal ramp, through a set of giant steel doors, and into a long carpeted hallway. Two other giant guards joined us, falling in behind our group. While we passed many doors, I couldn't see inside them nor read what must have been writing on the wall plaques. The hall led to a spacious room full of light. Its gray metal walls gave it a sterile appearance. The presence of a long stainless steel table with matching chairs gave the room a corporation look. The eight occupants grabbed our instant attention though I must admit they latched onto Bev and my appearance just as much. They each wore a translation box.

"Welcome to the Flagship Kanika. I'm Admiral Baba Skaggs, your host. I am from Azizi-D."

Of those present, he looked much like any human male

I'd seen. As expected he wore a green uniform, only his had many gold stars on his sleeves and on his shirt pocket flaps. He stood six feet with a robust build. Like Bev, he had a no-nonsense attitude that came across as a stoic, stern disposition. His hair was black and close-cropped. Bushy brows accentuated his dark brown eyes. I sensed no malice in his attitude, rather intense curiosity with Bev and me. He didn't hide the fact his attention rested on our large bosoms.

He continued. "Your emissary, Mr. Travis Jones." He pointed to a non-descript man, possibly thirty years old.

Travis nodded, a pleasant smile on his face. He was four inches shorter them me, brown hair and blue eyes, and wore a plain business suit. Mr. Jones was the type of man that could vanish in a crowd. Unremarkable in all ways. I had no idea we had an emissary. I panned my attention across our group, but only Admiral Rossi recognized this man. 'What emissary?' was the common thought among the rest of our group, save Airla who had no thoughts.

Admiral Skaggs pointed to the other six, paired men and women, all of whom looked strange to us. "These are the Federation ambassadors who wish to hold this meeting with you. Ambassadors Dara and Kiri Sim of the Varin race of Dian-C."

Both were extremely short, four feet tall, but incredibly stocky with bulging muscles, especially Kiri's. Dara wore a dress, not unlike Earth cotton day dresses. Embroidered flowers I'd never seen before covered her dress. She had long light brown hair and a pleasant smile that lit up her roundish face. Kiri wore a pleated kilt, reminding me of pictures of Scotland. His short arms were double the thickness of my legs. These were very strong people. He bowed to us while she curtsied. They had brownish skin tones. I considered them to be dwarves.

"These are Ambassadors Dasha and Midas Pappas of the Lana race from Liatos-D."

Talk about contrast. Wow. Midas stood close to eight feet, his head almost touching the metal ceiling. Both were giants. Only inches shorter than her husband, Dasha was also a large person. Both had musculature befitting their enormous height. A fancy blue gown, satin-like, suited her skin tone and light blond hair, which she had up in a stylish fashion. I found her azure eyes captivating. Midas wore an expensive silk suit— looked like silk to my eyes. Gray and blue tweed. His hair was black as was his mustache. Everything about these two spoke of a scaled-up human. Their skin had a yellowing hue to it.

"Senior Ambassadors Sanura and Aba Fenuku of Zahra-C."

Now I stared! Both stood about six feet with brownish skin tones, but each was drastically different in appearance. Aba's head looked like a tall tin can. His forehead rose cylindrical in shape, making his head appear as though it was twice the size of mine. It reminded me of images in history books of men wearing stovepipe hats, only this was his head. Combed black hair adorned his head. He too wore a silk-like suit, very similar in style to that worn by Midas.

If he was shocking, Sanura was even more so. Yes, she wore a satin-like yellow dress that complimented her skin and pale blue eyes. She had her hair done up like Dara's. Rather what caused me to stare was her upper lip. It had been slit, forming a lip loop. A golden disk about eighteen inches across stretched the fleshy loop out, hanging down onto her chest cleavage. A pair of outstretched hands reaching toward each other was etched onto the lip plate that masked all facial expressions. Reading her would be challenging. Plus, I wondered how could she even talk or eat. My gaze then focused on her earrings. Much like exotic chandeliers, sparkling crystals set in gold fittings and chains hung down, resting on her chest just above her breasts. Dozens of the two-inch stones reflected the brilliant light, and I wondered if they were diamonds. I imagined the weight of her earrings stretched her earlobes to the tearing point.

In the background, I spotted Major Airla Baker nodding to Travis. Conclusion: they knew each other. Airla introduced us, beginning with Dimitri and Natalie, followed by Admiral Rossi and Bev, before introducing me and then herself.

As I looked at these ambassadors, I felt small and insignificant. Focus, Molly Focus. I'm a good PI with a high IQ. Plus, I have telepathic skills. Now's not the time to feel sorry for yourself.

Admiral Skaggs said, "Everyone, please take a seat. Let's get this meeting started. Now then, here's the situation. The Sixth Invaders are attacking the fledgling Sol Empire. If the Sol Empire joins the Federation of Planets, then as the admiral in both the Azizi-D Empire and the Federation of Planets, my armada will drive off the Sixth Invaders and guarantee the future safety and freedom of the Sol Empire worlds. If you agree and join the Federation, allow six hours for my armada to arrive. I assure you, we've dealt with these invaders many times. They will flee rather than press an attack. Ambassadors, the meeting is yours."

He sat and poured himself a drink. I sensed his boredom and that he didn't like being thrust into the diplomat role.

"We're the senior ambassadors," Abu Fenuku said, "so we'll begin the negotiations. First, let me handle the geography."

His wife, Sanura, flipped a control bringing up a 3-d holographic image of half the galaxy. It floated above the table, filling that space.

It looked so real Bev had to see if she could touch the stars and gas clouds. "Way cool. Do we have a projection system like this?" Bev asked.

"If you join the Federation, you'll get them," Ambassador Abu said, grinning. "Now then, let's look at the spiral arm sections. Your sun, which you call Sol, lies in the Orion spiral arm, here."

Ambassador Sanura highlighted these groups and arms in different colors. Impressive. Labels written in English floating among the stars and dust lanes.

Ambassador Abu continued. "The Sixth Invader empire lies in the more distant, outer Perseus arm that contains what you call the Crab Nebula, a supernova remnant. When that star went supernova, it obliterated many worlds in the Sixth Invader Empire and is one reason they're so keen on conquering new worlds. Only recently have the Sixth Invaders moved from their Perseus arm into your Orion Arm. The Cygnus arm is even closer to the galaxy's outer edges, and the

Sixth Invaders are much more active in that region than in your arm."

While he talked, his wife indicated these locations using a laser pointer. He continued. "Our four empires—the Azizi, the Varin, the Lana, and the Fenuku—lie in the Sagittarius arm, closer to the center of the galaxy. Our empires are many thousands of light years from Sol and are next to each other. The Scutum-Crux arm is even closer to the center, while the Norma arm is attached to the bar spoke at the nucleus of the galaxy. The Federation of Planets is run from Bela Prime located in the Norma arm."

Natalie said, "Fascinating. We thought our Sol Empire was it—the only space-faring people in the galaxy. Except for the Sixth Invaders." Her arm swept over the holographic display and the group of aliens. "All this is new and exciting to us. Our astrophysicists have only mapped hyperspace to a radius of twenty light years from Sol."

Dimitri added. "To us, you're aliens, too. But I guess we're aliens to you. The real question is what do we have to do to join this Federation? Honestly, we have no choice. The Invader fleet is three times ours. So what's this going to cost us?"

Chapter 15 Negotiations

The meeting room could well be a corporate room in the GD skyscraper. Its gray metal walls gave it a sterile appearance though spacious and brilliantly illuminated by recessed lighting. A long stainless steel table with matching chairs made me feel both more at home and uneasy because I didn't trust our corporations.

As I glanced at those on our side of the table, I sensed urgency in Natalie, Dimitri, and Admiral Rossi, who were desperate to save Earth from the overwhelming Sixth Invader fleet. But Bev eyed every gun or weapon she could, drooling with envy. I still wasn't sure why they insisted I come. How was I supposed to detect lies and such? One thing was certain: their minds were open. Except that of Major Airla Baker and Mr. Travis Jones, our emissary who had arranged this meeting. Again, I picked up nothing from them; no thoughts at all.

Even stranger, the Universal Language Translator devices strapped to our waists translated these alien languages into English and our words into theirs. Yet, I didn't need them to understand thoughts the aliens had. Yes, they looked at us as though we were the weird aliens, especially me.

"No need to change rooms. We'll hold your lengthy discussions here," said Admiral Baba Skaggs. "My Flagship Kanika is vastly superior to anything the Sixth Invaders have. We'll be completely safe, so take as long as you need with your discussions."

He came from Azizi-D, and of every alien here, looked much like any human male I'd seen. His green uniform with many gold stars on its sleeves and shirt pocket flaps had been crisply pressed. He shared Bev's no-nonsense attitude, making him appear stoic and stern.

As my gaze moved down the line of aliens on the opposite side of the table, I lost focus. At least that's my best description, rather like fogging out or even doping off on a sleepy afternoon. Someone talked. "To join the Federation, Earth must..."

Boom. A eardrum shattering explosion on the other side of the door that we'd entered slammed into me. All traces of air rushed out of my lungs. Crushed. It felt as though an elephant had landed on me or perhaps a piano falling from a second story window I once saw in an ancient film clip. The concussion smashed our bodies into the back wall. Across the table, I saw the same happening to the aliens, though the arm muscles of the giants and dwarves rippled as they attempted to hold their positions at the table, legs flying back toward the wall.

A terrible creaking from the area of the blast followed, but with shattered eardrums, I wondered how I could even hear it. Then, I saw it. The explosion severed one end of the hexagonal tube structure containing this room. Black space and stars appeared. I remembered to breathe, but my body didn't respond. Worse, a tornado chose this moment to strike. Okay, it wasn't the weather, rather the air inside the meeting room rushed out into the vacuum of space, creating a tornado-like effect.

My body flew from its crumpled position at the wall's base towards the gaping opening where jagged bits of the hull structure gleamed like shark's teeth. Even though I didn't have any, I flailed my arms, trying to avoid being gutted like a fish as my body flew through the opening. Cold. Intense cold. That's the last sensation I detected from my body as it both exploded and flash-froze, leaving me drifting alongside it.

Looking back, I watched my sister and dear friends join me, along with the aliens who were only trying to help us. The body of Admiral Skaggs drifted past me and then Bev's. I couldn't even cry.

"Molly. Psst. Molly, wake up. You're sleeping through the meeting," Bev whispered and shook my shoulders.

"Huh? Bev? Are you alive? We aren't blown up? What just happened?"

Bev's eyes opened wide. "Did you just have one of your vision things? Hey, everyone. Wait a minute. Molly, what did you see? What's blown up?"

I exhaled deeply and looked at the many faces now staring at me. I'd had one all right. But was it going to happen or was my imagination running wild? Worse, with all eyes on me, I had to say something.

"I—I just had a vision. Someone detonated a huge bomb just beyond that door. It ripped one of the hexagonal sections of the ship loose. A gaping hole with jagged metal edges formed. All the air rushed out, pulling our bodies with it. We all died. I—I think there were several more explosions around the ship. The last thing I saw were the Sixth Invader ships heading towards us. We aren't safe in here. Admiral Rossi, we should head back to our ship."

Bev stood up. "Hey, you should listen to her. Molly has these visions of the future. If she says there'll be an explosion beyond that door, there sure as hell will be. I agree. We should head back to our ship, Admiral Rossi."

Admiral Skaggs looked at Admiral Rossi and then at Bev, Dimitri, and Natalie. "I suppose a bomb placed in the right position could break the joints holding this section in place. But who would do such a thing? How long do we have?"

I said, "I don't know. Probably not much time. It's something I'd expect the Sixth Invaders to do—what with their body swapping machines and all."

The giant Ambassador Midas Pappas rose too, his head inches from the ceiling. "Admiral, we couldn't help noticing dozens of shuttle ships coming and going from the Kanika. I wouldn't be surprised if the Sixth Invaders didn't try something sneaky like this. They're too cowardly to meet you in open battle. For safety, we should all return to our ships."

The other ambassadors nodded their heads, but Bev barked. "Hold on. Molly glimpses the future. We can change it. Look, we did just that in Chicago. Check for bombs, suspicious people; put the ship on high alert. Just prevent her vision from happening."

"Everyone, stay here," Admiral Skaggs yelled. He barked orders into his shoulder mounted comm device. Within seconds, a wailing siren echoed throughout the ship, and a red light flashed just above the door. "We're on high alert. Going to battle stations."

Six men burst in through the "doomed" door, saluting Admiral Skaggs. "Sweep the corridor. You're looking for a powerful bomb. Check on any unauthorized personnel in the hallway. Secure this room."

They rushed out and searched, moving methodically down the hallway. Another officer appeared and installed an invisible blast shield in front of the door which Admiral Skaggs kept open. He watched his personnel as they used hand-held devices, sweeping them across every inch of the corridor.

"You can relax now. The bomb would have had to be closer to the door than the men are now for it to create the effect in Molly's vision. Besides, the force field will deflect the blast. We're perfectly safe in here."

At this point, the personnel had cleared the first twenty feet of the hall. A man wearing a blue enlisted man's uniform walked towards the busy men. One stopped and barked. "Halt. Let's see your authorization to be on this level, ensign."

By now, everyone in the room had moved to positions behind the admiral, watching the search proceed. Me, too. I peered into the ensign's glazed eyes, and I knew. Don't ask me how I knew. I've no way to describe it. I just knew and yelled, "He's the bomber!"

Before anyone could react, the ensign detonated the bomb. Later, we learned he wore a bomb vest. The fiery explosion swept down the hallway, but the force field held, deflecting the flames and the concussion. But the six bomb searching men perished. Because of the wrong location of the explosion, the hallway suffered only cosmetic damage.

"Darin Rats!" exclaimed Admiral Skaggs. "If that bomb was only twenty feet closer, Molly's vision would have been accurate." Into his shoulder comm device, he barked more orders. "Total lock down. Be alert for suicide bombers—our people controlled by the Sixth Invaders." Turning to us, he said, "You folks. Continue your meeting. I've a ship to manage."

Boom. Boom. Several distant explosions followed.

"Darin Rats. More of them." Admiral Skaggs lowered the force field, ducked past it, restored the field, before stepping over his fallen men and racing down the corridor.

Ambassador Midas Pappas looked at me closely. "Thank you for saving our lives. But we best follow what's happening to the Kanika. If it goes badly, I'll escort us all to our private ships in the docking bay." He fiddled with some dials. The wall behind the aliens turned into the largest monitor I'd ever seen, at least ten feet wide. After more dial-switching, we had a broad view of Admiral Skaggs and his Command and Control Center with its many external view screens.

Everyone watched. No one was interested in pursuing the meeting—not with the Sixth Invaders making a move on the Kanika. The giant explained, "Ah, the other bombs weren't as effective as they might have been. See there, they tried to knock out the defensive fire computers. That would have cut down on the Kanika's ability to defend against a swarm of small fighters. That one there missed taking out all communications with the Command and Control Center. And that one almost knocked out their hyperdrive. Mrs. Parkinson, thousands owe you a thank you for saving their lives. So how do you have these visions of yours?"

Again, all eyes stared at me. "Dunno. They just come. But you should thank Admiral Skaggs. His fast action saved us." I hoped to deflect attention off me.

"Hey, look at the Sixth Invader ships," Ambassador Dasha Pappas interrupted. "They must have detected the explosions. Their ships are moving toward us. Midas, should we head to our cruiser now? For safety?" The giant woman sounded worried, though I picked her emotions up directly, not from the translator box whose speech was a dry monotone.

"The Kanika hasn't had any significant damage, so we're safe right here," Ambassador Dasha Pappas said. "They'll probably execute a light probe to verify the Kanika's defenses are compromised. When they see they aren't, they'll back off. Trust me. They're basically cowards and slime balls."

We stared at the big screen and the smaller screen

images of the hive of busy crew. We saw what the admiral did.

"Here they come," the ambassador said. "Now if I were Admiral Skaggs, I'd pretend the Kanika is badly damaged. Then, when the Invaders get real close, bam!" He slapped his giant hands together. I figured he'd have no trouble squashing a melon or someone's head for that matter. These giants were strong, really strong.

He wasn't Admiral Skaggs, who ordered his defensive batteries to fire when the Sixth Invader ships got within range. While two smaller ships took damage and limped away from the battle, the others in the fleet dropped into hyperspace, reappearing at their former distance, some ten light years away. The admiral now put his attention onto damage control. One small monitor showed the names of the victims. I counted twenty-three, presumed dead. Already a repair crew appeared outside our door; their first action: cleaning the soot and debris.

My guess is a half hour passed before Admiral Skaggs rejoined us. "Repairs are under way. Twenty-three dead, including the six bombers. Mrs. Parkinson was correct. The Invaders captured one returning shuttle. They transferred some of their amazon warriors into our men's bodies and strapped on bomb vests. Their orders must have been to take out six critical areas, including our hyperdrive unit. I issued a warning to the Invaders. If they try anything else, I'll order our entire Federation Armada to come and destroy every one of their spaceships, if we have to follow them back to their home world. So I think we'll be safe for now. I presume you've carried on with the meeting?" He glanced at the faces in the room.

"Hardly," Ambassador Midas Pappas said. "Your CCC was far more interesting." Several others chuckled. "Okay, Ambassadors Sanura and Aba Fenuku. As Senior Ambassador, Sanura, the meeting is yours once more." My attention shifted from the
giants over to the two strange looking people.

Senior Ambassador Sanura wore a satin-like yellow dress, complimenting her skin and pale blue eyes. Her golden upper lip disk, which had to be about eighteen inches across, stretched the fleshy loop out and hung down onto her chest cleavage. Again, I stared at the pair of outstretched hands reaching toward each other etched onto the lip plate. Once more, I marveled at how well that disk masked all facial expressions. Her earrings looked more like exotic chandeliers, sparkling crystals set in gold fittings that rested on her chest just above her breasts, the many two-inch stones reflecting the brilliant light.

"I should explain about us ambassadors. There are two levels of ambassadors. Within each empire world system, local ambassadors work with neighboring empires and planets. My husband, Abu, is one of our local Zahra-C ambassadors. Midas and Dasha Pappas are local ambassadors for Liatos-D, while Ambassadors Dara and Kiri Sim are local ambassadors of Dian-C. They represent their worlds in local affairs such as these with your Sol Empire."

She cleared her throat. "I, on the other hand, am the Senior Ambassador of our world and empire of Zahra-C. I represent our world in the Federation Circle of Ambassadors. We are charged with making the laws of the Federation and the handling of worlds who break Federation laws. The Federation Circle of Admirals handles the enforcement of said laws. It is they who will guarantee the Sol Empire's safety and security from the Sixth Invaders, once you join, that is. Admiral Skaggs is their immediate representative in this matter."

She paused a moment while nodding to the admiral. "With all these ambassadors, the Federation needed a way to separate the most important Senior Ambassadors from the local ones. Hence, centuries ago, we came up with these decorative and highly beneficial lip plates. Only Senior Ambassadors are allowed to wear such disks. It is a requirement of office. Also, the lip plates make reading facial expressions nearly impossible, further aiding our internal negotiations." She winked at me. "And the lip disks have other benefits, too."

She shook her head slightly causing her earrings to rake

against her skin. "Each female Senior Ambassador also wears earrings like mine. The crystals help dampen out the emotions of those around us, enabling us to remain impartial and not be unduly influenced by the emotions of others." Again, she winked at me. "And they have other uses, too."

I flushed. Why? Okay, I got curious and peered into her mind and saw her raking her earrings over his face and chest, arousing him. Damn, why did I have to probe? She smiled at me. While the lip plate hid the smile, I sensed it and saw it in her eyes.

"To business," she continued. "The requirements to join the Federation of Planets are simple. First, each world or empire must donate a half percent of their yearly net profits to the Federation. These funds pay for the large defense fleet, the running of the Circle of Admirals and Senior Ambassadors. Second, you must allow free trade between all Federation worlds, and all goods and services must meet fair market values. No undercutting or overcharging another world or empire. Third, you must agree to a free exchange of technology and methods. For example, your hyperspace coordinates are incredibly primitive. Once you join, you'll receive an update; you'll have total access to all such coordinates any world in the Federation has. Also, you'll experience a rapid exchange of technology. You may have some the Federation doesn't, but the reverse is more likely, considering the number of worlds and empires in the Federation of Planets."

I chuckled. From all I'd seen today that was the understatement of the year. I sensed Bev drooling over acquiring better guns while Admiral Rossi was imagining a larger space fleet.

Senior Ambassador Sanura Fenuku said, "Fourth, you will be required to send one top of the line battleship and admiral to sit on the Federation Circle of Admirals. If action is needed, you will need to supply the required space vehicles. Don't worry. You won't be asked to provide what you don't have. Fifth, based on the population of your Sol Empire, you must send one or more Senior Ambassadors to hold your place in the Circle of Ambassadors. These are the most important people in your realm, for they represent your world within the Federation. It's a vital and critical position. You must have one Senior Ambassador for every five billion people on your world or empire. Only one admiral, though."

She again looked at me. "Of course, any Senior Ambassador you send will have their upper lip split and the regulation sized disk supplied. Females will also receive a pair of these magnificent and emotion-dampening earrings, too. Male Senior Ambassadors are not so easily affected by nearby emotions. It's a body's gender thing. Male bodies have over double the resistance to electricity than female bodies. A universal thing, I'm told. So males don't need the dampening earrings."

Ambassador Abu Fenuku laughed. "Men don't wear gaudy earrings." Several other men chuckled, too.

"Sixth," she continued, "you agree to abide by all Federation laws. You'll be provided several copies today so you can scan over them. I'm told at first some worlds object to some rules. Don't know why, though. They are set up for everyone's benefit."

She chuckled. "That about sums it up. There's no downside to joining the Federation of Planets. There are tremendous benefits to do so."

The dwarven ambassador Dara cleared her throat. Sanura glanced at Dara, her earrings swinging in large arcs. "Oh, yes. There is another minor detail. Mind you, this isn't a requirement for joining the Federation of Planets. Several worlds are facing severe overpopulation. From what we've learned of the Sol Empire and Earth in particular, you were once over populated, but now are underpopulated."

"Yes, that's accurate," Natalie said. "We were fortunate to be able to colonize many nearby worlds. Two thirds of Earth's population chose to begin new lives on our sister worlds."

"You are very fortunate. Not so with Dian-C and Liatos-D. Both the giants' world and the dwarven world are terribly overpopulated. As a result, for the last two decades, they have made arrangements with other worlds to have some of their people immigrate there. The giants and dwarves would love to work out an arrangement with the Sol Empire so they could transplant some of their people to Earth. It is understood that those who do so would become citizens of Earth and the Sol Empire; they'd give up their citizenship of Dian-C and Liatos-D."

She continued. "They'd be subject to the local laws of Earth and the Sol Empire."

"Er, how many are we talking about?" asked Dimitri. To me, his mind was an open book. He saw how strong these giants and dwarves were and saw that as a huge benefit to his security forces. He had an ulterior motive in mind. I had to grin, but no one noticed me.

Ambassador Dara Sim, the dwarf in the simple cotton day dress with embroidered flowers, spoke up. "Dian-C would like to send about five million, as would the giants. We'll screen those who want to come to your world. No criminals. Only productive members of society and those who wish to migrate to another world."

"Precisely," said Ambassador Midas Pappas. "Five million. No criminals. We giants offer you enormous strength. Liatos-D is a light gravity world. Our people evolved to take advantage of this. Our people grew taller than normal, and compared to others, we have giant strength."

"But," said Dara, "Dian-C is a heavy gravity planet. We evolved short and stocky. Our strength exceeds the giants. Dwarves are master craftsmen. You can't go wrong by adding dwarves to your world population."

Dimitri said, "But if your people move to our world, won't future generations become more like us?"

Kiri Sim said, "Hurrumphff."

"Our people will risk it," said Midas.

"There is one other slight problem," Dimitri said. "Corporations run our world. Other than some common sense things, we haven't any codified set of laws anymore, not for several hundred years. I know in our distant past, there were so many laws people had to follow that it took lawyers years to figure them out. But they all got dumped. You can't murder people, rob others, beat up people, or harm people. You know, common sense things. Trouble is, until recently, the corporations were corrupt and could dictate what they wanted to be *right*. Molly has helped to bring some of the corporate crimes to light. I welcome both giants and dwarves, but be advised we're in a transition era."

He looked at Natalie, who nodded. "So what do we need to do to get started joining the Federation of Planets?"

I found myself attracted to the Sims. These dwarves were unpretentious and polite, even though they stood only four-feet tall. Okay, the giants at eight-feet tall seemed too domineering to me at a little over six-feet in my heels.

"We fill out the petition to join the Federation," said Senior Ambassador Sanura Fenuku. "Abu and I will help you fill out the application since you can't read our language. There's been some discussion in the Circle of Ambassadors about making one language a Federation standard that everyone must learn, but nothing has come of it. Admiral Skaggs, while we fill out the forms, call in the Federation fleet. Let's chase these Sixth Invaders away now."

"Yes, ambassador. I'll send word now." Admiral Skaggs left.

Dimitri and Natalie moved beside the Fenuku's, who began filling out an electronic document. Meanwhile, Admiral Rossi and Bev chatted with the giant ambassadors, so I moved to sit beside the Sims. Dara and Kiri's faces broke into smiles as I sat down.

"Love all that intricate embroidery," I said.

Dara smiled. "Yes, I did it myself. I'm so glad you're willing to accept so many of our people. But don't you have a hard time? I mean without any arms?"

I laughed. "One day, maybe that won't be the first thing on people's minds when they see me. Life is more challenging for me, but I don't let it stop me."

I touched their minds lightly. As I expected, they felt sympathy towards me, but thank heavens no pity. Right now, I couldn't take the pity of others. Perhaps there was something to the dampening effect of the Senior Ambassador's giant earrings. I made a note to follow up on that when I could. However, in touching Dara's mind, I also sensed she desperately wanted to talk to me about something. Now, how to get her to do so without my giving away that I probed her mind?

Chapter 16 Brainwashed

The meeting room wasn't all that conducive to the exchange of personal feelings and ideas. But soon the admiral returned with an invitation for lunch, and we adjourned to the Kanika's mess hall. Again, I did my best to ignore the stares. They were curious about how I could manage. Whatever the food was, it tasted like chicken, though I later learned that was merely an olfactory stimulus broadcast throughout the room.

That done, we broke up into the same small groups. "I know a quiet space where we can talk," Dara said. She and Kiri led me to their personal quarters on the Kanika.

"So, what all did the Sixth Invaders do to your world? We heard a rumor they were there for thirty years. Didn't your people know that?" Kiri asked.

"Nope. They used their body swapping machine and took over the CEOs of the two empire-wide ruling corporations." I spent an hour outlining what had happened. They asked many questions about what had happened to me, particularly my recent deaths and body swapping, along with my strange ability to foresee bad future events and telepathy. Dara bombarded me with questions about our therapy and how it cured Bev of her insanity. I was pleased they were asking such questions, for I was expecting to be grilled about how I could survive without arms.

"So that does it. I've no control over when I glimpse the future. But I'm glad it happened today. I'm tired of these Sixth Invaders killing me."

Dara said, "They got to my sister, Lara. She's—I mean was—our Senior Ambassador to the Federation—before they got to her."

"Wow. What happened to her?"

"They used that mental implant device on her. Rather like what they did to your sister, General Blythe," Dara said. "She's now insane, locked up in the ship's brig. She has to kill every admiral and ambassador she sees, but she's fighting those urges. We've got her locked up for her own safety as well."

I didn't need telepathy to know what she was about to ask next. "Do you suppose your therapy thing would work on Lara, a dwarf, a non-human?"

I sighed. "I've no idea. My sister, Celeste, is the expert. But I can try. No guarantees, though."

I sensed Dara's huge relief. Her face broke into a broad smile. "Thank you. We should try before you have to leave. But I suppose we could bring her to your world later on if you prefer."

"Let's go see her. Then, I can make a better decision."

We walked down corridor after corridor, but I was lost after the first turn. All right, I was lost long before we even got to the mess hall.

The brig looked formidable and puny at the same time. Kiri explained, "Force fields. They padded the walls so she can't hurt herself. She tried that twice, smashing everything in sight to break free. Dwarves are strong, but not against escalating force fields. Their resistance increases proportionately to what's trying to defeat it."

Lara looked much like her sister. Perhaps four-feet tall, she had a roundish face with brown hair. Dara told me she'd removed the chandelier earrings and her large lip plate, her badges of office. Her upper lip loop drooped down below her chin. But the crazed, insane look in her eyes told all. My translator device converted her constant babbling into something I could understand.

"Gotta kill the admirals. Gotta kill the ambassadors. Can't kill my sister. Can't. But I just gotta do it. You must kill all the admirals and ambassadors. But I can't. Let me outa here. Gotta kill them. Can't kill them. Let me out." Lara pounded on the walls reinforced by the force fields. Sparks flew, but the fields held. After pounding on them for a couple minutes and ignoring Dara's pleadings to calm down, Lara stopped and slumped onto the crude bed, the only furniture in the room, besides the plastic latrine.

Dara sighed. "Don't expect you can do anything for her. These damned Sixth Invaders have brainwashed her. Admiral Skaggs thinks we should kill her. But she's my sister. I just can't. We'll take her home with us, but there's no hope for a cure on our world. Whatever they did to her is permanent."

"Hey, life is precious. Let me try. But I have to get in there with her."

Kiri said, "That's risky. She could crush you and not realize it. Dwarves are much stronger than you humans. Besides, she's crazy. You saw how hard she smashed into those force fields."

"I'm not an ambassador or admiral. I should be okay, but I need to be sitting beside her."

"You heard her, Kiri," Dara said. "Officially, we aren't responsible for what may happen to Molly, if we do as she asks."

I slipped off my heels. Walking without them was challenging, but I didn't want Lara to use my spikes as a weapon. Besides, if she broke them, they'd have to carry me everywhere. While Lara mumbled to herself, Kiri lowered the field, and I slipped into her cell. I hoped I wasn't being foolish or stupid, but I felt the need to try to help Lara, just as Celeste, Randi, and Eve had not forsaken Bev.

One thing I hadn't considered: what would happen if Lara should break the translator. How would I communicate? I sat down beside Lara. First action: find a way to get into communication with her.

She looked over at me, her gaze passing from my mouth to my ears, before resting on my shoulders. I smiled. She was the first person to notice something about me other than the obvious. "I'm Molly."

"Gotta kill the admirals. Gotta kill the ambassadors. Can't kill my sister. Can't. But I just gotta do it. Let me outa here. Gotta kill them. Lara. Get me outta here."

Fascinating. While ranting and dramatizing her implant and struggles against it, she told me her name. What a hopeful sign. "I want you to return to when you first ran into the Sixth Invaders who did this to you. Okay. Now move through the trauma and tell me what happened. What are you seeing? What are you smelling?"

I resisted the urge to just probe her mind. Entering an insane mind probably wasn't wise. Besides, I trusted Celeste's therapy methods. While her body was very different from mine, she was still a person. A spiritual being, as Celeste was so fond of saying. Being plus mind plus body. That seemed to be a universal pattern.

Lara ranted on, reciting her implanted words interspersed with her personal protests against those orders. I listened carefully. Just as before with the protesters who had been implanted at the Moscow facility, Lara did her best to answer my questions with her answers buried among the implanted words. I sensed or felt Lara's immense relief; someone actually listened to her.

Within a few minutes, I was able to block out or ignore the implanted words, focusing instead on Lara's attempts to tell me what she was experiencing. Trouble was, that was very rough going. Think about it. You're unconscious and thus helpless; your head is being blasted with electrical pulses generating unbearable headaches; your body is drugged and feels nauseated; a voice endlessly repeats the commands you must follow. Assuming it lasted for a half hour, as Bev said hers had, what part of the trauma is easily confronted or faced? None. I guessed it must be like a large black ball surrounding Lara's head, one filled with commands, intense pain, and unconsciousness.

At first, Lara could re-experience receiving flowers akin to roses from an unknown donor, smelling them, seeing them emit a gas that knocked her out. She awoke and tried to kill fellow ambassadors, unsuccessfully though. Total time to get this much from Lara: three hours. Well, I expected as much, based on how things went for the protesters I helped.

We had to break for supper. A soldier brought a tray of food for Lara along with a single plastic-like spoon. No knife or fork, obviously. As I slipped into my heels, I noticed Dara's ghastly complexion.

She said, "It's not working, right? No hope for my

sister? You were in there three hours. Most of the time, I held my hands over my ears. Kiri couldn't take it and left hours ago. Come on. Let's head to the mess hall. At least you tried." Dara sighed heavily.

"No, Dara. We've made progress. Lara's telling me what happened. She's only able to get a word or so out in between the implanted words, but she's doing what I'm asking her to do. Someone sent her flowers which emitted a knockout gas. That's how it began. These Sixth Invaders' implants are incredibly nasty things. Not only is she unconscious, but she's enduring intense head pain. On top of that, they keep repeating their orders to her for at least a half hour. Lara's doing wonderfully to have seen as much as she has today. It will take us days, but I think I can help her recover."

Color returned to Dara's face. Her eyes turned brighter. "Oh, thank you. Thank you. I thought it wasn't working. They replaced her—as our Senior Ambassador, I mean. Do you need help with supper?"

"Huh? Oh, no. Well, yes, if you can carry a tray for me." For a while, I'd forgotten my own disability. Reality slammed me. Crap. I'd gotten used to our silly robot helpers and my sisters, who just did things for me without my having to ask.

Bev joined us. "Hiya. How's it going?" She sat her tray down, a pleased look on her face.

"Making headway. Slow going, naturally. So you look happy. Going to get some new guns?" I knew that look on her face.

She grinned. "You betcha. Big guns. If we'd of had them back on Brussels, we'd of wiped the robots out when we first encountered them. These are darn cool blasters. Makes ours look more like pea shooters. You know what? They don't have Glocks, so we're going to send them some to test out. Our antique weapons work well in a space battle when a hole in your spacesuit means a quick death. It's exciting times we're in, sis."

After a pause, she added, "Natalie and Dimitri are having difficulties. Government troubles. Or corporation troubles I should say. It's crazy that we don't have a codified set of rules and laws. All these other worlds do. And the pay thing. Big troubles. Our corporations subsidize everyone. Lord knows your original GD salary barely covered your rent. Well, with these new dwarves and giants coming to Earth, all that's gotta change. Fair market rates. That's the buzzword now. Corporations have'ta pay what's fair. No more ripping us off. Folks are gonna love that, but the corporations aren't. Glad I'm not in Dimitri and Natalie's shoes."

After we finished eating, Dara and I returned to Lara's cell. I picked up where we left off. After another two hours, we ended; exhaustion slew Lara. "Don't worry," I said. "I'll be back in the morning. You eat a good breakfast."

When I returned to our ship and my quarters, escorted by Dara so I wouldn't get lost even though I actually was lost on this huge ship, Bev played us a recording she'd made earlier this afternoon. "Watch."

She had her phone focused on one of the view screens in the Kanika's CCC. I watched hundreds of warships, a multitude of shapes and sizes, appearing, dropping out of hyperspace. Almost at once, the entire Sixth Invader fleet vanished.

Bev said, "I kinda wish they hadn't fled. Then, this Federation fleet could've wiped them out. No more Sixth Invaders ever. Ah well. At least they're gone. Admiral Rossi has sent our fleet out on patrol duty to make sure they don't sneak back to Earth or any of our worlds."

Dara said, "They are sneaky fiends. They never do stand and battle, General Blythe. Covert infiltration is their hallmark. It's wise to guard against them trying to sneak back to your world."

"Yeah," Bev agreed. "Plus, Admiral Rossi, Dimitri, and Natalie are planning to address the entire Sol Empire soon, announcing all these changes. Shit'll hit the fans when they do that. Course, I think bringing all these giants and dwarves to Earth is a good thing. Heck, two out of three buildings in Chicago are abandoned. We could use more people. And Dimitri told me something today that I never knew."

"What's that?" I asked, knowing Bev expected me to be

curious.

"Guess what job has more people doing it than any other job?"

"Dunno. Security guards?" I guessed.

"Nope. Home maintenance and care. Someone has to keep all those vacant homes in good order and demolish those that aren't. Only garbage recycle personnel make lower wages. But you're right, security guard is the next most populous position. There are four home maintenance workers for every security guard. I never knew that."

"Fascinating. I always wondered what became of us high school kids after we graduated. So you're saying half my class was sponsored as maintenance people to keep up abandoned buildings?"

"Righto, sis. Just ask Kyle or Hank sometime. So many are just plain dummies. You'd call them low IQ people. We don't even take 'em in the army. Dimitri says half of Earth's population are almost morons and in apathy. That's scary. I sure didn't know that. Course, these people stay in the background and cause no troubles. Still, I had no idea. When I get home, I'm gonna ask Kyle why this happened. Or maybe Hank. Now you see why I'm so excited to get all these giants and dwarves coming to Earth. Unless they're dummies, too." Her face cringed. "Hadn't thought of that. Maybe they're dumping their undesirables on us."

Dara laughed. "No chance of that, General Blythe. Our hens would be fried if we did that. No, you're getting educated, valuable immigrants, looking for a better life."

"Fried hens?" Bev asked.

"Deep trouble," Dara said. "Local saying. Sorry. These translator devices don't handle idioms well."

From Bev's face, I knew she didn't remember what an idiom was. "Bev, like shoot the moon doesn't mean to blow up our moon, but to bet everything in a card game or leave without paying your bill. Sometimes a phrase doesn't mean what the individual words would suggest. So these fancy translator gadgets have limitations. Good to know, Dara."

The dwarf smiled and said good night, promising to

fetch me in the morning. After she left, Bev said, "Tomorrow, they're giving me gunnery practice with these new blasters. I'm so excited I don't think I can sleep a wink." I laughed.

No laughter came from our therapy sessions either, not for days. Dara became my helper, picking me up from my quarters, escorting me to the mess hall, handling my food tray, leading me to and from the brig. She had above average patience, but then Lara was her sister. Still, she must have had nerves of steel to sit there for eight hours each day listening to what seemed like the same old implant rantings. I hoped she was picking up on what Lara struggled to tell me in between those ravings.

On the fourth day, bone-freezing screams replaced some of the ranting. Lara contacted the deeply buried, electrical-caused head pain. I wished I'd had earplugs. Dara plugged her ears with her hands, but I could only endure it. By the sixth day, the implanted words lost their power to force Lara to recite them. On the seventh day, Lara didn't speak the words at all. Rather, heavy yawns took over, and I knew we were erasing this awful implant.

By day eight, Lara still wasn't laughing, wasn't cheerful, so I asked her if there was a similar trauma that happened earlier. She fished around for several minutes before she found it. "I'm dying on a battlefield somewhere. There's this awful hole in my head."

"Okay. Return to the beginning of this trauma. Go through it and tell me what's happening as you go through it. What are you seeing, feeling, touching, smelling?"

"Oh, my husband is hounding me. Join the army. Fight for us. Over and over, he keeps pounding me with these ideas. I didn't want to fight. Oh!"

Lara brightened up. Until now, her face was as pale as a ghost. Suddenly, a healthy pinkish tone appeared. Her eyes fairly shone. She chuckled. "That was just like this Sixth Invaders' implant trauma. Force me to do something I refuse to do. Got my head blown off just like the implant's pain. Boom." Lara began laughing, heartily.

She continued to roar. "Like a pig." More laughter.

"Boom." "Hole in my head." Occasionally, Lara spoke a word or two before laughing even harder.

Dara could stand it no longer. She opened the cell door, turned off the force field, and joined us. She hugged Lara.

"Dara. You look wonderful," she managed to say above her laughter. "Pig. Boom. Hole in my head." She continued rolling in laughter. Dara hugged her sister even more, though it was hard because Lara's body shook from the laughter.

Lara's reaction reminded me of something Celeste once told me. "Sometimes people erase so much pent up energy that they laugh for hours while all the harmful bits and pieces vanish. The laughter is indicative of vanishing trauma." Celeste used big words, but this was the first time I experienced someone blowing away so much traumatic energy. Lara didn't stop laughing for over two hours.

When she did stop, she said, "I'm so hungry I could eat a dropper."

Dara laughed, and I couldn't help but peeking into her mind to see what a dropper was—some kind of large, furry animal.

As we walked to the mess hall, Lara said, "Dara, I feel like a new dwarf! I'm so full of life I'm bursting. Oh, who are you? You've saved my life. Did the Sixth Invaders get to you, too?"

"Molly Parkinson. Human from Earth, Sol Empire. Yeah, they got to me, indirectly so to speak. They've used genetic mutations on some of us, but they killed me twice now."

"Incredible. Killed twice? I have to hear about this. I owe you my life, Miss—"

"Molly, just Molly."

"Okay, Molly. I was totally crazy. Why my fellow dwarves didn't just kill me is beyond comprehension. Whatever you did, it's gone. Totally vanished. Oh, I can remember what those wicked Sixth Invaders did to me, but it doesn't affect me anymore. Dara! Do you realize what Molly's done? She's erased a heavy implant. That's never, ever happened before. Everyone knows you can't undo these mental implants."

"I know, Lara, but we heard rumors these Earth people had undone Sixth Invader implants. I had to try. I was going to take you there and see if I could find someone who knew how to undo it, but Molly came to us, part of their delegation. Her Sol Empire is petitioning for admittance into the Federation. They had to join up. The Sixth Invaders sent their whole space armada to conquer them."

"Dara, you're the best sister ever. But Molly, how did you ever learn how to do this thing? Wait. I've another question. That second traumatic incident—that happened before I was born. How can that be? And I was seeing things even though I was unconscious during that implant—like I was floating above my body."

"My sisters taught me how to do it. The Sixth Invaders implanted Bev and other female soldiers, forcing them to become sex Dolls. They worked their magic on them. Unfortunately, our people got their implant technology and began using it on our own people who were protesting corporate crimes. So many were harmed that I just had to learn how to do it."

I then explained what I'd discovered about myself—that I was an immortal spiritual being. Over lunch, I told them what had happened to me during the last two years.

"That's not all, Lara," Dara interrupted. "She can see the future. Molly prevented the Sixth Invaders from destroying this battleship and us." Dara told her what I'd done.

"Now wait a minute, Dara. Are you saying that Molly can see the future and that she can read minds?"

Rather than let Dara fumble about an explanation, probably getting it wrong, I spoke up. "I noticed after I had received countless hours of Celeste's therapy that I could pick up other's thoughts. Today, I'm pretty good at it, but nowhere near as skilled as my three younger sisters. I think telepathy is more tied to spiritual beings than to our bodies. And yes, a couple times I've glimpsed the future and told others who were able to alter things. Admiral Skaggs saved us by believing we had saboteurs on the ship. Bev believed me and confiscated the awful genetic mutation stuff that the Sixth Invaders were going to use on the men of Chicago where I live."

"Incredible," said Lara. "Genetics is my field. This is what we in the Federation often face—genetic mutation. It's one of the many diabolical weapons the Sixth Invaders use. I used to work in a genetics lab developing cures for some of the other mutations these fiends have inflicted on others. But then I was asked to be the Senior Ambassador for Dian-C. How could I refuse them? It's one of our world's highest positions. I take it I've been replaced." She chuckled.

Dara grimaced. "Yes, as soon as they learned you had been implanted and were insane. They were going to kill you, but Kiri and I rushed to Bela Prime and rescued you. We ended up here on the Kanika because—well, we had to keep you confined in and unbreakable brig."

Lara chuckled. "Good thing you did. I could have killed everyone."

"No, you wouldn't. You kept fighting the implant," Dara insisted.

"Well, Molly, I owe you a life debt. Tell me more about this current genetic mutation agent."

My face flushed, but I admitted. "Sorry. I'm ignorant of so many things. Eve knows the most about it, probably as much or more than our corporate scientists. You'll have to ask her."

Lara said, "That's okay. None of us knows all about everything. If we did, why, we'd be a god. But when you began your story, you mentioned a DNA database."

"Yes, that's what started everything. Galactic Defense and Galactic Medicine thought it would be a good thing to have every person's DNA on file. That's when my sister clone, Janine, discovered our DNA was absolutely identical. She'd enter my DNA and get back her ID—that sort of thing. So yes, the DNA database has nearly everyone's original DNA in it, before all these mutations happened. Why? Is that important?"

Lara pulled on her drooping lip loop, deep in thought. I resisted touching her mind to see what so intrigued her. She looked up. "Molly, if we have a sample of your original DNA, there's a good chance I can work up a genetic mutation to make your body change to its original form. I'm going to try, so, Dara, I'm returning with Molly to her world. You can come and be our ambassador to this Sol Empire of theirs, helping them get introduced to the Federation."

"If you think you can help them, Lara, Kiri and I are with you. We'll make the arrangements." She left to do so.

Once Dara was gone, Lara said, "One thing worries me, Molly. You didn't have telepathy and future visions before they mutated you. So if I return your body back to its original form, you might lose both abilities."

I chuckled. "Caught between the devil and the sea." Lara looked quizzically, so I said, "Damned either way. Life's a bitch without arms, but I will really miss not seeing a disastrous event coming my way. I don't care about telepathic skills."

Lara inhaled sharply. "Gotta lotta, Molly! You don't know what you're saying. True telepaths are exceedingly rare within the Federation. Corporations and wealthy individuals would pay you millions of credits a year for your skills. You could become fabulously wealthy in only a few years working for them."

"Wow. I had no idea. What would they do?"

"Spy on others. Make sure your corporation or boss isn't being taken advantage of—that kind of thing."

I laughed. "Ah ha. Sorry, that's not something I'd ever do. Originally, I wanted to be a private investigator. While I still love doing it, there's so much more I feel I should be doing. Worst thing is I don't know what that is. Not really. I know how dumb I am. No degrees, and PI school doesn't count. Eve, Celeste, and Randi—each has three doctorate degrees. Even my husband, Ted, has two doctorates. Me? Just graduated high school. Sometimes, I feel so stupid. But I'm not interested in being a housewife like my mother was. I need to do much more than clean house or look pretty for Ted. And while I'd like millions of credits, I'm not about to be a spy for someone. So don't fret about the telepathy thing."

That got me wondering. "Say, I'm pregnant. Do you think my baby will be born handicapped too? Will they have my telepathy? Is that even possible? Are our mutated genes inherited? I've also adopted two teenagers like I said. I wonder if they're developing telepathy?"

Lara said, "We can find some of the answers right away. We're on a battleship. They have state of the art medical facilities here. Let's ask someone for directions to the medical center."

An hour later, Lara and I looked at the high definition images of my baby on the monitor. I was going to have a baby girl, but her body lacked all traces of arms. My stomach felt as though someone had crushed it with giant pinchers. She'd have a hard life, too. Damn it. But I couldn't fool myself. I'd suspect this would be the case since I first learned Dr. Janet Padella had injected this nasty genetic mutation agent into my body that was on life support and brain dead.

"We can't rule out your genes being inherited, Molly, since you were genetically altered after you were pregnant," Lara said.

"And shot and killed and brain destroyed," I added. Yes, I couldn't avoid sarcasm.

"Excuse me." Senior Ambassador Sanura Fenuku interrupted us. She'd found me here in the medical center. "I've been meaning to talk with you, Molly. It's okay to call you that, isn't it?" I nodded. "Is everything all right with your baby?"

"As right as can be expected," Lara growled, answering her before I could. "Her baby won't have arms either, thanks to the Sixth Invaders genetic mutation agents."

"We're okay," I said. "Molly's fine with me. But how should I address you?"

I heard a chuckle coming from beneath her lip plate. Since the round eighteen-inch golden lip plate hid most of her face, I couldn't read her facial expressions.

"In public places, Senior Ambassador is required by all. However, in private as we are now, please, just Sanura. I'd like to talk with you when you've time. Lara, it's amazing to see you cured. You were insane when I first saw you. Molly, you realize no one has ever cured the Sixth Invaders' mental implants, don't you? This is an incredible breakthrough. Brainwashing can be undone. That's real news."

"Hey, I am truly alive, Senior Ambassador," Lara said. "That insanity—it's completely gone."

"I'm glad for you. Would you mind letting me chat with Molly for a time? I promise to return you to her when we're done talking."

Lara left, but not without a backward glance at me. I sensed she was worried, but about what I had no idea. I wasn't about to pry into her mind, though.

"Follow me. I want to talk to you in private," Sanura said.

Chapter 17 Texture Sensualism and the Offer

I followed Sanura to her private quarters. Along the way, I joked. "Gosh, I hope you know where you're going because I'm lost again."

I had questions, too. Like how come her husband's head looked like a tall tin can. Ignoring that, they were a little taller than I was, though, in my heels, I was taller than both. He wasn't in their room, so she must have arranged this meeting. Why? I had no idea.

Sanura had a brownish skin tone which made the satin-like yellow dress look perfect on her. As we walked, I got a closeup look at her split upper lip and the golden disk that stretched her lip flesh into a giant circle eighteen inches across. It bounced off her chest while her chandelier earrings rubbed against her upper chest. I studied her exotic earrings. Sparkling crystals set in gold fittings and chains hung down, resting on her chest just above her breasts. Dozens of the two-inch stones reflected the hallway light. They were clear stones, quartz or diamonds?

Her quarters were larger than mine, but then she had a high position. We sat on soft chairs facing each other. Now I could see her legs. They were encased in some kind of stockings, black and shiny. Her heels were perhaps two inches tall.

"On our world, Zahra-C," she began.

"Excuse me. Is that the name of your world? And what does the C mean?"

From her eyes only, I had a sense she might be smiling, but I resisted touching her mind.

"Zahra is our sun. Ours is the third planet out from the sun. Most civilizations within the Federation have a proper name for their world and a local one. The proper name uses the numerical count out from the sun. That way, no one is ever confused. Your world is officially being called Sol-C. Dimitri has agreed to that. Everyone has a local name for their world. Yours is Earth. Ours is Tagara. However, off-world, we always use the proper name. Less confusion that way."

She cleared her throat. "I should explain that each world in the Federation has its own ruling system, though corporations play a huge role on each. On our world, all rulers come from the upper-class, the haruna, which translates to wise or intelligent person. Haruna men have their heads tightly bound just after birth. The binding forces their heads to grow upwards, giving them their distinctive giant heads. You've seen Abu's head. They have frequent headaches while growing up, but that's the price men pay for their upper class position."

"His brain isn't any larger, is it? Seems rather barbaric to me."

A chuckle came from beneath the golden disk. "Scientific studies have shown haruna men's brains are the same size as all Tagaran men, and they aren't smarter either. No, I'm afraid the reasons for this are lost in our ancient history. Still, we follow our traditions, just as all people do."

"What defines haruna women?"

Again, I sensed a smile, more from the slight expansion of the creases around her pale blue eyes. "We're texture sensualists. For us, tactile sensations are everything. That's why I wear these dresses. The fabric is slippery, silky, and smooth. I believe your word for this type of material is satin. It slides across our skin. Then we all wear these incredible stockings. The fancy polymer is formed right on our legs and feet, providing a super tight feeling. Even better, if you even wiggle a toe or twitch a muscle, the stockings send that sensation up your whole leg. Indescribable tactile. You use your toes, but they can be formed around your toes, much like fingers in a glove, so you, too, could experience what it's like to feel your whole leg at one time. Plus, they are slippery and silky, just like my dress. I wish you had hands so you could run them over my dress and stockings and feel what I'm talking about. Ah well."

She took a breath. "There's more to this texture sensualism. Abu and I have found my lip loop adds a whole new dimension to our love making. Plus, I use these earrings, which really do dampen my reception of the emotions of others nearby, to feel and caress my shoulders. No one is the wiser, either. My lip disk does that, too. So there are many aspects to our sense of touch, and we try to experience as many of them as possible during the day."

Once more, she paused for air. Sanura was definitely a talker. "But this isn't why I wanted to meet with you, Molly. I've got a selfish reason and an ambassadorial one."

I laughed. "How about the selfish one first?" Given she was so impressed with Lara's recovery from obvious insanity, I expected questions along that line.

"Okay. What you did for Lara—that's, well let's say until now, undoing one of those Sixth Invaders' implants was not possible. We put the miserable and insane victims out of their misery, quickly and painlessly. That was supposed to have happened with Lara, except her homely sister, Dara, arrived and took her away from us at the Federation Circle of Ambassadors. Of course, you saw how she had to keep Lara locked up and surrounded by force fields. Those dwarves are very strong. Never doubt that. I saw Lara once pound her fist onto the Round Table where we meet, breaking the edge off. It was a metal table, mind you.

"And yet you did something to her over eight days—I know because I kept track of the days—comes with being a Senior Ambassador—nothing escapes you unless you're a masochist or wish to get blind-sided at a meeting. Whatever you did, I believe it was also done to General Blythe and many others on your world—people whom the Sixth Invaders implanted, though I'm still vague on just what this whole Galactic Doll thing was all about. She alluded to that fact when we talked, but she didn't know how it was done. Only that it worked superlatively."

I saw my chance to say something. "Right. My three younger sisters invented it. It's a therapy that has the person re-experience the trauma and erase it. With these infernal

Sixth Invader implants, it often takes many days for the victim to confront, to face, all that pain and unconsciousness."

"I see. And it works not only on you humans but also the dwarves?"

"I think it would work on any sentient being, Sanura. We're all immortal spiritual beings that have a mind and inhabit a body. The therapy addresses the spiritual being via their body and mind. It takes a lot of patience, I've discovered, and a real will to help the victim recover."

"So it would work on me, assuming I even had a trauma in my life?"

"I think so."

"I see. Good thing I've had no trauma."

Okay. Having had untold hours of Celeste's miracle therapy sessions, I couldn't keep from giggling. "Of course, you've had at least one trauma. You were born, right?"

Sanura's face flushed. "Oh!" After a long pause, she said, "Well, good thing that isn't affecting me, not like Lara's insanity."

Oh how I wanted to say, 'Okay. Let's return to the first moment of your body's birth this lifetime,' but I resisted. How could I know whether she had any ill effects from her birth still influencing her life? I couldn't, so I kept quiet. Then, I realized she hadn't yet shown me any pity or even sympathy. She'd mentioned my use of toes, but that was all. That impressed me.

"I'm asking about this because from time to time, some of our people fall victim to these evil Sixth Invaders and their implants. As I've said, in the past, we've terminated them—I believe that's your word for it. However, when and if it ever happens again, perhaps we could bring them to your world and let your people see if they could erase the effects of the implant."

"Sure. But there's only a few of us who know how to do it. Still, we'd try to help them. Oh, about the Galactic Doll thing. Before they killed him, I learned a good deal from their Chief Science Officer. With their species, both males and females have breasts the size of their heads, and their males do most of the nursing of young. Roles are reversed from us humans."

Sanura laughed. "Ours too and others who make up the Federation of Planets."

"According to him, their leader wanted to discredit all ruling men and let women fill those positions, making Earth into another Sixth Invader-like world. They genetically mutated most women of Earth into their erroneous idea of beauty. And they nearly wiped out the males of Central Chicago, too."

"That agrees with what I was able to get from General Blythe."

"And what was the other thing you wanted?" I was more curious about her ambassador mission.

"I'll get right to that point, Molly. Within a few weeks, your petition to join the Federation will be approved. No doubt about that. Then, you must provide one admiral and a proportional amount of Senior Ambassadors. Based on Dimitri's rough population estimates, your Sol Empire will need to provide two Senior Ambassadors, perhaps three. Molly, this position is the most important one in the galaxy for your world—for any world. I've gone on record suggesting that you, Molly, would make a perfect, nay, ideal Senior Ambassador for your Sol Empire. You'd make a powerful representative. From all I've heard, you never stop trying, and you don't take any crap from others. We need determined, strong Senior Ambassadors. You'd be ideal for the position."

I hadn't expected this. "Dara said all Senior Ambassador women must wear those lip disks. But I need to use my teeth to help me do things. That would be a difficult barrier for me. I think I could deal with the earrings, but not the lip disk." There, I had to mention my disability. What a reversal of roles.

"I took that into account and made some inquiries. If you'll take the position, I will arrange for you to always have a personal assistant with you. She'll attend to your needs, freeing you up to focus your attention onto what really matters: your world's representation within the Federation.

Please consider my offer, Molly. You'd make a powerful Senior Ambassador."

"But I know so little. Others are far more knowledgeable about our empire and its affairs."

"Knowledge only goes so far. Trust me when I say determination and will go much, much further. Plus, before you leave the Kanika, I'd love to give you a pair of these incredible stockings. Actually, it's a machine that forms them around your legs and feet. They wear out after about a week of continuous wearing. Your husband will certainly appreciate them when you get back. General Blythe will get some before she leaves. Shall I get you set up for them too? My thank you gift. Goodwill among worlds and peoples."

"Let me talk to her first. Are you sure they won't interfere with using my toes as fingers?"

Again, I heard a chuckle from beneath her golden disk. "Of course, they won't interfere, unless you want a mitten appearance instead of a glove fit. Seriously, Molly, please consider my recommendation to become one of the Sol Empire's Senior Ambassadors."

"I'm trying to set up a Department of Investigations and Justice, to bring illegal corporate actions to light and get justice for the victims. Earth is desperate for such a department. I don't know if I can leave them right now. Dimitri and Natalie depend on me to get the department operational."

"I'll discuss the matter with them again. I've already made my recommendations known to both, but I guess I'll have to be a bit more persuasive." She chuckled, and I suspected she was also smiling.

"What do I do about my family?" I asked, trying to find a way out of this. "Ted is in Galactic Robotics' Department of Research and Development. We've just adopted two teenaged twins who are like Ted and I am. Armless. What about them? I can't just leave them behind on Earth."

"I'd kick you on your bottom if you did that. No, they should move to Bela Prime with you. There, they can have the very best education within the entire Federation, all at no cost to you—a perk of being a Senior Ambassador. I'm sure someone with his credentials can find appropriate employment. Robotics people are in demand on all worlds. Plus, you'd have your own home, luxurious and free. Your only expenses would be personal items, food, and entertainment. Even that personal assistant I promised you would be provided to you at no cost. Okay, I'll see that he and your children also have their own personal assistants, if you wish. Anything to remove the barriers to your agreeing to join us as a Senior Ambassador."

I laughed. She was definitely hard selling me on the idea. "Okay. I'll discuss this with Dimitri, Natalie, and my family. No guarantees, though."

"I'd think less of you if you didn't. You have everything to be gained and nothing to lose, especially your children. Besides, Bela Prime has the best medical care in the Federation."

"Another inducement?" We both laughed. "You'll have to walk me back to my quarters."

That evening, I chatted with Bev. "Sanura wants me to be our Senior Ambassador."

"Yeah, she said as much to the rest of us. Gonna take her up on that?"

I laughed. "Hardly. And not without discussing everything with my family. Did she offer to give you those fancy stocking things?"

"Yeah, I accepted, too. I think Gail will love the feel. We'll be importing many new things. New guns, too. Don't you think so? It's like a whole new world has opened up. Kinda wild, if you ask me. Still, the Sixth Invaders have flown the coop. That's a very good thing," Bev said. "I think Natalie and Dimitri are still counting on you getting the Investigation and Justice Department up and running. Also, how can I see my niece if she's half a galaxy away from me?" We both chuckled.

Chapter 18 Recovery and Actions

Captain L'Grina, a pilot, was the sole survivor of the Sixth Invaders Recon Force 125. Earthlings had killed the other twenty-nine members, forcing her into hiding just as she was about to conquer Earth. Her threat of mutating all humans in other cities had worked. Six of Earth's largest cities had already broadcast their unconditional surrender to her, if only. If only. That had been the ill-fated story of her squad for the last twenty-five years—entirely too many if only's.

Approaching fifty years old and still in her youth, L'Grina had a well-muscled, gray-skinned body with short, jet black hair and matching eyes. By Earth standards, her bosom was gigantic, each breast the size and shape of a soccer ball. Each hand had six fingers, long and dexterous. Now she had one goal: to contact the arriving Sixth Invaders fleet and get rescued. The Earth fleet had located and destroyed her light cruiser. After that, they destroyed all their escape shuttles, forcing the few survivors to travel on foot. Well, she soon stole a two-man shuttle craft.

If only she could contact the fleet and tell them Earth was nearly conquered. Fear. She had created intense fear among Earthlings, so much so that cities surrendered, if only she had the means to accept their surrender. If only that infernal Molly Parkinson hadn't interfered with her plans. If only Admiral Rossi hadn't destroyed her ship. If only their backup sites hadn't been located and destroyed. If only's haunted Captain L'Grina.

She wasn't defeated. Not yet. Using her disguise projector which wrapped her alien body in an image of the average of the surrounding humans, she sneaked into Channel Nine's broadcast facilities in downtown Chicago. Quick blaster shots eliminated the two workers. She stared at the equipment, cursing. If only all her science officers hadn't been killed. After a frustrating hour, she finally opened the proper frequency.

"Captain L'Grina of Recon Force 125 calling Invasion Fleet. Come in please." She repeated this four times before she heard a reply.

"Verification Phrase."

"Tango-Alpha-Morango." She hoped the decades' old code still worked.

"Verified, captain. Please stand by."

"Admiral L'Tara here. What's your status? Over."

L'Grina sighed. It was over. God, how she'd hated this assignment, forced to live amongst these filthy, barbaric humans. "I'm all that's left, but we've nearly conquered Earth. I need rescuing." She related what had happened, including her deceased commander's attempts to mutate the entire population.

"Excellent work, Captain L'Grina. We'll have to draw Earth's space fleet away from the planet. Then, we'll send down a rescue ship. Give us coordinates and stand by."

On a separate channel, she heard Admiral Rossi issuing orders to bring Sol's entire fleet out of hyperspace just beyond the outer limits of the Sol Empire. She glanced at the incoming comm signals sent by the Galactic Entertainment corporation. Soon she grinned. Images of Earth's entire space fleet appeared on the screen. In the distance, she could see her own fleet, three times the size of Earth's puny force. She turned up the sound coming in, while laughing to herself, knowing soon she'd be on board and off this miserable excuse for a planet.

Just as soon as the entire Earth space fleet responded, as promised, a cloaked shuttle landed on the roof of Chicago's Galactic Expansion skyscraper, picking her up. Minutes later, she walked into the admiral's CCC.

"Reporting in, Sir," she saluted Admiral L'Tara.

"Captain L'Grina," the middle-aged admiral said, "you are hereby promoted to commander. While my staff is going over your logs, report to the quartermaster and get your new uniforms and stars. Well done."

Admiral L'Tara was perhaps eighty, but lithe with a no-nonsense attitude. She wasn't attractive, but that mattered not. Her command of the battlefield had earned her this top position. L'Grina saluted; her left arm shot out horizontally, palm down.

"Damn, damn, damn." Admiral L'Tara pounded her powerful fist onto her desk. She spotted the Federation's battleship Kanika dropping out of hyperspace about half way between her armada and the puny Earthling space fleet. "The Federation is meddling in our affairs again. Yes, I see. They're sending along Sol Empire representatives. See if we can identify who they're sending and if Admiral Skaggs is still in charge of the Kanika."

Many scurried to carry out her orders. Soon, they established contact with their spy on the Kanika. Commander L'Grina arrived in time to hear the report.

"Yes, Admiral Skaggs is in command. According to him, the Sol Empire's top Admiral Rossi is arriving, along with Earth's leaders, Dimitri Leonovich, Natalie Mantovo, and Molly Parkinson. Over."

"Dingo's crap! Not her again. We've killed her twice now. That woman won't stay dead. Last time, we put a blaster shot to her head. Admiral, she's real trouble," Commander L'Grina said.

The admiral chuckled. "Watch and learn, Commander. I aim to take out the Kanika this time."

Many smaller ships came and went from the giant docking bay of the Kanika, not just the lone Earth ship. One of these was a routine supply ship. Admiral L'Tara ordered it to be captured, leaving its personnel unharmed. Hours later, six of her soldier volunteers lay on cots next to the unharmed ensigns, while the male science officers attached the head harnesses of the Transference Machines to their heads. Minutes later, the soldiers awoke, finding themselves inside these ensign bodies.

They marched the men to the armory where they donned compact but powerful, explosive vests. After receiving specific orders from Admiral L'Tara, they returned to their small shuttle and departed from the battleship Riga. Soon, they docked in the enormous bay of the Kanika. The six men went their separate ways.

While this happened, the admiral explained the operation to L'Grina. "My soldiers are transporting the bombs to six critical areas. Our on board spy told us where the meeting is being held. One will detonate there, and if our analysis is correct, the explosion will jettison them into space. Let's see your Molly survive that. Others will take out their hyperdrive unit, their combat defense computer, and so on. Then, we'll launch our attack and destroy the helpless Kanika. I'll send a message to the Federation. Never mess with us."

An hour later, Admiral L'Tara's smile vanished as she issued the back-off orders to her fleet. They'd detected the explosions, but something must have gone wrong. The defense computers functioned as did their CCC and hyperdrive. She only picked battles she could win. A fully functional Kanika wasn't one of them.

Later, their spy contacted them, reporting what had happened. "Yeah, they've issued the stand down orders now. That Parkinson woman—she alerted them to the attack somehow. Something about a vision, but the admiral bought her story. Your orders?"

"Lie low. Notify us of any changes. Over and out."

"That Molly Parkinson woman has more lives than a dingo rat," Commander L'Grina said.

"Hum, things are getting more complicated. It's certain the Sol Empire will petition to join the Federation. Our contacts in their Circle of Ambassadors must be advised of the situation. One is on the Kanika now. Use subspace transmission and contact her now," Admiral L'Tara ordered, before muttering, "How I hate dealing with those freaks with their stupidly big heads."

She heard a woman's voice and activated the Universal Translator. "Are you trying to kill me? If Molly Parkinson hadn't gotten wise to the bomb, I'd be dead." The woman bitterly complained.

"Accident. Are the Sol Empire people petitioning to join the Federation?"

"Yes, they are. It's a done deal."

"No way to stop it?"

"Not with your fleet camped on Sol's door."

"Okay. This Parkinson woman—she's been real trouble for us for the last couple of years. We need her out of the way."

"I'm not an assassin. What if she becomes the Senior Ambassador for the Sol Empire? She'll be on Bela Prime. Is that out of the way enough?"

"Ah, perfectly so. Make it happen."

"As long as you continue to supply me with Rubidium chloride and Rubidium silver iodide. We need that biological DNA marker chloride and that iodide for our thin film batteries."

"Of course. You'll get your next shipment on schedule. Just deliver Parkinson to Bela Prime."

"Consider it done. Have to go now." The subspace transmission ended.

"Who was that? Or should I not ask?" Commander L'Grina chuckled.

Admiral L'Tara smiled. "It pays to develop contacts within the Federation. Watch and learn. Now then, let's meet with my staff to decide on a new plan for this Earth. It's nearly surrendered. How can we make that a reality? This way, Commander."

The number of top personnel in the conference room impressed Commander L'Grina. Six senior science officers and a dozen commanders sat around the meeting table. Once more, she outlined what had happened on Earth and how she'd used the genetic mutation agent to force the surrender of a half dozen major cities. She added, "We've made that agent widely available. Because the Earth's ruling corporations are so corrupt, many people are now protesting them and using the agent to mutate those who work for the corporations. We've been covertly aiding them. Most of Earth's population live in fear of us and our attacks. If only we had a way to take advantage of this."

Admiral L'Tara said, "In some ways, the late Commander R'Ina's plan to mutate Earths population into forms similar to ours has merit. As far as our scientists have determined, the mutation changes are dominant and will be inherited by their offspring. Since all women were mutated—by the way, what is the meaning of their term Galactic Doll?"

Commander L'Grina chuckled. She told them about the children's toy.

"Since their women are now Galactic Dolls, all their children, whether male or female will also have that form. So in another short twenty years, their adult men will look like they should, and they can help raise their young like any respectable male ought to. But this latest modification, the one that renders them armless, this bothers me. Our objective is to acquire a source of cheap labor. It seems doing this defeats our goal. Ideas?"

They held discussions for several days. Periodically, their spy reported on events on the Kanika, mostly high-level discussions about joining the Federation. Admiral L'Tara also sent a small recon group to Chicago. Their orders were to remain invisible and to monitor their communications. On the eighth day since the standoff began, the recon group reported some unexpected and startling news.

"These latest mutation victims, the ones who lost their arms, they are all developing telepathy. Yes, men, women, and countless children. Thousands of them. As far as we can tell, those Sol representatives on the Kanika haven't heard this news. It's creating a firestorm of interest among their corporations and their wealthiest people."

One of the science officers spoke up. "This is both good news and awful news. Good in that the galaxy has almost no true telepaths—at least that we've discovered. We could use some in our service. Awful in that these mutants will be able to detect us when we use our Transference Machines to take over one of their human bodies. Admiral, you must address this issue at once."

"How could the mutation have brought this about? That seems the key question," the admiral said. "Something caused it, not just their mutation into Galactic Dolls and their loss of arms. I'll instruct the spy group to acquire samples of the agent. We need to find out what DNA alteration results in telepathy. Will it work on our people? And you're right. We need some of these telepaths working for us. We'll kidnap some and use our implant machines on them to make them loyal assets."

She paused a moment. "Commander L'Grina, you'll take a re-enforced recon group down to Earth while their fleet is still standing by out here. Cloaked of course. Bring us back suitable telepath candidates."

Commander L'Grina cringed. The admiral added, "It's only a short assignment. At least for now. We've still got to come up with an overall plan for Earth. I'm not about to abandon all the hard work Recon Force 125 put in here. Now then, ideas?" she asked her staff.

"I think we should base several disguised units on this world," suggested another commander. "Have them continue to foment protests and riots. Provide the protesters with the mutation agent and instructions on how best to infect an entire building. Let the Earthlings do our dirty work."

Several nodded their agreement. Another said, "Is it possible to infiltrate their leadership like Recon Force 125 did? What do you think, Commander L'Grina?"

"That was beyond dingo's crap." Her body shook involuntarily; she recovered. "Right now, their leadership is a complete mess. Their top corporation leaders are dead both those for the Sol Empire and for Earth. This Dimitri fellow and the woman Natalie are making a power play, setting themselves up as Emperor and Empress. The other corporations don't like that and are protesting it. Perhaps going so far as to not accept them as leaders. There are all kinds of ways we could foment trouble, but if they join the Federation, how do we conquer them?"

Admiral L'Tara said, "Our spy on the Kanika reports these Sol Empire people have agreed to accept about ten million giants and dwarves. This will give us even more openings. You know how dumb the giants are."

A science officer said, "But not the dwarves." That sobered the group for a minute.

Admiral L'Tara said, "Don't worry too much about the dwarves. We handled one who was a Senior Ambassador. She's insane and you know what dwarves do with their insane." She made a throat-cutting gesture.

"As long as your contact can get Parkinson off this world, we stand a chance," Commander L'Grina said. "That woman has caused us no end of grief. It's because of her that Commander R'Ina was killed. Wait a minute. Did you say this insane dwarf Senior Ambassador was on the Kanika?" Several nodded. "Dingo's crap! Parkinson is there, too. Fifty to one Parkinson gets to her and cures her insanity."

"What?" exclaimed Admiral L'Tara. "These Earthling bumpkins can alter our powerful implants?"

"They can erase them, as if they never happened," Commander L'Grina said. "We implanted several dozen of their female soldiers, and every one of them has been completely cured. We checked on them. No trace of the implanted behavior is there. Hell, we implanted their General Blythe, but she acts as though she never was implanted. What's good and bad is that the humans have borrowed our implant technology and have been implanting those they genetically modified to have no arms. And even those have been cured. It's as if none ever had an implant. I tell you some of these Earthlings are damned dangerous, especially that Parkinson woman. If she's on the Kanika, I wouldn't bet a credit that your implanted dwarf Senior Ambassador remains insane."

"Dingo's crap! This is far more serious than I thought," declared Admiral L'Tara. "Okay, part of the landing party's assignment must be to discover how they are undoing our implants and ferret out those who are doing it. We need more bright ideas. Come on, staff. Put your minds to work."

The admiral's Chief Science Officer, who had been reading over the twenty-five-year log Commander L'Grina had brought back, spoke up. "Say, here are interesting details no one has paid much attention to. You were so caught up in that plan to mutate these Earthlings that you missed something. It says here two in three buildings are vacant. Populations migrated to nearby moons and habitable planets."

"Well, yes, we extensively used of a few of these vacant buildings. What of it?" L'Grina barked, annoyed that a *male* dared suggest she and her deceased commander had overlooked an important detail. "They have an extensive workforce that maintains them, though some are scheduled for demolitions. Evidently, that's why they're permitting dwarves and giants to migrate to their world." She glared at him.

"With that many empty dwellings, they must have a very large workforce to maintain them," he continued.

"Their Galactic Housing employs—rather, sponsors is their term for it—more people than any other corporation, including food production. What of it?" Commander L'Grina retorted, her eyes boring into his head.

"Have you looked at these workers and their mental capacities?" he continued, not seeming to be bothered by her hostility. "If I understand your log, when an Earthling finishes schooling, which makes them around eighteen years old or about thirty percent of their average useful lifetime, one of the corporations sponsors them, paying their salary for the duration."

"Yes, that's correct. Pitiful amounts, barely enough to survive on. But then, they have little to waste credits on."

"I'm looking over this Galactic University statistics report on the IQ levels of these high school graduates. Something about using them to pick those to sponsor for further education. What does it mean by the term moron— those whose IQ number is below eighty? I don't know that local idiom."

"Idiot or dun-der-pate in our terms. Imbecile. Stupid. Why?" She bit down on her lip. Her brows rose slightly.

"Ah, that was my initial hunch. Isn't this fascinating? Half of all high school graduates are dun-der-pates, barely able to work. And ninety-nine percent of them are hired to deal with the maintenance of these vacant dwellings." He smiled, satisfied he'd made his point.

Commander L'Grina glared at him, but Admiral L'Tara said, "G'Dun, what *is* your point? I fail to see it."

He raked his hands over his face. "Look, half the population of this Earth planet are idiots, of no worth to society, so they give them the job of what—mowing grass, dusting, and washing windows. No brains or intelligence needed. What do we do with our dun-der-pates?"

"We put them out of their misery," Admiral L'Tara shot back without thinking. She paused and inhaled sharply. "But the Earthlings don't. Instead, they put them to work on menial labor tasks requiring no higher thought patterns. I think I'm beginning to see your point, G'Dun. These morons would solve our shortage of workers in our fuel mining industry."

The admiral grinned at her Chief Science Officer. "It's obvious these Earthlings don't know what to do with their morons. According to our spy on the Kanika, they're eager to import millions of intelligent giants and dwarves, probably to make up for their deficit of intelligent people. With these immigrants moving into these empty dwellings, what will the Earthlings do with the morons they have doing maintenance that's no longer needed? We need to take an entirely new approach. This Galactic Housing corporation—where is it located?"

Commander L'Grina said, "Complicated. There are thousands of local Galactic Housing corporations running the affairs of their areas. Then, in Moscow, the Earth-wide Galactic Housing corporation controls these local ones. Finally, in Chicago, the Sol Empire-wide Galactic Housing corporation runs their many worlds' corporations."

"So we need to focus on this Moscow place or Chicago. All the major actions have taken place in Chicago, right?" L'Grina nodded. "And this is where Dimitri and Natalie want to dwell to run the empire, right?" Again, she nodded. "So it makes sense we should focus on Chicago's Galactic Housing, not just the one in Moscow. Wait, these other worlds. Do they have a dun-der-pate problem?"

Commander L'Grina chuckled. "Hardly. None, as far as I know. All the morons live on Earth. By dingo's crap, I don't know why that's so."

"That's a detail that should have been examined. But it's not your fault, Commander. You were their pilot. Commander R'Ina is the one who didn't do her job."

L'Grina exhaled and relaxed her muscles that had inexplicably tensed up.

"We'll hire millions of these Earthling morons and put them to work mining our fuel," the admiral said.

"You're kidding? Pay them credits?" one of her aides asked.

"Don't be ridiculous. Of course, they'll never be paid. They'll eventually die from the constant exposure to the fuel ore's dust, just as our people do even with the best precautions taken. No, we'll promise them good wages to make the Earthling corporations feel this is a good use of their morons. Once gone from Earth, the corporations won't bother to worry about them. Out of sight, out of mind."

"But we're considered their worst enemies," Commander L'Grina countered. "They'll never agree to send their morons to us."

"Don't be silly. Of course, they wouldn't. We'll need a go-between, a believable one."

"What about using our Senior Ambassador on board the Kanika? Have her work on the deal," suggested an aide.

Admiral L'Tara rubbed her face before replying. "No, she's too valuable to risk on this project. Too many things could go wrong. I won't risk her this way. We must find another believable ally who will act as our go-between. L'Grina, you know what things appeal to these Earthlings or perhaps the dumber ones. We'll need a mockup of what the mines look like. Make them appear highly appealing to these future miners. Of course, the mockups don't have to look at all like our mines. We'll need literature to help support how wonderful it is to work in the mines but keep it darn simple to understand. We're dealing with dun-der-pates, after all. In fact, it will be best if our go-between doesn't know the actual working conditions in our mines. Let them be sold by the appealing literature. More believable. Now who can we get for this critical sales job?"

"What about using one of the Zahra-C local ambassadors?" asked an aide. "We don't want to risk the Senior Ambassador. Besides she has to get that Parkinson woman to Bela Prime. But we have two other local ambassadors in our pay. Why not use one of them? They'll have to send local ambassadors to Earth anyway."

"Brilliant. Yes, we'll use Bahiti and Bennu Bomani. Have our Senior Ambassador on the Kanika make the arrangements. Contact her using the subspace channel right away."

An aide dashed off to do that while another went to the hyperspace relay center to send a message to the Bomani couple on Zahra-C.

"Well, Commander L'Grina, I'm afraid it's back down to Earth for you. I need you to coordinate these efforts, beginning with making the slick sales brochures to entice our new miners."

L'Grina groaned.

"I know it's torture, but it's vitally needed. You know more about this culture than any of us. Besides, I'll send along three light cruisers, triple your original force."

"How long? I was hoping to return home soon. It's been a quarter of a century," she grumbled.

"Couple of years at most. Until we get the situation under control. When you return, I'll see you are given command of a heavy cruiser. How's that?"

Commander L'Grina grinned. "I'll hold you to that. I should brief the three crews."

"Yes, take a couple of days to groove them into the situation around this Chicago place. I've a feeling things will become more chaotic and soon. Just get us those moron workers."

"Hey, make darn sure Parkinson isn't around. If she is, you can count on her messing up your plans," Commander L'Grina added.

Chapter 19 Mom, What a Surprise We Have For You

Bev strapped me in. Time to return home on board our shuttle. Dara and Kiri Sim came with us as the official ambassadors to the Sol Empire from Dian-C. Lara Axe-head, Dara's sister and geneticist, came with us, too. Yes, I held out hope Lara could find a way to regrow our arms, if not undo the other mutations. Also, Senior Ambassador Sanura promised me she'd send two ambassadors from Zahra-C within a week, ostensibly to help the Sol Empire transition to a valuable partner in local spiral arm affairs and learn about the Federation of Planets.

I'd upset Senior Ambassador Sanura by not accepting her offer of her fancy stockings machine or agreeing to become the Sol Empire's Senior Ambassador to the Federation. Still, I didn't probe her mind to find why she was so annoyed with me. We had far more pressing worries. At least, the imminent Sixth Invaders threat evaporated. Their fleet vanished from our sensors and screens. They'd not been seen for the past five days, and I prayed we'd seen the last of them.

"Want a beer or whiskey to dull the jump into hyperspace?" Bev asked me as she guzzled down her third tiny bottle.

I started to say I didn't when the jump happened. My stomach felt as though I had the flu, but that sensation lasted a split second. "Guess not. We just jumped. Right?"

Bev gave me a sheepish grin. "Yeah. I hate them. Home soon. Boy, do we have things to tell everyone. I've got new gun samples, too. I wish you could shoot with me. Maybe Lara can get your arms back. Then, we can go out to the range."

I sighed; I'd forgotten about that loss. My loving Glock. I loved that 9mm and used to be a crack shot with it. Now, it lay at the bottom of my clothes drawer, gun lock in place.

Memories of going to the police shooting range with Frank Wells came to mind. I changed the topic.

"I miss our twins, Isabella and Bernardo. I can't believe we adopted two eighth graders. Nothing like being an instant parent."

"I'll drink to that," Bev declared. "Just a little though. Gotta think of my baby."

Dimitri dropped by. "We'll drop you and the dwarves off at your new condo at Ace Leisure Acres. Tomorrow, we'll hold meetings with everyone. Natalie will let you know the specifics. We've a lot to handle and so little time."

"What are we going to do if the corporations don't accept what we've done?" I asked.

He sighed. "Ram it down their throats. Hell, I don't have any bright ideas yet. This whole thing has become a continuous nightmare. Even Natalie thinks so. We'll figure something out. She'll contact you tomorrow."

With that, he moved over to talk to Admiral Rossi, and I thought about my family. The kids had just gotten enrolled in their new school and had their course schedules, but that was days ago. September had come while I was away, meaning my twins would be in school. I hoped Ted helped them if they needed something with their schoolwork. I could help, but I wasn't good at math or science. This reminded me that Isabella was taking Calculus, but she was only in Eighth Grade. Well, I never did take much math, let alone all the science she was taking. Then again, I'd never studied Bernardo's main subjects either. He wanted to be a chef. Well, I could boil water for tea.

Then, I wondered about the last exchange we'd had just before Armageddon Day when I left to meet with the Federation people. Both teens and Ted showed signs of developing telepathy. Thinking about that occupied my thoughts until my stomach lurched as we came out of hyperspace far above the blue planet with many white clouds below. Home.

***

"I'm home," I called out as I walked through the giant common living room of our new condo. Bev and Major Airla came with me to help the three dwarves with their many crates.

We all got telepathy, mom! That was Isabella in my mind.

Yeah, and some corporations want to pay us a million credits a year to be their corporate telepath. Dad says we can't. Cause we aren't spies. That was Bernardo.

This is so cool, dear. Glad you're home. Kids are a handful. We've all got telepathy—everyone who was exposed to this new armless mutation. We need to talk soon. That was my husband, Ted. "And who are these folks?"

"Ted, Isabella, Bernardo, these are dwarves from Dian-C. Ambassadors Dara and Kiri Sim, and Dara's sister, Lara Axe-head. They are staying with us for a while." Turning to the dwarves, I added, "Sorry, I can't point you out."

"Wow! Real dwarves?" asked Bernardo. I thought his eyes couldn't get any wider.

"Aye, son. But I've never met any unreal dwarves," Kiri said. We adults chuckled.

"Are the giants coming too?" asked Isabella.

"Yes, but later on. Kids, show them to our guest rooms, please. I need to talk to Ted. We'll have a big family chat at supper. I want to know how school is going. Has Ted been helping you?"

"Yes, mom," Isabella said with a look that suggested I'd just asked a stupid question. She perked up. "Come follow us. Lara can stay in the smaller guest room."

"This is way cool, mom," Bernardo said. "Follow us." He and Isabella led the three dwarves off with Airla and Bev following along lugging more shipping crates.

"So Ted, how much of our meeting with the aliens has been broadcast here by GEnt? Does everyone know we're joining this Federation of Planets and that we're accepting ten million immigrants from the giant and dwarf worlds? Does everyone know the Sixth Invaders have fled?"

"They showed all that. Special news coverage every evening, especially since that first day's confrontation and explosions. I thought for sure you were being blown up. Boy, was I ever relieved to see you at that table with all the others the next day. So yes to all those. But we got problems of our own now.

"It's like the kids said. Everyone infected with this new alien mutation agent that makes armless Galactic Dolls has become a telepath. There's thousands of us here in this living complex. You better believe the corporations learned of it. We've been bombarded with employment offers from all the corporations and wealthy individuals, including off-world companies. In fact, it's more like a bidding war for us. Going rate is a million credits per year. But today, some are adding a time limit. 'Sign a contract to work for us for ten years for a million credits a year; then, retire in luxury.' That's the latest gimmick."

"Isabella and Bernardo?" I asked.

"Yes, they've received five offers each, but the high school children received upwards of twenty or more offers. Heck, they're even trying to sign up five-year-old preschool kids, but their contract wouldn't take effect until they finish high school. It's gotten crazy. Everyone wants their own telepath. Honestly, it's scaring me."

"You?" I asked in disbelief. I'd never seen much that frightened Ted.

"Yes. My own Galactic Robotics wants me to sign a ten-year contract as their R&D telepath, spying on others to make sure no one is selling secrets. I'd make ten million credits, though. But I don't want to spy on others, probe minds, that sort of thing. I want to do robotic research and development. Now, they're saying I can't do that because I don't have arms and hands. That I should use the telepathic gift I've been given."

"Oh boy. This is getting wild. With that kind of money, who can resist? Well, some good news. Lara is a geneticist and believes she can use our worldwide DNA database to restore our bodies to what they originally were. Now everyone can have hope for the future."

"Now that *is* good news, but I should warn you. Some are serious about taking these offers. Ten million credits is quite an inducement."

"I best get Lara into a lab somewhere fast. If she can develop a mutation agent that would give me back my arms, I'll take it in a flash. But I can see others might well sign a ten-year contract and get their bodies restored after that when they retire with ten million in their pockets. Crap. This isn't a good situation at all."

Ted chuckled. "It'll only get worse. The mutation agent is widely available. Plus, these traits are dominant. Some want to breed telepaths while others are offering contracts to normal people to get mutated into an armless Galactic Doll telepath and work for ten years making a fortune. Now, if anyone can have their bodies restored, this could become a widespread practice. Good lord. Become a helpless telepath Galactic Doll and be a corporate spy for ten years, receive your ten million credits, and get your body restored."

"I see what you mean. Nevertheless, I want Lara to see if she can restore us."

"Hey, don't get me wrong, dear. I'll jump at the chance to get my body back to what it should be. But can we convince the kids? Ten million credits is one hell of an inducement," Ted said. "By the way, our whole gang is coming over to welcome you back. They're bringing lunch, compliments of Gail, whose bringing Bev's favorites. Oh, and there's a bunch of meetings scheduled for you and the others tomorrow. I sent the list to your computer and phone, dear."

Later that afternoon and after everyone had met the dwarves, Eve, Lara, and the CEO of our local Galactic Medicine left to show Lara the DNA database and the genetics research facilities here in Chicago. Lara's optimism over finding a cure was catching.

Dimitri and Natalie dropped by and picked up the Sim ambassadors, so finally I had time to sit down with my family and chat. Of course, telepathy and the many lucrative offers became the major topic. Isabella began, but not without sharing something silently with her brother.

"Mom, what do you think about Galactic Expansion's job offer?" She pushed a document over the table to me. "They're offering me two different positions. Each is a ten-year contract. Well, they offered me a third, but I turned that one down right way."

"What did they want you to do that you turned down?" I asked, curious to learn what she rejected.

"Ten million credits to give them four babies. Like no way. If I have babies, they are mine. I'm not about to give my babies away to a corporation. Jeesh. What are they thinking?"

I smiled, pleased that she had common sense.

"They'll give me ten million credits for ten years working on an exploration or first contact ship. They want me to help their linguists work out the language of the people on the newly discovered worlds. Mental thoughts, we've discovered, are independent of language. They're concepts. Mr. James—he's the recruiter—thinks I'd be a natural at it. Plus, I can continue my astronomy studies on board the space exploration ships. So in ten years, why, I'd have my high school diploma and college degrees too. Everything is online these days. So it'd be easy to study on a spaceship—just as easy as here. I really like this offer, cause when I get my degrees, I'll have ten million credits in my bank account, so I'd be able to do what I want. Besides, maybe Lara Axe-head will have a cure for us by then. Anyway, I really like this one because I'd get to do something valuable. Mr. James says the hardest part of discovering a new world with inhabitants on it is learning their language—at least enough to communicate basic ideas. So I'd be really valuable, don't you think so, mom?"

Whew, she wound down. She was certainly an excited thirteen-year-old. "Well, Celeste would agree with you," I said, and watched her grin widen. I'd guessed right. She'd already discussed this with Celeste who, via therapy, had recovered all her last lifetime training in anthropology and xenology.

"Yes, she does. She says being able to pick up a stranger's thoughts and tie them to their local words would be invaluable in building their basic vocabulary. She said that since she earned three doctorates while living on the remote atoll, she didn't see why I couldn't earn mine on board a spaceship. Besides, I'd be rich, mom, not like you and dad, who can barely pay the rent."

Ouch. Well, like most, my stipend, didn't cover all my monthly expenses, particularly now that we had a family. Rather than commit, I wisely asked, "And the other offer?"

"Oh yeah. Well, Galactic Expansion has offered me a ten-year position overseeing their various business dealings. Ten million too, but I'd be able to live here at home and go to school—well mostly, except when they needed me at meetings and such things. I kind of figured I'd be a glorified spy. I'm not sure I like being a spy so much. And I'd be living here. Don't get me wrong, mom, dad. I love it here, and I'd miss you so much if I left, but you know, it's not like being an adult and away from home."

"But you're only thirteen, Isabella," I argued, "and we've only been in this place a few weeks. I see your point. On the spaceship, you'd be a grownup."

Isabella flushed. "Well, yes. We're going to be fourteen soon, so we're almost adults anyway. The point is either way, in ten years, I'd be independently wealthy, mom. I could buy a mansion, hire caretakers, or buy anything I wanted."

"But what about boyfriends? Finding the love of your life?" I tried another approach. I'd only gotten a "family" weeks ago and didn't relish losing them so soon.

Isabella's face reddened, and her jaw clenched. I hit a nerve I didn't know was exposed.

She sighed. "Until today and Lara, it's like who'll want to marry me? No arms makes life a challenge. Worse, my babies are going to be like me, even if they're boys. No normal guy'll want anything to do with me. So spending ten years on a spaceship isn't going to make any difference that way. But I see your point. Staying here, taking that second offer—that would allow me to meet more boys that are like us, like Bernardo. Maybe that might work—like you and dad. But you have to admit, mom, boyfriend possibilities for me are limited, almost non-existent. So staying here for that reason doesn't seem all that smart, does it?"

She's clever. "Well, I admit finding a boyfriend or girlfriend like Bernardo could be difficult."

"Exactly, mom. So you see why I'm leaning toward being a space explorer linguist for ten years. Maybe when I got back, someone will have invented a way to regrow our arms. I know I'd be gone for ten years, but I'd be doing something very valuable. Celeste thinks so, too. When I got back, I could help everyone financially."

"But when I lost my arms on that atoll, I had Ted to help me. You'll be on your own on a spaceship filled with older adults. They won't want to help you. They have their jobs to do. You'll be on your own."

"I have to be independent. You keep telling me and everyone that. Well, I aim to be independent, too. Besides, as Lara said, when they restore our bodies back to the way they were, we're likely to lose our telepathy. So I'd have my ten million credits and my college degrees when I got back and got my body restored."

"But what if she can restore our bodies, say by next month, honey, then you'd not have to spend ten more years like this? Surely, you don't love not having arms."

She twisted at her waist. "Well, no, of course not, but then I might not have telepathy next month and wouldn't have tons of money coming in. Aunt Deanna says having lots of credits is a very good thing because it allows you to be free and independent and follow your own goals, not some corporation's notions. She should know. She's a billionaire."

Isabella had covered her bases well, probably having bounced arguments off Ted while I was gone. Wisely, he said nothing at all. This was between me and our daughter. "Well, what about Bernardo? You still want to become a chef, right?"

Isabella nodded toward Bernardo. "Well, yes. Think what I can do with ten million credits. I can buy my own restaurant, mom. I'd only be twenty-three when done. With all that money, I can make my dream come true. They made me similar offers, too. I'm not about to help women make babies. That's just not right at all. Isabella and I would be on different exploration ships. Honestly, mom, I can't see any downside helping them learn a new people's language. We're kind of already multilingual anyway. Spanish and English. There's gotta be a lot of inhabited worlds out there waiting to be discovered. Look, you've just met a whole bunch of advanced worlds we didn't know existed a month ago. So there must be more for us to discover."

He grinned, "I won't have to worry about finding a girlfriend, not on a spaceship. If I stay here, it keeps bothering me. Face it. I look like a freak. If that wasn't bad enough, I've no arms. No normal girl will want anything to do with me. Besides, I wouldn't want a normal girlfriend anyway. They say my genes are dominant, so any babies we'd have would look like me. That's enough to keep everyone away from me."

Bernardo sighed. "Besides, I'm not smart like Isabella. So getting ten million credits means everything to me. I can get my own restaurant. Otherwise, being a chef isn't too likely. After all, mom, be honest. How many armless chefs do you know? This is the only way I can see to making my dream come true. Well, until today when Lara hinted she might be able to find a way to restore us. If that happened—which would be the greatest—then I'd have to work hard to become a good chef. Having my own place would have to wait years and years until I could afford it. But she can't promise me when a cure would be ready. If it's years, why, I'd be better off taking this exploration ship linguist job. I can count on having ten million in the bank in ten years. But I can't count on anything if I get the cure soon. My future is bleak if I don't get the ten million credits. She can get good jobs and earn lots, but I won't make much until I get my own restaurant."

I looked at Ted. He shrugged his shoulders. *Heard all this,* he sent me. *Told them it was up to you, not me.*

I sent back, *So you're making me the dictator?*

Ted grinned sheepishly.

I asked, "So kids, if you sign these contracts, when do you start working for Galactic Expansion?"

Isabella said, "As soon as possible. Like right away."

"You realize the corporations are corrupt? I wouldn't put it past them to hold onto your ten million credits until you return home after ten years. And on your way back, you accidentally fall out of an airlock."

Bernardo's eyes opened wide. "You think they'd murder us to keep from paying up?"

"Yes, I certainly do. It's a simple thing to arrange for a fatal accident, drastically cheaper than paying you both ten million credits. Look what GD ordered me to do to General Clay Homes, the man behind making us clones. They tried to make me terminate him without even giving him a trial, even kill his wife, who was innocent of everything. If you kids are determined to do this, we need safeguards built into the contracts."

"Like what?" asked Isabella.

"Like depositing your wages into an account here on Earth each month, an account we all have access to. That way, there's no reason to kill you at the end of the ten years, since they've already paid the money. Even if they kill one of you, we have the money and can give it to the survivor. I don't know. Maybe I can think of more safeguards. Look, if a deal sounds too good to be true, it probably is, what with the rampant corruption in the ruling corporations."

Ted backed me up. "Molly's right, kids. Early this year, Molly was temporary CEO of Galactic Defense, charged with rooting out the corruption. I helped with all the computer probes. In those four months, we uncovered almost two hundred illegal, corrupt acts. They were more, but the Sixth Invaders who controlled Galactic Expansion thought we were getting too close and ended her term. So yes, kids, mom's right. Expect and plan for corruption, lies, and crimes from the ruling corporations. If you want to go through with this, give us time to find some lawyers and work out safeguards for you. Okay?"

They agreed and headed off to work on their homework while Ted and I discussed their wishes.

"Glad you're back. They've bombarded me with these offers, questions, and ideas for the past week. Honestly, Bernardo's got a valid point. Assume Lara can restore arms soon. He's got a long road ahead to first learn to be a good chef and then to save enough to afford his own restaurant. It's also hard to argue with Isabella. She's awfully sharp. They'd be doing good, valuable work. I asked Celeste about it."

"So with safeguards, you're fine with two thirteen-year-olds taking off on exploration spaceships and for ten years?" I asked.

"I'm for what's in their best interests, dear. Bernardo's life could be formed by having the ten million credits in his bank account. My hunch is that Lara will be successful. We'll have our original bodies back but lose our telepathic skills. That's okay with me. I'll take the Galactic Robotic's offer, for now, spying or whatever they want. We'll salt the money away for the future. Then, if I lose my telepathic skills, no big deal. I'll go back to my R&D work, which I love. What do you think?"

I sighed. "Okay then. We best find a lawyer and get safeguards built into their contracts. I don't want the corporation killing them to avoid paying them when their tour of duty is up."

I'd only had these kids a short time, but I already loved being a mother. Or perhaps having two teens not too far from my own age appealed to me. Well, once I had my baby daughter, then I'd know better what I was feeling.

Chapter 20 The Meeting

The following morning, General Bev again escorted me to the top-secret meeting in an abandoned warehouse. Even though the Sixth Invaders had abandoned their plans for Earth's conquest, we took no chances. This time, the two dwarven ambassadors attended, along with Lara, who refused to leave my side. Dimitri, Natalie, Admiral Rossi, Major Airla, and many others were already there, along with many of our local corporate CEOs. I spotted Helen Hugo, who waved at me. Her husband, Casper, now had telepathy and had just gotten financing for three additional cruisers.

The front wall held hundreds of giant screens, each displaying six separate feeds from other local and world CEOs of the major ruling corporations. I couldn't even estimate how much work it took to set up this conference. Someone had pasted labels beneath each giant screen so we knew their location and who they were. Most of the participants were CEOs of Galactic Defense and Galactic Expansion, the two largest corporations and the most powerful ones.

However, I noticed three other Sol Empire-wide CEOs were with us, including Galactic Medicine, Galactic University, and Galactic Housing. Why were these lesser corporations here? The Sixth Invaders mostly ignored these smaller corporations. True, many of their men had been mutated into transgendered men along with the rest of us, and many women had stepped up to fill their abandoned positions. So I wasn't surprised to see these three female CEOs, but why they were here?

I found the first part of the meeting boring. Admiral Rossi, Dimitri, and Natalie went over the results of our meeting on the Kanika, outlining the benefits of joining the Federation of Planets. They covered its cost and obligations, too. Then, they reviewed the spiral arms and the locations of the other known civilizations, giving everyone a true sense we weren't the only space faring civilization around. Humbling, or so I hoped.

Next, they explained the local ambassador concept and introduced Dara and Kiri Sim, the Dian-C ambassadors to the Sol Empire. At last, they told everyone about accepting ten million immigrants from the giant and dwarf worlds—five million each.

Dimitri said, "So with these new arrivals, we must rethink how we choose and pay our workers. These new arrivals must receive fair pay. That's the most significant law we must follow. I've sent you a copy of the fair market pay. It lists the jobs and the minimum pay we must provide. We can always pay more. An accompanying list outlines basic goods and raw materials and the minimum price for them. Again, we must pay these minimum amounts, but we can charge more if desired. The idea is to provide a standard pay scale and cost of goods and services scale across the entire Federation of Planets. This facilitates commerce. Expect new trade routes and partners to begin within a month. We're in for a *huge* boom to our economy."

"But what about the Sixth Invaders?" asked the LA GD CEO, who had already "surrendered" to them.

"They're gone," Natalie said. "If they should appear again, the Federation will send their entire space armada to wipe out every last Sixth Invader spaceship. I think we've seen the last of those fiends."

I wanted to share her optimism, but...

The CEO from LA said, "While you were gone, ostensibly saving us from the Sixth Invaders and joining this Federation, the rest of us here on Earth and off-world have been meeting to work out just how Earth and the Sol Empire will be run, to be ruled. But before we get into that, there have been startling developments while you were away that must be addressed first. So I want you to allow CEO Mildred Winks of Galactic Medicine to speak."

I once met her deceased husband, who was the CEO before the alien mutation struck. Unwilling to live as a male Doll, he killed himself. She stepped up to run this vital organization. So I knew she was nearly fifty, but looked barely twenty-five, compliments of the mutation.

"Hello, everyone. I hate to be the bearer of bad news, but it falls to me to make this officially known throughout the empire. We've had time to study these genetic mutations. Thanks to Mrs. Parkinson, we know the Sixth Invaders' goal was to make our bodies look more like theirs. But women should look like Dolls. So we have a why behind the Galactic Doll phenomenon. However, a side effect has now been completely verified. It is no longer speculation, but a fact."

A hush fell over the room, but I had a hunch what she was about to say.

"Most women on Earth have been mutated. Any children she has will inherit her genes. That is, her daughter's body will also be a Galactic Doll, so don't be surprised to see young infants learning to walk having to wear tall heels. But it's much worse. The entire next generation of children, both boys and girls, will also have the Doll form. We are working with pediatricians and podiatrists to see if the malformed high arches of the babies can be corrected so they can walk without wearing the tall heels. There is hope this will be the case."

She inhaled before continuing. "As you know, the aliens created a corrected mutation agent that left the Doll also armless. It's confirmed; any child from such men and women will also be armless Dolls. A mutated male plus normal woman equals an armless Doll of either gender and vice versa. Today, those who've suffered this latest, nightmare mutation have been moved to Chicago and are under the oversight of Mrs. Parkinson and her group. It doesn't matter who marries one of these victims, male or female, their offspring will be armless Dolls. This genetic mutation is dominant. I wish I had better news. As of today, we've proven what many of you speculated. It's now fact."

Mildred exhaled slowly. "That means from this point forward, no one who has been genetically mutated may migrate from Earth to any other Sol Empire world. We must keep this awful mutation contained here on Earth. In light of the fact our next generation of men will be Galactic Dolls, it is fortuitous we're accepting new immigrants from the giants and dwarven worlds. Of course, we don't know if humans can mate with these newcomers."

The CEO from Pylon spoke up. Considering the time delay of five minutes, I suspected he and Mildred had timed her speech. "I want to re-enforce what CEO Winks has just said. No Galactic Doll with or without arms, male or female, may immigrate to any world or moon, whether married to a local off-world man or woman. The rest of the Sol Empire insists that this mutation is confined to Earth and Earth alone. No exceptions."

The CEO of Galactic University, Mrs. Henklebottom, spoke next. Again, considering the smooth the transition from Pylon, they had to have prearranged this. She too looked twenty-five, but probably was many years older.

"First, with the soon to be arriving aliens, the giants and the dwarves, it's crucial we learn to speak their languages. Yes, they have translator devices, just as we do. However, I'm told they are pushing the immigrants to learn our language as much as they can before arriving on Earth. We should do likewise. Thus, all major universities will offer basic language courses in their two languages. I encourage everyone who may come in contact with our new immigrants to learn as much of their languages as possible. Let's make friends as soon as they land."

She cleared her throat. "This brings us to the latest discovery and most unexpected situation ever. There has been an unpredicted side-effect to the corrected alien mutation agent that leaves the Dolls armless. Telepathy. Yes, you heard me. Every one of these mutants has developed telepathy. They can send and receive thoughts; even the infants are doing this. Of course, they just want to be fed."

Several chuckled before she continued. "This is monumentally important. A true telepath is extremely rare. In fact, until now, I've never known one to exist. Today, Earth has almost two thousand of them, from infants to adults, though most are children. As many of you already know, every corporation and many wealthy are trying to lock in the services of these vital telepaths. This past week has seen utter chaos around these individuals. We CEOs have reached some agreements. To be fair, the minimum going rate for a telepath will be one million credits per year. That gives everyone a solid notion of the incredible worth and value of these special people.

"Contracts for their employment are to be one year, five years, or ten years, depending on the needs of the host. No one may sign up a telepath for a longer duration. After the elapsed time is up, both parties may agree to another contract, if they so choose. Their salary will be deposited monthly into their bank accounts, each of which must have a secondary signatory, in case of the death of the telepath. This precaution is mandatory. Given the extensive corruption within several corporations, we are guarding against the corporation killing off the telepath when the contract is up and before paying them. Further, it is now a high crime to knowingly harm a telepath, physically or mentally. These are rare, highly valuable people, even if they are mostly helpless. We will not stand for any abuse of our telepaths."

She continued. "Galactic University has prepared standard contracts for hiring telepaths. These will be emailed to you today. When anyone hires a telepath, a signed copy of this contract must be sent to Galactic University. We will be the repository of these documents. Anyone is free to access them and verify they are being upheld by both parties. Finally, telepaths may travel off-world. The Doll travel ban does not apply to hired telepaths, who will return to Earth upon termination of their contract.

"Next, new telepaths. Several corporations expressed an interest in making their own telepath Dolls. The alien revised mutation agent is widely available at your local med centers and through GMed. So obviously, additional telepaths can be made. To prevent criminal abuse, Galactic University has prepared another contract for those wishing to undergo the mutation and become a telepath. They must be eighteen or older to sign. Further, if they have a sponsor who wishes them to undertake this mutation, the standard hiring contract must also be submitted, signed by both parties, and the duration must be for ten years with at least ten million credits remuneration. Those signing the personal contract also must sign off that they understand any children they have after being mutated will also inherit their mutation.

"These changes impact our off-world corporations and the wealthy. Many complained all the currently eligible telepaths will have signed contracts before they get an opportunity to meet with them and present their offers. Thus, we anticipate others being desirous of undergoing this radical mutation to become a telepath and earn these fabulous wages. We've installed safeguards for their protection. At this time, I'm turning the meeting over to Galactic Housing's CEO, Mrs. Steel."

Another youthful looking Galactic Doll rose and stood before the broadcasting system. I'd never met her and wondered what Galactic Housing wanted from this meeting.

"Greetings. Thank you for allowing me to address everyone today. First, I want to share some shocking news that probably none of you knew about before today. It's common knowledge that two of three buildings in most cities are vacant. For centuries, Galactic Housing's guidelines have been to keep as many of these in good repair as possible and to demolish only when repairs aren't feasible. With so much housing available, our new immigrants will have their choice. But this isn't the shocking news.

"Rather, it is the workforce we sponsor. These are the personnel who keep the grounds and buildings in good repair and clean. It doesn't take a rocket scientist to mow a lawn or scrub a floor or install a new roof. In fact, over one-half of all high school seniors end up being sponsored by Galactic Housing. Among all corporations, we choose last and for a good reason. What few know is the IQ level of those on Earth has been dropping steadily over the last two centuries. Currently, one-half of those graduating high school function at the moron level. These people are not capable of doing much in our technical society.

"But they can mow lawns and mop floors. Galactic Housing hires half Earth's workforce. This situation doesn't exist on the other worlds and moons of the empire. It's unique to Earth. Until now, the slow increase of morons hasn't been a problem because as buildings age, they need more upkeep. Hence, more workers are needed.

"With the arrival of millions of new able bodied workers, many dwellings will become occupied once more, lowering the need for these lowest paid, unskilled workers. We've discussed what to do with the millions, who have such pitiful IQs. Termination seems inhumane. Two days ago, a wonderful solution appeared.

"Actually, our new ambassadors from Zahra-C contacted us. It seems another world, Felt-D, desperately needs unskilled workers to do routine maintenance work. Their corporations will pay our workers double wages if they immigrate to Felt-D and work for them. I am sending along a brochure that describes the world and job offer. We're limiting applicants to only those who work for Galactic Housing. Felt-D officials don't want high IQ people because they would find the menial work utterly boring. So during the coming months, Galactic Housing will cull its sponsored personnel, making them aware of this incredible offer. Those who wish to take advantage of it will be transported to Felt-D via that world's deep space transports.

"Our new ambassadors suggested that ten million workers are urgently needed. We will try to meet those numbers as quickly as possible.

"It occurred to me to ask why the IQ level of Earth's people has been in such a steady decline during the last two hundred years. I've no theory, but I posed this question to Galactic University. They will investigate, so expect a report possibly early next year. Thank you."

She returned to her seat. From Kyle and Hank, I knew the IQ levels were dropping. Rather, the sheer numbers of low IQ people shocked me. My deceased father worked for Galactic Housing. This could only mean he was a low IQ person. Wham. It hit me. Now I understood so much more about my father and his behavior and overall apathy. He seemed to grasp things so incredibly slowly, particularly whenever I explained my PI mysteries to him. But I didn't love him any less.

CEO Mildred from Galactic Medicine rose again. "My last topic is controversial. That those sent to our assisted living homes are given a drug that brings on dementia has become widely known. Further, if they are given any of the various Galactic Doll genetic mutation formulas, their bodies not only take on the appropriate Doll form, but their biological age clock is reset to about age twenty-five. Many protested this treatment. Many wish us to give those aged sixty and older the Galactic Doll mutation formula so that their parents or loved ones could rejuvenate and continue to live. We've given this serious thought and reached a conclusion which has already been accepted by many local Earth corporations and which we will now follow.

"Low IQ people will not be given the rejuvenation Galactic Doll formula. Already they have lived a near non-productive life. There's no valid reason to extend it. Thus, that half of Earth's population will continue to be retired at sixty and terminated as their health dictates."

I noticed she hedged here. Exactly what determined their T-days? Would they be given the dementia-causing drug? I didn't like what she was saying. Under her plan, my dad wouldn't be eligible to be rejuvenated although he was a kind, loving man and father. His IQ was too low.

"All others will be given a choice when they reach age sixty. If they wish to be rejuvenated and have their bodies become youthful Dolls, then those wishes will be honored. But under no circumstances will they be administered the dementia-causing drug. Henceforth, Galactic Medicine will give the older higher IQ people their choice to be rejuvenated or not. This change of policy should satisfy all those who were protesting the corporations. Thank you." She sat.

Honestly, I felt as though I was the dummy. How could I have lived twenty-three years and never known half of our population were morons and that the only jobs they could do were maintaining and cleaning abandoned buildings? I felt stupid but then I realized no one else had been aware of these facts either. Many facets of our society remained invisible to all, including those with doctorate degrees.

That got me wondering. Why would another world want to hire these kinds of people and at double their current wages? I had a gnawing sense that something didn't add up. Perhaps my suspicious, untrusting PI attitude had raised its head again. I promised myself I'd look into this later on, But now the entire focus of the meeting changed. Rulership of Earth and the Sol Empire came to the fore.

Eve's thoughts appeared in my mind. *Sis, we need to talk about this telepathy thing and your adopted children. Drop by our place after you're done with the meeting.*

Chapter 21 Rulership Changes

The Galactic Expansion corporation had been in the leadership position for at least two centuries. That's what I recalled from my high school history book. The Sixth Invaders' body swaps into the CEOs of the Sol Empire-wide GPan and GD had been a clever move. From those positions, they controlled or at least oversaw the activities of all other major corporations—a brilliant move. Controlling Galactic Defense ensured their success. Now the hundreds of personnel who made up the empire-wide GPan and GD corporations were dead.

Into that vacuum stepped the Earth-wide GPan and GD corporation officials based in Moscow. And now they were dead, too, except for Dimitri and Natalie who had stepped up to be the Sol Empire rulers, establishing themselves as Emperor and Empress and leading the successful war against these Sixth Invaders. Okay, they brought us into the Federation of Planets, learned of many other alien space-faring races even more advanced than ours, and even arranged for the immigration of very strong aliens, the giants and dwarves.

Would the corporations accept Dimitri's power grab now that the threat was over? As far as I was concerned, it was a grab, a justified one, but a grab nonetheless. I say justified because in war there can only be one leader. A group doesn't win wars, but bickers among themselves. Well, I was supposed to be setting up their Department of Investigations and Justice, but I had doubts I'd be doing this after the meeting.

While the Sol Empire had two dozen official members, Brussels, Tau Ceti, and Pylon, Epsilon Eridani, were the two most populous worlds besides Earth. In fact, during the last two centuries, half of Earth's original population immigrated to these new worlds. There were several smaller moons and independent space stations in the empire, but those two had the largest populations, each approaching two to three billion people. Thus, I wasn't too surprised to see their CEOs ushering in the next phase of this meeting.

"I'm Phil Carlson, CEO GPan Pylon, Epsilon Eridani. I'm here on Brussels, Tau Ceti."

I saw a tall man wearing a gray business suit, otherwise indistinguishable from any other CEO. He had blond hair and blue eyes. Standing beside him was another wearing a bluish business suit. He had black hair and a small mustache. The other man spoke next.

"I'm Jose Ricardo, CEO GPan, Brussels. Together, we represent the bulk of the Sol Empire. Yes, we have been in constant communication with the other partners, such as the Ceres Colony. First, we would like to express our sincere thanks to Dimitri Leonovich and Natalie Mantovo for stepping up and defending the empire from the Sixth Invaders, for bringing us into this new Federation of Planets, for bringing new peoples into our civilization, and for forging alliances with those nearby space faring civilizations." He and many others on the wall monitors politely applauded.

"However, we're now entering a new era of peace, cooperation, and expansion—some say unheard of expansion, what with all these new civilizations and technology that can be shared. Traditionally, Galactic Expansion has always coordinated and led our empire as we entered the space travel age. As any businessman can tell you, expansion is the key to prosperity. No company or individual can long survive if they are staying the same or shrinking. Staying the same is akin to balancing on the point of a needle, for soon you slip off.

"Expansion is the grease of prosperity. We've seen what can happen when all power or shall we say too much power is placed in the hands of one or two men, namely the late Mr. Armstrong and Mr. Hardy of Chicago's Galactic Expansion and Galactic Defense. The Sixth Invaders took over their bodies and ran our empire for close to twenty years. We cannot let this happen again. Changes must be made.

"We've discussed their idea of having an Emperor and Empress running the Sol Empire, but putting all power into two people is setting up another Armstrong and Hardy scenario. All the worldwide major corporations agree on this point. We cannot have such a power arrangement. It's far too risky. With this body swapping technology, if all power is concentrated in one or two people, then anyone could take control.

"We've also seen what can happen if all power resides on only one world in our empire. We on Brussels, those on Pylon, and all the others have sat by helplessly watching Earth's two top corporations become puppets of the Sixth Invaders. Folks on Ceres saw what was happening, but had no authority to do anything about it. Twenty-three members watched Earth crumble, powerless to avert it. That can't be allowed to happen again.

"To that end, we're forming new ruling groups. First, we're establishing a Council of the Senate, charged with making laws and policies. Each world's top corporations will provide two senators each, so the group will consist of forty-eight members. Yes, Galactic Expansion is giving up its topmost ruling position. We must if we're to avoid the mistakes of the past. Each senator will serve a six-year term. The top corporations of each world will hold elections for their two senators. This gives the smaller moons an *equal* say in the running of our empire.

"Next, we're establishing the Council of Admirals and Generals. Each member world elects one of their spacer admirals and one of their grounder generals to this council. Their terms will be for ten years. These forty-eight admirals and generals will enforce the laws of the empire as set forth by the Council of the Senate.

"Each of these two groups will choose a president who will conduct their meetings and affairs. Should we ever again face a conflict, these presidents will be the two leaders to lead us forth, just as Dimitri and Natalie have today. However, we need to preserve continuity. So we are appointing Admiral Rossi to the Council of the Admirals and Generals. We also appoint him as its first president. Thus, he'll wield total command of our space fleet, just as he has today.

"Finally, we recognize that injustices have occurred in the past and that there has been some corporate corruption. Thus, we see the need for a third body, the Council for Investigations and Justice. Each member world will choose a Senior Investigator and a Senior Judge to serve on this council, which will ferret out corruption and crimes, and handle the justice aspect. The older Galaxy Detective Squad's members will become part of the investigation personnel of this new group. We recognize Dimitri and Natalie's efforts to man up a similar organization. Thus, initially, we anticipate using those existing members, while the member worlds elect their personnel.

"Where to house these three new groups has been hotly debated for many days. It comes down to existing lines of communication. There's no argument. Chicago has been the seat of the empire-wide corporations since their founding over two centuries ago. Currently, those buildings with their infrastructure are vacant. So it makes sense to set up these councils there. The Council of the Senate will occupy the upper floors of the Chicago Galactic Expansion skyscraper while the Council of Admirals and Generals will occupy the upper floors of the Chicago Galactic Defense skyscraper. We've made arrangements for the Council for Investigations and Justice to be located in the vacant Monroe building, which is where Dimitri's new Investigations and Justice group is located. We're maintaining continuity as much as possible.

"Earth will need to create new Earth-wide GPan and GD corporations, which were in Moscow before they moved to Chicago and were destroyed. Presumably, those two new corporations will also be in Moscow, along with the nearly two dozen other major Earth-wide corporations.

"Next, the Sol Empire must choose ambassadors to all these new worlds and two Senior Ambassadors to go to Bela Prime. We need to send off local ambassadors to Azizi-C, Dian-C, Liatos-D, and Zahra-C within the next couple weeks. Husband and wife pairs are suggested, but not mandatory. It is wise to send male and female ambassadors, for obvious reasons. Ordinarily, the Council of the Senate would elect these ambassadors, but since they aren't operational yet, we've made an executive decision. Earth will choose two ambassadors to Bela Prime and the Federation of Planets. Pylon will pick two local ambassadors to Dian-C, while Brussels will elect a pair for Azizi-C. The minor worlds will choose two pairs, one for Liatos-D and Zahra-C.

"Earthlings, we've heard from Zahra-C's Senior Ambassador Sanura Fenuku, She strongly advised us that Mrs. Molly Parkinson should be one of the Senior Ambassadors from the Sol Empire. Take her suggestion seriously. At this time, I want to turn the meeting over to Mr. Leonard Hadder, the CEO of LA's GPan."

Our eyes glanced over the wall of monitors until we found his image. Someone had pasted a label below the images on the giant screen, one of which was the LA feed. Crap. Mr. Hadder sent his unconditional surrender to the Sixth Invaders, just before we departed Earth to meet with the Kanika. A spineless traitor now had power.

"Welcome everyone and to our returning saviors Dimitri Leonovich and Natalie Mantovo." Again, polite clapping resulted.

He made no mention of me or my role. Ah well, just as good. I still couldn't figure out why Sanura wanted me on Bela Prime so badly. She must have called these people about me. Why? Distracted, I put my attention back on what he was saying, hoping I hadn't missed too much.

"... we want her as our Senior Ambassador, but we should ask Mrs. Parkinson if she wishes that appointment. In any case, one of our Senior Ambassadors should be one of our new telepaths. That is a must; all CEOs agree on that point. We'd suggest General Blythe be appointed to be our general on the Council, along with Admiral Rossi. We need two senators, an investigator, and judge. Because we recognize the invaluable work of Dimitri and Natalie, we wish to offer them their choice of these top positions. Since you both have been instrumental in bringing us into the Federation universe and opening these new empires to us, having you both as our senators makes sense. However, we must elect someone to the unfilled positions soon. So you three, think over our offer. Or if you prefer, you could return to Moscow and reestablish the Earth-wide GPan and GD corporations. We'll be in touch with you tomorrow. Time is of the essence."

With that, the meeting ended. Abruptly. By some predetermined cue, all the monitors went black within a few seconds of each other. Considering the time delay, this had to be planned beforehand. I glanced at Bev.

"No way am I going to be the political pawn general on their silly council. Find another general," my sister said.

I smiled and saw Natalie and Dimitri's faces as they turned towards me. Ghastly pale.

He walked up to me and said, "Stabbed in the back. Looks like politics haven't taken a breather while we were gone."

Natalie said, "I was afraid something like this would happen when we left with Admiral Rossi. It stinks. After we just saved the whole damn Sol Empire, this is the thanks we get."

Casper and CEO Helen Hugo joined us. Casper said, "It's been brewing since the moment you announced you were going to be the emperor and empress. I told Helen the CEOs wouldn't stand having their power usurped."

Helen added, "But I told Casper they would compromise a little. After all, we're here and free only because of your actions. They had to reach a middle ground or risk further popular uprisings such as the protests over killing anyone over age sixty. I've never seen so many men absolutely terrified as I did around Armageddon Day. After that, I had thought they'd confiscate and lock up all that awful new mutation agent."

Casper laughed. "Fat chance of that ever happening. As far as I can tell monitoring their overall finances, the corporations doubled their orders for more. Soon, it'll be available in any corporation office."

"Good lord," I said. "Why?"

Casper smiled. "Telepaths. Everyone wants their own telepath. Honestly, Molly, I've never seen such a rush to acquire any kind of item as they are these people. They've tried to recruit me a dozen times. I keep telling them I'm working for Helen and no one else. It's hilarious; two weeks ago being mutated as we are was so hideous that most chose to die rather than live. Now, the CEOs and wealthy can't find enough of us to hire and are working on ways to make their own telepaths by talking normal men and women into getting mutated. You should see their comm center ads. 'Become a millionaire; become a telepath.' They still show Ted's image in the ad—you know, the same one the Sixth Invaders had in their prerecorded messages."

He smiled at Helen and added, "Being like this has been the best thing that's ever happened in my life, other than marrying Helen. With my telepathy, I am so close to her, it's indescribable. Best thing ever. It's almost as though I'm one with her."

Helen nodded. "He's changed even more since his telepathic ability blossomed. Casper's become the love of my life again, only more so. I don't know how to describe it. I feel seventeen and madly in love." She giggled.

Casper added, "Don't forget to come to her art show. It's in three weeks. You're gonna love it. I sure do. I was a total idiot to have forced her to stop taking images after we got married. Hell, I don't know how she ever put up with me all those years. I'm the luckiest man in the universe because she did." He looked at Helen again. "And I can also feel our daughter-to-be. What an incredible thing to be able to do. Sense and feel the new life growing within her. Thank you, Universe."

Helen chuckled. "He gets a little carried away since his telepathic skills blossomed. So what are you three going to do? I'll back you no matter what, though my opinion isn't all that influential."

"We'll try to figure that out now," said Natalie. "We got blind-sided by the off-world corporations. We'll let you know."

I said, "Ted and I are supposed to meet with Celeste, Eve, and Randi. I'll keep you posted. Dimitri, Natalie, why don't you come with us?"

"Might as well find a quiet place to discuss our options," Natalie said.

Bev accompanied us to the apartment complex behind Costumes R Us. We entered Celeste, Randi, and Eve's home.

Eve was off working with Lara, but Celeste and Randi had tea and scones waiting for us.

Randi said, "We figured you'd need a pick-me-up after that meeting. It was televised across the Sol Empire."

As I sipped my Early Grey, Celeste said, "We three are very worried about this whole telepath thing."

"Why? Isn't it a good thing?" asked Dimitri.

She said, "Anyone with it can probe your deepest thoughts at any time, any place, and without your consent. Liken it to mental rape. Ethical telepaths wouldn't do that. But these new telepaths have no training in its use, no guidelines to follow. Anyone can spy on anyone's thoughts. Secrets for sale, dirt cheap. That's where we're headed. Not a pretty picture."

"But I've never done that," I said.

"Of course you haven't, Molly. You've earned your telepathic ability. You've had hundreds of hours of therapy, erasing all manner of traumas you've suffered and also caused to happen to others. Once you've faced all those barriers, your native abilities renewed themselves. Not so with these others. Their bodies just developed it. They haven't earned the right to possess such abilities by handling the unethical things they've done in this and earlier lives. One respects that which he honestly earns. But with these people, it's just been given to them as part of the mutation. Hence, their level of responsibility regarding telepathy will be low. So expect misuse and abuse.

"Consider this scenario. You're a corporate person with a dirty or vital secret. During the day, you cross paths with a telepath. How do you know you have? Easy. They're all armless Galactic Dolls. So what do you do to protect your secret? You have that person shot whether they saw your dirty or vital secret or not. Makes no difference. You must have that telepath terminated. Mark my words; we'll see many telepaths dying in all kinds of ways."

Celeste added, "There has always been corporate wars—behind-the-scenes confrontations that were never publicized. I've been discussing this history angle with Hank. Galactic Expansion didn't become the leader of the other corporations by logical voting."

"But shouldn't my twins be safe enough as linguists on space exploration ships?" I asked. I grew more paranoid by the minute.

Celeste sighed. "Learning a new civilization's language is a fabulous job for a telepath. Isabella and Bernardo discussed this with me while you were gone. Ted asked me, too. So yes, on the surface, it's a rewarding and valuable job for telepaths. As long as the corporation is forced to make payments to them each month and that other family members have access to that account. You need to guard against the corporation terminating the telepath and then confiscating their bank account funds using off-the-wall justifications. That aspect has me and many others worried. Which is why I think they added those clauses to all telepath's contracts. Still..."

"Yeah, still I wouldn't trust the corporations," I finished her thought.

"Eve and Lara believe they can make some genetic cures, perhaps not regrowing arms, but getting reproduction genes back to normal so offspring won't be cursed with the same mutation. If they get a total cure developed, those receiving it are more than likely to lose their telepathic abilities. Again, this could also be abused. Suppose your ten-year contract is up and you're looking forward to becoming a normal human again. Your corporation says, no, you're not getting the cure yet. We want you to sign up for another ten-year contract. After that, we'll get you your cure. That's something today's corporations would do in a heartbeat."

She added, "But Bernardo's got a valid point. After spending ten years as a linguist on an exploration ship, he will accumulate ten million credits, more than enough to buy his own restaurant. If by then an arm regrow procedure is in place, all the better for him. On the other hand, if he gets his arms back tomorrow, he's got a long, hard road to get his own restaurant—many years saving up his credits. You know kids—they want it now, not later." We laughed.

"So how do I make my decision?" I asked. "They'll hate me if I tell them no, you can't do this. Or you have to wait until you're older."

"I can't make that decision for you and Ted. It should be their decision because no matter what happens after that, they have to live with the result. I always opt for giving a person the responsibility," Celeste said.

That sunk home. My decision solidified. It would be the kids' choice.

"I wish all decisions were that easy," Dimitri said. He ran his hands over his face, ending with them on the back of his neck. "I had hoped they wouldn't have acted behind our backs while we were off-world."

Celeste said, "So many of the leaders are covertly hostile towards everyone, you should have expected it. Further, fear is playing a huge role in their actions."

"You mean fear of becoming and armless Doll? Wait, now they are the telepaths. How screwy can things get? Something dreaded and feared by the corporation leaders has become highly sought after," he said.

"Careful, Dimitri. Those very leaders are terrified of becoming armless Dolls. That alone has forced them to compromise on many of the decisions you heard today. They are marketing the telepathy aspect and the millions of credits as inducements to others to become that, while not becoming one themselves."

Randi said, "I can't help thinking that Sixth Invader science officer, that G'Karn fellow, purposely made this error. He felt guilty about using his science to make armless Dolls out of normal men, so he added something to offset the terrible downside of his mutation."

I laughed. "Randi, I agree with you. He was a gentle alien. I bet this was his plan all along, giving us a way to detect a Sixth Invader who has body swapped with one of us. I think he tried to give us a fighting chance."

"So what the hell do we do now? My emperor idea has been shot down," Dimitri said. "I feel betrayed by these other corporations. Shot in the back while saving their asses."

"We keep on doing all we can to better the world," I said. "Be true to our own goals and selves. You two could return to Moscow and rebuild the Earth-wide GPan and GD corporations and try to keep these many local ones in check. Or your could become our senators or ambassadors, even Senior Ambassadors to the Federation. What do you really want to do?"

Dimitri laughed. "I just wanted to marry Natalie, settle down, and live a quiet life. Let my dad and brother run the corporations. But Natalie doesn't want to lead a quiet life. She's into empire defense and all that. And dad and my brother are dead."

She sighed, "Well, my talents lie in defense. If I'm honest with myself, I should try to rebuild the Earth-wide GD corporation in Moscow. You should get GPan rebuilt there too, Dimitri. We owe it to our people and not abandon Moscow. If we don't do it, I can see that cowardly LA CEO trying to take over. Nature abhors a vacuum."

Dimitri ran his hand over his face again before exhaling. "Natalie, you're right. That's what we should do—rebuild GPan and GD in Moscow. Molly, what are you going to do? Are you going to become our Senior Ambassador to the Federation? Why the heck do those aliens want you to be our ambassador? That never made sense. Hell, they only knew you for a few hours."

I chuckled. "That's a darn good question. I was shocked to hear that same message today at the meeting. Someone sure wants me there. But..."

"But what?" asked Natalie.

"I'm a PI. I know Chicago and can handle investigations on Earth. But I know nothing about the empire's needs and wants. I'd make the dumbest ambassador ever."

Celeste laughed. "But Molly, that's not saying anything because we don't have any yet." Everyone roared.

"Seriously, guys. I'm not cut out to be an ambassador. Not my thing. Investigations are. I'm thinking about signing up to be our Senior Investigator if I can handle that position, handicapped as I am."

"Well, Molly, you'd make a good one," Celeste said.

I knew she meant well, but could I handle such a position? Physically, that is.

Natalie asked, "So what about this Senior Ambassador thing? They seemed insistent on sending a telepath, so that means an armless Doll. I'm surprised the Federation would allow it, considering our own empire is now prohibiting off-world immigration of the Dolls."

Dimitri said, "They don't want the mutation to take hold on their worlds. Rightly so. But as an ambassador, you won't be breeding with their local men and women. Still, considering those giant earrings and those crazy large lip disks, telepathy or not, an armless Doll will be severely handicapped by them. Don't you think so, Molly?"

I sighed. "Yes, that's one reason I'm not even considering it. Too inhibiting to me. You all know me. I must be independent or as independent as I can be, considering."

"So who are they going to get to be our ambassadors?" Natalie asked. "Will they take any input from us?"

"We should try, don't you think?" Dimitri said. "Look, if they insist on a telepath, then the second Senior Ambassador should be someone who can help the telepath. Meaning a normal person."

"Hey, they should know the empire's history, too," I said. "The Strawns. Aaron used to be a history professor at the U of C. Piper's a nurse. She knows the medical side of the empire. I wonder if they'd be interested in the position."

Celeste said, "They'd be ideal for it. Let's check with them today."

"If they want to do it," Natalie said, "then you can tell them Dimitri and I also back them. What about the Senior

Judge? They'll have awesome powers. Shouldn't they be telepaths, too? So they can make sure the person is guilty."

"I like that idea," I said. "Let me look over all those we have living with us at the assisted living complex. Maybe I can find us a judge candidate."

Dimitri laughed. "Or we could make one. Find someone who wants that position and make him or her into a telepath armless Doll."

"Good lord! You think any normal person would want to do that?" I asked.

"Just teasing, Molly. You take things too literally."

We chuckled. But I wondered if he might be right or if I was justified in being so literal and paranoid.

Chapter 22 Boom, Wake Up

After Dimitri and Natalie departed, I headed back to the complex via the MTES. September arrived with a chill in the air though the azure skies sent relaxing waves down my sides. It was good to be back. I would never be happy off-world and was glad I turned down the offer to be Senior Ambassador. Besides, I was fond of Chicago, even the sometimes smelly lake odor, the freezing winters, and the strong winds. It was home. I couldn't imagine another world feeling that way.

I found Aaron Strawn at home, struggling to make himself some lunch. "Hi, Molly. This darn robot cook machine leaves a professor much to be desired. I have to use only the simplest words. Not even four syllable words. Grr. Piper will be here in a few minutes."

I laughed. "Know what you mean. I leave the robot cook to Ted. He's the robot programmer. Say, did you hear the broadcast this morning?"

"Yes, I dismissed my nine o'clock class so they could watch it. If I hadn't, they'd of watched it on their laptops in class anyway. Besides, it's history in the making. Say, are you going to be our Senior Ambassador?"

"No, I'm not qualified, Aaron. I barely passed history in high school. Our ambassadors need to know much of our empire's history and what's needed."

"That makes sense. And I can see why they're insisting on one being a telepath. Hard to keep secrets from us. Say, can I ask you something?" I nodded. "Since my telepathy turned on, Piper and I are closer than we've ever been. I don't have words to describe it. Is it that way with you and Ted? Other married telepaths?"

"Yes, we're close. It's normal and common."

He relaxed and sat back. "Whew. I'm glad. I'll tell Piper. Oh, here she comes."

Piper bustled in on her lunch break and greeted me. As she fixed lunch, I told them why I was here.

"So they're insisting one be a telepath. I figure Aaron is perfect since he's also a history professor and thus knows all about our empire. Plus, you're married and can help him deal with those giant lip disks. And you understand our medical needs. Perhaps, other worlds have medical cures you can bring back to us. What do you think about my idea?"

Aaron said, "I agree with you. We need someone there that knows our history and someone we can trust, not these untrustworthy corporation men. Piper, it's a golden opportunity for us. My life can actually matter, rather than being a nearly helpless college teacher. What do you think, honey?"

She grinned. My hunch was correct. "Think of the possible medical cures I could bring back to Earth, not to mention getting your arms back. It's almost too good to be true. Do you think we can really do this? Will they allow us to be the ambassadors?"

"Dimitri and Natalie will back you, too, so I think you've got a good shot at it. They want to send a telepath, and there aren't too many of us adults. So unless some normal person wants to undergo this mutation, I think you've a great chance."

"Good grief," Piper said, twisting her face. "Who in their right mind would want to get this mutation done to them? Even with your help and all those videos, Aaron isn't very independent though the robots help some."

"Money and power, Piper. Those are strong motivations."

"Well, some people have no common sense. Aaron is really struggling to live like this. We don't know how you manage."

"Hey, it's a bitch for me, too. I've had more practice, that's all. I'll see if I can get an answer for you both as soon as possible."

Aaron said, "Thanks for thinking of us, Molly. Whether they'll take us or not, I'm impressed you thought enough of us to want to ask us to be the Sol Empire's representatives. Heck of an honor."

I laughed. "You might not think so when you wear that giant lip disk thing. But she told me they have a way to undo the lip slitting when you're done being the ambassador. At least something can be undone."

I raised my shoulders, and he laughed. I left and headed home to notify everyone of our choice for Senior Ambassadors. So far, so good. The kids would be home from school before too long. Time to have the talk I dreaded. I enjoyed being a mother to two young teens, but if they took the corporation offers, I'd not likely see them for years. Funny how I felt like a mom so quickly, only a couple weeks after meeting them and having them move in with us. I wondered if my mom had similar thoughts when she adopted me when I was a baby.

Boom. A loud explosion vibrated the ground. It was distant, perhaps coming from the Loop where all the major skyscrapers tried to touch the sky. "Turn on Channel Nine News," I said to our automated comm center.

Within a couple minutes, a reporter and crew appeared at the sight of the blast. My stomach lurched. The explosion knocked out an entire floor of the Galactic Robotics skyscraper where Ted worked.

"Minutes ago, an explosion rocked downtown Chicago. From what we can see, one floor of Galactic Robotics has suffered extensive damage. Police report no fires, but as you can see, that floor looks devastated. Officials are not citing a cause as yet, focusing on retrieving the casualties. What's that? Yes, okay. This floor housed the Research and Development Department. Several are dead. Emergency workers are setting up a triage center in the Galactic Defense building."

"Call Ted," I barked into my phone. "Damn. Went to Voice Mail. Call Deanna."

"Hi, Molly. Are you watching the news?"

"Yes, it's his department. They're taking them to GD. Can you go there and see if you can find out anything about Ted? It'll take me a quarter of an hour to get there."

"Okay. I'm on my way. I'll phone the second I hear anything, and I'll get Leslie to come over and watch for your kids coming home from school."

"Thanks, Deanna. I'm out the door."

Thanks to this mutation, running wasn't really possible, so I stayed out of the "fast lane" of the MTES. Tall heels made walking tricky anyway. While I wanted to race there, such wouldn't make any difference. I'm not a doctor. Besides, without hands, I would be darn useless if Ted needed anything. As the minutes passed, my stomach grew tighter and tighter. And I knew.

Later when we talked about it with Isabella and Bernardo, I explained somehow I knew Ted's body was dead, kind of a sickening feeling. The ME's autopsy revealed massive concussion damage to his major organs. "Nearly soup," he'd noted on the form. Many others crowded into the GD building where Helen had her people directing and informing us.

I found Deanna. "Sorry, no news yet. They're bringing another group of bodies here now. Maybe he survived."

I said, "I think he's gone. Kind of feel it."

"We need a new body for him," Deanna said, "like we did with you. Twice. Wait a second. Isn't Irina's body being kept in stasis at the Med Center?"

"Right. Yes, yes, it is. Call Holly Ann."

"Molly, we're watching it now. Is Ted?"

"Don't know yet, but can you bring one of the body swap machines to the Med Center? We've still got Irina's body on ice."

"On my way, Molly. Call me when you know for sure. It looks really bad on the monitor. Bye."

Helen Hugo spied us and walked over. "Molly, I'm so sorry. It's Ted. I'm so sorry." She hugged me.

"Can we get his body moved to the Med Center right away?"

She looked at me with raised eyebrows. "But he's—oh! Body swap. Right. I'll have my security men move him now. You and Deanna—come with me."

We ducked down a back way, took the express elevator up to the sixth-floor temporary triage center. I saw two dozen bodies laid out in a line, all extensively damaged and dead. Helen's men picked up Ted's body. Deanna and I followed them to the elevator. On the roof, we climbed into a GD EMAC and headed for the Chicago Med Center.

Thirty minutes later, I stood beside the two bodies, while Holly Ann attached the head harnesses to both. A doctor detached the stasis lines and injected a wake-up drug. Deanna kept an arm around my waist, steadying me, though I barely noticed her touch. Salty water trickled down my cheeks, but I couldn't do anything about that, scarcely daring to breathe. Was this what Ted went through when I was killed, twice even? God, I'd not wish this on anyone.

Holly Ann was the essence of calm. "Okay. Here we go." She powered up her device while I held my breath. This just had to work. I didn't want to lose Ted, not ever. Funny thing is, we saw nothing. The activation energy was in the kilo-yattahertz range, that white, incredibly pure aesthetic energy. "Done." She flipped off her machine.

I watched and gasped, having forgotten to breathe for too long. As if in synch with me, Irina's body inhaled sharply and jerked. Thank god, it was alive. But was my Ted in her body?

Deanna said, "Breathe, Molly."

Somehow, I made my body do so, but all my attention was focused on Irina's body. But then I realized how stupid and foolish I was being, so I closed my eyes and telepathically reached for Ted.

Can't breathe. Can't breathe. Oh, body's breathing again. Gotta get up. Molly? That you? I'm dead. Sorry about that.

We body swapped you into the Irina body. You're waking up. Come on, Ted. Wake up. Please, wake up.

Irina's body lurched and gasped. Eyelids fluttered. The gorgeous blonde woman with enchanting blue eyes, Miss Moscow, woke up. Holly Ann helped her sit up.

"Oh, I'm alive. I died. Wow, that body's crushed, isn't it? Oh, I'm in Irina's body, Miss Moscow. Shit. I'm a woman now. Crap, Molly. I'm a woman now."

Tears streaming down my cheeks, I said, "Don't you ever die on me again, Ted Billings. I love you so. What happened?"

"God, that body is really crushed! I don't know what happened. We were working on our latest robot controls when the whole floor exploded. I felt this impossible weight on my chest and have been trying to breathe ever since. Wow, you guys saved me. No, swapped me. How many died? What caused the explosion? I feel funny. This isn't my body."

Deanna said, "I've been following it on my phone. Massive explosion. Cause unknown as yet. The point of origin: next to your office. Ted, do you have enemies?"

"My office? That's where I was when it slammed into me. I'm gonna need some of Celeste's therapy. Molly, you do too. You've been killed twice now. Enemies? None I know of. Why would they be targeting me?"

"Working on something top secret?" Deanna asked.

"Hardly. A boring leg control. Minor improvement. Why would someone target me?"

"I don't know, but I sure as hell will find out," I said.

"Let's get you up, dressed, and out of here," Deanna suggested. "I've told everyone your body died, but that you're okay. I told them about the body swap, but to keep that detail a secret. Someone might be targeting you. If they learn that you're alive in a new body, they might try again. So for now, we'll pretend you're dead. Besides, we can't call this body Ted. You're a female now, Irina."

"I suppose you're right. Okay, but I want to be Irina Billings. How's that? Maybe she was my aunt or something."

I laughed. "Yes, Ted's Aunt Irina, come to Chicago to bury her nephew. Makes it plausible."

"Crap. This body is incredibly stiff. Going to take work to make this one limber enough to do much of anything."

"I know, honey. We'll work on it tonight. I'm thankful we got to you in time. They're carting your body off to the morgue already."

"Get a copy of the ME's report. I need to find out what happened. I've never been blown up before—not that I know of. What will we tell the kids? I don't want to lie to them."

"We can trust them. Besides, we'll have to let them make their own decisions about becoming linguists for exploration ships."

Deanna took us home before dropping Holly Ann off. Leslie welcomed us home. She had a hot supper waiting for us.

"Wow, is like that you, Ted? Miss Moscow like is right. Wow. Now you can like wear some of my fancy fetish outfits and like look super-hot."

Irina glared at Leslie before breaking into a laugh. "But I'm not a guy anymore. Okay, I didn't look like one for a long time, but this is different."

"Don't worry, *Irina*," she winked. "Your secret like is safe with us. I'll like measure you now and like bring a new line of fancy clothes tomorrow."

"Thanks, Leslie. I appreciate it. We'll pay you for them. We think someone may have tried to kill me."

She laughed. "Irina, they like did kill you."

We all laughed. Isabella and Bernardo heard us talking and came to see their dad. "Gee, dad. You look—well, really different," he said.

Isabella said, "Just like that old image we found online for Miss Moscow. You're not a day older than you were when it was taken. You're a knockout, dad. Wow. Wish I looked as pretty as you do. But are you going to be our dad now? Can you?"

Irina laughed. "We're pretending I'm Ted's Aunt Irina Billings. We have to because we think someone wanted to kill me."

Bernardo chuckled, "Well, they did that, dad, er Aunt Irina."

Irina grinned, "Yeah, they did. Body was crushed. From what I know about explosions, I bet my insides were turned into mush. Molly's going to get the autopsy report for me."

Isabella said, "Why dad? Er Irina. Why would you want to see that?"

"Dunno. Just curious. Hey, it's not every day someone kills me."

"Well, you be careful," she said. "Deanna said you're out of bodies to use for swapping. I don't want you to die, dad."

Irina gave her a sheepish grin.

"Okay. I'm like heading home," Leslie said. "Supper's on the table. Holler if you like need anything."

"Bye, sis. Thank's for everything," I said, while everyone headed to the dining room.

After dinner, I said, "Okay. Family powwow time."

"What's a powwow?" asked Isabella.

After that digression, I explained our position. "Ted, er Irina, and I have discussed your desires to sign up for the ten-year contract with GPan to be linguists on their space exploration ships. There is danger involved when making first contact with alien people."

Suspecting I was about to veto their grand plans, Bernardo interrupted me. "Heck, there's danger just going to work. Look what happened to dad."

"Right. Don't forget, I've been killed twice in the last month. What I'm trying to say, Bernardo, is we can't forbid you to go because the assignment can be dangerous. We both believe what you want to do is an admirable use of your new talents. As Celeste says, getting those first five hundred basic words of a new language figured out opens the door to communication. Fortunately, GPan has put in place some of the safeguards we wanted, like monthly deposits in your accounts. Plus, we can't deny you this chance on educational grounds. Ted got his two doctorates online without ever attending a university. Your aunts earned three doctorates that way. So I'm sure if you study hard in your spare time on the ship, you'll get all the educational courses you want."

"Mom, get to the point," Isabella said.

"I'm trying to, dear. We understand why you want to amass the credits, especially Bernardo. I feel bad we aren't wealthy and can provide you with that kind of money. But once your education is finished, I suspect Aunt Deanna could help us with the financial means. Lara and Eve are hopeful they will one day find cures. But as you know, that could take a long time, which again argues in favor of your doing this job. The only negative detail is your age. Yes, you'll be fourteen in a few more months. But you are still growing and maturing. That you are survivors counters this. While so many others chose to be terminated when they awoke from the mutation comas, you've shown exceptional courage. You are both more adult than many real adults."

That brought smiles to their faces while Irina chuckled. She said, "Don't we know it. Casper used to be one of those." I had to laugh, too.

"So kids, we've decided to let you follow your own dreams, but not without as many safeguards as possible."

"Yeah!" Bernardo said, rushing me and pressing his body into mine.

"Yes!" Isabella said, emulating her brother. In seconds, all four of us squashed into each other, the best we could do for a group hug.

"Tomorrow, we'll see what we have to do to get this going," I added.

"The hardest part is calling you Aunt Irina and not dad, dad," Bernardo said.

We all laughed, and I sent the kids scampering off to their rooms to do their homework. Okay, in these heels no one scampers. Both were elated.

Ted, I mean Irina, and I retired to our bedroom. I'd promised to help him, er her, stretch and get her stiff body more flexible.

"This body feels so strange, so funny, so emotional, honey. Hell, I'm crying and I don't know why."

"It's okay, dear," I said calming him. "You've just had your body smashed and are swapped into this one. Remember,

I complained about how stiff and inflexible it was. Come on. Let's get to stretching. You can do it."

Sobbing, he said, "No, I can't. I mean I can—stretch the legs, but I've lost the one thing that still made me a guy for you. It feels so strange down there. I can't ever be your man now, not ever again." Irina leaned into me, crying on my shoulders.

What the hell do you say or can say to make things better? They would never be the same. Ted now was a woman. Even if Lara invented a cure, she'd be a whole Irina, not a whole Ted. I felt sick at my stomach. I'd done this without asking Ted if he wanted to swap into Irina's body or to find a new baby body. What had I done?

I have this tenacious hold on life, a willingness to continue trying to help others. But did Ted have that too? I'd forced him into being a woman. It had been one thing to sound and look outwardly like a Galactic Doll and quite another to have a female body. I did everything to keep my Ted with me. I wasn't going to lose the love of my life. But was I being selfish? I started crying, too.

I remembered something Celeste had once told me when she visited from her St. Louis clinic. "Molly, we made a strange discovery. Male bodies have 2.5 times the electrical resistance of a female body—12,500 ohms versus 5,000 ohms. We've no idea what this means, but it's been consistent across all dead bodies we've measured."

"Ted, if an electrical circuit has more than twice the resistance of a second circuit, what does that mean?"

"Irina now. We have to get used to calling me Irina. I'll never be Ted again. I can't be," she sobbed. His mind latched onto familiarity. Circuits were one of his specialties.

"Oh, it'll take more than twice the voltage to punch through the same current. Or if you keep the same voltage across them, the current will be half as much. Why?"

"Remember what Celeste once told us last year? Male bodies have 2.5 times the electrical resistance of female bodies."

"Huh? Yeah, I remember her saying that. So what's that got..." He paused and ceased crying. "This body has much less resistance. No wonder I'm becoming so emotional. I'll have to get used to it. Still, Molly, I can't be your Ted anymore. I've lost my manhood." His crying resumed.

"I know, dear. I should have asked you if you wanted to swap bodies into Irina's. But I couldn't let you die. I need you. I want you. I love you, but I should have asked you first. I'm so sorry, dear."

"Oh." Irina brightened up a little. Her sobs lessened. "I hadn't thought of that. I love you, too, Molly. You're my dream woman. I would have said do it. I don't want to lose you either. God, you've no idea how I felt when they killed you, twice even. Oops. Well, now you know what I felt. But I'm not a man; I can't be your Ted."

"Don't be silly. You will always be the same person, my Ted. You aren't your body. I fell in love with you—not your almost mechanical mind nor your body which keeps on getting mutated this way and that. I love you. You're a being. Okay, I agree, we best not call you Ted. You can't wear Leslie's new male Doll apparel. And I think you are right. We best pretend you're Aunt Irina Billings come to help me. At least until we can figure out if someone was trying to kill you."

"They did kill me."

"Er, right. We'll pretend a while. Besides, Ted, Irina, it's not the end of the world. Look at Bev and Gail."

She stopped crying. Sniffling, she said, "That won't bother you? Me not having it anymore? How will I satisfy you? In bed, I mean."

I giggled. "We must ask Gail and Bev." We both flushed red.

"Utterly embarrassing. Hey, I thought it was grim years ago when I woke up on the Padellas' atoll with my body that of a male Doll, but this is much worse. At least there I was still male."

"I know, Ted, Irina. We should practice what we preach. Close your eyes. Okay. Now return to the first instant today when you thought something was wrong before the explosion."

"Oh, yeah. Right. Okay, I'm working on these new robot leg controls. We're perfecting them so they work more like those of a human."

He bounced over the pain of the explosion and hit the massive loss he felt after he woke up in Irina's body and realized he was alive but now a female. More sobs and tears filled the next half hour as we went over the whole incident several times. On the next past, he screamed when he confronted the massive pain from the concussion shock wave. After many more passes over the trauma, Irina still wasn't cheerful, so I asked if there was an earlier trauma that was similar.

He was in a space ship that exploded. The shock wave liquified his organs. Though still alive, he fought being ejected into the cold vacuum of space. "I have to escape, just have to." She laughed. "There I am, guts turned into soup, and I'm fighting against being sucked out into space. How stupid can you get? I was already dead."

She continued to laugh, so I ended the therapy session and relaxed for the first time since the explosion. He/she would be all right. Celeste's miracle therapy won again.

The next morning, as Irina worked on getting our robot cook to make us breakfast, Celeste and Randi knocked on our door.

Celeste said, "We've come to help you get going this morning and to give you both therapy sessions. We should have already worked on you, Molly. You've endured two murders that need to be erased."

Irina laughed. "Too late. You're too late. I was a basket case last night, so Molly ran me through it. I feel fine now. Confused a little about being a female, though. Embarrassed would be more accurate."

Randi said, "No problem. I brought a copy of the ME's report on your dead body. Its internal organs were liquified. So were most of the others who were closest to the detonation point. It must have been a powerful blast. Here. Let us fix breakfast. We want you both well fed."

"Hi Aunt Randi, Aunt Celeste," Bernardo said as he walked sleepy-eyed into the dining room. He brightened up. "Hey, they're going to let Isabella and me be linguists on the exploration ships. In ten years, I'll be a millionaire. Then, I'm going to open my restaurant."

"Good for you, Bernardo. But be careful out there in space," Randi said.

An hour later with the kids off to school, Celeste ran her therapy on me, erasing the trauma of being killed twice. Meanwhile, Randi worked a little more with Ted, beginning with his intense embarrassment feelings.

By noon, they finished up. I felt like a new woman again. Irina looked happy, too, which made me feel even better. Leslie dropped by bringing a dozen outfits for Irina and helped her get them put away while removing all Ted's clothing, which she promised to give to needy men.

After lunch, Natalie dropped by to check up on us. "Well, your idea that someone might have been after Ted could be true. My crew is still going over the floor looking for clues, but it was a bombing. High explosives. Directional charge, too."

"What does that mean?" Irina asked.

"Normally, an explosion fires off in all directions, in a sphere, until it hits barriers, which it damages. With a bomb this large, we'd expect severe damage on the floors above and below yours. However, they suffered nothing more than a few broken mugs that bounced off desks. It was constructed to blow outward. The focus of the blast appears to have been your workstation. Those who survived were on the outer edges of the floor."

She continued, "But we have no proof you were the intended target. Your spot was centrally located on the floor. Now, if your location had been near one side and the blast was focused there, then we'd have a stronger case you were the intended target."

I interrupted, "But wasn't this blast total overkill? They killed thirty people, according to the news."

"That argues against Ted being the target. Still, I agree. We should continue to pretend Ted is dead. Until we're certain, one way or the other."

"Okay. We're calling her Aunt Irina Billings, come to help me in my hour of need. But what about a job?"

"Yes, what about that?" Irina asked. "I'm a computer programmer and a robotics expert. That's what I do, er, did."

Natalie grinned coyly. "I've got Irina's DNA. I'll enter that name into our DNA database, along with your degrees and skills. I'll fabricate sponsorship information that you work for Galactic Robotics, Moscow. I'll let the local Galactic Robotics CEO know you've moved here to help Molly and are looking for employment. Since they lost so many key people, I'm sure someone will be calling you about a job offer soon."

"Thank you. You're a lifesaver," Irina said.

Chapter 23 Developments

The next day with Dimitri's help, we took the twins to our local GPan offices to get them signed up. Each signed a ten-year contract to be the linguist on board a deep space exploration ship.

The lawyer signing the forms for GPan said, "Their pay will be ten million credits, payable in monthly installments to their bank accounts, of which Irina and Molly Parkinson are the co-signers. Accidents can happen in deep space, so GPan always carries a million credit insurance policy on those on the ship. Beneficiaries will be Irina and Molly unless you wish to have others benefit. Mind you, this rarely happens, but we want all eventualities covered."

He continued with some new information we'd not heard. "Also, considering how valuable telepaths are when contacting a new people and considering we can now make new telepaths, all exploration ships will carry additional vials of that genetic mutation agent. If something should happen to Bernardo or Isabella, the commander of their ships will use the agent to make replacement telepaths. One of the crew members will sign a contract in which they opt to become the replacement telepath for the prorated contract benefits. Further, if something should happen to the designated telepath replacement, then the commander can inject any other crew member of his choice. All crew members must sign off on this new clause or they'll be dismissed. So you can see just how valuable you young people are."

He chuckled. "Also, you won't have to undergo the medical tests that the other crew members get. We know you're healthy because of your recent mutations. Everyone wins with you telepaths."

"What about hidden costs? Are you deducting such things from their monthly pay?" I asked. I'm not the trusting type.

"No deductions unless they willfully destroy things on the ship. That's never happened. But you have a point. Often, an exploration ship discovers a particularly valuable new planet, moon, or asteroid. In these cases, GPan pays a bonus to the crew. The telepaths will also receive such bonuses.

"And another thing—though I'm not yet sure how this will play out with the telepaths—all crew members are taught the basics of how to pilot and navigate the exploration ship. That's in case the commander, pilot, or navigator are killed or injured. We do everything possible to bring these expensive ships and highly trained crew home safely. I'm told that the commanders don't yet know if the telepaths can be trained to pilot or navigate the ships, but they'll work on that aspect during the flights. So welcome aboard, Telepaths Isabella and Bernardo Parkinson."

"Thanks. When do we start?" Isabella asked before I could.

"Isabella, you're being assigned to the Star Voyager. Bernardo, you're on the Path Finder. Here's a list of what personal supplies you're allowed to bring with you in a duffle bag. Report to New O'Hare next Monday. A shuttle will transport you to your ships, which are in orbit awaiting resupply and other crew members. With the addition of this new clause—that they could be turned into a telepath if you and the designated replacement are killed—is causing some turnover in personnel. Any more questions?"

I asked, "What if a cure is found while they're out there?"

"I assure you they will be given the cure when their contract is up, if they so choose. That's part of the contract. However, unless you know something I don't, no cure is on the horizon for this Sixth Invader mutation. I'm just thankful it's having such a win-win side-effect for the victims. We'll tell them if a cure is invented."

"Will they get periodical shore leave or will they be gone from Earth for the next ten years?" Irina asked.

Great question. I smiled at her.

"Depends. Sometimes, they're gone for several years, but they'll be back here for resupply at least every three years, sometimes less. When they are back, unless their duties require otherwise, they can call you and take a shuttle down to New O'Hare. Such visits are highly variable. No predict is possible. They are allowed one hyperspace phone call per month."

He cleared his throat. "In this case, I suspect there will be a resupply point within a year. Thanks to you, Mrs. Parkinson, and the others. We're getting a gigantic hyperspace coordinates upload along with tons of key data. It'll take time for GPan to assimilate this and work out where to explore next. So I would anticipate extended shore leave probably within a year."

With that, we left. I felt upbeat. Even though I still thought they were too young to be doing this, everything looked so positive. I relaxed a little for I realized I had been worrying about their futures ever since the mutation attacks. In ten years, they'd be independently wealthy and could execute their dreams. I wouldn't have to intercede on their behalf. But isn't that what a parent wants to do? Okay, I was ambivalent over this whole situation.

We spent the rest of the day gathering the essentials they needed, most of which we had at home: changes of clothes, shoes, boots, and personal grooming items. We did buy the regulation duffle bags.

That evening as I watched them eat supper, I couldn't help think about their futures. Ten million credits was more than I'd earn in my lifetime. Even if no cure was found, with such funds, they'd not be wanting or left destitute in some alley. That countered all the worries I had about their being too young for this.

The next morning, Natalie and Dimitri announced they would get married, before heading back to Moscow and rebuilding the Earth-wide corporations. Of course, we were invited. Further, via the news, we learned who our local ambassadors to Dian-C, Liatos-D, and Zahra-C would be.

Although I looked each up, I couldn't find fault with any of these choices.

Dara and Kiri Sim had been on the go these past days, visiting one corporation after another and in many cities around the world. Since our new ambassadors to their empire had been chosen, the four spent the daylight hours briefing each other on what to expect.

The ambassadors from Liatos-D and Zahra-C were due to arrive next Wednesday. Chicago planned a giant parade in their honor, giving Helen fits over security arrangements. A bored Bev lent her a hand. It promised to be an exciting week.

Monday morning, we saw our twins off on their great adventure. Irina and I managed not to cry until the kids, duffle bags over their shoulders, walked into New O'Hare. Our eyes watered all the way home.

We checked on the latest developments from the bombing. The bomb construction had been done with Earth-based supplies, including the burner phone detonator. They still had no clue who was behind it. Thus, we continued pretending Irina was my aunt. This was vital since, at one o'clock, we attended the cremation ceremony for Ted Billings. A few of his distant relatives attended along with my group. Helen and Casper Hugo already knew about Irina from our earlier adventures, and we had to let them in on the disguise and why. Casper thought we were wise.

"I'm sure someone wanted Ted dead. Now you only have to find out why and who."

I chuckled. "Easier said than done, but I'm diving into that next."

Irina said, "This is spooky—watching your own body being burned up. Weird too."

"I'm glad you're still with me," I whispered back.

We had little time to do sleuthing when we returned home. It seemed terribly quiet without the kids around as we got dressed up for Dimitri and Natalie's wedding. They had a low profile wedding. Only our large group attended. After congratulations and hugs, the new couple departed, heading back to Moscow. I didn't need telepathy to sense how disappointed they were. The corporation CEOs just didn't want to give up too much power, even though the pair was instrumental in saving the empire and bringing what we hoped was peace and prosperity for years to come.

The ambassador welcome parade lasted two hours Wednesday afternoon. An open topped EMAC hovered just above the MTES and navigated all around central Chicago. Crowds thronged the MTES as people jostled to glimpse the three pairs of alien ambassadors. How tall were the giants? How strong were the dwarves? Everyone wanted answers.

Since nothing new on the bombing had appeared by late Wednesday, Irina and I began our own private investigation of the attack. We began by downloading the various surveillance videos from his floor in the R&D department. There wasn't much to go on, though, just two camera feeds, but we got the prior two weeks' worth of video. We studied every minute of them on Thursday but found nothing definitive. By Friday late afternoon, we had to get ready for Helen's art showing and still had nothing to show for our efforts. Irina moped around the house while we got ready.

"Well, I can see," she said, "why no one knows anything yet. Disgusting."

We dressed up and rode the MTES across town to the fancy art gallery close to Lake Shore Drive. We arrived shortly after the gallery opened. Casper Hugo, wearing one of Leslie's latest male Doll's suits, greeted everyone at the door.

"Welcome to Helen Hugo's History of Chicago Architecture Images. Enjoy these incredible images and test your skill. See if you can recognize the buildings. The answers are in small print on the labels below the images. Irina, Molly, welcome. No need to fish out your tickets. I know you have them. So glad you could come. Helen will be pleased. Already, we have a larger turnout than expected. Lots of well-to-do men and women."

"You look good yourself tonight, Casper," I said, but we had to move on as others filed in behind us.

Helen looked regal in her red satin evening gown. She floated among the many visitors. Her face showed how much this showing meant to her. As Irina and I looked at the mounted images in their wooden frames, I saw another side of Helen, one I didn't know existed. An artist's eye for simple beauty and symmetry of lines, her works captivated us. Soon, we joined the guessing game.

"Isn't that part of the Cartwright building?" I asked.

"Certainly is. I've seen that gargoyle decoration many times," Irina said.

We checked the fine print. Correct.

"So what do you think?" Helen's voice broke in on the guessing game.

"Absolutely incredible, Helen," I said. "Each is a work of art. I can't imagine how you got some of these images, like the Cartwright building's gargoyle. Genius how you've drawn us into the guessing game. Wonderful."

"I figured that would appeal to my favorite PI," Helen said, raising both eyebrows slightly before grinning. "I'm so glad you could come tonight. Something like this helps relieve my stress. Casper is doing a good job welcoming everyone."

"He's one changed man and for the better."

"Who would have thought, but I'm thankful I didn't give up on him. When he shot Ted and kidnapped you, I almost dumped him. Now—well, let's just say it's wonderful. Excuse me. I should talk to her. She's the CEO of GMed."

Helen moved off while Irina and I moved onto the next image to continue the guessing game. When we finished and left, our score wasn't so good.

As we reached the door, Casper asked, "So how well did you do? Your score?"

Irina laughed. "Pitiful. I got six right, and Molly, five. Did you try it or did you already know what they were?"

"I didn't do so well. Only got three right. Helen's promised to take me on long walks around Chicago and point them out. 'View the world as an artist does,' she says. Anything for that amazing woman. Catch you later on. Welcome..." Another couple arrived, and he started reciting his welcoming speech, probably for the hundredth time or more.

As we walked home, Irina said, "Well, that was a nice diversion. I think we need more of them. Tomorrow is Saturday. The kids are gone. What say you to a picnic along the lake beach? Or maybe we rent an EMAC and go to the dunes?"

"Only if you're with me," I teased her. "You can't be invisible."

Irina stopped walking on the MTES. She looked at me, eyes wide. "Maybe that's what we are missing on the videos. Invisible. Suppose the perp was invisible when he planted the bomb."

"Terrific idea. Come on. It's still early. Let's have another look."

"Hi, Lara," I said as we walked into our commons. We'd seen so little of her this past week. She'd been holed up in labs with Eve.

"How was the art opening?"

"Very nice. Incredible actually. When you get a chance, you should visit it," I said.

"We had a bright idea about the bombing perp," Irina said. "We'll change into something comfortable and see if we can make it pan out. How's your research going?"

"Eve and I are hopeful. We're examining the actual changes in Molly's DNA when it was entered into the database and now. We were doing it for yours, Ted, but..."

"But now it doesn't matter."

"Yes, so we've gotten Irina's initial DNA, but she was mutated before it was taken. There's an outside chance we can get a sample from when she was Miss Moscow. If we do, we'll make use of it. But no matter what, I'll be here for you both. You saved my life, cured my insanity, so there's a life between us. Now, get going and find that bomber before they do more damage."

"Thanks, Lara," Irina said.

We spent a half hour changing, making use of our dressing/undressing machine. Then, we booted up our computers and studied the videos again.

"So how do we spot something that's invisible?" Irina asked. "What do I look for if I can't see it?"

"An anomaly. A distortion. A discontinuity in the image or position of objects. A wavering of light. Even invisible objects affect the things around them, albeit in a small way. Watch carefully."

By midnight, Irina had fallen asleep. My eyes felt blurry, but then I thought I spotted something. I rewound the recording and replayed it in slow motion. Bingo. Something not visible distorted or altered the ambient lighting near Ted's office cubicle. I checked the date-time stamp and made a note of it with a pen held between my toes. Curious. The date was the day the bomb exploded—four hours before to be precise. I left the recording at this spot and turned in. I was so wound up, so excited, that I thought I'd never get to sleep.

"So what's this, honey?" Irina's voice stirred me.

"Oh, morning. Hey, I found our invisible bomber. Hit play and watch the distortion of the ambient light. I wrote down the time-date stamp."

"Hey, you two. Need me to make breakfast before I head over to Eve's?" Lara asked from the kitchen.

"Will you? Please. We found the invisible bomber last night," I said.

Lara ran into the room. "Can I see?"

"Wow, that's tiny, but it's real. How did you ever spot that?" Irina said. "My eyes got so fuzzy I couldn't see the hologram."

"You fell asleep, kiddo. Replay it for Lara. You're looking for the distortion in the room's ambient lighting. It's visible. Something invisible passed through there," I said.

"Pickled Roosters!" Lara gushed. "You're right. Something did pass through there. Could it be the wind?"

Irina laughed. "You don't know how I *often* wished we had windows that opened. It's incredibly stuffy in there. Molly, are we going to the lake today or shall we work on this?"

"Lake. Just you and me."

Irina grinned. "Okay. You're on. Let's pack a picnic in one backpack and a blanket in the other. I feel like a heavy weight just lifted. Knowing someone put that bomb in there is a real relief. To me anyway."

The Windy City lived up to its nick. We had an awful time getting our blanket spread out on the narrow beach far from the pier. And the gulls got half of our picnic lunch, but we relaxed and chatted, something we both needed. Getting killed rather changes one's perspective. We appreciated each other even more.

Late afternoon, we showered and got back to our sleuthing. Irina wasn't a PI, so I gave her specific and doable tasks. She checked for more invisible persons while I did the heavy lifting. The perp was invisible when they crossed the room to his cubicle. But did he enter the building invisibly? That would be risky, considering the crowd of employees who entered at the same time. The time stamp indicated early morning rush hour. If the perp walked in while invisible, the odds bumping into people were huge.

Their leaving would also be a problem. Seeing a door opening and shutting with no one there activating the controls would raise a security alert unless the guards were asleep on the job. Thus, I was looking for someone carrying a large package and who didn't belong or seemed ill at ease or unfamiliar with the place. Hours passed.

Lara brought us supper, which I ate while watching the main entrance video recordings. I eliminated the vast majority of the recordings from consideration based on the time stamp. For the tenth time, I watched the morning rush of people entering Galactic Robotics. I even spotted Ted arriving and smiled.

"Thanks, Lara. Trying to spot the perp now. Hold on a second..."

I barked the rewind command, thankful the computer was voice-activated. Usually, I preferred my toes, but I needed fast action. "Slow motion playback." The computer responded.

Lara said, "Did you see something? I saw lots of humans walking in."

"There. Bingo. Molly wins again. Got you, you perp. Lara, Irina, come here. I've got them on video entering the building."

Lara and Irina crowded around my computer's holo display. "Watch the person in brown. Observe his face. Play back. Slow motion."

A minute later, I asked, "Did you see him?"

"Er, no," said Lara.

"Me either," added Irina.

I played it back again, only this time I pointed out the man with my right foot.

"Now look closely at his face. Here and now there."

"His face changed," Lara said.

"Oh shit!" Irina said. "Sixth Invaders!"

"Huh?"

She explained, "Lara, they have these devices that mask their true appearance by projecting an average of all the human bodies around them. Whoever that is, they are using a Sixth Invaders' belt device. General Bev has only recovered two of them. They're kind of spooky things. The perp's face changed because so many people around him moved off the right, changing the average appearance. What the hell's going on?"

I added, "Either someone has gotten a hold of one of those devices Bev captured or they stole one from the Sixth Invaders or they actually are a Sixth Invader."

"Or a Sixth Invader gave it to someone to use here," Lara added another possibility. "This is interesting. Is this what a PI does?"

"Yeah, this is my thing. Now we keep on back tracking. We'll use the MTES video surveillance recordings and see where he came from. He walked into the building from somewhere. I'm gonna find that where."

Irina yawned. "Can it wait until tomorrow? I'm falling asleep again. See, Lara. I married the hottest private investigator around."

They chuckled, but I agreed to put it off until the morning. Sunday would be a most interesting day.

Chapter 24 Perp Tracking

"What do we do now?" asked Irina.

We'd gotten our systems running. Time to catch this bomber. Armed with the exact time the perp entered the Galactic Robotics skyscraper, I logged into the Chicago surveillance archives and downloaded the recording covering that period. Irina brought up the best head shot of the man and also the best overall image of his appearance as he entered the building. Now came the hard part. I had to spot this person as he or she walked in, completing the union of the videos.

Because the image of the perp was an average of the appearance of all humans around him or her, my task proved challenging. I finally identified the person by matching the perp's entry with a woman in a yellow dress as she entered in front of the perp. Outside, his or her appearance was different. Conclusion: this device made visible changes rapidly and in real time. That I could join the two videos amazed both Lara and Irina.

"Now comes the fun part," I said. "We backtrack and see where this person came from. Hey, that's cool." Because I played the video in reverse, the perp appeared to be walking backward, but at the corner, his blue suit changed to a brown suit and then to a gray tweed midway through that block. Rather amazing.

Periodically, I had to log in and retrieve another video from additional MTES cams. The perp walked in from south Chicago, traveling several miles on the escalators. Then, at ten o'clock, I found another key detail. The perp suddenly appeared in the middle of a deserted street, walked over to the MTES, and began his long journey down to the Loop district. This area housed deserted warehouses, many in disrepair and scheduled for demolition.

"So we hit a dead end," Lara said.

"Pretty much so," Irina added.

"Hardly," I said. "Now we download all street cams in the area for the last week. We're focusing on the area where the perp first appeared. If my hunch is right, an invisible ship landed there, and he or she exited it with the bomb."

Lara and Irina soon took naps. I admit watching surveillance video can be tedious. Around eleven, I felt convinced and woke the others.

"Watch this." I played about a minute of video. "Isn't that a cloaked ship landing?"

Irina said, "I don't know."

"Absolutely," Lara said. "I've seen that many times. Do you have cloaked ships?"

"Not that I know of. I'm calling Admiral Rossi," I said.

Soon I wished I had been given a direct number. My call bounced between this place and that before I ended up speaking to a knowledgeable officer.

"I've detected a cloaked ship here in south Chicago. The person who bombed Galactic Robotics came from that ship."

"Who did you say you were?"

"Molly Parkinson. Please, put me through to Admiral Rossi. He knows me. Please."

More delays. If this had been a real emergency, the crisis would have been over before I got through to him. Once I did, action followed. I relayed the coordinates to him. In the background, I heard him barking orders. I hoped I wasn't wrong, crying "wolf" when nothing was there. He gave me a channel number, and I had Irina power up our comm center and switch to it. Ah, I had a view from the CCC of some ship—a light cruiser I later learned.

Within minutes, it shot into position over those coordinates. As I looked down at the center of the deserted street with the MTES ending about a block away, I saw nothing but asphalt or what appeared to be that. We watched the streaming video. The cruiser opened fire with its laser cannons and disrupters. Suddenly, a protective force field twinkled as it dissipated the energy being poured onto it. The cigar shape of a Sixth Invader light cruiser flickered below the crackling field.

Things happened rapidly after that initial probe. Our light cruiser switched to firing all its cannons, quadrupling the energy blasts striking the enemy ship. Within minutes, dozens of our space fleet hovered over south Chicago, making exciting news coverage. Then, a giant energy pulse shot from the rear of the enemy ship. Like a bullet, it shot upwards into the sky, singeing the ground around where it had been parked. No need for stealth now. Our cruiser darted after it, followed by a dozen more from our fleet.

"Never catch it," Irina said.

"Nope. It's made the jump into hyperspace," Lara said. "I used to love to watch ships make the jump after takeoff on Bela Prime. But that was a Sixth Invader cruiser."

"So what's going to happen now?" I asked. "Will the Federation go after them? Raid their empire?"

Lara chuckled. "Hardly. Politics. Lots of talk, but little action. I'm glad I'm not an ambassador any longer. Hated it."

"So why are the Sixth Invaders back here? Why blow up the R&D department of Galactic Robotics? Was Ted the target? If so, why? Ted, what the heck were you really working on?" I asked.

Irina flushed. "Hey, it wasn't even secret work. You remember those robot soldiers? Well, we were trying to improve their walking skills. They only really functioned on level ground. The ones used on Brussels, Tau Ceti, could barely climb up the river bank, and then only pitifully slowly. That aspect was more or less overlooked during the battles there. I swear we weren't working on anything critical, just useful. I can't imagine why the Sixth Invaders wanted to bomb us. Why would they even want to kill me? I'm not important. Molly, you are much more important than I ever was. You've been a thorn in their side for nearly two years."

"Then, why not bomb me? I just don't get it. If your people really weren't working on a secret robot project—"

"We weren't, Molly. I swear it. Routine R&D work. That's all. Oh, and we weren't scheduled to work on any secret project later on, either. Honestly, most of the work R&D does is mundane and boring—making robot machines work better."

"Okay. So you weren't working on a secret project. Stopping R&D doesn't prevent some new weapon or robot thing from appearing—"

"No, I assure you there's no new weapon or robot thing coming in the future," Irina insisted.

"Then, why kill you? You were the target. From the dispersal pattern, the blast was directed at your workstation, Ted. Why kill you?"

"I don't have a clue."

"But there must be a powerful reason for the Sixth Invaders to return to Earth, build a bomb from our supplies, sneak it into the building, plant it, and then remotely detonate it. That's a hell of a lot of risk and effort for only destroying the local R&D department. They should've gone after the empire-wide leaders. Now that would've been a reasonable attack, but not this. Killing you makes zero sense."

"But I'm dead all the same. Well, more or less dead."

"I could see them trying to kill me again. What can they gain by killing you?"

Irina shrugged her shoulders.

"Maybe they were trying to get to you through Ted," Lara said.

"Huh?"

"If they killed Ted, then maybe you'd be more willing to do whatever they wanted you to do."

"But what did they want me to do? I've not talked to these Sixth Invaders since we captured their science officer, G'Karn, months ago. What the hell could they want me to do?"

"Don't know, Molly. But you have to admit you've been a major problem for them. Most recently saving everyone on the Kanika. If Ted were dead, what might you do differently?"

"I'd cry a lot, but that doesn't count. Gosh, I don't think I'd do anything differently. I'm still waiting to hear if they want me in the new investigations group."

"What about that Senior Ambassador post?" asked Irina. "Some wanted you to do that, but I can't see me being dead would make that more likely."

"Well, that's pretty weird. I mean I just met Senior Ambassador Sanura, and she wanted me to be the Sol Empire's Senior Ambassador. She doesn't even know me, except that I saved the battleship. And why would their new ambassadors who have never seen Earth be pushing for me to be our Senior Ambassador? That's what's strange, but it has nothing to do with the Sixth Invaders."

"No, I can't see how it does," Lara admitted.

Irina tightened her lips. "You know, maybe it does in a round-about, twisted way. You weren't likely to accept such a post because of our family. Taking the twins to this Bela Prime turned us both off. Now they're off exploring new worlds. Would you go and leave me behind? Hardly. So I'm dead and the kids are gone. Wouldn't you be more likely to say yes and go?"

"Well, maybe. I still wouldn't want to leave everyone else, but I see your point. No kids, no husband, will travel. But what does this have to do with the Sixth Invaders? From the few ships I've seen, that one had to be theirs."

"Dunno. Probably nothing, I suppose."

Someone knocked on our door with rapid taps. Lara answered it for us because she was much quicker than we were.

"Major Airla. Hi. Heard the news?" I asked.

She grinned and nodded. "Molly Parkinson gets another +1 while the Sixth Invaders get another o."

The major had an unusual sense of humor, a bit strained perhaps.

"Come in. What's up?"

She looked quite the proper professional woman today. Plaid, pleated skirt done in subdued grays and white blouse. Her curly brunette hair just touched her shoulders. Deep blue eyes focused on my own eyes. Yet, she was one of the few people whose mind I couldn't sense, but then I didn't try. Not without asking first.

"Need your PI help. Some of the young telepath children have gone missing."

"Shit. Well, it was bound to happen. Some people are just plain greedy," I griped.

"Margot and Phillip Rothham, age six. Twins. They live at the far end of this facility. Never returned from the playground yesterday."

"Playground? Ours?" Airla nodded. "Well, there's surveillance cameras there. You should be able to see what happened to them."

She waved a portable drive. "I've already got it and watched the video. But..."

"So who took them? But what?"

"Well, I need you to look at the video. I'll cue it up."

I watched many younger children playing on swings, teeter-totters, and the merry-go-round. "Which ones?"

She pointed to two who were sitting on swings, moving slowly, trying to keep their balance. Okay, swings are a challenge without arms. I blinked, and the girl vanished. A moment later, the boy also disappeared. She stopped the playback.

"I don't know what to make of this."

"A snatch and grab," I said, rewinding it. "Play back. Very slow motion."

Once more, I was glad for voice-activated devices. I wondered how our ancestors got by without them.

"Oh shit! Sixth Invaders got them."

"Huh? How can you tell that?" Major Airla asked.

"Oh no," cried Irina.

"You're kidding, right?" said Lara.

"The perps are invisible. Watch the right side of the girl's neck. Wait for it. Crap. Even with slow motion, I can't control it fast enough. Irina, is there a way to make it play back one frame at a time?"

"I thought I saw something," Major Airla said.

"Lemme at it," Irina said. She fiddled with the holographic controls with her toes. "There, it'll be slow, a two-second pause between frames."

"Okay. Watch her neck. Can I tell it to pause? Thanks. Whatever would I do without my computer genius?"

"Yeah. Just bark that command, dear. Why, you couldn't do without me." Irina teased me.

"Pause!" I yelled my command. That frame froze on the holographic display. A thin gray hand with six fingers holding a rag arced towards the girl's face. The hand was visible partially in the previous frame, clearly visible in this one, and almost gone in the next, as was the girl who was knocked out by the fumes on the rag while being pulled into an invisibility field.

"Incredible. How did you ever see that?" asked Lara.

"I missed it, too," Major Airla said. "Now I know what to look for. That has to be a Sixth Invader's hand. That makes sense. I found heavy boot prints in the sand behind the swings. So many kids have been over the ground since the abduction, I couldn't follow the trail. How did you ever spot that, Molly?"

"I've a knack for it, I guess. What do the Sixth Invaders want with a couple six-year-old kids? Telepaths?"

"Telepaths is the likely reason," the Major said. "I have to call this in."

She stepped out of the room into our large commons.

"So any way we can find the kids?" Irina asked. Lara listened closely.

"Maybe, but if they took them into their spaceship, then probably not. I don't know anything about spaceships. Another damned hole in my pathetic knowledge."

"Hey, I don't know anything about spaceships either, dear. Don't be so hard on yourself. You spotted what no one else did," Irina said.

Lara laughed. "I've flown all over the galaxy in them, but I know nothing about them, except I get weird sensations in my stomach when we jump into or out of hyperspace."

"Well, my guess is their ship is nearby and cloaked. These aliens are strong, so they could carry the kids some distance, but it's more likely they didn't. Crap. That means they are close to us, too, Irina. Too damned close."

Major Airla returned. "I talked with Admiral Rossi. He's sending part of the fleet to hover over this facility. They're going to look for mass anomalies around here. Perhaps their ship is parked nearby. If not, they'll have to lug those kids some distance away. There's just too many large buildings this close to the Loop. We might get lucky and find their ship as we did earlier. Of course, I've no idea if we could rescue those children. Admiral Rossi doesn't think so. But I've got General Blythe standing by with a tactical team if we can take them on the ground."

I was about to comment when my phone rang. The ID said Galactic Medicine. "Accept call," I commanded. "Hello."

"Molly Parkinson?"

I said so but was surprised to see a holographic image of the caller appearing. So this person had one of the expensive and fancy phones that streamed a live holo image of the caller.

"I'm Francis Roth, chief Investigator for Galactic Medicine, Chicago branch. Could you possible come to the Med Center today? I would like to consult with you about a delicate matter. I've asked your sister, Celeste Sawyers, to come as well."

"When is Celeste coming? What's this about?"

"She said she'd come with you whenever you're free and if you'll do it. How does one o'clock sound? At reception, ask for Francis Roth. Thank you."

"Okay. I'll check with her. One o'clock then."

Celeste knew no more than I did, other than this must be important. She explained GMed had their own investigation group to track down medical fraud. What that had to do with us remained a mystery. Celeste volunteered to drop by and pick me up.

As she and I took the MTES from our condo into the Loop and the sprawling Med Center, Celeste had some news for me.

"Leslie has designed new dresses for you and Irina. They look sleek and elegant. They encase your shoulders, rather like a form-fit from your neck down to your waist, though the neckline in front looks like see-through lace. The dress flairs out at the waist and is knee length. It most definitely highlights your shoulders and lack of arms. A person with arms can't even wear it. I've seen her prototypes, and they look fabulous. Ah, here we are. I must admit my curiosity is roused, but not enough to probe this GMed woman's mind." We both chuckled.

Ten minutes later, a security woman led us into a small conference room on the third floor, where Francis waited for us. She was a tall brunette Galactic Doll, with a round face and stern, gray eyes.

"Welcome. Please have a seat. Thank you so much for coming without knowing what I wanted. Do you want anything to drink?"

"We're good," I said, as Celeste pulled out a chair for me.

"Okay then. I'll get right to business. Earth has a problem. Has had for a long time, one that few know about, one that has been getting steadily worse. Today, one-half of Earth's adult population has an IQ of 80 or less. In the past, Galactic Housing has been their sponsor, putting them to use maintaining the countless abandoned homes and businesses or demolishing them. Gardeners, cleaners, all the usual actions that must be done to prevent total deterioration of a building.

"With two-thirds of our buildings vacant, we needed these people to handle this maintenance. Either that or demolish good homes and businesses. The trouble is that over the years, the number of low IQ adults has been steadily increasing. We don't allow them to migrate off-world. We only allow higher IQ personnel into the colonization efforts."

"Have you taken that into account in the growth rate?" asked Celeste. "If you remove higher IQ people from the total population, then it will seem like the low IQ people make up a larger percentage."

"Yes, that's factored into the figures. It's a very real phenomenon. I've been asked to investigate it because of the recent request for these people. You've heard that Felt-D, wherever that world is, desperately needs unskilled workers to do routine work. They will pay our workers double wages if they immigrate to Felt-D and work for them. Galactic Housing has made a listing of those who meet their criteria: low IQ and age thirty or less. It turns out there are millions of them, and the figures captured the attention of the GMed CEO, who asked me to investigate why we have so many low IQ people."

"Have you discovered the reason?" Celeste asked before I could.

"No. I've run every medical test we have on them. Nothing unusual has shown up, not even on those who've become Galactic Dolls. I've heard about your special therapy from our St. Louis branch, Miss Sawyers, and we all know how good a PI Mrs. Parkinson is. That's why I've asked you here today. Could you put your special talents to work on our problem? Why do so many of our adults have such a low IQ? At first, I thought some chemical in our air or water might be harming people's brains. I've ruled that out. Frankly, I'm baffled."

Celeste looked at me before replying. "Okay. We'll take a look and see if we can discover the cause."

Chapter 25 The Drug Effect

Francis gave us the names of a dozen young men and women who worked for Galactic Housing and who wanted to take advantage of the Felt-D employment offer. As I looked over the list of names, addresses, jobs, and monthly pay, I understood why these people were so eager to immigrate to this unknown world.

My PI pay barely covered the rent on my office, forcing me to have to work to cover the rest of living expenses. That hadn't been too difficult to do. However, these people's monthly pay was a third of what mine had been! I couldn't imagine how they could get by on such a low stipend.

I thought of my dad. Then, I remembered he remodeled homes, so his pay must have been more than these people were getting. With the new access code that she gave me, I did a quick check on the pay for men who remodeled homes. I smiled. Dad received about three-quarters of the pay I received. I sighed, now understanding why credits had always been so tight in our family and why my parents were so thankful to move into the assisted living home when dad turned sixty. Their new apartment was much nicer than our tiny home.

Time to investigate. We picked a young man on the list and paid him a visit. We took the MTES to the western part of Chicago, where many empty, single-family dwellings lined long streets. The houses looked very nice, ready for occupation, a compliment to the continuous work of these people. Jasper stopped raking leaves as we walked up to him. I guessed he was twenty-five. He seemed fit and probably handsome if he wore something other than the bib overalls with patches on its knees.

"Hello. Are you Jasper Jenkins?" Celeste asked.

"Yup. That's me. If ya came to see the house, I can't let you in. Have to see the realtor. Not sure which one."

I glanced at the for sale sign, which had the realtor's name and phone number clearly visible.

"No, we came to see you, Jasper. Can we ask you some questions?"

"Sure thing."

"You've put in a request to immigrate to Feld-D."

"Um, is that the name of the place? Can't remember what it's called. Lots of money. I want to make lots. Can. If I move there. Are you here to take me?"

"No, we're checking up to make sure you want to move to an alien world."

"Okay. I hope they don't reject me because I dislocated my shoulder last week. It's a little sore but I'm fine, really I am. Then, I can marry Margaret. She wants to come, too. We'll be rich enough to buy a house. Do you think they'll let her come with me?"

"Sorry. I don't know," I said. "Maybe we can find out."

"So your shoulder is still sore?" Celeste asked.

"Yes, a little, but I'll be fine. No need to go to the Med Center. Then, it'd be on my record, and they might not take me."

"Is anyone inside this brownstone home right now?" she asked.

"No. I've already mopped the floor. Cleaning up outside now."

"Let's go inside. I want to see if we can do anything to help you with your shoulder. I promise we won't tell anyone."

Jasper agreed and let us in.

Celeste sent me. *I want to try my therapy on him. Keep an eye on how he responds. Maybe we can get a clue. He's able to communicate, but I can sense he's not too bright.*

I nodded my agreement as we sat down on the steps that led to the second floor.

"Okay, Jasper, I want you to close your eyes and see if you can recall the first moment when you injured your shoulder."

He twisted this way and that, as though struggling to remember, but eventually believed he was there. My curiosity rose, and I peeked into his mind to see why he was having such a hard time with this.

Oh brother. Peering into his mind reminded me of walking Chicago during a heavy fog. Gray-white masses moved this way and that, obscuring and obstructing his mental processes. His ability to recall an image or perhaps his ability to form a mental image was poor. When he said he'd found it, I knew he had because I saw it too. Jasper had a difficult time re-experiencing the trauma incident because the swirling cloud-like masses kept moving around, sometimes blocking his view of the images for a few moments.

Two hours later, Celeste ended the therapy session. A cheerful Jasper explained the pain had magically vanished. He moved his arm about to prove it to us and to himself. Celeste thanked him, and we left, heading for the MTES and the long trip home.

"Once blocks away on the escalators, Celeste chatted. "So did you see all that whitish and grayish stuff in his mind?"

"Yeah. It was like walking around in a dense fog. Mists swirling around with things coming into view and then vanishing. What was that? It's almost like the mental energies of the Sixth Invader implants."

"Good analogy, Molly. I'm almost certain it's the results of accumulated dementia-causing drugs. Imagine living ten lives in which the last five years of each you're given the dementia drug which ruins all mental faculties. I believe it's a many lifetimes buildup effect. Layer upon layer of the dementia drug. That's my theory."

"So how do we prove it? Can anything help half the people of Earth?" My own parents had been victims of this, so I had a vested interest in finding out.

"I'll have to ask Eve and Randi and get their opinion. I would think therapy should undo it, but..."

We stopped by their apartment behind Leslie's Costumes R Us store. Eve shoved her books aside and helped us. After Celeste described the situation with Jasper, I sent her my memories of the gray-whitish masses I'd seen in his mind.

"Well, I think your diagnosis is correct, Celeste. Accumulated effects of the dementia-causing drug over many lifetimes. As far as Hank could tell, they've been using it for two hundred twenty years. A person could well have endured it across four lifetimes or more by now. We should correlate it with the observed drops in IQ over this period."

"How can we do that?" I asked. "Didn't Kyle have graphs of that?"

"Not that exactly. But I know someone at Galactic University who owes me a favor. I'll send it to you as soon as I can get it," Eve said. "Be thinking if it's possible to use therapy to erase it. That, I don't know. I'll ask Randi later. Oh, Leslie wants to see you, Molly, before you go home. New dress design for you."

While Celeste and Eve chatted, I went across the narrow alley and into the back entrance.

"Hi, Leslie."

"Hey, Molly. Guess what? Like you probably already know. Come on. I've like designed a smashing gown for you women. Ta da! What like do you think?"

She knew I liked light blue. The satin gown was a sky blue, but what caught my eyes was the bodice with its lace-like neckline. She'd removed the mannequin's arms, and the bodice snugly encased its empty shoulders, while the lace rather sparkled around the heart-shaped neckline.

"Wow. This looks gorgeous. Smashing. Can I try one on? Ted's gonna love this."

Leslie got me out of my Galactic Doll blue gown and into this new one.

"I love how it feels on my shoulders like someone's wrapped a towel around me. It certainly shows off my form."

"You like look perfect in it, Molly. And love the little flair around your knees. Not confining, so you like have better use of your legs."

"Leslie, you've outdone yourself this time. I'll take a bunch and some for Irina too."

"I thought so. I like made you both a dozen. All I ask is like when you get comments about them, like tell them where to find them. Costumes R Us."

"Don't worry, sis. I'll tell everyone about these and always wear them. Love how my shoulders are encased in the bodice. Can I pay you for them? You can't go giving that many dresses away."

She protested, but I insisted on paying for half of them. Leslie boxed them and sent for a delivery person. I wore one home, knowing I'd get an awful lot of stares. I wasn't disappointed. Many people traveling on the MTES stared at my new gown and the obvious lack of arms, exaggerated by the form of the bodice.

"Wow! Oh wow! You're stunning, dear." I thought Irina's eyes would pop out of her head.

"Leslie sent along a dozen like this for you. Should be here soon. What're we going to do if we both look stunning?" I teased her, but I'd hit a nerve. She wasn't a male any longer.

Her introversion didn't last long. The door answering machine announced a delivery. At least the young woman carried the boxes into our bedroom for us, so we didn't have to wait for Lara to come home.

"Come on. Let's get you into a red one," I suggested.

Using my teeth, I pulled up the back zipper for her.

"This is incredible. My shoulders love the tight feel of the satin on them. It's like I've wrapped a warm towel around me. How do I look?" Irina said.

I chuckled. "That's what I said to Leslie. Feels like a towel. Look in the mirror. You're hotter than hot."

We pushed into each other and exchanged passionate kisses. Just then, Lara entered. "Oh. Excuse me."

"No, come on in. These are Leslie's newest designs just for us. What do you think?" I asked.

Lara whistled and said something in her native language. From her tone, I knew she, too, thought we looked stunning and sexy. "Well, that's one dress I can't possibly wear," she teased.

We laughed. I felt alive. The smile on Irina's face electrified me.

After supper prepared by Lara, Celeste dropped by with some graphs.

"You both look just fabulous." Cheshire grins dominated our faces.

"Okay. Business." She laid out the graphs. "The IQ of seniors in high school is shown over the last two hundred years. It's almost a shallow parabola. Not an exponential drop in IQ, but it's increasing at an alarming rate. Rather, I should say IQ dropping at a steep rate."

"What's the dotted red line at the end?" I asked.

"Oh, I extrapolated it out to see what happens if nothing changes. In another hundred years, the IQ levels will be so low that people won't even be functional outside an assisted living home. We must get them to cease using that dementia-causing drug. Otherwise, within two centuries, the highest IQ on Earth will be that of a moron."

"That's awful. Now that the CEOs are changing their ideas about drugging those over sixty, we might be able to do something about that," I said.

"Yes, but we must discover a way to undo this."

"I agree. Mom and dad got wiped out by that damned drug. So I suppose in their next lifetimes, they'll be even dumber than they were this time."

"I'm sorry, Molly. But you're right. Tomorrow, we will figure out a way to undo this. Okay?"

"Count me in."

Chapter 26 Change of Plans

"Yes, Admiral L'Tara. We've kidnapped two young telepaths. But that Molly Parkinson interfered again. Somehow she discovered our cloaked cruiser and send the entire Earth fleet to attack us."

The admiral barked, "Damage estimates?"

"As you can see, my right arm is badly burned, but I've got my repair crew working on the ship's damage. It should be operational in a couple days."

"What about the assist for the Zahra-C ambassadors? Have you killed that male of hers—that Ted fellow—for the ambassadors? Sure don't know why they wanted him dead."

"Yes, my bomb killed him and many others. But your plan failed. In spite of ambassador pressure here on Earth, Parkinson refuses to become a Sol Empire Senior Ambassador. Instead, she's somehow discovering our cloaked ships. I told you, this woman is big trouble. We've killed her twice now, but she keeps coming back."

"I see. Commander, I'm sorry I didn't believe you. I'm convinced. We're changing strategies. Back home, central planning has had a change of plans, too."

Admiral L'Tara cracked a grin before continuing.

"Has your team secured goodly quantities of the mutation agent?"

"Aye, sir. Enough for a large city. Are we going to use it or supply it to the human resistance movement?"

"Have our science team prepare enough skyscraper 'bombs' to take out a hundred story building like you did before. We'll need fifty of them to begin with. A major operation is about to begin, but first you must handle this Parkinson woman. Commander, I agree with your assessment. This woman is an acute danger to our plans. We can't allow her to interfere any longer. With this new plan from home world, we dare not have her interrupt us. It'll be my head, not just yours. Is that understood?"

"Aye, sir. Kill her again?"

"Don't be silly. She's come back twice now. Kill her again and she'll only be back once more. No, we must take her *out* of the picture. Kidnap her and hold her on your ship. Eventually, we'll take her back to home world along with the two small children."

"Consider it done, sir."

"It had better be done soon. The Felderans arrive on September 20 to pick up the first of our new miners. Time the bombs for that morning. Here are your sealed orders; follow them to the letter. With this Parkinson woman in your hands, this time nothing can go wrong. Dismissed."

Commander L'Grina watched the image of her admiral fade from her eyes and monitor. She slumped in her seat. She had been fighting the searing pain in her right arm, fearing the admiral would relieve her of her command if she saw how badly she was injured—all because of the infernal interference of Parkinson. Well, she smiled in spite of the pain; that woman's days were numbered.

***

"Hi, Dimitri. It's the middle of the night here," I said. My phone displayed 3 am.

"Sorry, but this is important. I got a call from the local GMed CEO in LA."

I grumbled and certainly didn't care that he'd gotten a call from LA. However, I was polite. "And?"

"They're getting ready for the arrival of the Feld-D transports to ferry the Galactic Housing workers to their new employer."

"Yeah, they're getting people interviewed for that here, too." I resisted the urge to add a sarcastic "so."

"One of those men came in begging to become a millionaire telepath. So they ran his DNA, just as they're doing to all those workers who want to take advantage of the doubled wages."

I resisted the urge to yawn. "And?"

"And my ID came up. They entered his DNA a second time and Ted's ID came up. Then, they called me. Molly, do you know what this means?"

Okay. Now I was *fully* awake. I felt as though he'd splashed ice-cold water on my face. "Another of the male clones has shown up."

"Not only that, but he wants to become a telepath. Here's Ted's golden opportunity."

"We should go there and check it out."

Dimitri chuckled. "And take a Body Sswap machine with you. I've told them you would pay them a visit tomorrow."

He gave me contact information. My talking woke Irina, who became too excited to go back to sleep. "If he wants to be a telepath, he's welcome to this body."

"Figured you'd say that, dear."

Early morning, I called Deanna Cartwright and told her what Dimitri discovered. She offered us her corporate Airliner. Around eight, Holly Ann met us at New O'Hare, bringing along one of her Body Swap machines.

"Wow, Leslie's new gown designs look fabulous on you two," she said as she strapped us into our seats.

"And more comfortable too. Less confining on our leg motions," I said. We chatted, making the flight time to LA vanish.

The GMed CEO met me at LAX, but I kept Holly Ann and Irina on the liner. The less anyone knew about this the better.

"Yes, we've already had six men volunteering to become telepaths—well, armless Dolls so far. We've got them at an assisted living home, where they are watching the many how-to videos and practicing using their feet and toes. We're monitoring how soon after the mutation their telepathic abilities mature. It's the sixth day for four of them, but nothing yet."

"In Chicago, it took over a week for telepathic skills to appear and then they gradually built up," I explained.

"Say, I like this new style gown you're wearing."

I told her about Leslie's new designs as we walked to a side room, where a man waited for me. I blinked and would have rubbed my eyes if I could. Here was the splitting image of Frank Wells, Dimitri Leonovich, Ted Billings, and Felix Baker before the latter two were mutated into male Dolls. Another of the male clones had appeared.

"Hello. I'm Molly Parkinson."

"Wanna be telepath. No wanna be alien gardener. Make me telepath. Make millions credits."

"He's been saying that from the beginning, so we checked his DNA. That's always the first step for anyone wanting to take advantage of the Feld-D offer of double wages or to become a telepath. The new DNA database has a few glitches in it, but we don't know the cause yet. I've assigned people to look into it. Anyway, we've verified he is Derrick Jones, age twenty-six. No living relatives. Adopted as a baby. Parents deceased. Worked for Galactic Housing for eight years now. I've no idea why you came all this way to see him, but I'll give you a few minutes alone with him. We should decide what to do with him today if possible. He's a good candidate for the Feld-D offer, but we've no idea about the telepath angle. Any advice you can give us will be appreciated."

She left, and I studied Derrick, lightly touching his mind. There was the same gray-white foggy masses I'd seen yesterday. "So you want to become a telepath?"

"Yes, telepath. Millionaire. Be one. You make me?"

"You must learn how to do things with your feet and toes like I do."

"You telepath. Me want be telepath. You make me? I learn. Work hard."

I doubted he had graduated high school, but then I never paid attention to most of those in my class other than Frank Wells. Maybe they didn't worry about having passing grades to graduate. Here was another thing I wanted to investigate.

I tried to hold a conversation, but soon gave up and met the CEO again. "Okay, I believe I have a body exchange that will allow him to become a telepath. He'll need to join the others at your assisted living home so he can learn how effectively use his feet. Will that be acceptable?"

"Yes, of course. Solves the problem for us. We'll monitor how good he is as a telepath. Then, we'll publish our findings. I'm sure other med centers are getting many lower IQ Galactic Housing men and women wanting to become telepaths. This way, we'll have a good idea if such is feasible. Thanks. How do you want to proceed?"

"I'll take him with me onto the liner and make the exchange. Back with him, er her, shortly."

The CEO chuckled, knowing what I meant. All telepaths were armless Dolls. I had Derrick follow me onto the Airliner where he met Irina and Holly Ann.

Irina took me aside and asked, "If I take his body, will I be that dumb?"

"I don't think so. The drug mass is in his mind, not his body. This body hasn't been given the dementia-causing drug, so I think he's taking that with him."

"Okay, then. Let's do this," Irina said. The excitement in her eyes shown like sparks. In a flash, I knew why. She'd be a male again. Only now did I realize how much that meant to Ted.

Ten minutes later, Holly Ann turned off her machine. The two awoke.

"What a miracle! I'm me again, Molly." Ted's exuberance rubbed off onto all of us.

"I feel funny. Hear thoughts. Oh, I telepath. I be millionaire," Irina said.

"Your name is Irina Jones. Come with me. You've got to work hard now."

"Irina. Irina. I work hard. Irina work hard. Hear thoughts. Fun."

I explained to the CEO, "Here's Irina Jones. Already, she's hearing thoughts. But she'll need to watch those how-to videos and practice a lot. Still, she's hearing others' thoughts already, a good sign she'll be a useful telepath."

I left her with the CEO and headed back onto the Airliner and my exuberant husband.

"Look at me, dear. I'm me again. Arms and all. Let me hug you. God, how I've wanted to do this for so damn long." His arms encircled my shoulders, pulling me up tight to his body. Okay, I felt light as a feather. I had my Ted back. Maybe there was something to Leslie's Lucky Gene idea.

When we landed at New O'Hare, Ted volunteered to help Holly Ann get her machine back to the Cartwright skyscraper. I wanted to chat with Celeste, who I knew had been working her therapy on the man we'd met yesterday. Had she been successful in breaking through that drug mass that obscured and dampened his mental faculties? I could use telepathy to find out, but I preferred to talk face to face.

"You guys go on. I'll take the MTES over to Celeste's. Back home before dark. Promise."

Off I went. I watched the puffy clouds in the sky and smiled at other women, many who stared at my unusual gown's bodice encasing my shoulders like a towel wrap. I made a note to tell Leslie how much attention her new style was getting before I headed home.

I inhaled deeply, but the fishy smell of the lake wasn't there. Oil and grease from the spaceport along with exhaust tickled my olfactory senses. And something else. What was that smell? It grew stronger, like a sickly perfume. I looked behind me but saw nothing. Still, the odor grew. Suddenly, I saw a gray hand with six fingers holding a rag reaching around my face. The odor came from the rag. I tried to turn and resist, but the drug knocked my body out before I could see my attacker. The daytime changed to the blackest night in less than a second or so I thought. My legs gave way, and I wondered what I should do about them. Then, nothing.

***

"Look, she's awake," a soft voice whispered.

My head was mush, but I forced my eyes open, though they weighted a ton. Disoriented. All my senses went crazy. I was sitting in a soft seat, a safety belt around my waist. The space was brown and smelled metallic or plastic—couldn't tell which. The brown resolved into the curved walls of a ship. My mind finally connected the dots. I was in a Sixth Invader spaceship. I sensed motion. The ship was flying. My eyes found the origin of the voice.

A small girl and boy sat on cushions on the floor at my feet. Both were armless Dolls, but at least the boy wore Leslie's new male clothing. A shirt and pants.

"Who are you? Where are we?"

"I'm Margot Rothham. He's a really a boy, Phillip. We're twins and six years old. Who are you? Are you a telepath, too?"

"Yes, I'm Molly Parkinson."

"Oh, you're the one they wanted. We want to go home. Can you take us?

"Are we their prisoners?"

The two shrugged their shoulders.

Another voice broke the silence. "For now you are my guests. I'm Commander L'Grina."

I turned in the seat and saw her sitting next to us. Heavy bandages covered her right arm. She radiated pain.

"Molly Parkinson. We killed you twice, but you just keep coming back. This time, we've captured you so you can't meddle in our plans. Your last intervention caused this." She pointed her injured arm. "You brought dozens of blasters firing down on my cruiser, giving me severe burns before we could escape. No more meddling. Things are about to happen. This way, you can't interfere. So sit back while we fly to our new destination."

Another soldier walked up. I noticed they'd fastened a translator device to my waist. Hence, I could understand them and vice versa.

"Commander, we're above LA now. Your orders?"

"Land at that abandoned stadium place, but not the one where our field excursion team has landed. Prepare to coordinate the extractions."

The woman saluted and briskly left the cabin. The commander turned. "You're in my personal quarters. Thanks to you, I have to minimize my appearance in front of my crew until my arm heals. We never show weakness."

"What are you going to do with the children? Leave them out of this."

"Ha. Fat chance, as you Earthlings say. Well, plans change, so I shouldn't be so snide. You knew me as CEO Hardy. What a laugh that was. Ran you through the hoops as your people say." Her face grew taut. "You interfered way too much for your own good."

"Well, your people interfered with us way too much for your own good," I bandied back at her. Not much else I could do. Yet. "So you were CEO Hardy. Bet you had a good laugh at Ted and me when you invited us to that formal ball."

"Smirk. That was my attitude towards you. Still, had we known just how much trouble you would be to us, I'm sure Commander R'Ina would have had you killed. I take it you've made use of the Transference Machines?"

"Yes, you didn't give me any choice but to use it. I don't like giving up and starting over as a baby."

"Huh? What the devil are you talking about? Baby? Once you're dead, you're dead, unless you have another body at hand and get swapped into it before yours dies. Somehow, you keep on doing just that, so our Admiral L'Tara had me kidnap you to stop your meddling. I can't see why I shouldn't kill you. If I blow a hole in your head, there's no way anyone could get you to a Transference Machine before you die, not when I've got you here with me."

"I'll behave. I've no death wish." Dark lines creased her face, and I guessed her arm must be throbbing mercilessly. Still, she did talk with me. If I could gain her trust, I could learn a great deal about our enemy. Then, an idea popped into my head. "Say, we have something that could help relieve some of the pain and speed healing."

"I wouldn't let you touch me. I'm not a fool."

She didn't reject my offer. I wouldn't let her touch me either if things were reversed. "Sorry. No hands to touch you with."

That brought a brief flash of a smile to her grimacing face.

"So what's this thing you have? Our medical man is good with field wounds. This is the best he can do. My body's going to need time to heal."

"Therapy. I'll show you if you have time and are willing."

She glanced at a dial. "I'm not needed for two of your Earth hours. Will that do?"

"Sure. It's all done by voice commands. I'm locked into this chair, so you don't have to worry I'll get up and strangle you. No hands."

That seemed to relax her. "Close your eyes. Okay. Now return to the moment when you first discovered Earth's ships had found your cloaked ship. Good. Now move through the trauma and tell me about it as you go along. Tell me what you're seeing, smelling, touching."

I didn't know if Celeste's therapy would work on a Sixth Invader, an alien. But it had worked on the dwarf. As far as I knew, everyone was a spiritual being, just inhabiting different species of bodies. I was about to find out. As it stood, I was at her mercy, as were the twins. If there was any way out of this, it would have to be through Commander L'Grina. The only thing I had going in my favor was that she knew me from her stint as CEO Hardy.

"Yeow!" She cried when she contacted the brunt of the searing pain. The many blaster shots overloaded their shields, which shorted out some machinery, sending shooting flames over her right arm. I continued to run her through the incident several times, and more specific information came to light with each pass. Conclusion: the therapy method worked on Sixth Invaders, too. But I doubted that I'd have enough time to finish it. She never became cheerful about it before a gong warning sounded, and she abruptly ended the session. She nodded and left the cabin.

"Did you help her?" Margot asked.

"I hope so."

"Why? She's our enemy."

"Good point. But if we have any chance of getting home, we must create goodwill between us."

Phillip volunteered. "We're supposed to learn to be their telepaths. I don't want to. I'll make them kill me first."

"Well, I'm here now. I'll try to find us a way home."

A male brought in a large tray of food. "Hope this Earth food is edible. Doesn't look like it, but the food robot made it." He set the tray down on the floor.

"Excuse me. Can you undo my belt so I can eat?"

He studied me, staring at my dress-covered empty shoulders, before grunting and undoing the belt. Okay, I could have undone it myself, but the more these people believed we were helpless, the better.

"Has the food been any good? Have they treated you well?"

"Can't tell any difference. Robot always made ours," Margot said, moving into position to help herself.

"Isn't poison," Phillip added.

"Where do you sleep? Is there a bathroom? Have you been brushing your teeth?" I tried to ask all the proper mommy questions while I could, hoping to get a better picture of our captivity.

"Some man helps us," Margot said.

"Over there," Phillip nodded to bedding lying on the floor in the corner farthest from the door. Nearby was a cot built into the wall, presumably the commander's.

He asked, "Are you going to take us home? We wanna go home."

"I'll try, Phillip. We best eat. Keep up our strength."

Chapter 27 Secret Strike

"Yes, Admiral L'Tara. We're in place. Awaiting your order," Commander L'Grina said.

Until they captured the twins and me, I believed the Federation representatives who claimed the Sixth Invaders had fled the Sol Empire and wouldn't be back. Yet, here they were, apparently stronger than ever. I didn't know what was about to happen. What orders?

"Execute now. The Feld-D transports have arrived at ten Earth space ports."

"Aye, aye, sir. Strike Teams, execute Operation Gas," the commander said.

That was all the commander did, for she sat back and relaxed, her hands behind her head. I noticed she'd replaced many of the bandages on her right arm with smaller ones. She turned from her chair and controls. If she'd just positioned the monitor more my way, I could have seen that admiral.

The male returned. He removed the empty tray and secured me back into the chair beside the commander's, though the twins remained sitting on the floor.

"Well, now the fun begins." She laughed. "That pathetic CEO in LA who surrendered to me is getting his worst nightmare as we chat."

"Can you tell me what's going on? You know me— always the curious one."

She flexed her injured right arm. "It's remarkably better, you know. After that thing you did for me. Much of the burn has healed unexpectedly fast. Amazing. I suppose I owe you for that. Besides, you're here with me and have no way to interfere this time."

"No, I'm stuck here." I re-enforced her idea.

"Back home, High Command has changed their plans. We no longer want to conquer Earth. Not sure about the rest of the Sol Empire though."

"Why the change of heart?"

"It's all because of the concatenation of errors our stupid Chief Science Officer, G'Karn, made. No one expected his blunders in the genetic mutations of your species would cause the creation of telepaths. Talk about blind, stupid luck. Home world is well aware your corporations are now offering pay rates of a million credits per year for your telepath's services."

She let out a 'Ha.' "Telepaths will put a severe crimp in the way we take over worlds. Our disguises as the two top Earth CEOs would have been blown within days of our body transferences instead of the two decades that we got away with it. Telepaths are also bad for our spies and agents on other worlds. Bad for business."

"So?" I wished she'd get to the plan.

"So, High Command wants us to get into the telepath providing business. We're already doing your world a big favor by using many of your morons."

"What do you mean using our morons?" She'd mentioned two actions. I could understand the telepath angle, but what about our low IQ people? They were supposed to be going to jobs on a world called Feld-D.

She laughed long and hard. "Feld-D is one of the worlds we dominate. They're transporting your stupid and young people to our world for us."

"But aren't they supposed to get double wages? Is this all another Sixth Invader lie?"

"We've never figured out why the Federation calls us Sixth Invaders. No matter. We need fuel for our space fleet. Mining for the raw ore is toxic to our people, bringing on severe illnesses and very short lifetimes. We've found the mining fumes are not toxic to humans, so we're hiring your dumb, but young and strong, to mine for us. Why dumb? So they can be manipulated into doing the mining. Yes, we're gonna pay them, but we'll mind wipe them before they return to your world with credits in their pockets. So it's darn convenient your world is full of dumb people we can use."

"So you will return them and pay them?"

"Of course. We want this to become a self-sustaining operation. Besides, it's a benefit to your world. These people can only perform menial labor. We're doing you a favor."

I laughed. "Did you ever stop and think about this? All you had to do was ask politely. Our CEOs would have jumped at the chance to put these low IQ people to work. We would rather call them that than morons, which sounds derogatory. You could have set up something completely above boards. Besides, we've figured out why their IQ is so low."

Commander L'Grina looked baffled, but she said, "Okay. Why is their IQ so low? Different genetic makeup? Different sub-species?"

I chuckled. "No. Nothing as profound as that. It's the dementia-causing drug that's behind half of those on Earth having very low IQs."

"Oh don't be silly. We're talking about young people in their twenties, not your older people."

"Correct. We've been drugging our older people for over two centuries. That drug wipes out mental functions in horrible ways. When that body dies, the person and his messed-up mind picks up a new baby body and starts a new life. These people have had their minds messed-up by the dementia drug at least five times, which leaves their current minds in a confused, gray-white drug mass, barely able to function. That's the real cause of their stupidity."

"Huh? You're nuts. When you die, you're dead dead dead. Don't be silly."

"When you have more free time, I'd like to finish that therapy session we were doing on the trauma to your arm. Perhaps that may shed light on what I was saying. Anyway, what's this about the telepath providing business?"

"Oh. Yes, it has helped my arm—remarkably so. Anyway, that's our current operation—one you can't interfere with. When we discovered that the genetic mutation goof by G'Karn created real telepaths, High Command tried it on our people. Alas, the genetic mutation only works on you humans. Our species is immune to the bio agent. So we're making a self-sustaining group of humans to be our telepath breeding population."

"What?"

"Yes, we're acquiring around four thousands of you humans, mutating them into telepaths first, and then bringing them to our Home World, where they'll be trained and bred. Soon, we'll market telepaths to anyone and any world who can afford their services. Talk about an incredible get-wealthy scheme—this one is fantastic and can't fail. A sure thing. No wonder High Command has jumped on this so quickly, abandoning their plans to conquer the Sol Empire."

"So where are you getting these people?"

"We have to avoid getting those low IQ people you harp about. We want bright minds. So we're mutating many of those who run your major corporations. I've teams at several dozen corporate buildings in large cities like LA. They've released the mutation agent into the air circulation systems of several skyscrapers. By now, thousands of bright people will be in their mutation comas. We only want top minds of Earth, you see. At night, my people will slip into the buildings, invisible of course, retrieve the bodies, and bring them to our waiting transport ships.

"They'll arrive on Home World in twelve hours, where, as I understand the plan, they'll be placed in homes and provided a computer loaded with all those how-to videos Commander R'Ina assembled for her failed plot in Chicago. Already, my team has raided the Galactic Robotics' storage facility and stole thousands of the hair and nail machines, the dressing/undressing machine, the cleaning/cooking maid, and even the latest robot that feeds your kind. Oh, and we'll also copy this new style dress you're wearing. It's damn alluring. Too bad you aren't a male."

Was that a flirting smile she gave me? I tried not to react. A call came in, and she took it.

"The five corporations in LA have been secured. We're going in now to retrieve the bodies. Have the transports standing by."

The commander looked at the dial. "Right on schedule. Excellent. Transports one through five, stand by to receive bodies."

She looked at me with a broad grin. "Done. LA's GPan, GD, Galactic Robotics, Galactic Entertainment, and Galactic University corporations' personnel are in their mutation comas as we speak. Now, my invisible team is retrieving the bodies. I'll have a head count soon. We've grabbed everyone from these same corporations in New York City, Philadelphia, Miami, and Mexico City. The mutation bombs detonated while most were present during working hours. For your information, it's now nighttime, which helps hide our activities."

She smirked. "Your leaders are completely confused. I timed this to occur when so many of your people were dealing with the thousands being transported by our Feld-D people. Clever, eh? By the time your people realize what's happened, those in their mutation comas will have vanished without a trace."

She laughed long before taking another call. I relaxed a little; they hadn't harmed any of my dear friends. With little I could do, I tried to estimate how many people were affected. These were local offices, not the larger hundred story skyscrapers filled with personnel who ran the empire or even ran all the local offices. I guessed perhaps five hundred people might be in any one building. That yielded twenty-five hundred from LA alone, and five times that from all those cities she mentioned. Wait, that couldn't be right. That would yield thirteen thousand victims. She had said her High Command wanted four thousand. Wait. Did this mean they were planning to sell off the excess nine thousand victims? I felt sick.

Where would they sell these people? Would a Federation world buy telepaths? If I let the ambassadors know about this, would they allow worlds to buy them and make slaves out of them?

Molly? Thank heavens we found you! Where are you? What happened to you? It was Celeste. She'd reached me with her telepathy.

Commander L'Grina kidnapped me. She's the Sixth Invader who was CEO Hardy. I'm with her in a spaceship, along with the two six-year-old twins, Margot and Phillip Rothham.

I told her about the mutation attacks and kidnappings and about the trickery surrounding the Feld-D deal for our low IQ young people.

No, I've no idea where we are. I'm trying to get more information. Contact me later.

It's magical what the gentle touch of a dear friend can be when you're in an awful situation. She calmed me down so I could think more clearly. Facts. I needed more facts, though I knew Celeste would let the ambassadors know about the telepath situation.

I tried to analyze the situation. Many corporations and others wanted to employ telepaths. Isabella and Bernardo were using their abilities for valuable purposes. Yet, corporations would use others as spies, and I suspected many would be used in that manner. Perhaps, secrets would become a thing of the past, since little could be kept from one of us who could pry into nearly anyone's mind. Did these Sixth Invaders know what they were doing?

"Five thousand three hundred six future telepaths on their way to Home World. Excellent job, Commander L'Grina," said Admiral L'Tara.

I twisted around but just couldn't see her face from my seat. While I'd been musing, the commander had received more communications. Apparently, the entire operation ended.

"Very good, sir. No casualties on this end. In fact, no trouble at all. The plan worked to perfection."

"Of course. You're to stick around Earth a while longer until all the new workers have been handled and are on their way here to mine for us."

Commander L'Grina's face twisted before morphing into a grimace. "Aye, sir," she replied, a note of hostility in her voice. Without touching her mind, I sensed how much she detested being on our world and around us. The admiral ended the transmission.

"Navigator, take us back to Chicago and our landing base in the abandoned stadium."

She turned. "Well, that's that. When you aren't around, our plans work perfectly. Anyway, I've got several hours free right now."

I smiled and took advantage of it. "Okay then, let's continue where we left off. Close your eyes."

I returned her to the trauma incident in which her arm was severely burned. After running her through it a few more times, I popped the key question, asking her if there was a similar trauma that had happened earlier.

Her birth came up. The doctor scalded her while cleaning up the newborn baby. After running her through that several times, she still wasn't cheerful, so I asked for something even earlier.

"Of course, there can't be anything earlier. Everyone knows that."

"Well, just take a look. Do you see anything, a faint image, a mass, anything?" Okay, I took a quick glance at her mind. I saw something was there, but how to get her to spot it became my challenge. She kept insisting there wasn't anything before her current life.

"Damn, my arm is throbbing again."

"Is it coming from an earlier trauma? What are you seeing?"

I debated whether to point her to what I was seeing. I decided not to do that. If I did, she would end up depending on me and not her own self.

"Oh, there's this funny reddish thing."

"Good. Let's go to its beginning. Move on through it and tell me what's happening as you do so."

Funny thing. I had seen something bluish, but she was seeing something reddish. So I was thankful I hadn't outright told her about what I saw. For all I knew, what was red to her might be blue to me.

She began going through it. "I see a spaceship. One of ours. I seem to be piloting it. Ah, we're in a dogfight. Oh crap! The ship is hit. Exploding. Burning. My arm is burning up. I'm helpless to do anything about it. Oh! That was me. I was alive in another body. I have lived before. How interesting. Wow."

I ended the session. She was not only cheerful but laughing. The last residual pain from her recent burn had vanished.

"Commander, we've landed. Local time is midnight."

"Okay. Post guards. Let's get some sleep," she ordered.

"Say, since you've got your thousands of telepaths, you don't need these two small children, do you?"

"Well, not really. The plans changed."

"Right. And now you're about to leave Earth, so you don't need me either. Why keep on holding me? You surely don't want to take me to your world where there's no end of trouble I could cause."

She laughed. "Point taken. Lord, I'd not wish you on my people. I've already killed you twice. What good has it done? No, if I ever have to return to this miserable world, I'll see you're captured before we take any action. In fact, holding you captive has, for the first time, kept you from interfering with our plans. So beware. I might snatch you again. Come on. I'll walk you to the exit ramp. You did me a good turn so I ought to reciprocate."

Five minutes later, I breathed in the chilly fall air of Chicago. The twins were at my side as we found our way to the MTES from the old ball stadium, still being maintained for unknown reasons, just as two-thirds of all buildings were.

Chapter 28 Recovery

Although midnight, we had enough light to see via the MTES system. I led us a couple blocks to the lake. From there, it was several miles to the Loop, paralleling the lake, but we had only a short distance to go. Our assisted living home was not too far inland from what had once been a zoo. By the time we arrived, many others had gathered to welcome me back.

As we walked up, Leslie ran up to me. "I like thought I'd like never see you again. We're like super lucky." She hugged me, before adding, "You like look good in my new style dress."

All my sisters were there, but Ted stayed back, grinning at me.

"Let's get inside. Everyone wants to hear what happened to you," Deanna said. "How on earth did you get away from them and rescue the twins as well?"

Once we sat down on the common area couches, I explained. "Goodwill. Celeste, your therapy works on the Sixth Invaders, too."

I talked for an hour while Ted brought us tea and cookies. Graciously, he put the two youngsters to bed in what had been our adopted teen's bedrooms.

"Yes, it's like a big disaster," Leslie explained. "It like was all over the news. LA, New York City, Philadelphia, Miami, and Mexico City. They like lost everyone who worked in the GPan, GD, Galactic Robotics, Galactic Entertainment, and Galactic University corporations. Thousands."

Deanna said, "Yes, fifteen mutation attacks. Tanks inserted into the air filtration system. The workers had no chance at all. Around five thousand people, we think."

I corrected her. "Five thousand three hundred six, according to the Sixth Invaders. I can't believe they're going to sell telepaths as if we're a thing."

Celeste said, "With that many men and women, they could easily begin a breeding program since biological clocks have been reset to around twenty-five for everyone that old or older. We've notified the Federation representatives, but don't hold your breath."

"Why?" I asked.

"Because everyone wants their own telepath working for them."

"We've ordered extra security for your condo and all others here," Deanna said. "Helen Hugo wants you telepaths guarded 24/7 from now on. She'll even have security guards at the schools. The corporations recognize telepaths are their most valuable commodity."

"Hell, I'm not a commodity to be bought and sold."

Everyone chuckled. Since the hour was late, my extended family and friends gave me a hug and left.

"Ted, get me out of these clothes and into the shower. I'll let you help me so we can go to bed sooner."

"You got it, dear. Mind if I chat while I wash off my precious wife I thought I'd never see again?"

As he assisted me so everything went quickly, he explained how he felt. "It's quite a shock to have telepathy and then one day wake up to find it's entirely gone. I'm still coming to grips with it. Kinda like I lost a whole perception sense or something. Still, while I can't just know what's on your mind anymore, I promise to pay more attention to you."

"Don't worry. I'm happy your body looks like it should have looked before all that genetic mutation stuff changed it. You're still you—the man I love more than I can say."

As we snuggled in bed, something that alien commander had said continued to bother me. "The commander said something about you that's strange. She had her crew make and plant the bomb that killed you."

"Ah ha. So you've proved the Sixth Invaders were after me."

"Well, yes, but..."

"But what?"

"She said they only killed you as a favor to some Zahra-C ambassadors. Now, why would Zahra-C ambassadors want you dead? Have you even met any of their ambassadors?"

"Huh? I've never even seen these Zahra-C aliens, much less done anything to them. Are you sure you got it right?"

I continued to doubt what I'd picked up from the commander. Why would aliens that we've never met want Ted dead and go to the trouble of having the Sixth Invaders do it for them? Just trying to make sense of this made my forehead ache.

"We have to be missing something, dear, something huge. Think about it. Aliens we know nothing about and who are part of the Federation and who came to our empire's rescue has our enemies killing you as a favor to them? What's the connection between Zahra-C and the Sixth Invaders? Hell, according to that neat holographic galaxy display, the two civilizations aren't even in the same spiral arm. Tell me again what your R&D people were working on."

"Can't it wait until morning?"

"Okay, okay." I wiggled a little, snuggling down beside him, his arm around me. Oh, how I liked that—how I'd missed his touch. Sleep finally came.

I saw the cigar-shaped Sixth Invader cruiser setting down on a strange world. Other spaceships sat on the tarmac, bustling with humans loading and unloading them. In the hilly background rose a medieval castle whose walls must have been thirty feet tall and enclosed a taller central manor house—all built of dark gray stone. Unknown writing covered a large sign over the passenger station, but I could read it. "Thromstead, Blackwell-C" How weird. As I watched the Sixth Invader ship, a side door opened and a gray-skinned, six-fingered woman in her fancy green uniform stepped down.

Her translator box around her waist translated her language into that of the imposing man wearing a gray suit as he walked up to her. I couldn't recognize either language, yet I understood them.

"Welcome to Blackwell-C. I'm Barron Blackwater, ruler of our largest city, Thromstead. Do you have what I ordered?"

"Aye, sir. Do you have the payment?" the woman answered.

I saw the well-dressed man hand over a large pouch. She took it in her dexterous, long fingers and poured a few gemstones into her palm, stones which glistened and sparkled in the dim light of this world. Satisfied, she slipped them back into the pouch and signaled her ship.

A green-uniformed woman assisted an armless woman down the ramp. She wore the same style gown Leslie had invented for us, one which encased our shoulders like a towel. She had waist length blonde hair, our massive bosom, and wore our very tall heels. The woman with the bag of gems spoke.

"This is Melissa Gray, a telepath, age twenty-one. We've cut out her tongue as specified in your order."

"She is perfect. Thank you. Miss Gray, this way. You will become my baroness and help me rule this city and maybe even all Blackwell-C."

He led her to a metal vehicle with four rubber-like wheels and side doors. After helping her inside, he got in. Then, the vehicle made noise and moved off over the ground, while the Sixth Invaders returned to their ship. It lifted off.

Weird. I watched similar deliveries. But each world was entirely different from the others. Usually. They dropped off one telepath, and payment was gemstones or precious metals. I recognized gold and possibly platinum.

Then I followed a delivery spaceship back to the Sixth Invaders' home world. Not far from where it landed, I saw a huge walled mini-city. As I floated over the outer walls, I saw thousands of armless Galactic Doll telepaths. Though I couldn't tell their sex, I saw many small children, so some must be male Dolls. I had no doubts the Sixth Invaders were raising and selling telepaths throughout the galaxy.

I woke up in a cold sweat, shaking so much that I woke Ted, too.

"Bad dream?" he said.

"Mega-bad dream, but maybe I glimpsed the future again, an awful one."

Ted dabbed the sweat off my face. "Tell me about it."

"So they really are going to go into the breeding and selling of slave telepaths," Ted said after I told him about it.

"I don't know if it's just an awful dream or an actual vision of the future."

"Trust yourself, Molly. I think once more you got a glimpse of the future as terrible as it must be for those poor people."

"Okay, if I did, how the hell do we change it? We don't even know where their Home World is or if they even took our mutated people there. Even if we wanted to stop them, the Sol Empire's fleet is a third of theirs. So why did I get a vision of a future I can't do a damn thing about?"

I felt frustrated and helpless. While I suspected many of those who were attacked and mutated had been corrupt corporate officials, they didn't deserve to become breeding stock and sold as telepath slaves. No one did.

"Come on. Let's get up. I'll make you breakfast this morning."

"Ted, you can barely boil water. You mean you'll program our robot chef to do it."

He roared with laughter. "Bingo, dear. Still, it's the sentiment, right?"

I couldn't disagree, especially when he pampered me, dressing me and brushing my hair while the robot whirred and whined in the kitchen.

As we sat down, a sleepy-eyed Lara walked in. "My, you're up early this morning. I thought you'd sleep in. Gee, even have breakfast waiting."

Ted laughed. "Yeah, I know. But I'm treating my honey this morning. She had a bad vision last night. Perhaps because she kept thinking what that Sixth Invader commander told her."

"What was that?"

"That Commander L'Grina killed me as a favor to some Zahra-C ambassador, who wanted me dead. Lord knows why. I've never met any of them."

"Hum," Lara said. "Molly, tell me about the vision or was it a dream?"

"More like one of my visions. It was so real, far more vivid than a dream. Besides, I rarely dream." I told her what I'd seen. "So what do you make of this?"

Lara sighed. "From what I know since I used to be our Senior Ambassador, the Federation has always had trouble from these Sixth Invaders. You must admit, Molly, having a telepath in your employ can be a most desirable thing. These aliens are filling a vacuum. While many Federation representatives and corporate officials will openly condemn the breeding and selling of slave telepaths, behind the scenes, they will want to buy their own from the Sixth Invaders. About the only way to stop them would be to create enough of a political stir within the Circle of Ambassadors that they and the admirals have no choice but to overtly stop them. Tough path, since behind the scenes, most will want their own personal telepath. Spies and such."

"So it's hopeless?"

"Not exactly. These are or were your people they've kidnapped. In the Circles, a good argument could be made that since these are Earthlings, the Sixth Invaders are infringing on your rights to make and trade in telepaths. If you can make the case strong enough and if Earth is still providing telepaths, then the Federation admirals could act to end the Sixth Invaders' trade. That's the only practical route I can see. I'll chat with other Senior Ambassadors I know and get their opinions."

"Thank you, Lara. I appreciate it."

She smiled. "Now what's this about Zahra-C wanting Ted killed?"

I told her what little I'd picked up from Commander L'Grina.

"So what were your people working on, Ted?" Lara asked. "And don't use technical terms. I'm a geneticist, not a robotics expert."

She and I giggled. Ted smiled.

"Okay. In simple terms, early this year, Galactic Robotics had invented the humanoid robot soldiers via the Sixth Invaders. Not the tin cans that were used on Brussels,

Tau Ceti, but the ones they later used as guards around the GPan and GD skyscrapers—the ones who gunned down so many women when the Sixth Invaders tried to wipe out Chicago with their dual genetic mutations. These new robots had artificial intelligence and could be very useful robots. On the back burner, so to speak, was the human robot. These look and act like normal humans. Their positronic brains were supposed to be the latest in AI—an intelligence which learns via experience just like children do."

He continued. "Ten prototypes were built just before the Sixth Invaders launched their dual mutations on central Chicago this summer. During that mess, the ten vanished. We still don't know where they went—probably destroyed during that fiasco. Anyway, we're currently working on building better legs and feet for a new set of this kind of robot—feet which would give them improved mobility. The fancy robots haven't been built yet. We're trying to improve all aspects of those original, lost prototypes. So really, it's nothing. No big deal. Nothing top secret or even remotely like that. So I can't see why some other aliens would want me dead over such a silly thing."

"I can't either," I said. "Those original ten—they just vanished?"

"Yeah, never found after we eliminated the invaders. When Helen's security forces got control over things, the ten were just gone. No trace has yet been found. Mind you, I wasn't involved in their actual fabrication, but I worked on internal programming, coding—that sort of thing. In fact, I've never even seen one. For unknown reasons, all images, all videos of them, are lost. In fact, even the original plans have vanished, but bits were recovered from archived databases. Anyhow, that's what Galactic Robotics is working on today. Mechanical men of the future. Kinda boring, actually."

Lara said, "Well, I can't see any reason someone on Zahra-C would want you dead over that. I'll do some checking."

"How's the genetic research going?" I asked.

"Slow but sure as your saying goes. I know how badly you and the others would love to have your arms regrown. That's the hardest part. Eve and I think we've got a handle on breast reduction and foot repair, but the rest is challenging. I believe it's possible to create a complete cure for each of you whose original DNA is in your database, but it would be prohibitively expensive and time-consuming to invent three billion separate cures. So, we're looking at doing it in stages. Speaking of which, I'm supposed to meet her at the lab in five minutes. Better rush. Many transports are due to arrive today bringing immigrants to your world. Catch you later."

After she left, Ted said, "Well, should I go back to work at Galactic Robotics or not? Should I reappear from the dead? Publically, that is. If not, what am I going to do? I can't sit around the house much longer. I suppose I can offer helping arms to some of the thousands in our assisted living condos."

I bit my lip. "I don't want to lose you. We have no more backup bodies—god, does that sound strange! So if you or I get killed, we've no spare bodies." I sighed. "But we can't sit here and do nothing. I'm not helpless, just handicapped in some ways, and now you're whole again. That's a hell of a miracle, so let's be cautious."

"But I gotta do something. So do you."

"Good point. Neither should hole up and do nothing so we don't get hurt again. That's not living. That's not life. Okay, you go back to Galactic Robotics. Say you got your body healed somehow. Make up something. Then, see what you can find out about the project you were working on when the bombing came and also find out what happened to those ten missing prototype robots."

"Whew. I agree with you. It's not living. I'd rather die living than be a hermit doing nothing. I know you would too. But let's promise each other we'll be extra careful. I don't know what I'd do if I lost you."

His arms encircled me in a solid hug before we exchanged a passionate kiss. I admit I loved to feel his arms sliding over my shoulders. I almost suggested we head back to bed.

He headed to the Galactic Robotics skyscraper in the Loop while I walked to New O'Hare. I wanted to join the CEOs and other important leaders greeting the arriving giants and dwarves. Millions of each were coming to Earth, and Chicago promised new homes and jobs to a hundred thousand giants and an equal number of dwarves.

I took the MTES and watched the clouds building up as a front moved closer. Many women noticed my new gown and either smiled or commented they loved the new look. Leslie certainly had a great fashion sense.

A crowd of dignitaries milled, and a large GEnt video crew readied their cameras. I spotted Helen Hugo and Casper and joined them.

"Say, your new dress looks good on you," Casper said.

"Hi, Molly. Join us. The first of the new immigrants is scheduled to arrive shortly," Helen said. "I've got security guards around but not prominently visible. Don't want to frighten these families. Heard you got abducted by the Sixth Invaders. We thought they had fled, that the Federation would handle them, but I guess not. We must get our ambassadors chosen and sent off soon. Perhaps they can press our issues. Glad to see you're okay. How about telling us about it while we wait."

"How'd you know I got kidnapped?"

Helen grinned. "Leslie. She can't keep a secret."

While we waited, I told them about it and that they were behind the kidnapping of nearly five thousand people in five major cities.

"You mean they intentionally mutated all those people?" Casper said. I nodded. "That's criminal of them. But why did they cart away their bodies? What can they want with that many helpless men, women, and children?"

"Simple. They want to breed and sell telepaths across the galaxy. With the numbers they've taken, they can start a breeding program and sell the children when they mature."

"And I thought I'd done some despicable things," Casper said. "But this is inhumane, grotesque. Can't anything be done to stop them?"

"We can't. Duh. Our fleet is a third of theirs. Lara thinks if we get a Senior Ambassador on the Circle of Ambassadors to press our case, then they can force the Federation to stop them."

Casper's face grimaced. "It's as I predicted, honey. Remember, I told you telepaths were extremely valuable and highly sought after. Only I figured the corporations on Earth would do the breeding and selling, not the Sixth Invaders."

"Well, the CEOs have made it clear they're offering any normal adult the mutation if they'll sign a ten-year contract for ten million credits," Helen said. "But they aren't *selling* them to people on other worlds—to aliens. That's gotta be criminal. I know Aaron and Piper Strawn are being briefed on what's needed and wanted for the Sol Empire. I've heard they'll travel to Bela Prime and the Circle of Ambassadors on October 1. I'll see they learn about what the Sixth Invaders are doing with our people. Maybe they can stir the pot as we CEOs say. I hope so."

Suddenly, her facial expression changed from concern to shock. "You don't suppose someone will try to kidnap Casper?"

I was looking at him when she said this. All the color faded from his face in an instant but slowly returned.

"I hope not, Helen. Casper, if I were you, I wouldn't go anywhere without a guard with you. CFO personnel are valuable, where PIs aren't."

"Don't sell yourself short, Molly," Casper insisted. "Look. Ships are arriving."

From inside the terminal, we heard them more than saw them. Soon, the arrivals walked in from the tarmac. The giants' new Earth ambassadors led the first of the seven to eight-foot tall aliens towards us and the video crews. From a different door, dwarves entered; most they stood less than five feet, but were broad and stocky. Both were definitely not homo sapiens.

The giants had my attention. Their heads were round balls, but with eyes, noses, ears, and mouths. The men either had no hair on their heads or shaved them, while the females had shoulder length hair, mostly shades of brown and black. The males wore business suits like those worn by our men, except they had colorful sashes around their collars and not ties. Their women wore loose fitting dresses, much like mine in that they flared out at their waists. Their shoes were practical, soft-soled flats. Our CEOs and dignitaries formed a welcome line, and we found ourselves in the middle. Our new dwarven ambassadors, Dara and Kiri Sim, slipped in beside us.

The giants wore translator devices around their waists. "Hello. We're the Liatos-D ambassadors to the Sol Empire. You may call me Pat and my wife Penny Angorotha. We're certain you cannot pronounce our first names, so we've shortened them for your benefit."

"Galactic Defense Chicago CEO Helen Hugo. My husband and our finance wizard and telepath, Casper. Our dear friend Molly Parkinson, also a telepath."

"The Mrs. Parkinson? The one who saved everyone on the Kanika?" Pat said.

"That's me. Pleased to meet you. Welcome to Chicago, ambassadors."

"We'd so hoped to meet you. Thank you for saving our ambassadors and everyone on the battleship. How do we greet you? Forgive us. We've never been around someone like you and Casper."

"A hug will do fine. I can't hug you back," I jested. He smiled and hugged me before moving down the line.

Pat said, "Ah. Our dwarven counterparts. We meet again, Dara, Kiri."

"Yes, welcome. You'll find Earth to your liking. We've never seen so many well-preserved buildings just waiting for people to move into. The gravity is much lighter than either Liatos-D or Dian-C, so expect your strength to be even greater than at home. Penny, good to see you," said Kiri.

After several thousand giants walked past us, many with small children, the dwarves had their turn. Dara and Kiri introduced the more important dwarves to us. Their women also wore dresses but with pants beneath them. Theirs were full of colorful embroidery. Each dress was different and a striking work of art. The males wore heavy work clothes, similar to what I'd often seen construction workers wearing. They, too, brought many children with them. Some were still babies.

The procession lasted an hour. Helen and other CEOs had EMACs waiting outside the terminal. When a sufficiently large group gathered, they climbed on board an EMAC, which took them to look over potential new residences. Thus, when the last had passed through the line, behind us, the terminal was empty, save for the GEnt crew packing up their equipment.

"Well, that went well," Helen said. "Can I buy you lunch, Molly?"

"I think the ambassadors are looking for you." I'd sensed Dara and Kiri wanted to chat with her, but also Pat and Penny had returned, heading our way.

Helen turned and chuckled. "Ambassadors, would you all care to come to lunch with us?"

"Yes, we returned to ask to dine with you, as head of GD and security here in Chicago. But please, can Mrs. Parkinson join us? And you two, Dara, Kiri. We have lots of questions for you," Ambassador Pat Angorotha said.

"Yes, you're welcome to dine with us anytime. I know just the place, only the fanciest restaurant in Chicago. Follow Casper and me."

I suspected we'd have an interesting lunch and afternoon, discovering more about our races or should I say species? I thought of them as people, albeit with different characteristics, but people nevertheless, even the Sixth Invaders.

Chapter 29 Decisions

Helen asked me to help get the dwarves settled into life in Chicago while she worked with the giants. Besides needing a home, furnishings, and groceries, they also needed employment. Comparable Federation wages had to be paid, and that meant our wages had to go up to be equal to these new arrivals. If not, expect riots.

Thus, every major corporation and many smaller ones, such as Deanna's Cartwright Enterprises, had to adjust their entire pay scales. With the profits I knew that GD made in the past via my four-month stint as temporary CEO, they could afford to pay fair wages. I had hoped my new sponsor, GEnt, would up my monthly stipend so I wouldn't have to work quite so much to pay the bills. Still, I was much better off than at least half of the people on Earth, those who maintained abandoned buildings for Galactic Housing.

I spent Monday talking to families and showing them how to order groceries and furnishings online. Each was very surprised to learn someone would deliver them within a half hour of the order. Of course, bank accounts had to be set up, but GD backed bank transfers from their home world or assisted in the conversion of precious gems into our credits. Yes, Helen and the other major corporations were busy.

Also, at least one member of each family or each unmarried adult had to have a sponsor. Thus, everyone took the standardized aptitude tests along with an interview to help determine the proper sponsor. Someone, such as me, had to read the questions for them, while their translation devices converted it into their native language. At least, the online ordering systems used images more than words. Today, I understood why that was: half our population could only relate to images rather than words.

When I got home at suppertime, Ted was already there. From his downcast eyes, something wasn't right.

"How'd it go today?"

"Not so good. They canceled all research and development for at least a year while they work on rebuilding our floor. They wanted to reassign me to clerking duties, but I turned them down. I've spent most of the day searching for smaller companies that could use my skills. Perhaps you and I should move to this Bela Prime place. Perhaps they're hiring robot building geniuses like me." He laughed.

"Sorry, it's not working out so well. Come on. Let's get some supper."

"Oh, I almost forgot. Celeste wants you to drop by her place when you have time."

"I'll go after we eat. So what are you programming our chef to make for us tonight?"

Later, we dined on chicken and wild rice with pea pods. While we ate, Ted wanted to talk.

"Since I quit work today, I've been giving things a lot of thought. If that vision of yours is accurate, we have to get our people back or stop them from breeding and selling telepaths."

"But we can't do that from here."

"I agree. We'll have to lobby the Senior Ambassadors and get them to—I don't know—but do something about it. Possibly you should go to Bela Prime as a Senior Ambassador for our empire. I heard a bit of news at Galactic Robotics. The influx of these giants and dwarves is upping our population. So we'll need one more Senior Ambassador. That's what some CEOs think. Dara is looking into it for us. I wish we knew if becoming one would make a difference and get our people back or at least make them stop selling telepaths. Lara thinks there's a chance, but we'd have to, as she says, 'work the other ambassadors,' whatever that means. I don't have the temperament for such things.

"On the other hand, come Valentine's Day, we have to think about our baby girl and making a stable home for her. So I'm not sure going to this Bela Prime is such a good idea. What a pickle, eh dear?"

I chuckled. "Yeah, but we must make some decisions, especially since our adopted teens are off on their own. Since your body is back to normal, you should be the big breadwinner. But I wonder how much they pay our Senior Ambassadors? Anyway, I know so darn little compared to you and my sisters, it's not even funny. I'm certainly not qualified to be our ambassador—not by any means. Helping Celeste with her therapy is incredibly rewarding, but not financially. My PI work is often rewarding in that I help people, and I've been able to get by, though if they raise our stipend, that'll help."

"Casper told me they'll soon have to raise the cost of goods to help offset the pay raises. Catch-22 as they say."

"Well, you see where I'm at, dear. I'm physically restricted in what I can do. My knowledge is grossly insufficient. And I don't know what I should do, except be a good mother to our daughter when she comes."

"Any chance Lara and Eve will invent a way to regrow arms?" Ted asked.

"Who knows? Besides, that's only a physical limitation thing I have to deal with. I want to help people. That's always been there in one form or another. All these people, some five thousand—while many were probably corrupt corporate people—they didn't deserve to be genetically mutated, kidnapped, taken to a foreign world, bred as captive slaves, and sold off as telepaths to the highest bidders. Yet, how can I possibly do anything about that?"

"Dunno, dear. Dunno. But you should head over to Celeste's apartment now. Want me to tag along or can I keep on my job searching?"

"No need for you to come. It's just a stroll on the MTES. The dwarves were certainly impressed with our system today."

He headed back to his computer while I headed off on the escalator system.

Celeste welcomed me with a huge smile. Lara, Eve, and Randi were there, grinning.

"Lara has an announcement for you, Molly," Celeste said.

Lara said, "Eve and I have found a way to undo some of the genetic mutation side-effects. It's not a full cure, not yet."

"Coolest. Tell me about it," I said, scarcely believing the good news.

"Go ahead, Lara," Eve said, "tell her what we've invented."

"Based on your original DNA and that of many others, Eve and I have synthesized a simple genetic tweak that will reduce breast sizes and undo the distorted legs and feet. It won't regrow arms or anything like that. Our breakthrough came when Eve pointed out that the female version the aliens used this summer when they infected everyone with the sex-dependent versions also had an error in it. After a time, women's feet and legs returned to normal."

"Yes, that was wonderful. Made my life lots easier," I said, recalling how pleased many Chicago women were over that.

"So we found the error in that mutation sequence and fabricated a mutation cure," Lara explained.

I chuckled. "Already, you're talking over my head. How do I get the cure? Another coma? Are we going to cure all the women on Earth? Oops, all our clothes'll have to be altered. How soon?"

Eve laughed. "Just like the Molly we know and love. Just the facts, ma'am. All of 'em." Everyone chuckled.

"No coma. A gradual reduction over about a week. Just drink plenty of fluids to help flush the dissolving particles out of your body," Lara said. "We give you a shot. That's all. In about a week, breast sizes will be around the size of Leslie's. Still large, but acceptable we think. Also, you'll notice the tightness in your calves will lessen as your arches also straighten out. Flats in a week is our goal."

"Wonderful news," I interrupted.

She smiled and continued. "Leslie's been in contact with Galactic Manufacturing. They make all the apparel, including her new designs. Galactic Manufacturing has agreed to send a group of seamstresses to Chicago to assist in making the bust alterations to men and women's existing apparel. They're also willing to set up an exchange program. You drop off clothes that no longer fit and pick up ones that do."

Eve said, "As far as the Galactic Doll implanted ideas across the world, Randi and I figure enough time has passed, and if the changes are gradual enough, the women won't become debilitated by the implant. We'll monitor that aspect, though. We're using Chicago as a test to see how it works out. So, are you ready to get your shot?"

"You don't have to ask twice."

Eve injected me in my leg. "There, your bosom and feet should be normal in a week from now. Don't worry. We're still working on the arm regrowing process. What's complicating things," she said, "is that in restoring bodies, we're trying not to also destroy their telepathy. We know how upset Ted was when he swapped bodies from Irina and lost his telepathic abilities. So we're trying to preserve that if we can."

Randi, who had been silent, said, "Okay. That's done. Leslie is making a series of reduced bosom-sized gowns for you. She'll bring them by tomorrow morning. We aren't sure how fast you'll want to exchange dresses. You're our experimental case. Now, on to more critical details."

I laughed. "So I'm your lab rat. That's fine with me. I can see your point. If returning bodies to normal also wipes out their telepathic ability, some won't like that. What's critical? Also, since I'm here, can we talk about the five thousand who were mutated and are being bred and sold as telepathic slaves?"

"Sure. We've some ideas. First, I've been working with Galactic Medicine, Galactic University, and many corporate CEOs. I'll be involved in the merging of the Federation's hyperspace coordinates with our own. With the continued Sixth Invader attacks and those of our own people against us, statistically, more innocent people will be harmed, such as Ted and the other R&D robotics developers have. We can ill afford to lose people considered vital and critical to our world and the Sol Empire."

"What're you getting at?" I asked.

"The CEOs and others are aware just how valuable being able to body swap has been for us and Ted. Further, they're aware of how powerful the rejuvenation aspect of this armless Doll mutation agent is. They did tests—okay, experiments—on terminally ill people. Every one of them has recovered, though they're now the usual male and female armless Dolls with telepathy, of course. The point Galactic Medicine makes is that lives can be saved, especially those considered vital to our society."

"Ah, and they've identified those they consider vital," I said.

All right. I admit I was being sarcastic. I thought of my mom and dad, which I now knew were low IQ people. I recalled mom taking me to the parks to play before I went to kindergarten. Then, there was dad taking me for a ride in grandpa's tiny electro car. They wouldn't be considered *vital*, but they were to me.

"Yes, they have and are making a recommendation which the CEOs will implement today. On the quiet, mind you," Randi said. "It's a simple precaution. Each critical person will be given a syringe containing the armless Doll mutation agent, enough to mutate one person. These critical personnel are to have it on their person at all times. If they are injured, harmed, shot, then either they or someone with them will inject them with the syringe, saving their life."

"Like I'll inject myself when I took that gun shot to my head. Excuse me, Sixth Invader, but I need to inject myself before you kill me."

Randi chuckled. "Point already made to them. So they will put the syringe in a special red container along with instructions in its use. Then, they will make this widely known. Educate the public so when they see someone injured or shot, the first responders will check for the red container. If they find it, they'll inject the person, thereby saving their life. Here's your red container, Molly, and one for Ted."

I gasped. She said, "Don't worry. We all have one. Even Leslie and Felix if you're wondering. All us sisters and brothers and friends have one. The idea is not to lose one of us."

"Has anyone given any thought to the fact a person might prefer to die and get a new baby body to living a disabled life, even with telepathy?"

"No. I couldn't get that notion through to them. They believe you only live once. Thus, they're doing everything they can to prolong it. Some are saying we should use it on ourselves when we get old so we become twenty-five again. Honestly, Molly, I can see the day coming when none of us die, but are forced to be injected and re-mutated endlessly."

"Good lord. They can't do that, can they? Deny a person the right to die?" I said, thinking of Dimitri and Natalie's parents and the hundreds who chose to die rather than live as an armless Doll.

Randi sobered. "At the moment, Dimitri's ruling to respect a person's death wish is still allowed. However, with the distribution of these red pouches, that attitude is changing."

"What's our world becoming? Soon, we'll be breeding and selling telepaths."

"Oh, that reminds me," Eve said, "we've been exploring what we can do. Thanks to your kidnapping and vision, we know the Sixth Invaders' plan for the five thousand victims. Randi and I've been doing some checking on just who the victims were. Those of us who came here from Bahira were already telepaths. Celeste met them in her last lifetime. Several worked in Miami and New York City. It would be like kidnapping Randi and me. We would be pissed and able to take action against them."

"But what can we do? I so want to help them—to change that bleak future I saw for those people. I'm even considering becoming our Senior Ambassador so I can try to convince the other ambassadors to take strong action against these Sixth Invaders."

"We'll need one more Senior Ambassador. The immigration of the giants and dwarves has upped the Sol Empire's population enough so we get three. Anyway, as I was saying, we'll try to contact them telepathically when we guess they're out of their mutation comas. When we're ready to do that, we'll have you lend us a hand."

"Sorry. All out of hands at the moment."

Everyone roared, easing the tensions.

"One other thing," Celeste said as she led me to the door, "the initial tests on the low IQ people are done. Yes, they can be helped and that debilitating drug mass erased, but the required therapy hours has proved untenable. It's taking ten times longer to get results on them than the normal person. Our conclusion is that time will be the best cure. Give them several lifetimes of no drugs so the masses tend to de-stimulate and float into the distant past in their minds and not in the present as the masses are now."

"Makes sense. So if we stop using the dementia-causing drug, in time everyone will recover?" I asked.

"More or less recover. One day, they'll have to confront and erase those incidents, but they should be in a better position to do that after a couple lifetimes without the drugs," Celeste said.

"Thanks. So drink lots of fluids, and in a week my body will be closer to normal?"

"Yes, that's the plan. Lara will check your progress every day. Bye."

Night came early in late September. I headed home on the MTES with much to ponder. Not having soccer ball breasts would be a relief, but to have my legs and feet back meant more stability and range of motion, something I cherished, though I wished I could release tension by shooting my Glock. As I rode along, I became aware of changes. I saw both giants and dwarves on the MTES, sightseeing, I think. The world had changed. Aliens walked among us, but they seemed to be like us, as far as I could tell, just taller or shorter.

I exhaled deeply. So much had changed in the past couple years, but I still didn't know what I wanted to do with my life. That I ought to go back to school weighted heavily on my mind, but studying what? Pick a subject; I'd surely be ignorant in it, well, except investigations. Should I consider joining up with the Investigations Department, maybe become their Senior Investigator? Would they even allow a handicapped person to hold that position? And what about helping others? Celeste's therapy filled that role beyond all doubt. Then what about my baby girl? I was halfway through my pregnancy. Yet, I couldn't see myself in the role my mother had played in our family, a housekeeper. I had to make some decisions and soon, but I just couldn't do it.

"You mean if I get shot, someone's supposed to inject me with this so my body gets rejuvenated and mutated again?" Ted said.

I'd returned home and told him what I'd learned. He'd fingered his new red pouch, feeling the syringe inside.

"What about choice? Don't we get a say? I don't like this."

"I know, dear. I don't either," I said. "I thought we took a giant step forward with Dimitri's ruling that a person had the right to be terminated instead of going on living. I think some in power are paranoid about dying. You only live once. Ha."

Ted slipped his arms around me. "Honey, I've made my decision. As much as I love you, if something happens to this body—it gets shot or something—please don't inject me. I don't want to live another life as an armless male Doll—telepathy or not. It's not fair to you or me. A perversion of nature, that's what it is, a constant reminder that the Sixth Invaders harmed me. Besides, I don't like being handicapped and taking forever to do the simplest things, always having to stop and think how. It's unnatural. I'd rather go find a new baby body and start over. Promise me, Molly. Don't let them mutate me again."

"I didn't know you felt this strongly, dear. I need you. Our daughter needs you, so don't go getting yourself killed."

This was one of the hardest things I've ever done—to make him this promise. After a huge sigh, I said, "Okay, I promise not to use this mutation agent to keep your body alive and restored."

He hugged me for some time.

The next morning, a Galactic Robotics lawyer paid us a visit just as we sat down for breakfast.

After introducing himself, he said, "I'm here with the settlement over the recent death of your husband. All those who recently lost their lives in or after the bomb and while on the job at Galactic Robotics are covered under the corporate insurance policy. The beneficiaries are each receiving one million credits for their loss and suffering. Galactic Robotics doesn't want the families of their deceased employees to endure needless hardships based upon the loss of financial earnings. The settlement amount represents the theoretical earnings your husband would have received had he continued work until the retirement age of sixty. That amount has been deposited in your account, Mrs. Parkinson-Billings. If you will please check your account balance for me now..."

I gasped. Ted said, "But I've got this new body. I'm still me."

"The corporation is aware of your peculiar circumstances. However, there is no doubt your body was killed in the explosion. The autopsy proved it perished because of the bomb. Thus, legally, the corporation is responsible for providing your beneficiary with the legal death benefits. Perhaps in the future, the law will be altered. Please check your account, ma'am. Then, I need you to sign this document acknowledging receipt of the death benefits."

He stared at my dress that highlighted my lack of arms. "If you are unable to sign, then I can sign for you, but I'll need an independent witness."

"Don't be silly. I can write." I growled at him. It had been a long time since someone thought I was helpless. I felt annoyed. I was still a person, but I had different ways to do things. I fetched my phone, made the App connection using my toes, and gasped again at the incredible balance in my account. Then, I pivoted the display so the lawyer could see.

He handed me the document. It wasn't a paper, but an electronic document displayed on his small tablet.

"If you'll put it on the floor, I'll sign." Okay, I had to show off a little and took my time to make my signature look fancy. He touched the Okay button, stood, thanked me, and left as quickly as he could.

"You spooked him, dear."

"The jerk."

"Now you are rich. How weird is this anyway?"

That started me thinking. When Ted left on his job search, I took a long walk on the MTES to clear my mind. That didn't work so well since many people used it and most insisted on greeting me. While pleasant, I wanted to think, so I ended up sitting on a park bench overlooking the lake, listening to the distant roar of spaceships and the calls of the gulls. One flock of geese flew high above me, heading south for the winter.

Something about the lawyer's visit this morning touched a nerve but also formed the seed of an idea. Yes, I still wanted to alter that awful future I'd seen in my vision. The five thousand, who had been mutated, abducted, and now held in some monstrous telepath breeding and marketing hell, had to be rescued. I knew what had happened here in Chicago when the Moscow GPan and GD groups had come out of their mutation comas. So many adults begged for death. Their group terror and screams shook us to our cores. But the lawyer thought I couldn't even write my own name. That I was disabled and helpless. Hadn't he known so many of Ted's fellow researchers were also armless Dolls?

From my brief stint as the GD CEO rooting out corruption, I knew corporate lawyers seldom left their own offices and never took part in the actual workings of the company. So this man knew nothing about us Dolls, other than the frightening images shown on the comm center channels.

A way to save those five thousand people flashed in my mind. I focused my attention, attempting to make the strangest telepathic connection I'd ever done.

Chapter 30 Solutions

If asked how I knew Commander L'Grina was still on Earth, I wouldn't have been able to answer. I just did.

'Ah, Commander. Molly Parkinson here. Yes, I'm in your mind. I'm a telepath, after all. Look, I need to meet with you, face to face. This is important for your people and mine. Please. I'm sitting on a deserted park bench by Lake Michigan. I'm alone and unarmed. Of course, I couldn't shoot my Glock even if I wanted to. That's a joke by the way. Please. No trap. It's vital I talk with you. Oh, don't talk out loud. Just think what you want me to hear. Okay. An hour. I'll be here.'

She was still on Earth, but the commander wasn't in Chicago. More likely, she was in Moscow, checking up on what Dimitri and Natalie were doing. No way to tell via telepathy unless I wanted to deep-probe her mind.

I waited on the bench watching the water lap at the shore. The sun rose higher in the southern sky. I spotted one sailboat tacking towards the docks and wondered if sailing a boat would appeal to me. A person sat down next to me, bringing me out of my reverie.

"Well?" she said. Ah, Commander L'Grina.

"Hi. Thank you for coming. I wanted to talk to you about your people's plans to breed and sell armless Doll human telepaths, the ones you've mutated and taken to your world."

"What of it? Brilliant plan. Your own corporations are paying your telepaths a million credits a year. Home World is going to get very rich, very quickly."

"That's why I wanted to meet with you. To warn you. If your people continue down this intended path, the telepaths will destroy your entire world."

"Oh, get real. As you said, you can't even hold a gun, much less shoot me."

"No, they won't be shooting you, but the chaos they will cause and the damage they'll do to the mental well-being will end your entire race. Let me show you some things and explain others."

"What the hell are you talking about? You armless telepaths are almost helpless. You can't possibly harm us."

"You're partially right. While we aren't helpless, the humans you've captured won't be harming you directly. It's much more subtle and insidious—almost vicious. There are several aspects to this impending disaster for your people. It's been almost eight days now. They should be coming out of their comas.

"I'll put into your mind my memories of when five hundred came out of their mutation comas in the GPan skyscraper several weeks ago. While I'm sure your people won't be as humane as ours were, this is what your people will face."

I focused and contacted with her mind. Then, I recalled my memories of that day, as Dimitri and I headed into GPan to find his parents and brother. The screams, the almost physical solid wall of terror, the shock—these I transmitted to her, but I kept the volume down to what she could experience without freaking out and leaving me. Then, I showed her images of those who begged to be terminated and Dimitri's actions.

"I doubt your people will be moved by the sheer terror generated by our humans, but this is what they will be experiencing. Your people won't kill them, no matter how much they beg for it. Yet, unless you're very careful, they will find ways to die. I'll show you."

I replayed in her mind the images we had when Bev and I returned with Aaron Strawn and the others to the roof of the Cartwright skyscraper where we were getting ready to help them recover. She watched as two of them rushed and jumped off the roof, falling fifty stories. Next, I showed her how Mary Trout had dropped into sub-apathy, waiting for death to take her. I made sure she grasped the idea.

"Some victims will give up and sit there unresponsive until death comes."

Commander L'Grina cleared her throat. Yes, I'd made her uncomfortable. "I'm sure Home World has already taken such responses into account. Perhaps, that's why we took so many of your people, anticipating many wouldn't survive the transformation process."

"I presumed your admirals expected such losses. But that's not how your people will be harmed. I'm just getting to that part. You mutated many of the more able humans, our brighter minds. In fact, some were already telepaths, only they didn't tell others about it. Those who don't succumb will rise into violent anger and perhaps as high as antagonism. These spell the downfall of your entire world. How?

"By mental and covert means. First, they can torment your minds. I contacted you an hour ago, even though I had no idea where you were, but I hoped you were on Earth. I don't know if I can reach off-world with my telepathic connections. Think of what an angry telepath might do to and with your mind. Multiply that by several thousand. They can drive anyone into a raving fit, perhaps even convince them to blow their own brains out to silence the screaming in their mind from all the telepaths bent on their destruction.

"So you sell some. You can bet on two things happening. One, every secret your people have will be eagerly told to the buyers. Two, they'll fabricate lies to convince their buyers that they aren't telepathic or are dismal at it. They will also intentionally bring utter ruin to their buyers, hoping he or she will get so infuriated with them that either they'll kill the telepath ending their misery or the buyers will come back to your people with serious scores to settle because of the damage the telepaths have wreaked on them.

"Sell enough of the telepaths and half the galaxy will come gunning for your world. I wouldn't bet a credit that your Home World will survive another ten Earth years, Commander L'Grina. Could be less than that if you sell more telepaths quicker. Your world is doomed, just as if you'd taken a planet-busting bomb home with you. Commander, it's a certainty.

"Last night, I saw this happening. It's inevitable. While you Sixth Invaders have wreaked havoc on our world, you are still people. Your culture differs from ours, but Science Officer G'Karn saw that you and we are more alike than we are different. We're all people. I've shown you that you are a spiritual being, just as we are. Yes, our bodies are very different. But we are all people. I couldn't sit by and let this genocide happen to your people, not even after all the bad things you've done to my people. It's not humane, not civilized. I couldn't live with myself if I didn't both warn you and help circumvent the coming genocide of your gray-skinned people with six fingers per hand." I tried to lighten it up a little; she looked a tad pale if I interpreted her slight skin tone change correctly.

"Circumvent genocide?" she asked.

Now I had her.

"Yes, there could be a way to avoid the coming disaster to your people. It'll take effort on your part and on ours. First, you need to convince your people that I'm right about this. Then, you must return everyone you took, and I must convince my people to accept those almost helpless people back, telepathic or not. But we should go further. You need our people to be miners for your spaceship fuel, right?"

"Yes, the mine's fumes are toxic to us, but your people are immune thus far. The last report I had, your people are working out well."

"I thought so. What if I could get you a contract from Earth allowing you to import as many of these workers as you need, as long as they are well treated, properly paid, and returned to Earth when you're done with them? We could have a peaceful trade agreement between our worlds. Your people would win as well as ours. Millions of giants and dwarves are immigrating to Earth. They occupy many of the abandoned homes these low IQ workers were maintaining all these years. Some will be out of a job and will jump at the chance to make good wages mining for your people. What do you think? We both will have to do serious negotiating with our people, but I think it can be done."

Commander L'Grina rubbed her hands across her face before resting them on her thighs. She was using her disguise device, which made her appearance the average of those around her, namely me. So she presented an illusion that seemed to have almost transparent arms.

"You aren't lying. I kept a covert eye on what happened when they came out of their comas there in the GPan skyscraper. I admit it unnerved me, too. Okay, I'll take your proposal on up the lines. I can't guarantee you anything."

"Just as I can't guarantee you Earth will go along with my ideas. But you and I—we have to try. Then, I can rest if your people continue on and genocide happens."

"Why this sudden change in viewpoint?"

"Meeting these new aliens on the Kanika opened my eyes. There are many other human-like species in the galaxy. We are not alone. Yes, we've discovered a few primitive peoples on nearby worlds, but these are space-faring people, whose bodies are so different from ours and yours too. And they know much more about the galaxy and technology than we do. I was humbled and yet encouraged. I erased an awful mental implant that the dwarf Lara had—one that made her insane. I helped you recover from your severe burn. So I'm convinced we're all people, just with different physical bodies and cultures. I exist to help people."

"Okay. I'll contact my people. I'll be in touch."

"Thank you, Commander. That's all I can ask. Bye."

She vanished. I rose, stretched, and headed back to my new home in the assisted living condos. Now, I had to convince my people. First call went to Dimitri in Moscow.

"Hi. How's it going?" I grinned as my phone displayed his fancy holographic image, meaning he had one of the expensive phones. Because of the way I had to hold mine, he got a poor visual of me.

"Darn good. Natalie and I have nearly gotten GPan and GD corporations restaffed and ready to resume oversight of Earth's local corporations. The Sixth Invaders have indirectly helped us. The kidnapping of those five thousand key corporate personnel from LA has shifted the balance of power. Or should I say the bitter rivalry between Moscow and LA? I hope to begin re-staffing those fifteen corporations next week if I'm lucky. But it'll be hard to replace the highly educated men and women who worked at Galactic University."

I saw my opening and took it. "I think I have the answer. I've just proposed a deal with the Sixth Invaders. They'll return our people they've abducted and mutated. In return, they're desperate for more of our low IQ people to work in their mines. We set up a fair trade agreement with them for miners; they return our people."

"What? Are you nuts? Dealing with our sworn enemy?"

"No, I'm being practical. Think of what will happen throughout the galaxy when they start selling our people as telepaths to other worlds. Our sold telepaths will screw their buyers over big time, selling everyone's secrets. Everyone will blame Earth since these people originally came from here and since we're already making use of telepaths. Earth will get the shaft just as much as the Sixth Invaders. This is a way out. Besides, we'll get these highly educated people back, and you'll have far fewer people to replace."

"But they'll be helpless. They'll be like dad was, begging to be terminated."

I sighed. No matter what I wanted in my future, at this precise moment, I knew what I had to do.

"Look. I'll take full responsibility for the recovery of these five thousand people. I'll have them brought to Chicago and work with them to get them as independent as possible and ready to return to their former jobs, assuming they're still able to physically do them. You provide me with the treaty negotiations. Make sure our low IQ people are handled well. After all, Dimitri, since the giants and dwarves are buying so many of the abandoned buildings, thousands are no longer needed on their maintenance."

"Do you think these people can be salvaged?"

"Hey, I do okay myself, don't you think?" I felt annoyed that he'd even think such thoughts.

"Okay. I'll get on it today. I can't imagine how you can handle five thousand of them. Keep in touch."

I hung up and answered my doorbell. Leslie stood there, tapping a foot while holding onto a large clothes bag.

"Sorry, on the phone with Dimitri. Come in, sis."

"'Bout time. I like brought several modified dresses, each with decreasing bosom sizes, and a selection of flats and tennis shoes like you used to wear. Are they like any smaller today?"

She marched into my bedroom, plopping the huge bag on my bed. I'd been too preoccupied to check, but Leslie pointed out how baggy my bust appeared. Soon, she had me dressed in a new gown, exactly like my old one, but with a smaller bust size. It fit perfectly.

"I like don't expect this one like will fit more than a day or two. Eve and Lara like think the reduction will be fast. Now if they like could just get your arms back—"

"Yeah. Say, I might have found a way to get our five thousand abducted people back from the Sixth Invaders. If so, I've got to house them here in Chicago. Any way you can have enough apparel on hand?"

"Wow! All of them? Here? Oh, boy. Okay, I'll like get on the orders today. Bye for now."

She headed off at a rapid pace to handle such a large order from Galactic Manufacturing. Now, I had to find living arrangements for this many people and a place where I could work with them, showing and leading by example, something those here at the assisted living condos appreciated and needed to survive. This time, I'd be handling adults—if Casper Hugo was an example, a much more challenging group.

I called up Helen Hugo, GD CEO, to ask for advice. After explaining what I was trying to do, I asked for help. "I need a place where the five thousand abducted people can stay, where they can learn and adapt to their handicap, where I can work with them each day, and where they'll be safe."

"Let me make sure I'm following you, Molly. You think you can get the Sixth Invaders to return everyone they abducted and turned into armless Dolls and telepaths? All of them?"

"Yes, I have high hopes that will happen. But if they're going to have any chance at an independent life, I've got to show them the route. I have to set an example."

Helen whistled. "Okay, hun, I'll get on it. I think I've an idea that might work. How long do you estimate you'll need to get them all trained and able to be independent enough to return to their homes? After all, none are from Chicago."

"Best give them six months. Maybe it'll go faster, but winter's coming soon, probably before they'll be confident enough to venture off on their own."

"Okay. I'll get back to you. Say, I heard Lara and Eve have come up with a partial solution to the Galactic Doll mutation."

"Yes, I'm their test subject. My breasts are shrinking a little, but it's only Day 1. I'll celebrate when my feet and legs are back to normal."

Helen laughed. "I think we all will. Bye for now."

Ted wandered in. "Hi dear. Home for lunch. Took a job offer from Galactic Robotics. It seems they were upset that I quit, so they made me a better offer. Now, I'm the new Vice-president of Research and Development, but we don't have lab facilities yet, not until spring."

"Congratulations, Mister VP."

He grinned and headed off to program our robot to make us lunch. While we ate, I told him what I'd done.

"So, we might need thousands of computers with the how-to videos on them and all the various robots."

"Don't worry. There are millions of them in storage. The Sixth Invaders planned to mutate millions of us and were prepared. I'll put in a requisition for you."

After he left, I began education plans, working out how I could train these victims as rapidly as possible. What would be the most optimum method? I knew what I would be doing until next summer at least, long after I had my baby. I'd cast my die. I had to make a difference with these victims, giving them a new chance at life. Even if Lara and Eve developed an arm regrow method, I'd not have it until the last of these people had been trained, helped, and were on their way to an independent life.

Late afternoon, Helen called. I smiled as my phone displayed her fancy holographic image. She, too, had one of the expensive kinds. Now I wanted one.

"Good news, Molly. I've arranged for the Northeast Surgical Facility to merge with the central Chicago Med Center for the next six months. The NSF has about five thousand beds in that large facility, along with kitchen and dining facilities. Their auditorium seats around fifteen hundred. You should be able to address about a third of the victims at a time. How's that sound?"

"Fabulous, Helen. Thank you."

"When's this going to happen?"

"I've no idea. I'll let you know the moment I know."

I spent the afternoon on my special computer that had all the how-to videos on it. The objective: arrange them in an order best suited for teaching others and prioritized by the degree of criticalness to living. I presumed we'd all have our hair and nail machines, which used electrostatic charges and a gentle wind to untangle and arrange each hair. The dressing/undressing machine handled those skills, and every public restroom in central Chicago had them. The cooking/cleaning robot could handle those needs to an extent. Heck, Ted and I made extensive use of one. Manipulating their phones, writing, grasping and moving items were crucial since using them they could order clothes, food—just about everything—and have them delivered, but they'd have to put the items in proper places. I put things such as swimming near the end of the list because I didn't know if a pool would be available. The lake's too cold this time of year.

Just as I finished making my lengthy list, someone entered my condo's common room without knocking.

I rose and walked to the door. "Hello?"

"Ah, there you are. We need to talk."

I recognized her voice, Commander L'Grina. I took a deep breath and exhaled slowly, calming my suddenly racing nerves, and joined her. She'd already plopped down on one of our couches. As I entered, she turned off her disguise device.

She looked impressive in her green uniform, which blended with her gray skin and short black hair.

"Hi, Commander."

I sat down beside her. If nothing else, I demonstrated I wasn't afraid or intimidated by her. Nervous, yes.

She sighed once. "Well, as much as I hate to admit this, Mrs. Parkinson, you were right."

"Molly, please."

"Molly, then. First, I should tell you I relayed our conversation and the images I saw in my mind to Admiral L'Tara, who relayed them to our rulers. The humans were just then coming out of their comas. Their emotional reactions shocked our caretaker personnel, so much so they fled the auditoriums. Perhaps you underplayed just how badly they might react upon awakening."

"I didn't want to scare you."

"Thankfully, I wasn't there." She flashed a grin. "You were also correct about their wish to kill themselves. Last I heard, about a hundred found clever ways to kill their bodies. One drowned himself in the latrine—if you can believe that."

"I can. Waking up and finding you've been mutated into an armless Doll is very traumatic. Been there, done that."

"You win. After a lengthy discussion centered on what you told me and their direct observations—several had telepathic abilities as soon as they woke up—you weren't exaggerating. Our workers fled holding their hands over their ears trying to block the telepathic screaming in their minds. Home World agrees with your suggested treaty. We need the miners, but we can't handle these new telepaths. I'm here to arrange the treaty, but we'd like to return the surviving humans as soon as possible."

"Excellent."

"I mean soon. They are already being loaded onto transports, along with the various machines we stole to help support them in their new lives."

"Wow. You move fast."

"Of course. Were you able to get your world to agree to the treaty? I'm to arrange for the delivery of another hundred thousand miners over the next month, but our transports would like to return with at least a thousand once they unload your humans."

"I've got people working on it, but they are waiting to hear if your people would agree to the proposed treaty. Let me call Dimitri."

"You need help with that?"

"Just give me time to do this. It's difficult making feet work as hands."

She stared at me. While she must have seen the how-to videos and seen us, this was different. I was sitting beside her, maneuvering to get my phone out of my dress pocket and the connection made. With the phone between my right foot's toes, I propped my right leg on my left knee so it faced me as the call went through.

"Hi, Dimitri. I've got Commander L'Grina here with me. She's ready to return our people and get this treaty implemented."

His holographic image stood about a foot tall. Because of the angle of my phone, he could see both of us on his. One day I should spend the money to get me one of these fancy phones.

"Incredible. For real? They are returning our people?"

The commander said, "Right now, they're being loaded onto transports. We're also returning the various machines they need to survive—the ones we took to help support them. I'm authorized to arrange delivery of a hundred thousand miners, but on their return trip, our transports would like to bring along a thousand of your people. Same deal as those who signed Feld-D contracts."

"Amazing. I never thought your people would return ours. Okay then. I'll board an Airliner tonight and join you in the morning. We can work on the details. When will your transports arrive?"

"By noon tomorrow, your time."

"Okay. I'll be there by breakfast time. Molly, make reservations. I'll take everyone out to eat, and we can sign the treaty. At this point, I represent Earth corporations, but not the Sol Empire."

"Excellent. Cya in the morning. Bye." I ended the call.

"Mind if I ask you a question, Molly?"

"No, what?"

"How did you know this would be a disaster for us? More importantly, why did you even bother trying to save us from it? We've been doing our best to conquer Earth for thirty years. I would have sat back and watched them be destroyed."

"I've had to learn to live life with this handicap. I was there when the five hundred Moscow victims came out of their comas. You saw what we saw and experienced that day in the GPan skyscraper. Developing telepathy doesn't suddenly make our lives any easier. I took a gamble when I saw you were in great pain from the burns and tried our therapy on you. It worked because you are people, just as we are. So I could anticipate what would happen when five thousand woke from comas to discover their lives were shattered. Worse, I knew your plan was doomed. While I can never condone the many crimes your people have done to ours, I couldn't sit back, do nothing, and watch the genocide of your people. I wouldn't have been able to live with myself. So I reached out the only way I could. No matter which way it went, I had done what I could to prevent genocide. I could live with that."

Commander L'Grina said, "Molly, you and I are a lot more alike than we are different."

I took that as high praise. "I discovered your people weren't all wicked beasts via the actions of G'Karn. In his own way and at great personal risk, he showed us compassion and tried to help us survive as best he could. Today, I wonder if this current mutation was an error on his part or if he deliberately made the changes to make us telepaths."

"Hum. Yes, he continually defied Commander R'Ina by showing your people compassion. She almost killed him several times for his actions to help you humans. I can see that now. Funny, how I can see things more clearly long after the fact. Mind you, I'm a soldier first."

I laughed. "So is my sister, Bev."

She laughed. "Another thing. Don't you wish you could get your arms regrown? I've heard many of your geneticists are working on that project."

"Of course. I miss firing my trusty Glock. Yeah, they are antiques, but I relieved tension by firing at targets on the range. I miss not being able to do that."

She chuckled. "You and I are a lot alike. Okay. I best see to making more arrangements. I'll drop by around eight o'clock. Thank you."

She rose, engaged her disguise device, and left my condo, strolling through the commons just as Ted returned home from work.

Chapter 31 Recovery

"Who was that woman? I've never seen her before," Ted asked, as he joined me.

"Commander L'Grina. She used to be in CEO Hardy's body. The Sixth Invaders have agreed to my proposal. Tomorrow noon, the surviving people are being returned, a new treaty between our worlds signed, and more of our low IQ people are being hired at double wages to mine for them. Highly successful day, but I best make more calls."

"After we eat. Besides, I have news for you, dear. Let me program our chef first."

Over a chicken dinner, he explained what he'd uncovered. "Remember months ago when we thought we'd defeated the Sixth Invaders and I looked into what had been happening at Galactic Robotics? Recall I said ten robots vanished. Today, I've found more data on them. Okay, I recovered deleted files on the R&D server. These ten were experimental robots designed with the most advanced AI brains and to appear *indistinguishable* from humans. The laws of robotics had been installed into the first five of them, making them operational."

I laughed. "I'll bite. What're those laws?"

"Oh, that a robot can't harm a human, that they have to obey humans. All the usual safety precautions to keep the machine safe and to help humans, never harming them, that sort of thing. Anyway, those five have vanished. No records exist of where they went, who may have purchased them— nothing at all. But what's even scarier, the other five hadn't yet had the basic laws installed into their programming. Those have disappeared, too."

"Are they dangerous? I mean if they aren't programmed with these laws."

"When you put a loaded clip into your Glock, is it dangerous? All depends on who's holding the Glock."

"I see. Any idea what happened to these robots? What they look like? Where they were kept? Why they were built?"

"Ah, my Molly in action. Yes, great questions. I'm looking into them and more, but that has to wait until tomorrow. I only got these files recovered before quitting time. I also want to know who deleted these and all associated files. Someone went to an awful lot of trouble both to make these robots and to hide their existence from us."

I chuckled. "Curious minds crave to know."

Ted roared.

After dinner, I made several calls, alerting Helen Hugo to the arrival of perhaps five thousand of our people around noon tomorrow. She promised all would be ready. Leslie also said she had apparel ready for the people. All I could do now was wait and hope I could reach these terrified people tomorrow and help them take their first steps on the road to recovery. In my heart, I knew this was my calling, my way to help other people get through their darkest times. But could I do it?

Our assisted living condo complex was north of the Loop close to the Lincoln Park Zoo. The Northeast Surgical Facility where we prepared to house the arrivals lay about two miles northeast of us. New O'Hare Spaceport was four miles east of the surgical facility. I remember reading in my history book that to build it, they leveled the suburb called Norridge, tripling old O'Hare's size, which brought it closer to downtown. The question that bounced around my mind all night was what would the emotional condition of these five thousand people be?

Why did this keep me awake? You can't talk or reason with a hysterical person. By the time I gave up and rose, I had concluded these people would be either sub-apathy or hysterical. I didn't want to wake Ted so early, so I struggled to make myself a cup of Earl Grey. I say struggled because for me it's not an easy set of actions to do. As I did so, both my feet made loud popping sounds. Bolts of pain shot through them, but then both feet rested flat on the kitchen floor. My legs and feet had returned to normal or rather the way they were supposed to be. I wanted to cheer but remained quiet until Lara made her way into the kitchen.

"It worked. My feet are normal again. Thank you!"

Lara smiled and looked at them before heading to the coffeemaker. "One thing about this world I love," she said, "is the taste and smell of coffee in the morning. Beats our tea by a mile—to use your phrase for it. Glad our mutation worked. I wish we had the arm problem solved though."

"Hey, this helps a lot."

"Why are you up so early? I know you had a breakfast meeting planned when Dimitri gets here."

"Couldn't sleep. Worrying about the condition of the victims when they get here."

"Guess you'll find out in a few more hours. I imagine the condition they're in is awful. It can't be good."

While I hoped she was wrong, I had a hunch she was right. Wearing my new light blue satin dress that encased my shoulders and matching pumps, I stepped into the hair machine one last time, allowing it to adjust my long black hair. While I could have worn flats or more comfortable shoes, I didn't want to be the only one wearing them. It was important to be a role model, at least for today.

Ted joined us. "Well, dear. Today, I'll find out where those ten missing humanoid robots went or die trying."

I didn't like his expression, but his excitement showed. We kissed, but the doorbell interrupted us. I answered the door and was surprised to see Commander L'Grina standing there without using her disguise device. Dimitri stood next to the commander, while Natalie fingered her holstered gun.

The commander spoke first. "Well, we're here. Should I use my disguise machine?"

"Hi, everyone. Er, what do you think, Natalie? I don't want someone seeing Commander L'Grina and shooting her."

"I've got my personal protection shield armed. Your blasters and flying projectiles can't get through its force field."

"In that case, let's go get breakfast just as you are. Helen Hugo, our local GD CEO is holding it at the best restaurant in the Loop."

"Lead on," Natalie said. "I'm starving. Will you be able to eat human food, Commander? None of us thought to ask you?"

She chuckled. "Originally, I thought your cuisine was loathsome, but after twenty years of it, I've rather gotten used to it. I'll be all right, once I get coffee in me. That's the one thing this world excels in: superb coffee."

Helen and Casper met us at the door and led us to a private back room. "My, Commander L'Grina, I didn't expect to see you... Undisguised."

She laughed. "Mrs. Hugo, I've always hated using it. I love my body and cringed every time I had to hide it. Don't worry about someone shooting me. I'm not that stupid. Protective force field." She patted a small device strapped around her waist, its soft blue light blinking. "Also, I hate those darn translator boxes. Makes my voice sound tinny and weird. Having been stuck on this world for a quarter of a century, I've picked up your language. Ah, coffee." She poured herself a cup before everyone else was seated.

Helen helped Casper with his chair while Natalie assisted me. A waiter arrived, stared long at the commander, but snapped his fingers. Four others entered carrying Helen's pre-ordered breakfast.

The commander said, "Okay. Let's get down to business. There's been a tiny change in our plans which helps you. Our transports had wanted to make the return trip carrying a thousand new workers back with them. However, they've requested a week's layover here. It seems the five thousand humans have made an awful mess of their ships. Molly, your description of their state when they awoke was grossly understated. I'm told it's beyond awful. I've no idea how you can handle these people when they arrive."

"They aren't wounded or hurt, are they?" I asked.

"No, nothing like that. Hysterical is your word for it, insanely hysterical. They can't seem to do anything for themselves, not even using the fancy machines we had Galactic Robotics develop for them last year. One of our men can't handle the needs of forty. We should have foreseen this coming, but we didn't. As reported early this morning, conditions are filthy and smelly on board. Hence, they need a week to clean up after they drop off your people."

Commander L'Grina sighed. "I hate to say this, but my people owe a great deal of gratitude to Molly for contacting me and warning me about what to expect. Originally, I thought Home World had just come up with the best idea ever. Kidnap a sufficient number of your people, mutate them into telepaths, and then breed and sell telepaths across the galaxy. Who wouldn't want a telepath in their service?"

I laughed. "It might have worked if to become a telepath, they didn't have to be mutated into armless Dolls against their wills."

Casper interjected. "Hey, without substantial training and practice, even everyday life can be an utter nightmare. It's beyond terrifying to wake up and find your body like this. Hell, I took half a year to get up enough courage to even try to do anything for myself."

After that, Dimitri and Commander L'Grina looked over the proposed treaty. Both found it simple and acceptable. Then, they signed it, witnessed by Natalie and Helen. After that, Helen and Casper left to continue making housing arrangements, while Dimitri and Natalie left to find another thousand of our people who wanted to mine and make double their usual wages. The commander and I headed to New O'Hare to await the arrival of the first transports.

She explained each transport carried around two hundred of our people and that twenty-five were on their way.

"I'm told a few have already perished, just like you warned me. I heard they found creative ways to kill themselves. Damn it, Molly. You were dead on. I'm impressed, even more impressed that you chose to contact me and warn us."

"Thanks. Now comes the hard part: salvaging them and getting them able to live independently again. We were successful with the kids who survived, but the adults are far more difficult to handle. So you're right. We have an awful mess coming."

"I'd like to get more of that therapy thing you did for me, if that's even possible."

I grinned. "Okay. But first I've got my hands full with these five thousand victims."

Commander L'Grina laughed. "Molly, what a sense of humor. Between you and me, I don't know how you can survive as you are. If it was me, I'd have found a way to kill myself. So there is a difference between us. I couldn't face living like you have to live. I just couldn't."

"Don't sell yourself short. You might rise to the situation—if it ever happened, I mean."

Helen and Casper joined us, along with a large security force that cordoned off one section of the giant spaceport where the transports would land.

She said, "Precautions. We don't want any trigger-happy people looking for revenge against your people. Lord knows enough folks want to do just that. Plus, we have EMACs waiting, along with doctors and every nurse that could be spared in central Chicago. Don't worry, Molly. We'll get them to the new facility."

Casper said, "So Hardy or L'Grina, do you remember me from GD?"

"Now you look more like a male should, but yeah. I remember you, my Chief Finance Officer. You did an excellent job, for a male, that is. Helen should be pleased with your new shape: a proper male."

"On your world maybe," he said with a grin. "Not on this one. I don't know about having done an excellent job, but I was a conceited prick. I can't believe the stupid things I did, but that's in the past. Have to look to the future."

Commander L'Grina sighed. "Yes, point taken. It'll be awful for me—the future that is."

"Why? Aren't you headed home soon?" asked Helen.

"Hardly. Of all my people, guess who not only knows your language but is familiar with your culture? Duh, me. Only me, damn it."

Casper laughed and finished her thought. "So you'll be your people's ambassador to us?"

Her coal-black eyes glared into his before breaking into a smile. "Damned observant, as always, Mr. Hugo. Yeah, looks like I'll be stuck here for several more years until my replacements are up to speed and comfortable being here. So, Molly, I'm looking forward to receiving more of this therapy thing of yours."

"Hey, you've had some too?" Casper asked.

"Yeah. Don't know why she did it, but it opened my eyes."

"Same here. It's incredible stuff," he admitted.

"The first transport is on its way down," Commander L'Grina said in an official tone. A wrist device made a slight noise. She glanced down and pressed a few buttons. "I'm in constant communication with my cruiser via my comm bracelet. Ah, here it comes."

All heads looked upwards. A giant gray cigar descended, guided by a beam from the computer-run control tower. I couldn't see how such a thing could even fly, but that only illuminated my ignorance. The transport was at least three hundred feet long and perhaps forty feet across, sloped to a point at each end. A side door opened, forming a ramp. Several soldiers in their green uniforms disembarked, blasters in hand, and formed a cordon around the ship.

Commander L'Grina beckoned us forward as she walked to greet them. In our heels, we fell behind her. Her left arm shot out before her, parallel to the ground, her hand facing the ground, a salute I'd seen CEO Hardy use many times. The other soldiers returned her salute. The first of the exchanges began.

Shrieking high-pitched voices relayed the stark terror these victims felt. While they'd been provided clothes and heels, all were filthy and stank. At once, I knew why. Unable to deal with anything, they'd just gone to the bathroom wherever they were.

Casper and Helen flinched and grimaced, unable to deal with the awful noise and stench. Even Commander L'Grina stepped back, holding her hands over her ears. One of the guards that secured the perimeter pointed to her ears. She wore sound dampeners.

Soldiers carried the victims off the ship and placed them on their feet, just as dozens of nurses joined us. They led the screaming victims to the waiting EMACs.

"Horus Dalles! It's worse than what you told me, Molly," Commander L'Grina said. "Hey, private, bring me sound dampeners."

The green-uniformed woman dashed into the ship, returning with a pair. "We're moving to the designated parking zone. The ship needs a thorough venting and scrubbing. Worse, we don't have enough males on board to do it, so we're going to have to help them. Horus Dalles times ten," she said.

We endured this twenty-four more times, before Helen, Casper, and I headed back to the new facility to join the others. Commander L'Grina vanished, presumably rejoining her own ship.

On the way to the facility, I got the call—one I hadn't expected or ever wanted, but one that shocked me. The CEO of Galactic Robotics called me. My stomach knotted and twisted hard, and my legs nearly gave out.

"Molly Parkinson, I'm so very sorry. There's been a murder. An hour ago, someone shot and killed your husband, Ted Billings. Our new policy is to inject anyone suffering life-threatening injuries with this powerful genetic mutation agent. All our key personnel carries their red pouch with them at all times. Someone administered it to Ted, but he was already dead, shot three times through his heart. He died instantly. The assassin also poured acid on his computer, destroying it. I'm so very sorry for your loss. Soon, you'll receive his insurance settlement from us. His body is being transported to the morgue out by New O'Hare, the closest one to your home. Again, I'm so sorry."

He had talked long enough for me to react. "Did you catch the assassin? Know who he is? Identify them? Why kill Ted?"

"No. We've no idea why he was killed, but internal security and the Chicago Police are on the scene now. We'll find them, I assure you. Oh, I have to go. The detective needs my help. Again, I'm so sorry. Bye."

I'd left the phone on speaker phone, so Helen and Casper heard him. Helen put her steadying arms around me, preventing my collapse. Soon, she had me sitting on a soft seat in her EMAC.

"Should we take you home?" Helen asked.

I swallowed hard. "No, he would insist that I help these people. I can visit it tonight. I could use a water."

"Who would want him dead?" asked Casper.

"I don't know. No one. Wait. This morning, he said he would find out what happened to the ten missing special robots or die trying."

"Okay, Molly," Helen said, "I'm going to launch an official GD investigation into Ted's murder. Galactic Robotics won't be able to cover anything up. I guarantee you that much."

Casper brought my water bottle, cradled against his shoulder. He sat down, took off his heels, and opened the top for me. In that moment, I realized just how far he'd come in overcoming his handicap. I felt encouraged. If he could do it, so could all these others. During the short flight, I called Deanna and told her the news, and she promised to relay it to everyone else. When the EMAC landed, the circumstances pulled me into the present moment and out of my swelling grief.

A hive of activity encompassed the facility. Thankfully, the shrill screaming died down. When I entered the giant auditorium, I saw nearly a thousand of us from my assisted living condo complex. From grade school children, to high school kids, to the adults—everyone was there, including many of my sisters.

Already ushers led in the first thousand of the survivors. They had been bathed, dressed in clean clothes, and brought to the auditorium where I planned to give my speech before beginning their training.

Celeste said, "After your talk, I have an army of therapy givers lined up. We'll try to do a thousand at a time, spanning five days to get to them all. This first group is from LA. We're keeping them in their city groups. Leslie's handling their apparel needs. Felix has been coordinating with Galactic Robotics, getting the needed machines here along with the special computers. We'll coordinate therapy sessions. The goal is to just take the edge off their recent trauma, though I suspect my army will push on through to a complete erasure of the trauma and its side-effects. So sorry about Ted. We all heard. We'll deal with that tonight. Right now, the first batch is ready for your talk, if you're up to it."

"Not how I thought my day would go, but thanks for everything, Celeste. Maybe we have a chance to save them."

I walked to the front of the stage where a microphone hung down. As I did, a hush fell over the room. I looked out onto a sea of many colored satin gowns, just like my own, Leslie's striking new style. Most of the faces were those of adults, all around twenty-five years old. I swallowed and began.

"Hello, everyone. I'm Molly Parkinson. I've managed to get a treaty with the Sixth Invaders, one in which they returned you to us. In case you don't know, they planned to breed you and sell telepaths to the entire galaxy. The latest count says five thousand one of you survived. Three hundred five didn't make it.

"This attack mutated everyone who worked in the GPan, GD, Galactic Robotics, Galactic Entertainment, and Galactic University skyscrapers in LA, New York City, Philadelphia, Miami, and Mexico City. That's five thousand of you.

"Look around at those in this room. You've survived against all odds. Now, it's time to heal. This is not the end of the world. It's a new beginning. We'll provide each with the machines we have that'll help you with some actions that are now harder for us to do. Last summer, the aliens collected a huge number of how-to videos from the internet to show us how to do many things in life. Each of you will have one of these voice-activated computers. I've arranged these videos into various categories and prioritized them. My advice is to watch them in the order I've listed them.

"Your lives aren't over. Yes, your life has been made more challenging for you, tougher in many ways. I and the others who we helped the past summer are here today and will show you how to do things our way. Give yourself time to learn new ways. We armless Dolls have a saying. Stop and think how. That must become your motto too, for I've found that needed every day.

"We are *not* helpless. We aren't dependent on others to survive. But yes, we will be for a brief time, as we learn these new ways to do things, get as comfortable as possible with our new bodies, accept what has happened to us, and move on. Life isn't over. Not remotely. Further, you were leaders in your cities, vital corporate leaders. Five cities, your cities, face a gigantic crisis, the loss of their major corporate leaders. Your cities cannot hope to replace everyone, especially Galactic University.

"You're still important. You haven't lost your minds, your knowledge, or your leadership skills. Your cities need you back at your old job as long as you can still do it. That means you must work hard and never give up. If these children can do it, so can you. But never think it'll be easy. It isn't. Sometimes, I think it's a bitch, but I've accepted this is the way it is for now. Make the best of it, and get on with your lives.

"To do that, here's my plan for the near future. Starting today, the children and adults here will run a special form of therapy on each of you hoping to erase the emotional and physical trauma you're endured. Each day, I'll hold training sessions with you, showing you the best ways I've figured out to do what we all must do to live independently. When you're confident you can manage on your own and with your own set of these helpful machines, we'll return you to your city. Then, if you held a key leadership position, consider resuming your vital role. Your city needs you back and as soon as you are able.

"Casper Hugo, Junior, wants to say a word to you." Via telepathy, he'd told me he wanted to speak. So I let him.

"Hi. I used to be the CFO for the Sol Empire GD corporation. Look at me now. I'm like you. Yes, I've also developed telepathy. But that's not what I'm here to tell you. Rather, I want you to know I've done what Molly Parkinson has just told you. I learned these new ways to do things, accepted the way my body is. Today I'm contributing to GD once more. I'm doing financial work for our local GD corporation here in Chicago. So yeah, I'm back doing what I love to do. I urge you to do as she says. It's damned hard, but you can get your life back."

I continued. "We have our geneticists working on undoing these mutations. It's a tough assignment. Progress has been made in the last couple days. Our giant bosoms can be reduced. Mine are almost there now. Our feet and legs can return to normal. Only this morning, mine did. It hurt for a second when both feet popped back into their original positions. Now I don't have to wear these tall heels.

"As soon as possible, these minor cures will be given to you. Give our geneticists time to create enough of their curing agents. My sister Leslie will coordinate getting you proper apparel and shoes, especially as your body dimensions change. Will we ever get our arms back? No one knows. But I won't sit in my chair for years waiting for that to happen. I want to live life, and I hope you do too. Now, it's time for your first round of my sister's therapy. She'll run this portion of our meeting."

Celeste walked up to the microphone. She explained what was about to happen. Then, her army of volunteers fanned out, each one taking one of the victims aside. Amazing.

A girl about six years old at most, said, "I'm here for you, Molly. Please sit there. Okay. Close your eyes. Let's go back to when you heard about Ted's death."

Although it sounded almost as if Celeste had had the child memorize those lines, I couldn't help but follow her command. My shocking loss was right there in present time, right now. I did as she asked. As I ran through it, I allowed my suppressed grief to pour out. A bucket of tears later, the emotional loss discharged. I felt much better. This was what Ted told me he wanted. He was dead set against someone using the red bag's syringe on him without his consent, mutating him again. I accepted his decision, but I missed him terribly. That evening, my sisters and friends joined me, saying our goodbyes as his body was cremated.

I had no time to mourn his passing. Rather, the next week became a blur of activity at the facility. I rose before dawn, got there in time to help show others how to use the various machines when they arose in the morning, how to dine, and so on. I returned home long after dark, having spent the entire day showing others how to do things, coaching them, praising their efforts, and even running therapy sessions during idle times.

By the second day, the official tally of the victims consisted of three thousand males and two thousand one females. Almost all were adults, now biologically twenty-five. A third of the victims were married to other victims. All but five hundred were married, though most of their spouses were back in their respective cities.

As we wrapped up the seventh day, Celeste said, "Okay. All the therapy sessions are done, as far as we dare to go right now. While it is still early, I believe none of these adults will commit suicide right away. The therapy sessions salvaged them, unlike what happened this summer with the Moscow people at the GPan and GD skyscrapers. I was worried the children couldn't handle the adults, but the kids didn't take no for an answer."

I chuckled. "But they have become old hands at therapy giving. Heck, I overheard Bernardo running one on Isabella when she stumbled and fell. It's become a natural thing for them to do. I bet you wish you could get all these adults to run such sessions, too."

She laughed. "You bet I do, but I realize many of these people have university degrees and held key positions within their corporations. It's vital they return to their posts if they can handle them. Still, I can wish, can't I?" We both laughed.

On the eighth day, Med Center personnel came by and injected everyone with the partial cure, explaining the two changes would be gradual. During this second week, Leslie handled the ever-changing dress sizes due to shrinking bosoms. When feet returned to normal, the males cheered, for now, they appeared more normal and didn't have to wear tall heels. At once, they too noticed they had more stability when walking. Their voices were still high-pitched, and several wondered if the geneticists were working on that aspect.

On the fifteenth day, one by one, their telepathic abilities appeared. So much so that I had to stop everything and give them an ethics talk.

"Okay, it's happened. All five thousand and one of you are telepaths. Some of you have been anxiously awaiting this while others could care less. Telepathy gives us more responsibilities. We must use our gift wisely. Looking into someone's mind without their consent is akin to mental rape and shouldn't be done. Some may want to accept one of the million credits per year offers that many corporations are advertising. If you do, make sure you read the fine print. Above all, first, stick it out here. Practice everything until you're confident you can get by on your own, living independently. Only then should you consider returning to your former jobs, looking for new employment, or going after the million credits per year assignments.

"One other point. Many have asked if an arm regrow cure will soon be available. The honest answer is not right away if at all. Don't hold back on practicing and learning, hoping that cure will be here next month. It may or it may not.

"What is important is for each of you to learn to be independent again. We're not helpless people. Some call us handicapped or disabled. I don't like either term. Physically challenged is far more accurate. Yes, I know the word handicapped means having a condition that restricts a person's ability to act—physically in our case. But I don't feel like I have a condition. I'm not restricted. Rather, I have to develop alternative methods, that's all. Hence, I prefer to be called physically challenged, because that's accurate and has no other connotations or social notions. Never give up. Remember our motto. Stop and think how."

Someone yelled, "How much longer will it take us?"

"We're on uncharted ground. This past summer, the thousand children were doing well enough to move into assisted living condo homes, where there was an adult available if needed. But as you've seen, our children are remarkably adaptive. The more you practice, the sooner you'll feel confident you can get by on your own. That's the key thing. Do you feel confident you can? I'm working up a practice test, a 'see if I'm ready to graduate' thing. All the usual actions a person must do throughout the day will be on it."

Another yelled, "Hey, brilliant. Get that list to us ASAP."

Half the room laughed. I'd hit another home run. With Celeste's help, I spent much of the following day working up what should be on the test.

When we sat back looking at the extensive list, Celeste said, "Perhaps we need a second test, a real world version in which they go out onto the streets of Chicago and carry out actions. Someone could follow them in case they get into trouble."

"I like that. An in-house test, which if passed, leads to the outside test."

She added, "Which if passed, means they can return to their home cities."

We presented these to the five thousand the next day. At first, they cheered when they heard they could go home when they passed the outside test. However, when they looked over the in-house test actions, they discovered they needed more work on most actions. For example, we placed a time limit on retrieving their ID cards from their pockets, swiping it at the cash register to pay for something, and putting it away. Other customers weren't willing to wait thirty minutes while someone took this long to do it.

We kept those from a given city in the same general area within this giant complex. Why? Many of the roughly one thousand from that city knew each other or had been friends before the attack. By Thanksgiving, new friendships formed and old ones renewed. Comradeship. Again, I knew this would be invaluable for them when they returned home. They'd not be alone.

During December, graduations began, slowly at first. Most found it scary to be out in the city on their own, especially now that winter had come. Still, we kept pushing them and encouraging them. One by one, confidence grew. After the first dozen passed, the others followed in quick succession.

When Christmas came, the facility was empty, and the medical staff moved back into it.

Celeste and I reflected on what we'd done. She pointed out the obvious. "Every last person should have had at least a hundred hours more therapy. They had unworthy feelings, scared feelings, phantom arms and hands sensations, terror stomachs when first going outside on their own, to say nothing of feeling embarrassed with others staring at them and their unusual ways of doing things. All those should have been looked into and handled because underlying each one is likely a traumatic incident with pain and unconsciousness. But we don't have the people who could do that for them. Five thousand times a hundred hours is a half million hours of therapy to deliver. If we could have done that, why, I bet every one of them would be a superstar."

"I know. You surprised me by using the kids. That was brilliant. Saved the day. We would have lost many to sub-apathy when they gave up on life."

"True, and a few might have found creative ways to commit suicide, while others might have forced the issue by begging to be terminated like the Moscow adults did this summer," she said. "The question for you, Molly, is now what? I still can't get my head around the fact that Ted's gone."

Chapter 32 My Decisions

Even though Lara continued to live with me, sharing the nearly empty condo, Christmas this year was... Dismal. Ted was gone. I missed him. In six weeks, I faced raising our family alone, something my orphan background found hard to stomach.

With Celeste's help, I made telepathic contact with Ted, who had already taken a new baby boy's body. He overheard the doctor talking after he slipped into the baby's head. Thus, he knew his baby body inherited the dominant genes from his mother, and he would be a male Galactic Doll, just as many had been predicting for months. With the two cures available, he took this news in stride, hoping we'd find a complete cure before this body reached adulthood. We expected this would be the fate of all boys since most of Earth's women had been mutated into Galactic Dolls last year.

He and I talked. Yes, I told him I respected his decision not to have them use the red bag syringe to revive him. My acceptance filled him with hope and caused him to relax. We discussed his shooting, but Ted could only say he was working on the server trying to recover more of the schematics of those ten robots and their disposition when someone shot him. He had no idea who or why.

I kept an eye on the case via my contacts with the Chicago Police. Helen Hugo also kept me informed since she launched her own investigation. By Christmas, nothing had turned up. Now I was too pregnant to do much of my own sleuthing.

But then so were Leslie, Janine, Deanna, and Helen Hugo. Our due dates clustered in February, with Helen's moved back from early March to the last days of February. Deanna and Holly Ann already had experience being mothers—Jana and Carl eighteen months old at Christmas time. And both women gave us tips on what to expect.

Still, little things continued to crop up, reminding me of my loss or my situation. Celeste gave me additional therapy sessions, erasing every little thing that bothered me. I'm glad she did. Despite my protests that this was nothing, each "nothing" turned into a past traumatic incident with pain and unconsciousness, and usually happening during previous lifetimes. If I appeared sad one morning, Lara called up Celeste who ran over and delivered another short session.

Since the last of the five thousand passed our tests and returned to Mexico City, I had the days to myself. Leslie often dropped by, helping me order baby things, while Lara deciphered the instructions to put together a baby bed. I experimented caring for a toy Galactic Barbie Doll. That led to Lara cutting the legs off the baby bed, lowering it to floor level, where I could easily work with the doll. Yes, as I grew fatter, I grew more and more worried I might not be able to handle a baby on my own. Losing Ted loomed large.

But I also had the luxury of time and money. I received a second million credit insurance settlement for Ted's death. Then I received a settlement from GMed over their crimes against Ted and me last year. So money worries vanished.

Time. I had much to ponder. What was I going to do? Three years ago, I knew everything I ever wanted to know. I was a PI, doing what I always dreamed of doing, helping people. Via all the therapy I'd had, I discovered I'd gone that route because I had been an orphan and didn't want anyone else to have to live life as an orphan, abandoned by their parents. But I was a clone. Lord knows who our birth parents were.

While I was, er am, a good PI, that's insufficient. Months ago, events drove home to me how ignorant I am of so darn many things. Early summer, I vowed to go back to school and learn more, like my three younger sisters, Ted, and Deanna. Even Hank, Janine's husband, had gone back to school, working on getting his history doctorate. So in August, I had planned on getting some college education. But that changed, too.

Then, this past fall, Celeste's therapy took on a huge aspect of my life. I'd used it on two completely different species, a dwarf, Lara, and a Sixth Invader, Commander L'Grina. Here was a mental-spiritual technology that helped people. That we used it on the five thousand victims proved to me how valuable it was. Based on what happened late summer with the Moscow personnel who underwent the same genetic mutation, everyone estimated at least eighty percent would perish, either by dropping into sub-apathy, by committing suicide if they were clever enough, or by begging to be terminated. We lost none because we erased the trauma they'd endured.

So as I sat around my condo in late December, what I should be doing with my life constantly bounced around my mind. Making matters worse, Earth's corporations organized their new ruling bodies. The Council of the Senate, charged with making laws and policies, was ready for operations, occupying the top floors of Chicago GPan's skyscraper. Each of the Sol Empire's worlds sent two senators, so the ruling group had forty-eight members. They were scheduled to hold their first meeting in January. Someone suggested I be Earth's senator.

The Council of Admirals and Generals moved into the top floors of Chicago's GD skyscraper. Again, each member world sent along one of their spacer admirals and one of their grounder generals. General Bev refused the appointment; I knew she wanted nothing to do with politics. Admiral Rossi became Earth's appointee.

The third body, the Council for Investigations and Justice, had two zones, a Senior Investigator and a Senior Judge. Again, each member world sent along one of their people for each post. Further, the older Galaxy Detective Squad became part of the investigation personnel. Both smaller groups were housed in the refurbished Monroe building. Many corporation leaders on Earth begged me to take Earth's Senior Investigator position. I haven't yet committed to doing so, but I had Major Airla handling Earth's duties in my place.

The ambassador positions had to be filled. Those from Zahra-C pushed hard for me to be one of the Sol Empire's Senior Ambassadors, go off to Bela Prime, and help make the laws of the Federation. I declined the original offer, and we sent off Aaron and Piper Strawn to fill those posts. However, with the addition of millions of giants and dwarves to Earth's population, we need to send another Senior Ambassador. Again, many CEOs asked me to go. I've not yet decided. Part of me is intensely curious about these other worlds. If I was into being an ambassador, there were openings for local ones to represent the Sol Empire with Azizi-C, Dian-C, Liatos-D, and Zahra-C. I could have any of those posts. But with Ted gone, I had an excuse. They preferred married couples to be the ambassadors, like the dwarven couple, Dara and Kiri Sim.

As I sat around the last week of December 2352, I had many choices to consider. I could continue my PI work or even be the Senior Investigator with Major Airla as my assistant. I felt qualified to handle these two jobs. My lack of formal education made me shy away from being an ambassador. I had no idea what our empire's wants and needs were. I'd be a poor choice, and now I had an excuse that would allow me to turn down those posts.

I appreciated how little I knew and wanted to go back to school. In a way, I felt I needed to do that—anything to become better educated. But educated in what field? What would I do with that education? Unknown.

Celeste's therapy offered me the greatest personal satisfaction of all. With it, I truly helped another person.

Since I was a telepath, many Earth corporations and several off-world ones made contract offers. Since our adopted twins became linguists on space exploration ships, most such offers were for similar positions. From long talks with Celeste, I knew how valuable having a telepath was when making first contact with a new people. That would also be a rewarding career.

What to do? What path to follow? Around and around I went that last week of December.

With my mind completely confused, I made a list of the possibilities and then prioritized them by assigning a number 1 to 10, where 10 meant I was keenly interested in pursuing it. I scratched off all those whose number was less than 7, which left only three items: delivering Celeste's therapy to others, learning more via getting additional education classes, and being a PI. Being a good mother was understood to be the most important activity of them all.

I asked Celeste to drop by so I could discuss this with her.

"Thanks. I want to deliver your therapy to others. It's at the top of my list, but it isn't a job and doesn't even have a name—what we're doing. I've got Ted's insurance money we can use to get it started."

She said, "That would be wonderful, Molly. I have a small group doing it in St. Louis. They call it Spiritual Recovery and Healing."

"I guess that's as good as anything—to call it, I mean. We can use the empty office next to my PI office in the Parker Skyscraper. It's on the second floor."

She hugged me and chatted about our new business for an hour. The next day, we purchased used, but comfortable, chairs and desks. Next, we added a filing cabinet with folders and plenty of paper and pens, along with three sets of the various machines armless Dolls needed and three computers loaded up with the how-to videos. Celeste promised to handle the promotion actions if I would conduct the therapy sessions.

With that established, I visited Deanna and told her I was ready to get more education. I explained, "I'll be running therapy sessions for Celeste at our new place, Spiritual Recovery and Healing. But honestly, I need to do more than just be a PI. I have to know more—be smarter. I can't be an ambassador like so many want because I don't know enough. But I don't know what I want to learn or could learn. Math isn't my strong suit, but could I somehow improve it? What do I do?"

"Let's get you enrolled in a General Education program for starters. They have batteries of tests that can help you focus in on what you might be good at. The corporations are always using those tests though they modify them for eighth graders and then again for high school seniors. Come on. I'll walk you over to the campus and introduce you around.

"Most courses can be done online, but I'm a building person. I like walking through marvelous old buildings and even smelling old books—real books, that is. Kind of a musty and leather smell. You'll see. They have a fabulous library."

Deanna helped me don my heavy cloak. Together, we walked over to UIC. Yes, I shook slightly. Could I manage to be a college student?

A dozen Dorian columns held up the entrance portico of the Administration building. Inside, the Roman appearance yielded to the modern efficiency of concrete and steel. Deanna assisted me as I registered as a freshman in Gen Ed. For the last step, I posed for my ID photo.

"See, it's that simple," she said, as I stowed my ID card.

"Now if the courses were that simple."

We laughed. She said, "Their library is top notch. Most books can be viewed online, but they have underground stacks with *real* books. Thousands of them. When I was going to school, I used to love to curl up down in the stacks—they have comfy chairs and all—and just spend hours reading and doing my engineering work. It's a shame they don't make real leather-bound books any longer. Now that you're registered, I'll take you to my favorite spot in the stacks."

Deanna led me out of the back of the building and into an unremarkable looking, single-story building of red brick. In an arch of gray bricks, the word Library sat above the entrance doors, which opened automatically.

"This is the main floor where most students get access to the electronic books, if they are downtown or here on campus and not at home online. I'd say ninety-five percent of the UIC students are online these days—maybe more. Anyway, you can see all the kiosks for studying."

I glanced at the spacious area and saw one student and one older woman, also a Galactic Doll, the head librarian, who nodded to Deanna. Well, it was semester break.

"Just showing my sister the library and stacks," Deanna said.

"It's good to see you. It's been years. Enjoy the real books."

She flashed us a matronly smile. We took an elevator down to the basement.

"There are many more subfloors below here, each with special elevators. You'll see. But first, you have to be authorized to enter the stacks. Your ID card is all you need. Just pass it over the scanner. They have a librarian down here somewhere who will help you with whatever you might need."

After swiping Molly's ID card, Deanna led her into the stacks where the real books were kept. Books of all sizes, colors, and shapes lined the shelves—a veritable rainbow of books. I gasped at the sight.

Just then, a young woman walked up to us, her heels clicking on the concrete floor. At first glance, I believed she was another armless Galactic Doll—the tall heels, the knee-length golden hair, the exaggerated curves, and even the voice—a pleasant alto sound. "Hello. Can I help you find something? Oh, Mrs. Cartwright. Good to see you again. And Mrs. Parkinson. Wow."

She looked vaguely familiar. Deanna stared at the woman. Like most in Chicago, this woman had had the two known cures, though she still wore the tall heels and satin gown, a rust color that blended with her hair, giving her a professional appearance.

"Sam? Sam Kross? Is that you?" Deanna said, holding one hand near her mouth. "I thought your face looked familiar. Molly, he had just gotten his library position when I was here working on my engineering degree. Sorry I didn't recognize you right away. You look so—"

"Freaky. Weird. Different. Yes, it's me. I was with Aaron Strawn's protest group. Mrs. Parkinson saved my life with her therapy thing. I was ready to die, but after that, I wanted to survive."

"Oh, sorry, Sam. I didn't recognize you," I said. "You've let your hair grow some."

He chuckled. "You've helped so many of us. Anyway, I'm here to help you."

Deanna said, "Molly, Sam, here, is the most valuable resource in the entire library. He's got a knack for finding absolutely anything you need. I can't tell you how many times I've come down here to the stack with only a vague idea of what I needed. Just tell him about it. In no time, he'll have the book you need. Sam's a fountain of knowledge on just about anything."

"No, Mrs. Cartwright, these books are." Turning, he said, "I know these stacks well, but it's not instantaneous. The longest it's taken me to find what a patron needed was twenty-four hours. Got no sleep that time, but I found what he wanted. That's my job. I've been here for a dozen years."

"I've just signed up for courses," I said. "My sister is showing me her favorite places here in the stacks. I've never seen so many real books before. I can't believe there are so many."

He chuckled. "One million four hundred sixty-three thousand seventy-five. Five subfloors of books. It's my job to know where they are so I can help anyone find what they need. So what are you studying, Mrs. Parkinson? And thank you for saving my life and teaching us how to be independent."

"Oh, just Molly, please. General education. I can't figure out what I want to study. I just know I need to learn so much more, even history.

"I have your saying posted on my wall at home and here at my desk. Stop and think how. I have to do that several times a day. But I always try to appear professional while I'm on the job in the library."

"I bet you're saying it fewer times today than say last month. So that's why you are still wearing the tall heels. Rather wondered about that."

"Yes, I'm continuing to get the hang of doing things so differently. Flats and tennis shoes are comfier, but..." He sighed. "Since I look like a Galactic Doll, when I'm in public, I dress like one. Less embarrassing. Many men are wearing the new male Doll suits, but that draws attention to themselves. I'd just as soon have no one notice me."

I chuckled. "Well, it's working. I thought you were a woman when I first saw you. I'd forgotten I'd done that brief therapy on you. I can see how this would let you relax more when in public."

Deanna said, "Molly, Sam is blessed with a photographic memory. Once he reads a page, he can recall every word on it—as if he has a picture of it in his mind. He's right. He can find anything you need in this library. You'll be in good hands with Sam."

"Sorry, I've lost them hands," he joked.

After we both smiled, Deanna said, "I never thought I'd ever get turned into a Galactic Doll, so I guess I look freakish too. Hell, all women do now."

Sam flushed. "No, you don't look freakish, Deanna. That word is reserved for us men. My aunt—she hated to have it done, too. She was a big woman before—okay, she was overweight, but now she's so thin she thinks she's anorexic. Been to the med center about it ten times."

"Is she all right?" Deanna asked.

"Yes, her body looks much like yours. It's all in her mind. That's what the doctors keep telling her."

"Well, it is a genetic mutation, after all," Deanna said. "Many of my factory workers were big, robust men, strong men, and now their body forms are indistinguishable from those of a woman, and anything but robust and strong. I think men lost more body weight, more muscle mass, during the mutation than women have."

"Good point. I lost forty pounds. My arms didn't weigh that much, I assure you. As soon as I speak, my voice sounds female. So when people look at me, they think they see a Galactic Doll woman, until they see I don't have arms."

I added, "And even then, they aren't sure, right?"

He grinned. "Astute observation."

"Well, I'm due back at work. Sam, will you show Molly some of the cozy places here in the stacks where she can curl up with a real book?"

"Sure. That's what I'm here for."

"Thanks for getting me enrolled and setup. I'll see you later tonight."

After Deanna left, Sam said, "I know just the spot she used. Follow me. Almost no one comes down here. Deanna was a regular several years ago. Most everyone reads the electronic books. Has been that way for centuries. Can't say I blame them. Darn convenient. But still, there's something about holding a real book—its smell, its texture. Only now, I can't hold them—not properly anyway."

Sam led me to a side reading area, equipped with five small desks with chairs and one couch, worn and stained, but clean. Overhead lights were strong making this an ideal place to study.

He said. "So you're studying Gen Ed?"

"Yes, I really want to help people. That's why I became a PI, but I've found that's so limited. I'm not the brightest student, not like Deanna or some of my younger sisters. I can't imagine how much they must have studied to get three doctorates. I barely passed math in high school."

"If you don't know what you want to do, then Gen Ed makes sense until you figure it out. Me, I've settled down into wanting to be an astronomer and spaceship navigator—that is, until this happened." He shrugged his empty shoulders.

"You can't do those things now? Don't the ships have auto-controls or something?"

"I figure they'll take one look at me and point to the exit door. I don't want to be a linguist either."

"Well, their loss then. They've not heard our motto: stop and think how. We usually find a way, somehow."

Laughing, he said, "Yeah, somehow. It's been a real challenge for me. I have to pull the books off the shelves for people and then put them back up when they're done."

"All the way on the top shelves?" I glanced up at books that were about ten feet above the floor.

"Stop and think how." Sam grinned. "I had to thunk long and hard too." He laughed.

"But somehow you did it, right?"

He nodded. "Well, that's all that matters. You got it done. Wouldn't it be easier if you cut your hair shorter?"

"Probably. But I like it long. The fancy hair machine keeps brushed out properly, and I can feel my back with my hair."

I looked up at him, smiling. "Same here. I can't reach my back, but I can feel it using my hair. It's rather a silly thing, but—"

"It means everything to us, right?"

"Exactly. Before, I rarely had mine longer than shoulder length. After the mutation and this happened, by tossing my head, I can feel my back and sides. Well, there are times I need that feeling."

Sam sang, "No one knows what it's like to be me, behind blue eyes." We both laughed.

"Yes, you've nailed it. And you have gorgeous blue eyes too. You are so easy to talk to."

"So are you. I had a girlfriend, but after this happened, she freaked out and broke up with me. Since then, girls won't even look at me, except with pity in their eyes. I can do without that. Thank you very much!"

"I totally understand."

"Thanks. So when's your baby due?"

"Valentine's Day. She'll be my valentine. After Ted's death, I need this."

"I'm sorry about his death. I know how much he helped everyone with all the robots and machines. Have they discovered who killed him?"

"Nope. Nada. Not a clue."

"I saw where the last of the five thousand left for their homes. It must have been hard helping them when all you wanted to do was put on your PI hat and find who murdered him."

"Observant, too, Sam. Yes, dozens of times I wanted to stop and play PI again."

"Like whenever you got another update that said nothing new had been found?"

"Damn, Sam. You're good. That's precisely right. Helen—GD's CEO—she's conducting her own investigation independent of Galactic Robotics security and the CPD's investigations. How can nothing ever be found? Surely, clues are there somewhere."

"I have a knack for judging people. I've been avoiding using this telepathy thing. Kinda silly of me not to, but if they find a way to cure us, we're likely to lose that when our bodies return to normal. Why get dependent on something that might not be there tomorrow? Eh?"

"Good point, Sam. So do you think they'll be able to regrow our arms? Or make male bodies return to being males?"

"I believe one day we'll get our arms back. I have to believe that. If I don't..."

"Yes, too depressing."

"Bingo. As for me ever looking like a real man again, ha. Tell me another joke. No, those Sixth Invaders did a job on us. Say, I've seen the latest medical findings."

I looked at him, putting a quizzical expression on my face.

"Medical journals. Newborn babies to our Galactic Doll women are Dolls themselves, both boys and girls. Forty years from now, you're not likely to find a normal male anywhere on Earth. Then, there are the children from folks like you and me, the armless Dolls. Our kids will be like us. Oops, I'm sorry. I don't want to upset you."

"You aren't, Sam. You're being honest. I've known for a long time she would be like me. Sonograms. I'll love her just the same. Ted would have, too."

"Still, you find it a little depressing?"

His blue eyes drilled into mine. I felt a tingling up my spine. Sam was almost too observant.

"Yeah, a little. Still, I'm sure she'll do fine."

"I think it'll be a lot easier on her than losing them when you're an adult like we did. She won't know any other way. I can see why so many adults preferred death."

I laughed. "Yeah, that's why we had to run therapy on them as soon as we got them back."

"Speaking of that, can you tell me how that all came about? The news was vague on just how that all happened. How did our worst enemy suddenly have a gigantic change of heart and become friends with us? Wait. If it's an empire secret, you don't have to tell me."

I laughed. "No secret, but I have to use a bathroom soon. Deanna said I'll be going all the time in another couple weeks. I didn't believe her, but now I do."

"This way."

When I finished, I rejoined Sam.

"My shift is over, Mrs. Parkinson. I'll buy us supper if you'll clue me in on what the heck happened with the Sixth Invaders. I can't find any documents discussing it. You seem to be the one in the know."

Chapter 33 Falling in Love Again

"He's charming." I explained to Lara why I wasn't home for supper like normal. "He bought me supper. In return, I told him about how I negotiated the return of our telepaths."

"Why did he want to know that?"

"Curious, I suppose. He was more interested in our new therapy group, our Spiritual Recovery and Healing. That both dwarves and Sixth Invaders responded well to the same therapy that he received resonated with him. Now, he wants to get more therapy sessions from us. He's living in this center, Condo Number 53. But he has a north side home he inherited from his parents who were professors at UIC. Sam protested along with Aaron Strawn, so after his mutation, he moved in here along with all the others."

"Then, we should invite him over for dinner one night," Lara said. "Unless you don't want—"

"It's too soon to be thinking such thoughts, Lara. I've got my daughter to worry about right now. Still, he is a charmer. I wish he hadn't been mutated."

Lara laughed. "Hey, everyone who was sure wishes they hadn't been. Well, except for those who signed contracts for the million credits a year."

After a pause, she said, "It's good to meet young people your own age. Since you're going to college, it's a good idea to have someone there who can help you find things."

I giggled. "Books. Real books. This guy has a photographic memory, too."

"Well, there you go. A charmer who can recall everything. Good combo. Oops. Sorry, I forgot you said he's an armless male Doll—not exactly the handsome, gallant man."

I sighed. "I know. But then Ted was mutated, too. One thing Ted taught me is to look at who the person is, not so much their appearance. Besides, Sam also knows the truth—that all males born on Earth to a Galactic Doll mother—which is darn near all women—will be a Doll themselves, male or female. From that point of view, it won't matter much."

Lara laughed. "Unless you marry a giant or a dwarf male or someone from off-world—as if that's gonna happen. I'm surprised they haven't quarantined everyone on Earth."

"Besides, I'll have a daughter to care for in a few more weeks. Who'll want to marry me then? Statistically, that lowers my odds."

Lara laughed. "When have odds ever stopped love?" We both laughed.

"So are you going to go to the Midwinter Formal Ball on January 1? Helen's invited you. She's sponsoring it and has been hounding me to find out if you're going to go. I think she wants you to come, even though you're eight months pregnant."

"It's couples-only, Lara. I seem to have misplaced Ted at the moment."

Lara chuckled. "Good one, Molly. Good one. Say, how about asking Sam? If he's as charming as you say—it's a good thing to be seen in public again. You don't want to be hold up like an old maid. I bet he'll be your plus-one."

"Oh, I don't know. I'm so fat."

"Helen told me this year, she's providing many chairs, unlike previous years when men were in charge of the dance."

"Well, that'll be most welcome for those wearing heels. When Ted and I headed home from the dance, our feet throbbed so badly we could scarcely walk. Good for Helen."

"Why don't you ask Sam? It'll do you good to get out and enjoy a special evening. If I get it right, it only happens once a year."

"True. Okay, I'll ask him."

***

I spent the morning in my PI office, paying bills. No new cases. In the early afternoon, I worked at our new place, Spiritual Recovery and Healing Center, delivering two therapy sessions, while Celeste worked on several others. Many of those who had their eyes opened with that initial round of sessions when the Sixth Invaders returned them now sought relief from other unwanted feelings, emotions, and pains, usually related to their handicapped state.

Late afternoon, I visited the library stacks and found no one down there but Sam. I didn't know how to start this conversation.

"Hi, Molly. I've been digging into Ted's murder. Well, more like I've been trying to find out more about those humanoid robots you mentioned last time. The library has tons of documents, not just books. I found a monograph on The Prospects for Humanoid Intelligent Robots by a Professor Higgenbacher. He claims we'll see them in our lifetime. Robots that are indistinguishable from people. Robots that are highly intelligent and serve mankind. He was rather vague about how they would serve us, though."

"Fascinating. How does it tie into Ted's murder?"

Sam smiled, and I admired his unpretentious smile, his sky-blue eyes, enchanting. "I work here, you'll recall. I looked up who's checked out this document. It isn't on the must read list for students, not even those who work for Galactic Robotics. Guess who the last person to check out this electronic copy?" He paused a moment. "Ted. He checked it out a week before his death. Isn't this curious?"

"He did? A week? Okay, can I do that, too? I doubt I'll understand even a page, but who knows? If Ted thought this might be important, I'll read it."

Sam smiled, sending shivers down my spine. Again. "I thought you might, so I took the liberty of signing it out for you. You'll find it in your UIC Book Nook on your computer. I've also checked it out. I'll read it tonight, but I'm not sure I'll get much out of it either. Still..."

"Thank you, Sam. That's wonderful. Maybe we'll get a clue."

He smiled. Again. I took a deep breath, well, as deep as possible with my protruding belly. "Sam. The Midwinter Formal Ball is coming up on January 1, three days from now. Helen Hugo is hosting it. She's invited me and is begging me to come. It's a couples-only dance."

"Oh. Do you need someone to take you?"

Damn, he's observant. "Yes, if I go, I have to take someone. Sam, would you consider coming to the dance with me? I know. I look like a blimp or something, but I hate to disappoint Helen after all she's been doing for me."

"Hey, you don't have to ask twice. I'd love to take you. Consider it a tiny thank you for saving my life with your therapy back in August. Say, what do we wear?"

Okay, I felt so relieved that I had asked him and that he said yes that I said, "Clothes, Sam. It's best if we wear clothes."

Sam roared, and I grinned. "Okay, seriously, Helen's changed the dress format. When I went to CEO Hardy's Midwinter Formal Ball, the women all wore billowing ball gowns, which Ted and I couldn't manage. So we bought loose fitting gowns. This year, Helen's invite says normal Galactic Doll apparel is acceptable. I guess I must wear tall heels again, and I'll wear one of Leslie's new style gowns that covers our shoulders. I don't like cold shoulders."

"Okay, that sounds fine. What time should I pick you up?"

"It starts at six, so how about a half hour before that? We can take the MTES and be there in time. Sam, are you sure you want to do this? You'll be in the public eye."

Sam smiled. "I'll look like any other woman there."

"Hardly, Sam. Most will have arms. Men will likely wear Leslie's male Doll suits. Casper always does now."

"I'll endure it for your sake, Molly. What about dinner?"

"Hey, it's my turn. Drop by my place when you're off. I'll have something for us."

Sam's lower jaw dropped. I said, "No, I don't cook. Never, ever did. Lara will fix us something."

"Oh. You had me there. I can almost make a cup of tea myself, and I've been able to make coffee. But a whole meal? Wait, is she serving dwarf food?"

I chuckled. "No, our food. Now you mention it, I wonder what her native food is. Thanks. See you in a while. I'll get started reading that document on the robots. Bye and thanks."

"No, thank you for inviting me."

Once home, I turned on my computer and found my UIC Book Nook. There was the document waiting for me. Before diving into it, I fixed myself a cup of tea, using the microwave. Then, when Lara returned, I asked her to fix supper for three.

"Yes, I invited Sam over. You can meet him. He's agreed to take me to the ball. So that's that."

She winked at me. I felt my face flushing. I'm not a silly school girl, I told myself, but I don't think I believed it. Then, I dove into the monograph.

He described possible uses for a human-looking, intelligent robot. Mining and dangerous occupations occupied the author's mind. Toward the end, he referred to an ancient science-fiction author named Isaac Asimov, who presented the laws robots should follow. I found they made perfect sense on a first reading. Robots shouldn't hurt a human or fail to act to prevent a human from harm. Further, it should obey all orders given to it by us. I liked the proviso unless such an order violated the not harming humans. I recalled Ted telling me about the third point—that a robot should protect itself as long as doing so didn't interfere with the other two laws. Yes, they seemed to make sense. In a flash, I realized why these would be necessary in an intelligent, "thinking" machine.

I had to stop because Lara had dinner ready and Sam arrived. In spite of Lara's frequent winks at me, we three had an enjoyable meal. Then, I showed him what I'd found in the document so far. To my amazement, Sam recited the paragraphs describing the theoretical laws from memory.

"Yes, I got that far in the document, too," Sam said. "Can you imagine what might happen if one of these artificial intelligence, human-appearing machines didn't have these laws as part of its behavior? Is it even appropriate to say behavior? These are robots."

"Dunno. But I saw that too. Scary. Bev and her soldiers fought against robot soldiers on Brussels, Tau Ceti. Those robot soldiers had to be directed by humans, but still..."

"Right. Scary to even contemplate. Didn't you say Ted said ten of these supposed human-like robots vanished?"

"Yes, five had been programmed with robot laws, though I don't know what those laws were. Five had just been made and hadn't been programmed yet. Why?"

"On my walk over here, Molly, I asked myself how would anyone recognize a human-like robot."

Damn, I liked how this man thinks. "And how did you answer yourself?" I had to tease him, a little.

He gave me that smile of his. Again. More shivers. Damn.

"Well, that depends on how closely the robots can mimic humans—how well they were built. I recalled the footage GEnt showed of our soldiers fighting and losing to those robots on Brussels. Those moved slowly and clumsily. They acted rather stupidly, if you ask me. But suppose they improved the design. Suppose they could build a robot body that outwardly looked and moved just like us."

"Then, we'd have to have other ways to detect it."

"Right. We'd have to depend on its speech, but we both know that's already perfected in the robot machines we use to handle our hair and getting dressed. No, we'd have to detect them based on their mental—if that's even the right word—responses and actions."

"What about other physical actions?" I asked. "Like eating and drinking."

"Ah, those too. So assume someone has perfected the robot's body so it looks like us, talks like us, and acts like us. How do we tell it's a robot?"

"How?"

"Minds. All that's left is us and our minds. You've shown me I'm a spiritual being that has a mind. If they can perfect a mechanical body that looks and acts just like our bodies, then beings and minds are all that separates us from the robots. That got me wondering. How do we sense a robot's mind? Or would we even sense it? I mean with our telepathy. Ordinary people can't tell if either one was present. But we can. Sense minds, though I almost never do it. What would we sense? Electric circuits?"

"Damn good point, Sam. Our minds consist of images with full perceptions almost like a continuous video recording. A robot with a computer running an AI program would only make calculations. It wouldn't have any images for us to see."

"Wow. So only one of us telepaths could detect whether it was a robot or a human."

"I think that might be the case."

He laughed. "Glad there are only ten of them."

***

January 1, 2353, arrived, bringing a heavy snow with it. Wonderful for the Midwinter Ball. I dressed in my yellow gown, which covered my shoulders tightly, Leslie's fancy new style. As always, I let my raven hair fall down my back, though these past months it had grown and fell between my knees and ankles. At first, I tried to wear matching yellow tall heels, but as pregnant as I was, I took them off and wore soft-soled, comfy shoes. It's what Helen gets for insisting a pregnant woman come to the ball.

Sam arrived right on time. His golden hair was only inches longer than mine. His similar gown was a light rusty color; his tall heels matched his gown. As I looked at him, I realized no one would suspect he wasn't a woman, lessening his embarrassment. I made a note to add such things to his therapy sessions later on.

"Wow, Sam. You look great."

"I hope no one can tell. Molly, you look stunning, too. I was going to suggest you not wear tall heels. I'm glad you opted for safety and comfort."

"Not stunning, Sam. Like a bloated pig or something."

"No, a young mother close to bringing new life into the world."

Damn, he had a way with words too.

"It's snowing, so we're both going to have to be careful walking," he said.

Lara fastened my cloak for me. He and I stepped out into the falling snow. For once, I had secure footing, but Sam had to go very slow, trying to keep from falling down. Neither could help the other if they fell.

Meeting us at the door, Helen said, "So good of you to come, Molly. Sam. Don't worry. We've plenty of chairs this time. Lord knows I'll need to sit down often. We're both so pregnant. No wine for us tonight. I have a good punch, spiked with vitamins."

This time, I had a wonderful time at the dance. True, many leaders came up to chat or introduce themselves, but few chose to dance with a pregnant woman. I picked up surface worries that they might harm me by dancing. Silly people.

I honored Sam's request. When people asked who this charming, golden-haired young woman was, I responded, "A friend from UIC, looking after me tonight." While Deanna recognized him, only two people from the university did; they said nothing.

When the dance ended and others helped us don our cloaks, we found Leslie and Janine outside waiting for us, accompanied by their husbands, Felix and Hank. Both my sisters were as pregnant as I was. Besides wanting to make sure we made it home safely—snow depth now reached eight inches—both wanted to meet Sam and find out all about the ball. Slipping and sliding, we made it, though Sam had a very difficult time negotiating the slippery sidewalks.

The late afternoon the next day, I dropped by the library to see Sam. He surprised me again.

"Molly, I've been thinking about how we can detect a robot. The key is they don't have minds—not like we do. So all we need to do is lightly touch the subject's mind. If we find one, they're human or aliens. But if we detect nothing, they're a robot."

"Sam, that makes sense. Oh my god! Sam, I might just know of two of these robots. Wait, before I say anything, I should make sure. I don't want to start wicked gossip."

"Okay, but promise me you'll tell me what you find out. And be careful. Ted was murdered."

"But we still don't know why he was murdered. It might have nothing to do with robots."

Sam and I had dinner together. Again. At my place. Why couldn't I get this man out of my mind?

The next morning on my way to check my PI office, I stopped by the new office of our Senior Investigator. Theoretically, the post was supposed to be mine, but since I turned it down, they installed my assistant as our top investigator, Major Airla Baker. As I walked in, I wondered where that Mr. Travis Jones had gone. Somehow, he'd traveled beyond the known Sol Empire and found the Federation, bringing them to our aid. Had he not done that the Earth would be in the Sixth Invaders' hands.

"Hi, Molly. Are you here to relieve me?" Major Airla said. "I guessed I wouldn't see you until after your maternity leave ended." She had a wry smile. She was teasing me, of course.

"Hardly. Can we talk privately somewhere?"

She led me into her office.

Once more, I focused and attempted to read her mind's surface thoughts. Nothing. I probed deeper. Nothing.

"Well?" she said. "By the way, we're looking into Ted's murder, too. Something about it isn't right, but no one's got a clue yet."

"He was looking into the ten missing robots. Supposedly, no one can tell them apart from a human. Ted told me he believed five had been programmed with robot laws so they couldn't harm humans. The other five had just been built. Anyway, I've worked out a way to detect these robots."

Major Airla cocked her head to one side, her eyes staring into mine.

"Minds. Telepaths can sense minds—surface thoughts are easy—or probe even deeper into a mind. I've never been able to sense your mind at all. There's no easy way to say this, but I think you're one of these ten robots, one which has the laws programmed in them. I think may be Mr. Travis Jones is one too. So are you? A robot?"

I couldn't make it plainer. While I was saying this, I continually attempted to contact her mind or be alert to any emotional reaction to what had to be startling news. After all, it isn't every day that someone accuses you of being a mechanical man or woman in this case. Do they even have a gender?

"Five of us saw how close the Sixth Invaders were to conquering the Earth and its three billion humans. Our programming dictated we act. Travis took a huge gamble and won. The question now is what are you going to do with this knowledge? When the latest mutations began developing telepathic skills, we feared this day would happen."

"Me? I'm not doing anything. We owe you our continued existence as a free people. I needed my theory confirmed. So there's five of you?"

"Yes. We work in the background. Except me. I kept hoping you'd take this post of Senior Investigator so I could slip in as one of your many workers and not draw attention to myself. Will you take the position when you've had your baby? If not, will you get someone who's qualified to take this job? Eventually, another telepath will work it out. We aren't sure if your joining this Federation of Planets is a good move or not. Much work, much study remains to be done, but we saw it as the only way to save you from being conquered by the Sixth Invaders."

"I'll consider it or see if I can get another to take the position. I've got a ton of questions, but what about the other five, the ones who haven't been properly programmed?"

"They vanished. We've been trying to locate them, but so far, we've found no trace. Our bodies have been so well constructed that we can't tell one of us from one of you, not without some invasive probing. Or seeing them when they are recharging at a power outlet. This is why I opened an investigation into Ted's murder. Could it have been one of these rogue robots? If so, why kill Ted? We have too many unanswered questions to make a proper calculation."

"Okay then. I'll see what I can do to get someone in this position, Major Baker."

"Molly, if another telepath discovers me, I'll vanish. One feature built-in to our model is the ability to alter our appearance."

"If that happens, how can I contact you? If I need you."

She made a human gesture, biting down on her lower lip as though in thought. "Take this." She slipped a small device into my dress pocket beside my phone. "If you need me, push the button. It'll send an electronic signal I can sense and track. Works on an unused frequency."

I thanked her and left, a million questions left unasked. Okay, not that many, but a lot. I had to assume she was being truthful with me. Why make that assumption? If she had the robot laws as part of her programming, she couldn't lie. But did she have those laws in her circuits? Ah, that's the better question. Ted might have a way of finding out, but not me.

More snow fell later this first week of January. The bitter cold winds didn't help, so I minimized my outings, spending time only at the therapy center. Sam dropped by every night after his shift at the library. After dining, we spent hours chatting. As the end of January approached, he brought baby gifts: blankets and clothes. If I'm honest, I treasured his visits. I'd found a part of having children I didn't enjoy—these last weeks. Had my bladder shrunk to the size of a peanut? Getting around and using feet became a struggle.

Then the best news ever came one evening in late January. Eve and Lara rushed in. Lara said, "Molly, Sam, we've done it! We've made a mutation agent to regrow your arms."

After Sam and I cheered them, Eve took over. "There's one catch. God damned politics. Galactic Medicine has to sanction our discovery. When they discussed this breakthrough with the other corporations, the CEOs insisted on one change we had to make. That's why it's taken this long to develop the cure."

Eve sighed. "When arms are regrown, the telepathic ability must be undone. The pituitary gland is responsible for the remarkable telepathic skills of the armless Dolls. That mutation enlarged the gland threefold, bringing on telepathic abilities. The CEOs insisted it is shrunk back to its original size."

"The bastards. Why?" asked Sam.

"I can see their point, sort of," Eve said. "Today, if you see an armless Doll, you presume they're a telepath. While there might be an exception here and there—genetic birth defect, for example, this is pretty well a certainty. Their reasoning comes from fear. If we only regrew arms, then there'd be no way of knowing if the person near you was a telepath or not. They feel this would give telepaths unprecedented power over ordinary people. 'Temper power' was how the CEOs put it. Telepaths must be instantly identifiable by everyone. We had no choice if we wanted to release this cure to the thousands who need it."

Eve continued while staring into my eyes. "They don't know about us natural telepaths. With enough therapy, anyone can become a telepath. Even Sam could become a natural telepath, but he'd probably have to undergo a thousand hours of our therapy to get it. We believe spiritual beings once had that ability before they started using and being a physical body. That was eons ago. What I'm saying, Molly, is you aren't likely to lose yours, but Sam will."

"Wow. Incredible news. I can shoot my Glock again. I've missed that outlet more than any other."

"Hold on, sis. You can't get it now. You must wait until after you have your baby. Then you can have it done. Both you and your baby girl. Sam could get it done now."

He said, "Not just yet. I'm here to help Molly with everything. I'll get it done later on when she and the baby are doing okay."

"All right, Sam," Eve said. "I'm glad you're here to help look after Molly. I'm sure we'll have thousands wanting the cure right away. But it gives the CEOs another marketing tool. 'Get mutated into a telepath; work for us and make your millions; get your arms restored.' Great for the CEOs." She laughed cynically.

After Eve left and Lara headed to bed, I had a serious talk with Sam.

"You should go ahead and get it done now."

"No, I want to help you and your daughter get through this first. There's plenty of time to get it done later. I guess they could do it to her right after she's born. Then, she'll grow up being a normal girl."

I don't want to be normal. I'm taking this girl body because it's going to have telepathy. Don't you dare *take that away from me. I want to be a telepath!*

That appeared simultaneously in my and Sam's minds.

"What?"

Sam glanced all around the room but saw no one.

As I said, don't you dare *do that to my new body. I'm right here. Okay, I'll make the body kick.*

"Ouch! Stop that! Baby's kicking me."

"Yeah, baby, stop hurting your mother," Sam said.

Then don't let her get rid of its telepathic ability.

"Okay, I promise I won't," I said.

"Right. Molly won't do that if you don't want her to. Do you want to become a telepath? Like me and your mom?" Sam asked.

Duh! Of course. What a stupid question.

"Molly, it looks like you're going to have a bright girl."

We both laughed.

"Okay. I'm getting my arms back. If you don't want yours back, then okay."

Good.

Sam said, "Molly, she'll need a role model, someone to show her how to do things. Let me do that for you. I know how much getting your arms back means to you. This way, I can help your daughter learn."

"Sam, you can't do this. She's my daughter. You aren't obligated to help her."

"But I want to help you and her. Can't you see I'm in love with you."

My face felt instant heat. Had Lara turned up the furnace? I felt electricity shooting up and down my back, and it wasn't my baby acting up.

I want Sam to be my daddy.

"Sam, I love you too, but—"

"Hey, you deserve a whole man, not one that looks like I do. I want to do what I can for you and your baby. Help you both do well. I told you how my ex-girlfriend freaked out when she saw what I looked like after the mutation. So I want to be here to help you until you can find a proper man worthy of you."

In a flash, I understood Sam. "Are you in love with me or with this mutated body of mine?"

"Don't be silly, Molly. You. I love you. Everything about you. Oh, I see what you mean. I like your face, hair, and piercing eyes, but I'm in love with you, the person behind them eyes of yours."

"Then, why can't I do the same, Sam? Damn it. Marry me, Sam. Now. Before I have my baby."

"Are you sure, Molly? I look like some—"

"So do I. Yes, I'm sure. So shut up and kiss me."

Great. Now Sam is going to be my daddy.

That interrupted the kiss.

He can show me how to do things, Mom.

We both laughed. "Okay, okay. I can take a hint."

Hey, what are you going to call me?

"Vanessa. After my grandmother."

Yucko. Name me Nikita, Mom. Sam, make her name me Nikita.

Again we laughed.

"Precocious kid, Molly." We roared.

The next day, we told everyone. On January 31, we married in spite of the snowstorm. We kept the wedding simple. I didn't want my sisters who were also nine months along, to be traipsing through the blizzard, so we made use of a video conference. That way everyone could attend the brief service held in my condo. Sam insisted I not change my last name. He chose to be called Sam Kross-Parkinson, in my honor.

During the next few days, with help from Felix and Hank, Sam moved his few possessions from his nearby condo over to mine. Touring his fancy home in North Chicago had to wait until spring at least.

February became baby month. First, Leslie and Felix had a girl, Sandee. Janine and Hank had a boy, Reese. Sam and I had Nikita next. Deanna and Russell followed with a boy, Paxton. Then, Bev and Gail had a daughter, Sasha. On the last day of the month, Helen and Casper had a daughter, Veronica.

Nikita came the day before Valentine's Day, but she became my valentine anyway. Sam had a whole new experience. Well, I did too. Because we'd spent the last month in proximity, his body responded to the birth just as all male Dolls did. For the first few days, we shared breast feeding duties. When Sam and Nikita went home under Lara's care, I entered my mutation coma, knowing the worst was over.

A month later, I went home. My body had arms again, but now I had to exercise them to build up their strength. I found Nikita and Sam doing well. He'd worked out various ways and means for changing diapers, giving her a bath, dressing her, and feeding her. Lara always kept an eye on the pair, but she told me she never had to interfere. My milk dried up while I was in the coma, so I allowed Sam to deal with that aspect.

I realized the Sixth Invaders might have succeeded in transforming our society into one similar to theirs, where their males were the domestics, caring for their children. Spooky. Eve and Randi also had similar conclusions.

Watching Sam caring for Nikita, I couldn't help wonder how Isabella and Bernardo were faring on their exploration ships. Perhaps they'd call home soon.

After I settled in, Helen, Casper, and Veronica paid us a visit. Helen had a pressing question.

"Sam told me how Nikita wants to be a telepath. So he's not getting his arms regrown so he can show Nikita how to do everything—be her support. Incredibly admirable. As you can see, Veronica is also an armless Doll like her father."

Casper beamed.

She said, "She'll become a telepath, too. We've talked with Sam about this. Should we give her the choice to be a telepath or just go ahead and have the cures done? If she wants to be one, should Casper do like Sam's doing? Be there for her, showing her how and all that?"

Before I could answer, she added, "Casper's already been communicating with her via telepathy, their special bond which I can't share. How do we know what's best for her?"

Casper said, "Hey, she and I have bonded. This telepathy thing is indescribable. Beautiful beyond words. But I've spoiled her into wanting to be like me, a telepath. Maybe I shouldn't have gotten so close to her."

"Can you give me an independent view, Molly? I'm biased," Helen said.

I focused and touched Veronica's mind. I smiled. "Well, it's amazing, Helen. I would never have expected this, but Casper and Veronica have bonded just as Nikita and Sam have. Two peas in a pod is the image that comes to mind. You're right. I'd recommend letting her grow up and then give her the choice. In the meantime, Casper best be showing her how to do everything."

Casper puffed up. "See, dear. This is the best thing I've ever done. I'll raise Veronica properly. You'll see."

I said, "Casper, that means you can't get your arms back until she's grown up."

"I wouldn't dream of doing that."

Helen said, "I can't believe the changes Casper's undergone. At first, he begged me to get his arms regrown five times a day. Now that he can, he doesn't want to."

I laughed. "What some people will do to be a telepath."

After they left, I checked with Galactic Medicine. Three-quarters of those who had been mutated into the telepathic armless Dolls had already undergone the cure. Many of those who hadn't had already signed a contract putting their telepathic skills to work and becoming wealthy.

As spring 2353 came, Earth had changed. We now had giants and dwarves living with us, strolling the MTES. If you saw an armless Doll, you knew they were a telepath. The ominous underlying and unspoken problem was that all children were being born as Dolls, male or female. However, Ted's murder remained unsolved. Still, as I looked at my new husband caring for my new daughter, I felt whole, complete somehow. And Bev promised to take me to the range to

practice with my Glock, just as soon as the weather warmed up. Now, if only Isabella and Bernardo were here...
The End.

A Favor to Other Readers

How about helping other readers? Many readers rely on reviews to make the decision whether to buy a book. You can help them make their decision by leaving your opinions and viewpoint in a short review of the positive things of this book. Writing the review and expressing your opinion only takes a few minutes, and other readers will appreciate your efforts.

Click this link: Sol Empire Volume 2 Fear
https://www.amazon.com/dp/B07BQHXQ33/
scroll down to Customer Reviews; click on Write a Review, and enter your review. Thank you.

Author Information

Visit My Amazon.com Author Page
Vic Broquard Author Page

Follow My Blog
Vic Broquard's Blog

Follow Me on Social Media
Facebook
Google+
LinkedIn
YouTube

Other Books by Vic Broquard

Without Warning (fantasy)

The Trident Series: (fantasy)
>Volume 1 The Trident and the Book
>Volume 2 The Trident and the Scepter
>Volume 3 The Trident and the Resurrection

The Adventures of Elizabeth Stanton Series: (science fiction)
>Volume 1 The Evolution of the Path
>Volume 2 The Great Messiah
>Volume 3 Of Kings and Queens and Troubadours
>Volume 4 Chaos in the Aftermath
>Volume 5 Power Plays
>Volume 6 Age of Exploration
>Volume 7 Abducted
>Volume 8 The Emperor and Empress
>Volume 9 A Job Worth Doing
>Volume 10 Degradation
>Volume 11 The Second Crusade
>Volume 12 When Worlds Collide
>Volume 13 Dark Ages

The Lindsey Barron Series: (fantasy)
>Volume 1 The Rod of the Apocalypse
>Volume 2 The Board of Governors
>Volume 3 The Crown of Moses
>Volume 4 Dominus for President
>Volume 5 The National Health Care Program
>Volume 6 States Justice
>Volume 7 Cross and Double-cross
>Volume 8 Down the Dragon Hole

Zoran Chronicles Series: (fantasy)
>Volume 1 A Dragon in Our Town
>Volume 2 Dragons, Power, Courts, and War

Planet of the Orange-red Sun Series: (science fiction)
Volume 1 When Kingdoms Fall
Volume 2 Dark Ages
Volume 3 Age of the Towers
Volume 4 Difficillis Exitus
Volume 5 Age of the Lords
Volume 6 The Renegade Tower
Volume 7 Rebellions
Volume 8 The Aliens Return
Volume 9 Power Struggles
Volume 10 Guilds, Genetics, and Gods
Volume 11 Magi, Witches, Swords, and Superstitions
Volume 12 The Voyage of the Eagle's Seed
Volume 13 Eagle's Seed and Origins
Volume 14 Justifications
Volume 15 Responsibilities

The Return of the Wizards: Twelve Companions – The Making of Wizards (fantasy)

Slow Comes the Dark Series: (science fiction)
Volume 1 Creeping Darkness
Volume 2 Serendipity
Volume 3 Darkness Descends
Volume 4 Perversion Incarnate
Volume 5 Extermination Wars

Reclamation Series (science fiction)
Volume 1 For the Want of a Pill
Volume 2 Organ Donors

Dragons, Magic, and Me (fantasy)
Volume 1 The Box

The Sol Empire (science fiction)
Volume 1 For the Want of Humanity
Volume 2 Fear

<u>Volume 3 Greed</u>
<u>Volume 4 Power Moves</u>